Praise for _B_

_"Al has written a story that touche_____ values and small town ideals._ _Lance's jou____y ___ough the challenges of being a sought-after college basketball recruit stirs fond memories of my experiences as a college football recruiter and the hard decisions the young men had to make and the importance of those decisions on the rest of their lives. I highly recommend the book. You don't have to be a basketball fan or a sports fan of any kind to enjoy this wonderful story."_

Dom Capers
Former Head Coach, Houston Texans

"Knowing Al's background in athletics, anyone who enjoys sports, from high school, to college, to the pros will love Back Porch Swing."

Nick Saban
Head Coach, Miami Dolphins

"Al has created a tremendous story that shows how the values and principles developed through strong family relationships can be strengthened by participation in sport. It's a great read by someone who believes in what he has written."

Karl Benson
Commissioner, Western Athletic Conference

"Al's creative mind and intriguing story has the reader "hooked" and hungry for more as they turn the pages in Back Porch Swing. This compelling, sports oriented story has a terrific message for the reader about the "game of life." Al's passion, faith and commitment to educational values comes shining through in this novel."

Shelley Appelbaum
Sr. Associate Athletic Director, Michigan State University

"Having known Al for almost 20 years, I am not surprised at his ability to use an athletic back drop to tell a compelling story about the life challenges we all face. Sports are often used as a metaphor and that is done in a heart felt manner in the book. A Great read for not just the sports fan--it will touch you on many levels."

Bill Fennelly
Women's Basketball Coach, Iowa State University

"Finally, we have a book about big time college recruiting from someone who knows. Al Bohl, who, as a Division IA athletics director, worked with the likes of Jerry Tarkanian and Roy Williams, traces the fictional, but realistic, account of the recruitment of Lance Stoler, a small town high school basketball star in Kentucky. His choice for college seems obvious to everyone, but him. And when the recruiting wars begin, he is faced with pressure that tests both his personal values and sense of loyalty. In his book, author Bohl knows of what he speaks. This is a wonderful basketball yarn, but it is also a touching human interest story that transcends college athletics."

Rick Bay
Former Athletic Director at The Ohio State University, former Executive VP of the New York Yankeesm, former President & COO of the Cleveland Indians.

"Knowing Al for over twenty years, it's easy to spot his enthusiasm and knowledge of not only sport, but of spirit and integrity."

Paul Dinovitz
Vice President and Western Director, Hearst Foundation

"It is awesome! It is realistic and it is graphic!"
Jim Tressel
Head Football Coach, The Ohio State University.

Back Porch Swing

Back Porch Swing

Allen Bohl

Elevate is an imprint of Advantage Media Group.
Elevate, its Logos and Marks are trademarks of Advantage Media Group, Inc.

Published by:
Advantage Media Group
P.O. Box 272
Charleston, SC 29402
amglive.com

First Printing: June 2006
Library of Congress Control Number:
ISBN: 1-59932-025-8

Most Advantage Media Group titles are available at special quantity discounts for bulk purchases for sales promotions, premiums, fundraising, and educational use. Special versions or book excerpts can also be created to fit specific needs.

For more information, please write: Special Markets, Advantage Media Group, P.O. Box 272, Charleston, SC 29401 or call 1.866.775.1696.

Author's Disclaimer

This is a work of fiction. Names, characters, places, and incidents either are the product of the author's imagination, and/or are used fictitiously. Any resemblance to actual persons, living or dead, business establishments, events, or locales is entirely coincidental.

Acknowledgments

With special thanks to the following:

I have been blessed with many friends throughout my life. Thanking them all is my first acknowledgement. Their lives contributed to this first novel in countless ways.

Thanks must also be given to those who helped edit and publish: Mary Hubley; Ann Summer, a gift from South Carolina; along with a very competent young publisher, Adam Witty from South Carolina. A special recognition goes to author Don Snyder for his wonderful teaching, and to Jim White who introduced us.

But it is family that truly makes the difference. My three children Brett, Nathan, and Heidi have been spectacular.

Finally, this book came to life because of the editing, reading, and love put into it by the woman I cherish: Sherry, my wife.

Dedication

This book is dedicated to the memory of my dear friend, Jim Burbridge, a wonderful person who kept the dream alive for so many young people.

Chapter 1

Dust flew in the rustic gray barn. Indignant hens clucked as they scurried from the path of Hoover's blue Chevy truck. A second vehicle followed close behind.

Lance and his younger brother Greg had just spent an eternity sitting dutifully still in the fifth row of the small Baptist church that clung peacefully to the banks of Prater Creek. The boys met smiling eyes from relatives scattered in every pew. A lone ceiling fan was squeaking rhythmically above the congregation and it seemed to help give Brother Jacob's sermon its gusty second wind. Their father, Milt, was a more seasoned worshiper, but even he had to be nudged awake by Helen. She sat patiently still, hands folded across her bulging belly, silently praying their third baby wouldn't arrive before the sermon finally ended. Elder Johnson must have read Helen's mind. His soulful tenor began the strains of *Precious Lord, take my hand, lead me on, Help me stand...* The grateful flock happily rose to their feet, concluding the lengthy service.

When Milt turned off the engine, Lance shot out of the family van like a caged rabbit set free. He was five years old today and his grandparents were throwing a party. Lance saw Nana and Grandad Hoover step onto the wide porch that stretched across the front of their home. A swing and two ladder-back rocking chairs were the scant furniture grouped together on the porch's solid surface. The house was a duplicate of most of the homes nestled along the creek. They all seemed to have been built from plans ordered from Sears and Roebuck catalogues in the 1920s.

"Hey, Boy, doesn't your momma need some help?" Lance heard his dad shout. His sturdy little legs had already hurried him down the path to the porch, where he was kicking off his church shoes.

"Sorry Daddy," he called back. "Need to hurry and get me on some play clothes!"

Helen soon caught up with her two boys in the back bedroom. "Let me tuck that in for you, honey." She helped Lance with his tee shirt and jeans, kissed his chubby hand, and then laid it lightly on her belly. "Feel that?"

"No, I don't feel nothin'." Lance was anxious to be off.

"Wait a second," she urged.

His small palm felt a lump quickly form. Wonder filled his eyes. "The baby?"

"Your little brother or sister just wanted to say Happy Birthday," Helen beamed. Lance lowered his hand and hugged his mom. "Go ahead, now. I'll help Greg get changed."

Lance scrambled into the kitchen in hastily-tied Nikes. The savory aroma of a beef roast and fat hens stewing slowly on the stove welcomed him. A huge chocolate cake took up half the space on the kitchen table. It had thick, blue icing with LANCE spelled out proudly in red.

Nana was rolling out dough for dumplings; flour handprints sprinkled her checkered gingham apron. Lance grabbed the edge of the apron and jerked twice. Nana looked down. She winked.

"There's my sweet, darlin' birthday boy. You look more comfortable in them clothes."

"Nana, can I go get it?"

She stopped rolling dough and matched his serious tone. "It's still on the lower shelf in my bedroom closet. Be careful takin' it out of the box, now."

As he ran out of the kitchen he called over his shoulder, "Love ya, Nana."

Lance found the box prominently located at the front of the closet. Using both hands, he carefully lifted the ball out of the box. Nana let him touch it only on special occasions. He suspected that she, or Grandad, got the ball out and played with it when they were all alone, because it was always in great condition. It felt firm, with perfect bounce, whenever he had the good fortune to handle it. As the story goes, Grandad outbid everyone at an auction for this official UK Wildcats basketball, signed by Coach Joe B. Hall and one of his many championship teams. Grandad always joked that he was Nana's third love: first came the kids, second came UK basketball, and he was a lucky third.

Lance tenderly carried the basketball into the living room and met his brother.

"C' mon, Greg. Let's play us some ball." He held open the screen door with his bottom, allowing three-year-old Greg to toddle onto the front porch.

"Go get'em, boys!" Helen called after them. She placed both hands lovingly on her belly as she moved toward the kitchen.

Milt and Grandad Hoover sat on the porch, lazily blowing up a tub of birthday balloons. Milt glanced down, eyebrows squeezed with doubt. "What are you doing, Boy?"

"Nana said I could use it," Lance said, boldly, moving past them.

Milt chuckled. "That's too big for you to shoot with, son."

"Nana said I could." Lance frowned, holding the ball closer to his body.

"Let him give it a try," Hoover urged, running his weathered carpenter's hand across Lance's head. "Who knows, this might be the next Kyle Macy standin' right here on my front porch."

Lance started down the steps. *I'll make a basket,* he thought. *A real one.* He had made plenty of baskets with small balls and low hoops. That was baby stuff. He was five years old now. *I can make a real basket.* He stopped under the faded orange rim, secured to a gnarled walnut tree by several rusty nails. He looked up. His confidence faltered for a second. *It's high.*

He turned to watch his dad hustle over. Milt jumped up, easily slapping the hanging net. Playfully pulling the ball from Lance's small hands, he threw up the first shot. It hit the side of the rim and rebounded to the left.

Lance found his courage and sprinted to the ball.

"Don't let my grandson watch you shoot!" Hoover teased his son-in-law as he and little Greg joined them, in the side yard by the barn.

"Come on, Lance," Milt urged, ignoring the blow. Lance threw the ball to his father. "Good pass."

Once again, Milt shot. This time the ball rolled twice around the rim and then unceremoniously plunked through the basket to the ground.

Lance cheered. He chased the ball into the weeds. *I just know I can do it,* he told himself.

"Your turn now," Milt stood back. "We'll rebound for you."

Hoover and Greg circled around the yard. Greg giggled as Hoover held his tiny shoulders, then jumped over his head with slightly bowed legs.

"Dribble closer now," Milt coached. "You can do it."

Lance dribbled in the hard dirt. He raised the ball. Then pushed it up toward the sky. The ball veered off the side of the rim, landing next to Greg.

"That was real close, Bud," Hoover shouted, clapping his hands over his head.

Greg tried to kick the ball toward them, but fell, missing the ball completely.

"Give it to Lance," Milt ordered.

Lance took the ball, hurling it back at the target. This time it hit the tree trunk, bouncing toward Milt, who picked it up, ready to give Lance another shot.

Helen called from the kitchen. "Come on! Hurry and wash up. Dinner's almost ready. The rest of the family will be here soon!'"

Hoover scooped up his youngest grandson and twirled him around. "I'll bring Mr. Gregory."

Milt nodded. He smiled as he placed the ball under Lance's arm. "It's a big ball for a little man," he said gently. "Put it back where you got it, son."

"Yes, sir." Lance did not smile back. He softly rubbed the ball as he walked to the bedroom closet and opened the box. His throat constricted. It was the same feeling as when Greg and he were playing rough, and tiny hands grabbed his neck, squeezing unmercifully. He felt suddenly hot. Tears ran down his cheeks. He threw himself into the corner next to a basket of carefully folded quilts.

"Lance! Family's here! Dinner!"

He heard his name, but stubbornly ignored the call. Wiping his face on his sleeve, he looked up.

Hoover stood looking down at him. "Hey, bud. What's wrong? Cain't have tears on your birthday."

Lance sniffed, "I'm no good, Grandad."

Hoover kneeled down, took one of Lance's small hands, and spread it out on his own.

"Well, will you look at that," he spoke softly. "Your fingers just about touch my weddin' ring your Nana gave me forty-five years ago. Some day soon those fingers will reach further than mine could ever hope to reach. I've tried to make a difference in life with my hands, son. You will, too." Hoover pulled the boy into his arms with a tender motion. "Let's get ready to eat. You just need some of your Nana's good cookin' to make those hands grow powerful strong."

Holding his hand, the carpenter walked his grandson out of the bedroom.

When dinner was over, Milt struck a match to light five candles as Nana led the celebration with the traditional song. Small candles illuminated the darkened room. Lance filled his lungs with more than enough air to take care of the flames.

"Wish for what you're dreamin' for, Lance," Helen urged.

Silently he asked, *Lord, please let me grow tall so I can make the baskets. Amen.*

Eight Years Later

Fans were scrambling for seats in the upper deck an hour before tip-off. Lance and Grandad Hoover proceeded safely to their row while Milt stopped for popcorn. *How can Dad stop for snacks?* This was his first time inside the shrine. Ardently aware of the surroundings, Lance shivered. The floor. The benches. Those baskets. *Rupp Arena at last!*

"Some place, isn't it?" Hoover smiled.

Milt edged past Lance, balancing bags of popcorn. "What great seats!" He shouted. "Mid-court! High enough to see all the action!" Milt was almost as excited as Lance. "When Mr. Akers shows up, you make sure you thank him kindly for letting us share his tickets."

Mr. Akers owned a large construction company in Floyd County. He had given Milt the tickets and would be joining them for the game, along with his daughter, Wanda, a middle school classmate of Lance. Lance nodded absently. The crowd's attention was suddenly drawn to the floor as the pep band blasted the fight song. The Wildcats, dressed in blue and white warm-ups, were running onto center court. The arena roared its pleasure. Hoover commenced a detailed commentary on each player, followed by his inside scoop for the season. Lance was mesmerized by every word.

"Folks know how to dress around here." Milt stood, eating popcorn, while gazing around at the fans. "Some mighty fine furs and family jewels in this house tonight!"

Hoover declared, "Only Sunday's best will do for a Kentucky Wildcats game."

Lance watched in awe as each player shot. *It's like they're not real. They're so good. If only I could be half as good.* His full focus was on the floor. Unexpectedly, he felt a strong hand rest on top of his. "Someday you'll play on this court. I can feel it in my bones," Hoover reverently predicted.

Lance wanted Hoover's words to be true. He loved basketball, almost as much as he loved eating his Nana's good cooking. But he was a doubter. Maybe one of his buddies might be good enough to someday play on this hallowed court, but could he? In his mind, he'd be lucky if a small school took a glimpse at him.

He remembered a camping trip, last summer, with Bruce, Terry, and Dale. Each shared elaborate dreams of playing for the Wildcats as they passed around a second pack of Marlboros. The bet was, who could smoke the most cigarettes without getting sick. Lance lit his third in less than half an hour and coughed as Terry boasted how he would amaze the UK fans by scoring double digits every game and all the cheerleaders would be begging him for dates. Lance said nothing, letting thoughts bounce off golden campfire flames. He loved Kentucky, but an inner burning to fly beyond his hills was slowly developing, along with a queasy stomach. *What could he see? Who would he meet? What could be accomplished?*

Lance snapped back from his recollections. "Grandad, there's lots of schools that play basketball."

"We could sit here and name most of them," Hoover agreed. "But there's only one school good enough for my grandson."

"You tell him, Grandad. Go Wildcats!" cheered Milt.

Four years later

My best game so far, Lance thought as he gazed at the state tournament posters crowding the window of Bill Jack's Barber Shop. Posters were still prominently displayed all over Connsburg, weeks after the game had been won. *I got that shot off just in time.* He opened the door and was met by familiar smells of eucalyptus and old leather. The tarnished bell on the door jingled. He crossed the worn wooden floor, passing the potbellied stove that once warmed Bill Jack's father's customers. Lance smiled at the folks waiting in mismatched chairs by the stove and tipped his head at Bill Jack.

Bill Jack looked up. "For a minute, I thought you was Milt Stoler walkin' into my shop." He stood behind the only chair in operation.

"You ain't supposed to be lookin' at nothing but my head when I'm sittin' in this chair," Clinton Kidd ordered Bill Jack. Clinton, the owner of

Kidd's Grocery across the street, watched Lance take a seat. "Besides, Milt was never that tall. Same flat top, though."

"I know," Bill Jack pulled Clinton back into the seat so he could continue trimming. "I knew that was Lance walkin' in all along. You can't mistake the best three-point shooter in Floyd County!"

"The best in the whole commonwealth!" Clinton corrected. "Mornin', Lance."

"Mornin'." Lance glanced over at the faded, signed picture of Adolph Rupp and his 1958 basketball team that hung above the chairs. Lance knew the story. Rupp had been on a recruiting visit to Connsburg in '58. He had stopped by to get a haircut and dazzled Bill Jack, Sr. and the sprinkling of customers with story after story of his coaching experiences. The picture had arrived in the mail a few weeks later and had been displayed in that place of honor ever since.

"The man up there on the wall was probably smilin' down when you made that last shot in his arena," Bill Jack offered. "What a game."

Lance tried to suppress his smile.

"Mmm-Hmm," agreed Dr. Howell, who had been waiting patiently. He stood up and reached over to grab another back issue of *The Cats Paw* from the top of an old cedar chest recruited as a magazine stand. "The whole town must have been at that game," he told Lance. "Everyone who sat in my dentist chair the last couple of weeks has had to tell their own version of your game-winning shot." He sat back down and tapped Lance on the knee with the magazine. "You've never formally met my grandson." Dr. Howell motioned to a middle-grade boy sitting on the chair to his right. "Brady, you're finally meeting Lance Stoler."

"Hey, Brady." Lance shook his hand. "Nice to meet you."

"Hey." Brady was all smiles.

"You play ball?" Lance asked him.

"Yeah, love it," He paused. "You're awesome. Everybody on my team wants to be as good as you." His eyes sparkled. "We all went to the tournament, you know."

"Really?"

"Yeah." He sat back. "All the girls at school are in love with you." Brady wrinkled his freckled nose. "But you know girls, next month it'll be somebody else, probably some country singer."

Bill Jack took the towel off of Clinton's shoulders. "That Wanda Akers better not hear of all those other girls after her feller," he teased.

Lance felt his face heat up. "Naaa," he said. "It's not like that." He didn't want to look up. He focused his eyes on the stove. "We're just real good friends."

More teasing was cancelled by the jingle of the front door bell. They all looked up as the postman entered the shop.

"Morning," said Mr. West, as he took out a stack of mail and laid it on the counter. "Not much here today." He glanced around at the customers. "Well, hey, Lance." Lance returned the greeting.

"Lots of mail been goin' to your house lately. It plain hurts my back." He leaned against the counter. "How many coaches have sent you letters? I was tryin' to keep track in my head, but it just got to be too much of a chore." He chuckled as he rearranged his bag for the next stop.

"Sorry to be a burden, Mr. West." Lance silently loved the compliment.

Clinton Kidd reluctantly gave up his chair. "I'll tell you what." His words were for the postman. "Make it easy on yourself. Just dump all of Lance's letters that aren't postmarked from the University of Kentucky straight into the Big Sandy River. That'll make the whole town mighty happy."

West nodded in agreement, and headed back out the door.

Bill Jack dusted off his barber chair while motioning for Dr. Howell. "I know one thing's for certain. Your Grandad Hoover would have sure loved to have been at that game."

Lance was silent. His quiet gesture let Bill Jack know how much he appreciated the kind words as memories flooded his mind.

Chapter 2

A Few Months Later

Lance put his suitcase into the Tahoe before walking down the long driveway to pick up the morning paper. Dew lay heavily on the grass and early morning fog completely hid the house from the road. He loved this hour of the morning when even roosters were still asleep.

This was the hour he and Grandad would rush out, letting the screen door slam behind as they set off on their way to the barn. As a child, he would often visit the family farm nestled along Prater Creek. On those mornings, Nana would be lighting the stove to prepare a big breakfast she'd have spread on the table when her boys came, slamming the door, back into the kitchen after morning chores. Lance took a deep, lazy breath, remembering the feel of damp, country air, and cool, gritty dirt on bare feet as he tried to keep up with Grandad's quick stride.

Placing the paper under his arm, he walked slowly back up the driveway and found himself drawn to the back porch swing. He sat down, letting himself be cradled by familiar wood and comforting motion. Gentle breezes wrapped loving arms around him. He closed his eyes. *I don't have to go. This is my home.* Lance opened his eyes and spotted his basketball peeking over the top of the tattered wicker basket. Helen demanded that sports equipment be left in that basket before anyone stepped into the house. He reached over and grabbed the ball, caressing the object that would so heavily influence his future. His hands knew instinctively where to settle. Quietly, swaying back and forth in the swing, he began slowly to dribble, mindful of his sleeping family. The familiar feel of hand controlling worn leather eased his reservations.

Basketball. Milt had made sure Santa left one under the tree when Lance was a baby as a first Christmas present. He had said he'd rather have his first born grow up lovin' one of those, instead of some fluffy ole teddy bear. The magic worked. Lance was rolling a ball back and forth with his dad before he crawled. He learned to dribble before nursery school. Now a senior at W.A. Akers High in Connsburg, Kentucky, he was being recruited by major basketball programs across the country, and had finally narrowed his choices.

Today, Milt was driving Lance to the Lexington airport, where he would board a plane for his first recruiting visit. This was Lance's reward for grueling hours on the driveway, intense summer camps, and endless conditioning. The prize for forcing himself to make fifty free throws in a row, after making only thirty-three, then starting over because he missed. It was the payback for a hot gym in July, where he would shoot for so long that Helen often sent Greg to fetch him home. God-given talent, hard work, and a lust for shooting had put him on this path. There was nothing Lance wanted more. Nevertheless, it came with an uninvited guest: the sad realization that his life would never be the same.

He looked up, startled as Milt bounded out of the house wearing a pair of jeans, a favorite golf shirt, and an air about him that left no doubt that he was proud to be pulling this duty. He looked over at Lance. "All set?" The whole Stoler family knew this was a command, not a question. Milt reached for his keys as the screen door slammed.

Well, there goes the sleeping family, Lance thought.

Milt leapt down the steps and jumped carelessly into the car. Lance reluctantly followed. He reached the car and looked back at the house. Slowly he turned, got in, and closed the passenger door. *OK. This is it.*

Driving along the familiar banks of the Big Sandy River, they passed a small farm with a tidy white house trimmed in black shutters. The yard was comfortably enclosed by a well-preserved picket fence. It stood alone in the heart of a dew-filled meadow. Lance had passed this home hundreds of times and always wondered about who the owners might be. It suddenly weighed heavily on his mind, like an equation he couldn't solve during a math test. Rippling river water ran beside them for several miles, then disappeared, only to reappear. It seemed to ask, "Where are you going?" One hill softly ended and its neighbor began. It was as if they were playing a graceful melody. The scenery was imprinted on Lance's soul. Each view squeezed his heart and seemed to whisper, "Are you sure you're ready to pioneer your destiny?"

He wrenched his eyes away from the window and looked at his dad. "Is it crazy to be lookin' at a school so far away?"

"I have no problem with it," Milt answered. A moment later he added, "Don't know about the rest of the family, though."

"Kansas," Lance said in a throaty whisper. He cleared his voice. "Basketball is huge there." Lance looked out the side window again. "Phog Allen coached there. Kentucky's coach Adolph Rupp got started there. So did Wilt Chamberlin." *I can't believe they're lookin' at me,* he thought humbly.

"Wonder how long it would take to drive out there when we come to visit? We'd have to drive, you know." Milt was a high school principal and Helen a first grade teacher. "We'll tell everyone at school we're going off to visit Dorothy and the Scarecrow."

Lance's lips slowly curled upward, rewarding Milt for his attempt at humor.

His dad became serious. "What do you think about that coach?"

"Let me make the trip, Dad. You know, get a closer look." Lance was not completely comfortable with the head coach. He did have questions.

"You're probably right. But take a long hard look," Milt demanded.

The local country radio station faded in and out as the car twisted through the hills. Lance accepted the family rule: the driver picks the music. He leaned back allowing his mind to wander, almost drifting to sleep.

Milt didn't let him roam too far. "Let's get some breakfast."

They pulled into a restaurant. Even though the hour was early, the place was crowded with cars. The smell of hot biscuits fresh from the oven greeted them as they walked through the door.

"Good mornin', Darlins," called a plump, smiling waitress. She looked like anyone's Aunt Bonnie. "Sit yourselves down wherever y'all like. I'll be over with some coffee in just a minute."

Lance and Milt eased into a booth. Aunt Bonnie soon came over to their table to pour coffee. "Now, what can I get for y'all this mornin'?"

"Well, Ma'am," Lance nodded toward his father, "The old man will have a ham and cheese omelet, home fries, two biscuits, orange juice, and a little more coffee, please."

"Well, now." Milt leaned back, enjoying the game. "The little boy, there, will have the biggest stack of pancakes you've got in the house, sausage on the side, and keep some cold milk comin'. He's dry."

Aunt Bonnie rolled her eyes at the two as she wrote down the order. "Gotta be father and son, right?"

People often remarked about their strong resemblance. Lance was taller, but they shared the same strong jaws and piercing, brown eyes. Both were towering, sturdy men, blessed with large hands perfect for dribbling basketballs. Lance was in top condition and could eat immense meals without guilt. His muscles had spectacular definition, which seldom went unnoticed by Green Bear cheerleaders at Akers High games. He sported the same dusty blonde crew cut Milt had proudly worn some twenty years ago.

Milt couldn't claim such good condition. Through the years, strenuous workouts had slowly become just a memory. A second chin was gaining ground, a thirty-six inch belt was getting tighter, and he wore his hair longer in an attempt to hide a few bald spots.

Milt swallowed the last drop of coffee, then set the cup down next to his empty plate. They stood up to leave, weaving slowly through packed tables. Lance glanced back as he opened the door for his dad. Grandma Stoler had been a cook and a waitress before her fatal bout with cancer. Leaving grand tips was one of Milt's silent ways of honoring his mom's memory. He saw Aunt Bonnie's face sparkle as she picked up her money.

On the road again, full stomachs and more country music allowed each man to dwell on his separate thoughts. Lance was first to speak. "What made you pick Eastern Kentucky for your undergraduate school?" The uninvited guest, Anxiety, was attempting to power his voice. He tried his best to conceal it.

Milt rubbed his chin, hesitating for a second. "See your momma anywhere?" He glanced mischievously at the backseat. "She tends to tell the story a little differently." Milt described his version of how Helen had followed him to Eastern after they graduated from Akers High.

Milt set the cruise control and relaxed. "Eastern was a perfect fit for my undergraduate work. Not too far from home. Not too big. Then, for graduate school, U.K. was just what the doctor ordered for me and your momma." As the last words crossed his lips, Milt gave Lance a glance filled with compassionate understanding. He seemed to know why his son had asked such a question. Milt's voice softened. "Just remember where you come from, son. You'll do fine."

At the airport, Milt pulled up to the curbside drop-off and turned off the engine. Lance gathered his gear from the back and stood gazing awkwardly at his father. Milt reached out and hugged him. Lance held on tightly. Milt gave him two rough pats on the back, then walked around to the driver's side.

"Act like a relative!" Milt called out.

Lance tipped his head as if to say "I will," then watched his dad drive off into merging traffic.

He found his gate easily then sat down to wait. A broad smile spread across his face as he thought about their morning, especially Milt's last words, "Act like a relative." Lance remembered the tiny chalkboard, salvaged from an old Amish barn, hanging by the family's refrigerator. On its black surface, Milt had written this advice to his children: WORK HARD, BE HONEST, AND HONOR THE LORD. DAD. Helen had found the chalkboard at a country auction. Lance helped her clean it up before she hung it in the kitchen as a message board. After reading Milt's first message, Helen never changed what he had written. She let the advice stay. Lance knew what "Act like a relative" meant. It was a hint to remember his roots, to be true to himself, and to God, and to heed the chalkboard's advice. His throat felt tight. *Dad never changed the words on the board.* Simple but powerful, the words had steered him through some touchy situations. Because of those words, he had felt compelled to tell the truth to his ninth grade coach when he hadn't run the laps he was supposed to after practice. Those words had reminded him to lean on his faith as he dealt with the difficult passing of Grandad Hoover.

Lance looked up from his reverie. Many travelers at the gate looked frustrated, some irritable. One man was clearly being obnoxious to an airline attendant at the service desk. In ugly tones, he let her know the flight should have taken off by now, and complained she had not yet called for boarding passes. The attendant was clearly trying to be civil, but her tired eyes and stringy hair were clues that this was not going to be one of her best days. Lance tried not to stare. Several rows of people watched the irate man's antics. Lance got up and took a walk to be away from the unpleasant scene. He stopped by a newsstand to buy a sports magazine. When he returned, passengers were beginning to board. He found his seat, happy it was on the aisle. At least one lanky leg could stretch out comfortably. He fastened his seatbelt, then looked up to discover the irate man from the gate was placing a carry-on in the compartment above.

"Let me pass," he demanded. He squashed his short, stout body into the middle seat.

The belligerent man called a flight attendant over. "Get me a pillow and a glass of water," he ordered.

Lance glanced sideways. He watched as the man searched his briefcase. He pulled out a bottle of prescription medicine. When the attendant handed him a glass and pillow, he roughly took them without even a thank-you. The man downed the pills.

"Darn airplanes!" he grumbled. "I hate flying." He turned towards Lance. "Only thing that got me up in the air was my sister's funeral. Haven't seen her in fifteen years and it had to be at her funeral."

"Sorry," said Lance.

The man didn't respond. He closed his briefcase and slipped it under the seat in front of him. "What's got you up in the air this time?"

"On a basketball recruiting trip to Kansas."

"Gonna be a Jayhawk, huh?" The man's eyes brightened.

"Don't know, sir. Just visiting, right now."

"We get the Jayhawks on T.V. all the time in Dodge City. Can't get that coach to come out to cow country, though. Never been able to figure out why. We've asked and asked him. It'd mean a lot to the people out in western Kansas."

"Sorry." Lance didn't know why he was trying to apologize to the jerk. "Hope Booth will visit you this year." After takeoff, the medicine seemed to work. The man closed his eyes and settled into sleep.

Lance sat forward, trying to glance through the window. The plane was probably out of Kentucky airspace by now. He pushed the seat back as far as it would go, stretching both legs out into the aisle. *Bluegrass... It will always be in my blood, no matter what life hands me.*

Chapter 3

Kansas assistant coach Jim Holister was waiting for Lance when he walked out of the arrival gate in Kansas City. Jim was a big man with a friendly handshake. His freckled skin had the appearance of a permanent blush. Lance read in the media guide that he had been quite a player at Arkansas in his day and had been on Coach Booth's staff for several years. Lance pushed aside a nagging fear that Holister would hand him a return ticket for this afternoon and say they made a mistake.

"How was your flight?"

"Fine flight, sir. Pleased to be visiting."

"Well, you're going to be even more pleased when you see Lawrence and the KU campus," Jim boasted.

They walked to the short-term parking lot. Jim stopped at a royal blue Ford Explorer with license plates that left no doubt about the driver's team allegiance. They exited the airport and drove into the Kansas landscape. Lance was surprised the countryside was blessed with gentle, rolling hills not unlike Lexington horse country.

"I was told Kansas was flat as a pancake."

"Yeah, most people think it's nothing but big winds and dusty prairie," Jim drawled. "Kansas has real beauty. But like everything in life, you have to go lookin' for it. Doesn't come lookin' for you." They traveled on, talking about basketball camps and people they both knew.

Approaching Lawrence, Lance asked, "How does the team feel about this season? Do they see themselves at the Dance?"

"Could be. The players have been working hard during the off-season, especially Shane White," Holister slowed down for the exit. "By the way, Shane told me he has high hopes for you."

Holister didn't have to explain more about Shane. The whole basket-ball world knew Shane White, pre-season All-American. Came from a great family out of Oklahoma. Mom was a schoolteacher. Dad coached the high school team to a state championship his senior year. Last basketball season, most people thought Shane had been the main reason the Jayhawks went as far as they did. His senior collegiate season should position him to be a first round NBA draft pick. Shane was someone who could answer questions, especially about Coach Booth.

The Explorer turned off the Kansas turnpike. Soon they were driving up a hill at the school entrance. Bright fall sunshine glowed on the university's tree-lined streets. Leaves were in their full-color glory, vying for perfection in hue and downward spiral. *I'm like one of those leaves,* Lance thought. *In search of a good resting place.*

They stopped outside Allen Fieldhouse. The landmark was not one of the new sterile arenas being thrown up around the country. This structure was an old gentleman, standing alone in a park, who did not achieve dignity from outward appearances, but from stories of cherished medals hard earned on bat-tlefields. As they walked into the Fieldhouse, Lance thought with reverence, *If basketball were a plant, its roots were right here. The seed may have been developed out East, but it sprouted in Kansas.*

Coach Holister guided Lance right out onto center court. "Seventeen thousand screaming fans can't wait to watch you hit a three-point shot off this floor next year."

Lance eyed the empty seats. "That's a lot of people."

Milt had coached Lance well about sales pitches. He needed to keep his senses about him. Lance knew he couldn't be the only three-point shooter the Jayhawks would be recruiting. *How many others have been given the "Seventeen Thousand Screaming Fans" pitch?*

"Can we take a look in the locker room?"

"Later. Coach is waiting." Lance followed Holister as he headed off the court, noting the urgency in his footsteps.

A skinny, middle aged secretary greeted them as they walked through the office door. "We're so happy to have you on campus." Her warm smile put Lance at ease. "I'll buzz Coach to let him know you're here."

"Thanks, ma'am." He sat to wait. Life size posters of past players stared back from every wall. *Will some boy, years from now, stand here and look at my picture? Me on a championship team?*

A loud voice broke his daydream. "Lance Stoler, welcome to Jayhawk country."

Lance watched Coach Booth stride towards him. He had forgotten what a small man he was.

"I'll take him now," Booth dismissed Holister.

"Thanks for the nice talk," Lance said to the assistant as he turned to leave.

"Hey, you haven't seen 'nice'," Booth slapped Lance on the back. "Wait 'til you taste Wendy's cookin' tonight."

They walked into a room decorated with team awards showcased on each wall. Lance was drawn to a picture of the 1988 NCAA Champion team. Coach Booth walked around his desk and sat down. Lance wondered why the coach wasn't wearing KU colors instead of that nondescript golf shirt. Lance's high school coach lived and breathed Green Bear green and white; his players expected to see him dressed in school colors at his funeral. Here was the coach of one of the top ranked teams in basketball, and one might mistake him for a slick salesman just passing through town.

"How's your mom and dad?" Coach asked. "Sorry they weren't able to make the trip."

"Me, too. They had to stay for district conferences," Lance apologized. "There's no way Mom would skip meeting with the parents of her little guys. Dad might try to bring the family out for a game during the season, if that's OK."

"Sure, sure," Coach sat up in his chair. "But let's talk about you. Your team won the state championship last year. Repeating will be hard. Always is."

Lance defended his team. "Coach Hunter wants another championship bad," Rumors were circulating that Booth was furious at Lance's high school coach for trying to push Kentucky over Kansas. Lance figured Booth wouldn't waste any kind words on Hunter. He didn't.

"Yeah, sure," Booth quickly picked a new subject. "Tell you what, I'm impressed with your leadership skills." Lance attended Kentucky Boys State and was voted vice president of his senior class. He felt privileged to have been captain of both football and basketball his Junior year.

"Thanks. My dad's always preachin' leadership. I've got some pretty stiff competition, though. Dad's heroes are Abe Lincoln, Woodrow Wilson, and Robert E. Lee." Lance did a half grin. "When Dad's in one of his preaching moods, which happens frequently, the whole family says, 'Hold on, here comes another story about Woody, Abe, or Bobby'."

"Lee and Lincoln? Those two boys fought for opposite sides."

"Dad says they both had the highest character. Did what they felt was right."

"Well, at Kansas, by God . . . " Booth rested his elbows on the sides of his chair pointing a finger directly at Lance, "doing what's right is always important."

Lance thought, *He's really saying that "doing right" is what HE thinks is right.*

"By the way, you got that football out of your system. Right?" Booth commanded.

This coach wasn't that difficult to figure out. Lance nodded. He thought about Booth's question. Playing football was something he loved, but his bread was buttered by hoops. Lance had been an All Conference tight end his junior year, but hadn't gone out for the football team this year. He knew he needed to concentrate on basketball, and the tight end position needed to be filled by someone who could give the team one hundred percent.

"I'm here for basketball, Coach." Lance returned Booth's stare confidently.

There was a sudden knock. Lance looked up, amazed to see Michael Lee at the door. Lee was touted to be the best player ever to wear a Jayhawk jersey.

"Michael, come on in. Meet Lance Stoler," Booth introduced the two.

"They tell me you're the best shooter out of Kentucky in the last decade," Michael said, shaking hands with the awestruck youth.

"Pleasure to meet you, Sir. I don't know about being the best." Lance asked in disbelief, "Who told you that?"

"Some guy named J.C." Michael wasn't finished. "But he also told me he could score twenty on you with his left hand tied behind his back."

J.C. and Lance had first met in a summer tournament and had bonded immediately. J.C. scored twenty against Lance's team in the semi-finals. Twenty-two were actually made, but the game official ruled the last shot didn't count as the buzzer went off. His team lost.

"Wait a minute! J.C.? Bring him on! I'll show him who could score twenty." Lance now knew Michael was joking with him.

At that moment, J.C. Burbridge appeared at the doorway. He strolled into the room and over to Lance.

"J.C.!" Lance was happily stunned.

"I tried to warn them about you, but they didn't listen. They let you visit anyway." Both laughed, obviously pleased to see each other.

After a few minutes of small talk, Michael suggested, "Coach, J.C. and I could drive Lance to the hotel and get him checked in, if that's O.K. with you."

"Great. Sure. Lance, Shane White will pick you up for dinner." Booth walked around his desk. "See you guys at 6:00." They were all dismissed.

Michael grabbed Lance's arm, as they passed the athletic director's suite at the top of the stairs.

"Let's go in. Need you to meet someone," Michael urged. They walked into an outer office.

"Meet Lance Stoler," Michael said to the woman behind the secretary's desk. "Can't shoot a lick, but Coach Booth says we gotta recruit him anyways." He turned to Lance. "Dayle Jarrett's been with KU for over twenty years." Michael explained her competence. "This lady knows the workings of the athletic department inside-out, including where a few skeletons are hidden. She's been the secretary to five athletic directors."

Dayle's smile seemed genuine. She crossed her arms and stared at Lance with a gleam in her eye. "Michael, I got a feelin' this one might be just like you."

"How's that, Ms. Dayle?"

"Two seconds to go, Kansas down by one, everyone expecting the ball to land in this one's hands. The other team, probably Missouri, fearing it would."

"That's Stoler, alright," bragged J.C.

"That's kind of you, Ms. Jarrett." Lance felt ill at ease, not knowing if she was teasing or praising. She walked over to Lance, noticing him squirm, and laid a hand on his shoulder. "You'll really like the people of Kansas," she spoke with sincerity. "They love their wheat and feel even stronger about their basketball. Isn't that right, Michael?"

"Yes, Ma'am. Always have, always will."

The heavy paneled door swung open.

"Afternoon, Boss." Dayle quickly walked back to her work station.

The athletic director, Hugh Henderson, appeared in the outer office. Nearing his mid-sixties, Hugh was impeccably dressed with glorious silver hair and tanned skin, perpetuated by a love of the outdoors. He noticed the guest.

"Michael and J.C. brought a new recruit in to visit," Dayle explained, "Meet . . ."

"Lance Stoler," Hugh finished her introduction. "Guys, come on in for a few minutes." They walked into his office and everyone eased into comfortable stuffed chairs. "Been across campus in meetings. Made sure tailgating will be handled properly tomorrow."

Lance took a long look around the room while Mr. Henderson offered the three young men soda or water. He noted a picture of Abe Lincoln and a worn edition of *The Letters of Abraham Lincoln* sharing space on a lamp table next to a blue tapestry sofa. A framed copy of the poem *Footprints* hung on the wall beside bookshelves loaded with books from counter to ceiling. *Dad would love to meet this guy,* Lance thought.

"We are very proud of Michael," Henderson told Lance. "Not only an outstanding player for the Jayhawks but, more importantly, he's a great person. And J.C.'s early commitment means the Jayhawks are going to continue to be a force in the Big Twelve." He handed Lance a Pepsi. "Glad to have you visit."

Henderson's voice sounded sincere. Lance hoped his own face expressed appreciation, not his fears. *What if they change their minds? What if I'm not good enough?*

"Tell us about your family." Henderson seemed interested.

"My dad's a school principal and Mom's a first grade teacher. It's conference time. That's why they couldn't make this trip with me."

"I know the drill. I used to teach."

"I have a brother. Greg's a sophomore. You might want to keep an eye on him—he's one heck of a quarterback. But between you and me, my sister, Cherie, is the real athlete in the family. She's aggressive on the soccer field and off." Lance set down his pop can. "Especially when her brothers get in her way."

J.C. leaned forward clasping his hands. "Shoot, man. I can score twenty on you with one hand behind my back wearing ankle weights, and your little sister can push you around? What do we need you for?" J.C. punched Lance, playfully. Lance prayed Mr. Henderson knew J.C. was kidding.

"How does it look against Kansas State tomorrow?" Lance asked, in an effort to switch the focus.

"We haven't beaten those son-of-a guns in the last ten years. They're ranked fifth in the nation." Mr. Henderson's eyes twinkled. "Say, what are you doing about one P.M. tomorrow? That's when we kick off. Maybe the NCAA would let you suit up at tight end for us." Hugh eased back in his chair, stretching his hands behind his neck. He let out a deep chuckle. "I bet you thought I didn't know you play football awfully well too."

Lance beamed.

"We'll have a big crowd tomorrow. Problem is half of them will be wearing purple. In our stadium! Purple all over the place." Henderson leaned back, crossed his legs, and sighed. "Coach Malone has been working to improve our fate, but the Big Twelve is no place for the faint of heart. One of my main goals is to get a winning football tradition established here, like our basketball tradition." Hugh Henderson grinned. "Saturday's game against the Wildcats will be your first taste of just how bitter this rivalry is. They don't like us, and the feeling on the field is mutual. If we could upset them, well, it would be real special."

Dayle stepped in and spoke to Henderson, "Your four o'clock meeting is here."

"OK." Henderson acknowledged Dayle. He shrugged his shoulders clearly indicating displeasure in having to stop a joyful conversation to handle more pressing matters. To Lance and the others he said, "Sorry guys. I really enjoyed our talk." Hugh stood up and walked them to the door. "Hope you have a wonderful weekend." He spoke to Lance last. "You're in good hands with J.C. and Michael."

They stepped outside into radiant Kansas sunshine.

"Once Coach Booth sets us free tonight, we'll have some fun on Massachusetts Street." J.C. seemed awfully enthusiastic.

"Massachusetts Street?" asked Lance.

"The main street in town." J.C. looked at Lance as if he should have known.

"What's the main street in Lawrence, Kansas, doin' with the name Massachusetts?"

"Man, where's your history?" J.C. glanced at Lance. "I forgot. You're from the Kentucky woods. They don't teach history back there." Lance watched his sly grin grow. "The land you're standin' on was settled by the good people of Massachusetts."

The three walked to the parking lot. J.C. clicked his car's locks.

"This sweet thing is yours?" Lance asked, thoroughly astonished.

They climbed into a shiny black Cadillac Escalade that still had the scent of "new" clinging to beautiful tan leather seats.

Michael didn't say a word, but Lance caught a knowing glance exchanged between the two.

"My mom got it for me. A boy's gotta have some transportation. Especially since I drive back and forth from Kansas City a lot," explained J.C.

Michael continued to say nothing. Coach Booth had to know what J.C. was driving. It had been parked right outside of Allen Fieldhouse.

He strongly doubted if J.C.'s mom could afford this. She was divorced and worked as a secretary in Kansas City. Last summer, between tournament games, Lance and J.C. had spent quite a bit of time together. One rainy evening Lance had driven J.C. to his home where his mom treated them to a fantastic home-cooked meal. She welcomed Lance to her family's dinner table as if he lived just down the street, and she had known him all her life.

"Where did you say your mom works, J.C.?" Lance asked. "She must've hit the lottery to get you some wheels like this."

"I wish. Momma still works at Overland Distributors." J.C. peered at Lance through the rearview mirror, then back to the street. "Mr. Graham, the owner, has been good to us ever since I was in the eighth grade. That's when I started playing on the travel basketball team he sponsored. Got me my first pair of Nikes. Momma started working there two years ago, since right after our team made it to that summer basketball tournament in Vegas. Graham's a big donor alum. He flat out expects KU basketball to do well. No! I take that back! He flat out demands KU basketball does well. You know what I mean?" He glanced into the rearview mirror again. "The guy has skyboxes for both the Royals and Chiefs games. He's got eight basketball seats in Allen Fieldhouse, three rows up, center court. Brings his wife and his customers to the games. Likes to show off how he can talk to the players during warm-ups."

"It must be nice to have your mom's boss so interested," Lance couldn't help being inquisitive.

"Yeah. When I committed to the Jayhawks, Mom was promoted from Secretary I to Secretary II. Mr. Graham sure was happy about my commitment," J.C. answered. He was silent as he stopped for a red light, then turned the corner. His voice sounded sincere, as he continued. "It's nice to have someone care about my brother, sisters, and especially my momma. That don't happen much in my 'hood.'" He looked into the rearview mirror once again and shook his head, grinning at Lance. "I still don't know how you guys beat us last summer. And after my momma fed you her famous fried chicken the very night before."

J.C. pulled in front of the hotel. Lance sensed he was glad they were finished talking about his mom's work and his new car.

"I'll grab your suitcase." Michael got out of the car and walked to the rear.

"Hello? Is anyone looking?" Lance whispered to himself. *An NBA player is carrying my suitcase.* It was just a small bag on rollers. Even so, Lance was honored. Here was someone making over a million dollars a year and he was not stuck on himself. The bag's wheels whirred as they entered the lobby and walked across to the registration desk.

"Shane will be by to pick you up at 5:30," Michael reminded Lance, motioning to J.C. that it was time for them to hit the road.

Chapter 4

L ance noticed the big bowl of apples on the counter. He grabbed one, wiped it on his sleeve, and took a big, juicy bite. *I haven't eaten since breakfast,* he thought. *That snack on the plane couldn't possibly count as a meal.* His stomach was happily anticipating dinner at Coach Booth's house. He rolled his bag down the long, second- floor hallway while he enjoyed the last bite of apple. Entering his room, he walked to the balcony and looked over the rail at the Kansas River. Sun sparkled on its swift current. A shower of yellow and red autumn leaves danced past his balcony, settling gently on the bank below. Lance wondered who had traveled up and down this mighty river. *Which Indian tribes? Lewis and Clark? General Custer?*

"Dang, I must be sleepy," he said out loud. He walked back into the room. "Here I am on a basketball recruiting trip, and I'm thinkin' about Lewis and Clark." Lance flung his bag on one of the two psychedelic blue bedspreads. Then he stretched out on the other. His mind wouldn't relax. So far, KU was everything he thought it might be. He loved the beautiful campus and the aura of Allen Fieldhouse. Most of the people had been nice, but he felt he had more homework to do on Booth.

As he lay there, he wondered what his Mom would think. She would love Dayle Jarrett and would appreciate most of the other people he had met. Her judgment of personalities was uncanny, coming from years of working with six-year-olds and reading unspoken problems. She'd know if Booth could be counted on to "walk the talk", or just "talk the talk".

His mind continued to wander until five o'clock. A long, steamy shower helped wake him and focus his mind on the evening ahead. He debated between a couple of shirts, and had just finished buttoning the chosen one when there was a knock at the door. Lance glanced at the clock. Five-thirty on the dot. He opened the door to a tall lanky young man, obviously built for basketball.

"You must be Lance Stoler." The All-American introduced himself. "I'm Shane White."

"Wow. Nice to meet you, Shane."

"Better get going." Shane pushed a hand through his curly brown hair. "Don't want to be the unlucky stiff to arrive late."

They walked toward the parking lot chatting easily.

"You've enjoyed your years at Kansas?" Lance asked as Shane unlocked his car, a plain old Toyota.

"Kansas has been good to me. We've had a lot of talent, but just haven't quite been able to make it to the NCAA finals. My hopes are we'll correct that this year."

They drove on silently, each seeming to be pondering the last statement. Shane flipped on his blinker and turned down Twenty-Third Street. "Coach lives on a golf course out this way. Any more questions before we get there? I remember having a million questions when I was in your shoes."

"Gosh, well, why'd you choose KU when you were coming out of high school?" It was the first question that came to mind.

"Where do I start? Tulsa, Oklahoma State, and Rice were the three main schools recruiting me. Kansas came in late. I liked the campus right away, and, of course, the basketball tradition. My dad felt sure Coach Booth could use a combination shooting guard and point guard. It was close to home. I knew I could play either position."

"How have you and Coach Booth gotten along?" Lance was keenly interested in his answer, but tried to act normal.

"I've been a starter since my freshman year and I'm a basketball player. We haven't had many problems." Lance sensed Shane had measured his words carefully.

They arrived at Booth's house and parked. Lights were bright inside the large, one-story brick home. Lance wasn't surprised to find a basketball hoop on the concrete driveway as they made their way toward the front door. Lance paused to look back at the hoop.

His home in Connsburg had a great hoop. Milt made sure of that. Pick-up games were known to occur on a moment's notice as the Stoler brothers welcomed any two-on-two challenge. Greg was the picker and rebounder. Lance the moneyman. When they blended their talents, most competition went home disappointed. One-on-one was a different story. Greg and Lance were pretty even. Greg could always muscle inside and score. However, when the moneyman was in his zone, it was no contest.

If there were no pick-up games, Lance would go out by himself and shoot. He shot in heat, rain, and snow. Weather was not a factor. Early, late, time didn't matter. He would spend hours perfecting his shot, mastering his free throw technique. What he loved best, though, was bombing away the threes. Time and again, he would fire away, enjoying his mental announcer's script, "There are only two seconds left in the game. Stoler gets it. He shoots. And it's gooood!"

Shane was ringing the doorbell when Lance joined him on the front porch steps. Mrs. Booth greeted them with a smile.

"Come on in," she opened the door wide. "You boys won't be disappointed with the meal tonight. I have some real good-looking steaks ready to throw on the grill, the baked potatoes are about to come out of the oven, and Coach Holister's wife cooked up some of the best green beans and pork I've tasted in a long time. You like green beans, don't you?"

"Yes, ma'am. They're my Nana's specialty." Lance wiped his feet on the welcome mat and stepped into the vestibule. "She always says you're not a true Kentuckian if you don't love green beans."

"Get in here," Coach Booth shouted to Lance from the end of the hallway. "I've got some other recruits for you to meet."

Lance followed the coach into a huge room that stretched completely across the back of the spacious house, overlooking spectacular views of a well-tended fairway. Several young men were casually enjoying popcorn and talking ball. Michael Lee was the only one he knew.

"Everyone, this is Lance Stoler from Kentucky."

Lance began shaking hands, remembering what he had heard or read, about the other recruits visiting this weekend. First, he met John Jacobs, a center forward from Reno, Nevada. John was being recruited by Duke, Arizona, and Kansas. John and Lance had never competed against each other, but Lance knew he was a big time player. Next, he shook hands with Reggie Hamilton. Reggie was from Tulsa and probably the most athletic guy in the house. Besides being good in hoops, he was an All-State wide receiver and could high-jump six feet ten inches on a bad day. Sam Wilson stood up as Lance approached him last. Sam, a shooting guard from Dallas, was being aggressively recruited by Texas, Texas Tech, and SMU, as well as the Jayhawks. There was no way Sam and Lance would both sign with Kansas. One of them would get splinters if that happened. Eye contact between the two left no doubt each prospective player quietly understood this reality as they grasped each other's hand.

"Make sure you get something to drink," Booth bellowed, as he walked out to the patio with Coach Holister, each carrying heavy trays of steaks. "There's plenty of cold pop at the bar."

The group made itself comfortable again. Lance listened to the banter, getting a feel for the personalities in the room.

He heard John Jacobs ask Michael Lee, "What do you think is the biggest difference between college and pro ball, besides the money?"

"The pros are a business," Michael answered. "As long as a player performs to the expected level, he's fine. Good guy, bad guy, purple hair or tattoos, it doesn't make a difference. Any slippage in performance, though, and you're history."

"What else?" John questioned.

"Well, in college, team friendships and trust seem to be stronger. But, as you mentioned, the money is a whole lot better in the pros." Michael turned to Lance, teasing, "Unless you're at Big Blue Kentucky, that is." Everyone laughed, even the bluegrass kid.

Lance stepped over to the bar to get a Coke. *What about that car? Whose money is paying for that? Where's J.C., anyway?* Lance turned when he heard his friend's voice behind him.

"How's everybody doin'?"

J.C. was late. Booth did not hide the displeasure on his face as he and Holister walked in from the patio carrying steaming platters. J.C. seemed unaffected by Booth. What Lance really noticed was how J.C. lit up the room. J.C. mingled with genuine pleasure and self-assurance. He could make others smile, without their knowing why.

The meal was finally served buffet style on the dining room table. Lance carried his loaded plate to an empty place in the family room and dug into the beans first. *Good,* he thought, *but they can't touch Nana's.*

Cherie loved to boast that the best smells in the world came from Nana's kitchen. Green beans truly were a specialty, but Nana had many. Greg's all-time favorite was her chicken and dumplings. Any morning was first-rate if Lance sat down to her biscuits and gravy; and all it took to make Milt loosen the notch on his belt was one sniff of her apple butter stack cake. Whatever the season, food on Nana's table was always bountiful and delicious. Last August was the first time Lance noticed she ran out of fried chicken before her serving tray ever made it around the table twice.

Booth seemed to be anxious to gather the group around his big screen TV. He rushed them through their apple pie. Wives cleared the tables while Booth made a few light remarks, then started a video of last year's highlights. Kansas had made it to the Sweet Sixteen, but ended the season with a sad upset by Bowling Green. Jayhawk fans were visibly dazed and puzzled in the footage. Their expressions seemed to shout, "With so much talent, how could the game slip away?"

Watching the video with critical eyes, Lance clearly saw Shane would be playing in the NBA. He was gifted. He had an uncanny ability to get the ball up and down the floor, hardly ever forced a shot, and was an excellent defensive player. Shane's fundamentals were obviously very sound.

Booth turned off the power then gave his opinion of the Bowling Green game. He shouted his disgust with the outcome. He made it clear that the only players he wanted to recruit would be those who never let such a disappointment happen to his program again.

Lance thought surely the players hadn't wanted such a loss. Were the players the only ones at fault? He caught J.C.'s eye. His wry smile told Lance that the two might be thinking the same thing.

Coach eventually wound down and soon everyone was filing out.

J.C. leaned over to Lance and whispered, "I'll meet you at your room in half an hour. Better be ready for some fun."

"Hey, man, I stay ready," Lance whispered back.

J.C. took off in the "wonder machine". Lance and Shane piled into the Toyota for the drive back to the hotel.

"You need to be ready early tomorrow morning. I'll pick you up at 8:00 A.M." Shane reviewed the schedule. "The coaches want to meet us for breakfast at The First Watch by 8:30, sharp." He grinned at Lance. "You'll find that breakfasts in Lawrence aren't too skimpy, either."

Lance told Shane he was very impressed with his play in the highlight video. "You gotta be getting some great coaching here at KU to be able to play like that."

"Not bad. But, I must say, I think I learned more from my dad and his intense practices back home. That helped me the most." Shane shook his head, "Ya know, it baffles me. We have so much talent here."

Lance nodded. He was thinking the very same thing.

Chapter 5

Right on schedule! Lance swung the door open. His friend was not alone. J.C. swaggered in with a beautiful girl on each arm. "Lisa, Marla, meet Lance Stoler. Our job is to introduce this boy to Massachusetts Street."

Lance was not surprised J.C. had rounded up companionship, and such good looking companionship to boot.

"They're freshmen at K.U.," J.C. told Lance. "From back home."

"Do I need a jacket?" Lance asked as he turned out the desk lamp.

"Just put on a sweater. You'll be fine," Lisa suggested cordially. She had long, wheat blonde hair and beautiful eyes that peered out from behind dainty wire-rimmed glasses. She was only about 5' 2", but Lance instantly approved of every inch. He slipped on his favorite blue sweater and eagerly followed the three down the hall.

The night was clear and quiet. J.C. decided to leave the Escalade in the hotel parking lot. "It's probably the closest space we'll find, anyways," he explained. Chatting and laughing, they walked to their destination.

Massachusetts Street was a scene out of the past. It was Lance's vision of what Main Street America should be: a long, wide, tree-lined avenue with quaint shops, restaurants, and no shortage of bars, alive with business. Lance could imagine his mom falling in love with this street. However, he was certain his companions were not taking him to any of the places Helen might stroll into on a visit.

Their first stop was The Sandbar. Fish nets, papier mache whales, and sharks covered the walls of the tiny wood-framed building. A Miss Mermaid competition was taking place using the bar surface as a stage. Several girls from the audience had been chosen to wear Sandbar mermaid costumes over their own clothes. They walked onto the stage with great fanfare. An announcer introduced each contestant to cheers from friends. The mermaids threw plastic bead necklaces to their encouraging fans.

Lance cheered for a cute, chubby mermaid who was so overweight she couldn't zip her costume in the back. She held the top up with one hand, threw beads with the other, and laughed contagiously as she sashayed across the bar. She seemed to be at peace with being a big enough person to laugh at herself and enjoy the moment. A Miss Mermaid was dutifully crowned and the stage returned to a working bar.

Lance and the others squeezed around a table in the middle of the cramped room.

A male waiter visited their table. "Lisa and I will have a rum and Coke," Marla ordered, quickly.

"You can order, little lady, but I gotta see some ID first," the waiter demanded.

Lance was shocked when both girls produced IDs stating they were born twenty-two years ago.

"Yeah, you two hide your age well. Now boys, don't tell me you're twenty-four."

"I'll have a Pepsi," Lance ordered, ignoring his joke.

"Me, too," said J.C. He looked at the crowd, not at the waiter.

Lance was relieved that J.C. didn't order alcohol.

"Good choice, my man," Lance told him after the waiter departed.

Alcohol was a barrier to any basketball future. He tried not to judge his friends who drank, but Lance chose not to imbibe. It was hard enough guarding guys like J.C. He wasn't about to do anything that might slow him down.

"You, too, Kentucky boy." J.C. raised his fist for a quick tap.

Lance leaned over to Lisa and whispered, "Never would have thought you were twenty-two in a bazillion years."

"I'm not, but let's not broadcast that information. You can get a lot of things in the city. IDs are no problem. Marla got mine for me." Lisa quickly changed the conversation. "How did you meet J.C.?"

Their drinks and popcorn arrived. Lance waited until everyone was served before answering. He leaned forward in his chair.

"I first met him in a summer tournament. Why don't you ask him which team won?" Lance asked loudly, knowing J.C. had turned his attention away from Marla and was listening in.

"Don't be giving Lisa old news! I still say, and you can quote me on this, you guys were just plain ole lucky!" he huffed, dramatically.

"Maybe so, but the record book will always show Stoler 1-0 against the great J.C. Burbridge." *I would love to be J.C.'s teammate,* Lance thought. *No team could ever relax guarding that back court.*

J.C. had a lean, sculptured body that carried no extra fat. His statuesque frame was best displayed during games, when muscles exploded through the boundaries of a sweaty jersey. The Lord spent a little more time perfecting J.C.

"You learn how to pick yet?" asked Lance. "Ya know, Coach Booth will want to make sure I get a good look at the basket."

"Think assist, man. Your job'll be to get Burbridge the ball, then sit back and enjoy the show."

Marla pinched J.C.'s arm. "Are you guys going to talk ball all night, or are we going to have a good time?" Marla appeared to be one of those personalities who functioned best when all attention was focused on her.

"Sorry," J.C. rubbed his arm. "Where to next?"

"The Teddy Bear Lounge," Lisa suggested eagerly.

"Bottoms up. Let's go to the Teddy!" Marla commanded. She pushed away from the table. Lance and J.C. happily followed the girls.

The Teddy Bear Lounge was around the corner from the Sandbar. It was a typical college bar with noise so loud that patrons called it music. Numerous students, and some folk who would never attempt a college degree, kept the place alive. One couple sat at the bar, each sipping a mug of beer. The guy was smiling because each time his date took a sip, she wrinkled her cute nose with distaste. They made a striking couple. He was tall and confidently good looking in a heavily-starched oxford shirt. She was a spunky petite who could have just stepped out of a J. Crew catalogue. Lance and Lisa noticed them right away.

"Crazy about each other," Lisa whispered to Lance. "Definitely freshmen. Probably her first beer."

What kept Lance's attention was the look of complete adoration each had for the other. He wondered what their story was, silently wishing them a happy life together. Glancing back at Lisa, he noticed how cute her nose was.

Marla and J.C. had found a table and waved. Before they joined them, Lisa led Lance to the dance floor where a group was Texas Two-Stepping to *Boot Scootin' Boogie.*

"You dance in Kentucky, don't you?" Lisa teased.

"Let's see." Lance twirled her into the group. *Thanks, Mom and Dad, for years of Country Music 101.*

The dance ended too soon. Still holding hands, they briefly stared at each other, each wanting to say something, but not knowing quite what. They turned and slowly curved around a few tables to join Marla and J.C.

"Not bad, you two." Marla praised, in a slightly jealous tone. "I'm impressed."

"Come on, Lisa, I'll show you how to really move on the floor." J.C. took hold of Lisa's hand and led her, once more, through the crowd.

Lance sat down next to Marla and stretched his hands behind his head. He leaned back, noting her obvious displeasure at not being in the spotlight at the moment.

"Ya like being a Jayhawk?" Lance asked, trying to break her mood.

"Had no choice, really," Marla gave a flip answer. "My mom and dad graduated from KU. Destiny, I guess." She watched the dancers. "Couldn't imagine going anywhere else. The school is great and the parties are tremendous." She kept her focus on Lisa and J.C. "Lisa's dad went to Missouri. He wasn't all that happy when his little girl wouldn't even consider becoming a Tiger. He survived, as parents usually do, and everyone's happy now. Lisa's a good dancer." Marla glanced at Lance. "We share an apartment, you know."

"That's nice." He enjoyed watching Lisa on the dance floor. "She is good."

J.C. and Lisa returned just as a waiter stopped at their table. The girls quickly pulled out wallets when asked for IDs. Lisa turned to Lance and smiled, secretly. Lance suspected she thought he might blow her cover. Tonight, he wasn't trying to be anyone's guardian.

After finishing their drinks and sharing the dance floor a few more times, Lance looked at his watch. "Guys, it's getting close to eleven. Should be heading back. Coach said we have a big day tomorrow."

"Not so fast, my friend," J.C. stopped him. "Marla's adamant that we stop at The Wheel."

"What's that?" Lance asked.

"You'll like The Wheel," Marla promised. "It's a lot quieter than here. A bunch of former Jayhawks usually show up there on Friday nights before home games."

Lance simply nodded. He was clearly outnumbered.

Despite his nagging feeling that he probably should be heading back to the hotel, Lance followed them up a steep hill towards another watering hole. Inside, it was small, with several booths and a sprinkling of tables jammed together. Each corner of the dimly lit room held a television brightly broadcasting a Fresno State football game. Lance smelled pizzas cooking in the back and marveled at the bartender's speed cranking out draft beers. A waitress took their order, never asking to see IDs. Apparently, J.C. and his two friends were not strangers at The Wheel.

A tall, husky man walking with the strut of a former basketball star, approached their table.

"Hi, Jack," Lisa looked up with an easy smile. "Lance, this is Jack Morton. He was a player way back in the early '90s. Even claims he played in the Final Four."

"Nice to meet you," Jack propped himself against a post, commanding attention.

Lance simply nodded a reply.

Jack turned to J.C. "I was watching you from across the room. You're gonna make one great guard for the Jayhawks, but everyone knows we need two of you." Jack looked directly at Lance. "Word's out about you. I like what I've heard."

Jack took a sip of his beer, and continued. "All I know is that if the two of you line up as our guards, we'll make it to the Final Four again. It's been quite a while since that happened. Too long." he patted J.C. on the shoulder. "Marla, Lisa, always a pleasure." Jack stepped away, slowly relinquishing his space.

The gang talked and joked with others who surrounded their table. Lance knew it was getting late, but he hated to leave. He enjoyed being with Lisa, loved the conversation, and didn't want to burst the bubble of what had become a magical night. Bubble or not, he would have an early wake-up call.

"I hate to break up the party, but guys, Shane's pickin' me up at eight sharp." He stood up to leave.

Lisa surprised him by also standing up, then slowly placing a warm hand in his.

She stepped closer, "Come on. I'll walk with you. Wouldn't want you to get lost on your first night in Lawrence." She turned to J.C. and Marla.

"I'll meet you at the car in a few minutes. We should be headin' back to the apartment, too."

Lance was more concerned about not letting go of Lisa's hand than with his good-byes to the others. He vaguely remembered Marla offering a "nice to be with you" and heard J.C. say something about seeing him at Booth's pre-game tailgate party.

He focused on how he felt, walking in the crisp, autumn night with Lisa by his side. His head was spinning, and it wasn't from the Pepsi he had consumed.

Lisa broke his trance. "I'm happy J.C. asked me to come tonight. I watched you all evening. You must come from awfully good stock. I mean, it's nice to see someone with manners and who sticks to his values. You didn't even think about havin' a drink. Not even a beer. My crowd has been drinkin' on the sly since middle school, and we were the so-called clean-cut student government officers, cheerleaders, and jocks. My mom and dad would grin and glow like Christmas if they knew I was with a sweet guy like you."

"Whoa, Lisa." He raised his voice, slightly. "I like those Bud Light commercials on TV as much as the next person." He continued, "I'm not doin' anything to mess up my chances of getting a scholarship. Self-discipline is never easy. Am I making sense?"

"I know exactly what you mean. I wish I didn't feel like I have to drink when I'm with Marla and the gang. I've never been drunk." She hesitated, as they crossed another street. "I'd feel out of place if I didn't drink. Is that bad?"

Lance stopped and turned to face her. "Everyone wants to fit in, to belong. I guess my parents have helped me. My dad says there's only so much talkin' he can do. Sooner or later, he says that life will land on my shoulders and I'll have to carry the load alone. They can guide, but the way I carry that load is my choice. Doesn't mean all of their lessons hit home with me. I'm certainly not perfect."

They stopped briefly and looked in through the window of a closed jewelry shop. Lisa squeezed his hand and said softly, "You are quite definitely the closest to perfect I've seen."

The couple's walk back to the Marriott took less than fifteen minutes. They walked slowly, trying to stretch out their time together.

"Thanks for the walk back," Lance said. He hoped it wouldn't be the last time he saw her. "Will you be at the game tomorrow?"

"Of course. I'll try to stop by Coach Booth's tailgate, and I wouldn't miss Midnight Madness for the world."

Lance looked toward the parking lot and spotted J.C.'s car. "That sure is a nice set of wheels."

"My dad keeps asking about it. I tell him it's none of my business." They saw J.C. and Marla farther behind them walking towards the car.

They stopped, turning towards each other. "Well, thanks again," Lance pulled her into a hug. Electricity shot through him. He had held many girls in his arms, but none had given him the sensation of belonging. This one fit exactly right. Like a missing puzzle piece suddenly found. Reluctantly, they let each other go.

"Bye." Her voice was soft.

Lance entered the lobby alone. It was jammed with people splattered in purple. Lance's sweater caught their attention. One guy swaggered close then taunted, "We're gonna cook you birds tomorrow."

Anyone wearing blue could easily find a fight tonight. Lance kept walking. These K-Staters knew that his sweater was blue, but they didn't know it was really Kentucky Blue, a present from Nana at the beginning of his senior year.

Safe in the elevator, Lance thought about how the guys back in Connsburg would nail him. He could just hear them shouting, "Hey, Stupid, what were you doin' walking away from that Kansas City girl?"

"They're right," he scolded himself. He slipped in the key card, walked into the room, and threw himself onto a bed.

Chapter 6

Lance slowly stretched, and then he realized he had fallen asleep in his clothes. He rolled out of bed and walked onto the balcony. *Today will be special.* He looked forward to all the scheduled events, especially Midnight Madness. Lisa would be there. Sitting down, he put both feet up on the rail, shut his eyes and willed himself to see her again. There was the long blonde hair, small upturned nose, and slender body, barely as tall as his shoulder. She had worn a green sweater and jeans, but what he remembered most were her eyes. At first he had thought they were brown but the more he tried to recall, he saw flecks of green. Maybe it was the sweater reflecting in her eyes.

The telephone rang, jolting him out of contemplation. He sprinted over to the bed and picked up the receiver.

He heard his dad's voice say, "Mornin'."

"Hi. How's everything back home? Did we win last night? How'd Greg do?"

"Whoa, buddy. We beat them by four touchdowns. Your little brother threw for two. It was a fantastic night. All else is fine back here. How 'bout you?"

"Great. Tell little brother I'm happy for him. Trip's going well. Met a lot of good people. You'd like the athletic director. I thought of you when I was in his office. Get this. He has the exact same picture of Abe on his wall that you have behind your desk at school. I also saw a tattered copy of *Lincoln's Letters* lying on a side table."

"Sounds like a guy I'd like to get to know." Milt paused. "Booth?"

"Very cordial, but he made it known he doesn't like Coach Hunter. My guess is he still thinks Coach is pushin' me to UK."

"Doesn't surprise me a bit. If I were Booth, I'd worry a little bit about that, too, seein' you're Kentucky born and raised."

"OK, OK. Hey, Dad, remember J.C. Burbridge from the games last summer? He came over to my room last night and took me on quite a tour of downtown Lawrence. He's a great guy."

"Didn't I read he already committed to Kansas?"

"Sure did."

"You two didn't get into any trouble on that little tour of Lawrence, did you? The coaches should be watchin' out for that, too." Milt sounded like he was ready to lecture.

"No trouble, Dad."

"Better say hello to your momma. She'll pout if you don't. Have a good time today."

"Thanks, Dad."

Lance heard rustling on the other end of the line as his dad passed the phone to his mom.

"Hi, honey. How's Kansas treatin' my boy?"

"Real nice, Mom. How's Greg and Cherie this mornin'?"

"They're still sleeping. It isn't noon yet," she laughed. "They'll be happy to know your trip is going well."

"Better get goin'."

"Enjoy yourself, now. Tell Coach Booth we said 'Hello.'"

"You bet."

He hung up the phone, then stretched his hands toward the ceiling. Through the window, he watched the sun begin to brighten the sky. The wind was still. Great football weather.

The Kansas coach was in his first year. The media printed they had high hopes he might build a football program to equal KU hoops. Lance's interest in the football team was personal. He wanted to gauge if Greg might have the talent to play quarterback in this league. And, selfishly, he wanted to find out whether he might have been able to hold his own at tight end, if football had been his first passion.

Shane was right on time. "Get a good night's sleep?" he asked when Lance opened the door.

"Sure did." He walked with Shane to the elevators. "By the way, what happens at Midnight Madness?"

"It's one of the best kick-off shows in the country, and I mean it's a show." Shane's eyes lit up. Lance could tell he was happy to explain more. "People come over to Allen Fieldhouse right after the football game. Seventeen thousand fans pack the place and wait hours to watch. We have a bunch of music, entertainment, you young puppy recruits are given wild cheers, and then we do skits." The elevator reached the lobby and they exited. "Both the women's and men's teams perform. After midnight, the men's team comes out and has a short scrimmage. Early the next morning, after the fans have gone home to bed, the team comes back for the first real practice of the season." They reached Shane's car.

"Coach like all the madness?" Lance asked. He fastened his seat belt as they eased out of the parking lot.

"Think so. He normally complains about something, though. Like last year, the PA system wasn't working just right. He got on people pretty hard."

"Does he do that a lot? I mean, ride people pretty hard?"

"I've been told you shouldn't get on his bad side." Shane lowered the volume on the radio. "One time, the strength coach, a football man, a neat guy, asked a couple of basketball players who had taken their shirts off while working out to get their shirts back on. That's a rule of the weight room. Well, the incident got back to Coach Booth and he was livid that someone other than him was telling a basketball player what to do, rules or no rules."

"No kidding."

"It was no big deal, but the strength coach had no prayer of getting Coach to be cordial to him again. That strength coach couldn't survive at Kansas after that. He got a little revenge by leaving and then being scooped up by a NFL team."

Shane stopped the car in front of what looked like an ordinary, small-town strip mall. The First Watch sign hung above a little restaurant located in the middle of the mall. A few people stood outside drinking coffee, amiably waiting to be called for open tables. Lance thought his dad would love this place. It fit Milt's description of a good breakfast restaurant: lots of cars, lots of people, and great smells luring customers inside.

They walked in. Every wall was covered with Jayhawk memorabilia. From women's rowing, a sturdy oar was prominently displayed above the side window; two softball bats were crisscrossed behind the checkout counter; and a pair of track shoes were hanging behind the first booth. This place was a haven for all teams, not just football and basketball. He knew Cherie would like that very much. Lance followed Shane to the back. Coach Holister was waiting with John Jacobs.

"Hope you had a good night with no trouble to report," Coach Holister said to Lance as he stood to shake hands.

"No trouble, Coach. J.C. took good care of me."

Lance turned to shake hands.

"I saw you back in the corner at The Wheel last night, but didn't get a chance to make my way over to your table," said Lance. "Looked to me like you were pretty occupied with fans."

John grinned. "Yeah, I saw you, too. Who were those ladies?"

"Two friends J.C. went to high school with. They're freshman here."

"I'd say he knows how to pick some pretty good company," John said. He chuckled.

Lance nodded in agreement, remembering the instant sensation of wholeness and warmth that had pierced through him when he held Lisa close.

They waited for Coach Mills, the other assistant coach, to arrive with Reggie and Sam. J.C. had told Lance that Mills was Coach Booth's "do everything guy." He didn't have much of a role during practices, but whenever Coach needed something, Mills would quickly "gopher up" and make sure it was taken care of.

"Today will be a busy one," Coach Holister said casually. "After breakfast, we'll go back to the Fieldhouse to meet with academic people and trainers."

"Will we get our ankles taped? I wanted to prove I could take it to the hole against John," Lance boasted jestfully.

"Bring it on, little man," John shot back.

Lance just smiled and then noticed several patrons' heads turn, eyes bulged in amazement. Reggie and Sam strolled in with Coach Mills. The happy buzz in the restaurant rose in decibels as the basketball table welcomed the newcomers.

It only took a few minutes for everyone to get settled. The waitress easily saw she had some hungry customers and proceeded to take orders.

"I'll have a ham and cheese omelet with whole wheat toast and orange juice," Lance told her.

"Any coffee or hot chocolate?" she asked.

"No, ma'am, but I'd love a big glass of ice water, too." Lance gave her his best smile.

The waitress smiled back and stared a moment. She said shyly, "I saw you at the Teddy Bear last night. That was a pretty good two step on the dance floor."

"Thank you, ma'am. My partner was pretty good, too, don't you think?"

"Indeed."

The waitress left. The others teased Lance about showing off his two step.

Coach Holister tried to rescue him by starting to share stories of his basketball days. "Enough dancing, boys! Think hoops. You guys got it made today. When I was in high school, we would have been jumping for joy to shoot as much as you guys get to." Coach Holister seemed delighted. His audience was listening. "My coach made us pass the ball five times before we could ever consider a shot." He threw up his hands to start an apology. "Don't get me wrong, I loved my coach." His lips puckered. "But dang, I could've averaged thirty a game, if I'd had the green light."

Coach Mills couldn't hold back. "Holister, somebody like Sam would have been guarding you," he said. "Your coach was probably right. It was best that you passed."

Everyone was still laughing when breakfast was served. Lance looked around the table for the strawberry jam. *Please don't let this toast be ruined by having to put apple or grape jam on it.* He thought.

"Is there any strawberry jam in that container?" he asked Reggie.

"Plenty."

"Please pass some over this way." *That's it! I'm comin' to Kansas! Big steaks, great omelets, strawberry jam, and Lisa . . . greenish-brown. Her eyes were greenish-brown.*

Lance happily slathered his last piece of toast with strawberry jam and looked up to see a gentleman, obviously the restaurant manager, approach the table.

"Hope you enjoyed the food." He spoke with a cheerful voice.

"When have we ever been disappointed with one little thing on your menu?" gushed Coach Holister. "Lance is from Kentucky, too. From Connsburg. You know where that is?"

"You've got to be kidding me," the manager's words almost came out as a shout. "I grew up in Ashland. Connsburg is only about an hour south. What's your high school?"

"Akers High, sir."

"Whoa, you guys are really good. Didn't you win the states last year?" He explained to the others. "Akers High is always one of the better teams in the state. They can even beat Ashland, although I hate to admit it." He patted Lance on the shoulder. "It was nice meeting you all, but I have to get back to the kitchen." The manager gave the table a last look. "Have a terrific visit. Do come back."

"Hey Stoler, you pay him to say that stuff?" teased Sam Wilson. "How 'bout bringing your startin' five down to Dallas? It'll be showtime."

"What did you average? Thirty-two a game? Thanks, but no thanks," Lance fired back. "Daniel Boone taught me well. Never pick a fight with a grizzly." His grin let everyone know he had more to say. "I have to ask, though. Who are those midgets you're scoring thirty plus on anyways?" Table conversation suddenly turned into a friendly battle of challenges and put downs.

Coach Holister silenced the group as he slowly stood. "Time's up, guys." He looked at Shane. "Could you drive these squabblers over to Allen Fieldhouse? I need to talk to Coach Mills for a minute."

"Sure, no problem. Where do you want them to go?"

"Take them up to Miss Appleton's office. She'll be waiting for them." Holister ordered more coffee for Mills and himself then sent the group off with Shane.

The players approached Shane's car. "You guards hop in the back. Big John is going to need some serious leg room."

Lance wondered what the coaches were discussing. *Are they still interested in me? Do they think they made a mistake recruiting me? Am I good enough?*

John and Reggie were definitely good enough. Kansas would have to work hard to sign those two. Lance still couldn't quite figure out Sam. He seemed like an OK person, even though newspapers reported he had been in a little trouble back in Dallas. He had apparently been involved in a robbery and had some problems with a girlfriend. It seemed ironic they'd be interested in him, knowing Coach Booth's public persona of not wanting to coach kids with problems. But he might just make an exception for a kid who incidentally averaged thirty plus a game.

Lance gazed out the window at a tan brick dormitory perched on top of the hillside. *They wouldn't want me over Sam, would they?*

Shane assured the group they would like Miss Appleton. "She's the best," he told them as they drove through the campus entrance.

Shelley Appleton was the Assistant AD for Academics. Her goal was not simply to place athletes into majors to keep them eligible. Rather, she wanted them to get an education. She wanted them to appreciate having earned a degree when their playing days were over.

"The trainers are good guys, too, especially Mr. Shaffer," said Shane. "He's the head trainer and with my knack for getting banged up," Shane smiled, "well, he considers me a regular."

"What should we ask Miss Appleton?" Sam seemed baffled.

"Don't worry. Ask her anything you want. Remember, she's super. She'll talk to you straight."

"It's just I've been workin' on my hoops more than my studies. I qualified, though. Barely, but I did. Nobody can say I didn't," Sam mumbled defensively.

"All of us can't be like John," Shane said. "Didn't you blow the doors off the SAT, John?"

"I was lucky, I guess. Teachers have been real good. Had me reading in kindergarten. I've grown up loving books about as much as basketball."

"Lucky? Luck doesn't get you offers from Stanford and Duke," protested Shane. "I can read too. Read those recruiting magazines. Big John, here, is a merit scholar. Harvard and Yale are begging for him."

Lance was impressed, and he was not alone. His self-confidence started to stumble. *Those coaches want John. Not me. They're thinking they made a mistake lookin' at me.*

Shane parked in the garage next to Allen Fieldhouse. The group got out and strolled down the sidewalk. Lance was captivated again by the rugged charm of the sturdy old block building climbing several stories high. Shane and the recruits entered the building, climbed up a spiral staircase, and went down a long hallway. Miss Appleton's door was open.

"Come on in, guys. I was having some coffee, just waiting for the chance to put live faces with these files I've been reading. Very impressive stuff. All of you." She stepped around her desk and shook each of their hands with both of her own. "Sit down," she said. Everyone sat except Shane.

"If it's OK, I have to meet my parents in a few minutes," Shane said. "I have these puppies house broken, so they should be fine."

"Well, thanks for making sure the puppies arrived safely." She winked at them all. Shane left the room.

Miss Appleton started talking about her role when a distinguished-looking man appeared at the doorway.

"Well, hi, Doc," Miss Appleton said. She adjusted the frames on her glasses. "Meet an example of one of the great profs here," Miss Appleton said to the recruits. "I asked Dr. Fulton to stop by and meet you. He's a professor of speech and hearing -- he's received the KU Outstanding Teaching Award. Twice."

"Thanks. That was a very kind introduction." Dr. Fulton immediately made the recruits feel important. He explained that the whole department cared that the student-athletes perform well in the classroom. Fulton said enthusiastically, "We want you to have every opportunity to excel."

This is cool, thought Lance. *This guy doesn't seem like one of those bookworm teachers who'd come into the classroom, walk to the chalkboard, talk in a monotone for forty-five minutes, then say, "Class dismissed." He might just pass the Woodrow Wilson test.*

His dad measured good professors by his view of Woodrow Wilson. Milt often spoke of Wilson's early years, before he was President of the United States, governor of New Jersey, and president of Princeton. In Milt's view, Wilson's highest office was as the best political science professor of his time. Students at Princeton stood in line to get into his classes. A teacher who could inspire students so strongly to want to learn was "a Woodrow Wilson."

"Have any of you decided on a major?" Dr. Fulton asked.

"Not me," Sam seemed to panic. "Do we have to pick one? Can't you just tell us what we should do?"

"It's your precious choice," Miss Appleton counseled. "We don't want to limit your options."

"Yeah, you could major in engineering or something like that," Reggie said. He snickered.

"Are you sayin' I ain't smart? I'm a qualifier. I passed the SAT, same as you." Sam answered hotly.

Miss Appleton tried to calm Sam. He was turning red. "You don't have to decide now."

"Great advice," Dr. Fulton supported Miss Appleton. He nodded and glanced at his watch. "Gotta go. Big game today."

"And we've got an appointment with the training room." She led them out of her office.

The recruits were as large as the Grand Tetons compared to the diminutive Miss Appleton. She scurried to keep up with their lengthy strides through the hallway and down the spiral staircase.

Lance, last in line, mentally left the group for a few minutes. Through the two-story windows on the front wall of the athletics building, he could see across a parking lot. Several landscaped campus buildings were securely perched on a small knoll. He imagined himself sitting in one -- a big classroom -- the first day of the semester. It would probably be an eight A.M. history class, too early for Sam and Reggie to attend. John would be there, though, and the two hoopsters would love the fact Marla and Lisa had enrolled late for the class after checking the guys' schedules. Lisa would sit next to Lance, of course, and she'd take great notes when he would be on the road for a game and had to miss class. He could see it all vividly.

"Around to the right and down the hallway," Miss Appleton instructed, snapping Lance out of his classroom daydream.

The training room was smaller than Lance had expected. Despite its size, the room was well equipped with taping tables, whirlpools, and exercise equipment for rehab. Several student athletes were being treated. This time of the year, Kansas had quite a few teams in competition besides football, and beginning tomorrow, there would also be basketball.

As if on cue, Paul Shaffer entered the training room from a side door, acknowledged their presence, and shook everyone's hands. A short man, he had the face of a diplomat. Some people have the ability to immediately make others feel they understand their pain and are wonderfully empathetic. Shaffer was one of those people.

"So, Coach Booth wants you guys to play basketball for the Jayhawks," Shaffer said. "Well, take a look around, because you'll visit this place regularly. Every day we'll be taping your ankles, giving you cold medicine, listening to your problems."

Shaffer slowly ran a hand through his hair. "May God hear your mothers' prayers asking that you never be injured. But realistically, injuries and pain are going to happen. When they do, this room will become your caretaker." Shaffer cleared his throat. "Let me be specific: ankles, knees, hands, fingers, shoulders, elbows, heads, and for sure, noses. I have yet to see one of you skyscrapers not bang up your nose rebounding." He hesitated. His eyes sparkled. "Make note, though. I don't handle hearts." He placed one hand on his chest. "Any of you dribblers fall in love -- go see Miss Appleton. She has a much softer shoulder to cry on."

Shaffer finished, then turned. "Where do these scholars head to next, my dear?" Before Miss Appleton could answer, Shaffer quickly interjected, "Hey, I hope that I didn't scare any of you."

As if having practiced in a choir, their answer harmonized, "Naaaa."

"We're going to the stadium," Miss Appleton said. "Time to experience tailgating, Kansas style."

A van was waiting in the parking lot. A well-dressed student jumped out to help with the doors. Miss Appleton climbed up front, turned to the group, and introduced the driver. John Mattington was an administrative assistant to the athletic director, while currently working on a PhD. Driving people to and from their destinations on game days was one of his duties. During the week, he was Dayle Jarrett's right hand in the director's office.

"Nice to meet you, guys," Mattington said. "Say, which one of you is Lance? I read something in your bio that struck a nerve. My dad used to coach at Eastern Kentucky."

"That's me, sir," Lance leaned forward. "My mom and dad went to Eastern."

Mattington smiled as he started the engine. "Hey, you don't have to call me sir. I'm just a student, myself."

"How long was your dad at Eastern?" asked Lance

"He was an assistant coach for two years when I was just a little dude. He went on to North Carolina then USC. Now he's with the St. Louis Rams."

Sam leaned over the driver's seat and asked, "So, your dad's got one of those big Super Bowl rings?"

"Yeah. Super big." Mattington responded.

"Sweet." Sam leaned back in his seat, looking thoroughly impressed.

Lance called over the other voices, "How'd you like living in Kentucky?"

Mattington slowed the van, barely missing some students recklessly running across the street. "To be honest, my recall is limited. I was only two when we left, but my mom and dad always talk fondly of living there. Where's your home in comparison to Eastern?"

"Two hours east, next to the Virginia border."

"Then you're close to Pikeville," Mattington said. "One time, I drove through there on Route 23 when we were traveling from Ohio to Virginia. That's pretty country."

Lance was delighted. "That's right."

Sam perched over the front seat and said, "Enough bluegrass. Tell us truthfully; we gonna see a good game today?"

"K-State's mighty good. You know we're re-building. It will be inter-esting." Mattington tried to glance at Sam. "Now, basketball. Cause of guys like you, its big-time different. Kansas State never beats us in basketball."

The rest of the ride provided fresh views of the Mount Oread campus with its roller coaster hills. Lance wondered how students handled the steep, icy sidewalks during winter storms. Like little ski slopes, several streets curved quietly downward to town. They slowly drove by a row of huge sorority and fraternity mansions. Lance hoped he might catch a glimpse of the Beta Theta Pi house. Milt had pledged Beta Theta Pi, and Lance had grown up listening to Beta stories. Mostly about their parties, but the best was when he crowed about pinning Helen, a mere month before asking for her hand in marriage. They turned the corner by the education building. Mattington navigated the van down a winding hill toward the stadium. Lance was disappointed. No sight of the Beta house.

John Jacobs must have been scouting the fraternity houses, too, because he asked, "Do any basketball players join fraternities at KU?"

Lance thought that was kind of a silly question, but remained silent. He was surprised when Miss Appleton frowned. She answered with a sound of regret in her voice. "No, John. Coach thinks being on his basketball team is like being in a fraternity, and he's the coach." She looked back as if to apologize. "A lot of people feel strongly that being involved in campus life is a good thing, though."

Lance was sure he wasn't the only passenger upset with this informa-tion about Booth, but he remained silent. The van turned into the VIP parking area. Mattington stopped at the entrance and rolled down his window. The parking attendant laid both arms on the door.

"Well, if it isn't John Mattington. Why aren't you in the library studying, college boy?" He leaned into the van and looked around. "You didn't highjack these guys, did you?"

"I can't believe Mr. Henderson pays you big bucks to sit out here harassing people on game day." Mattington grabbed his hand. "Guys, this is Joe Ferguson. Every university in America wishes they had someone as great as Joe."

Joe blushed and waved Mattington on. "Try not to hit any of the big donor's cars."

Mattington pulled the van right next to the stadium. It was a gray concrete fortress, with blue scroll trim and it showed signs of recent remodel-ing. Plenty of people were already milling around even though kickoff was more than two hours away. Lance thought, *the athletic director's meeting on Friday must have gone well.* The parking lots surrounding the stadium were full of tailgaters.

The long-legged passengers filed out one by one. The smells of grilling brats, burgers, and chicken tantalized Lance as they approached a table where Mrs. Booth was working. She stopped to welcome the group. "You're the first to arrive." She smiled approval.

Lance was no stranger to this type of spread. It reminded him of the Stoler reunions. He loved going to Grandma Stoler's house for their annual Fourth of July picnic. Grandma would spend the whole week before baking cookies, pies, and cinnamon rolls that melted in your mouth. Aunt Elsie could always be counted on to bring at least five graham cracker crust pies and his mom would bring a juicy ham, baked to perfection. At night, Milt and his brother Gary would start a big bonfire in an old truck tire ring. As the cousins gathered around to roast marshmallows, Grandma Stoler would surprise them with a new, never-before-heard story of growing up on the farm during the Depression. The ending was always, "It was a hard life, but we made our own fun. We were poor, but didn't know we were poor. Just thanked the Lord for what we had." After Grandma Stoler had died, the family tried celebrating the Fourth at a different home each year, but it was never the same. Her vivacious, loving spirit was no longer with them.

Lance was finishing a second helping of Mrs. Booth's apple cobbler when he noticed a black escalade pulling into the lot. *VIP parking pass?*

J.C. was at Lance's side in seconds. "Morning. How's the food? Save me any?"

"I think there's one piece of cornbread and maybe a chicken bone. Where've you been? We just had a great meeting with the trainer and academic counselor, or do early signees have a waiver on meetings?"

"Had to get my beauty rest. Cornbread and chicken bones, my eye." J.C. walked over to Mrs. Booth and gave her a hug.

Wendy Booth smiled impishly, then scolded him. "You're late *again*."

J.C. loaded his plate and stood beside Lance as he ate. Two gentlemen who had been talking briefly with Coach Booth now approached them.

"I take it you're one of the recruits?" asked one, whose expensive tweed sports coat stylishly covered the build of what may have been a former offensive lineman. He had a dignified air, with piercing gray eyes that looked like they seemingly knew answers before questions were ever formed. The other man's silver hair, weathered face, and slight limp gave the impression he was much older.

"Yes sir, I am, and this is J.C. Burbridge. He signed early." Lance had watched Booth's body language while he had spoken with these men. He surmised they must be important to the University, or at least to the basketball program.

"I'm Hank Shipman," The man who looked like an offensive lineman offered. "Boys, we love our basketball. Like to start enjoying football again, but those darn K-Staters'll probably make life miserable for us today." He cocked his head and said, "My comrade is a great friend of the University. Meet Thomas Hillcrest, from Wichita."

"So you're the Stoler kid." Mr. Hillcrest quickly eyeballed Lance. "Folks in Wichita say you can really shoot it. Can we count on having you do that for the Jayhawks?" he demanded.

Lance wasn't sure how Mr. Hillcrest knew who he was, but answered, "Sir, this is my first trip. I'm delighted to be visiting Kansas and other than having to hang around J.C., the stay has been pretty good." J.C. swallowed a bite of his sandwich and returned Lance's grin. "But to be honest, Sir, I have already told Ohio State and Kentucky I would visit. We have several relatives in Ohio, and Cherie, my sister, she'd cry like a baby if I didn't visit Kentucky. Gave'em my word that I would visit."

Mr. Hillcrest scowled as he addressed Lance. "Well, Big Fellow, we'll wait and expect good news for Kansas." Then turning to J.C., he said, "The Jayhawk faithful were pleased to see you commit early, Mr. Burbridge. I'm certain you have enjoyed the *benefits* of your decision," he asserted.

J.C. was spared having to answer. Coach Booth joined their circle. "There's plenty of food. Join us."

The two declined. They were on their way to their suites, where they would be entertaining all afternoon. Mr. Hillcrest continued to converse with Booth, allowing Lance and J.C. the opportunity to return to the tailgate.

Lance picked up a few potato chips. "Strange dude. What did he mean about benefits?"

"I don't know. You know those Boosters." J.C. shrugged his shoulders and started to refill a plate.

Lance picked up a cold Pepsi, taking pleasure in the moment. Slowly, he became aware of the conversation behind him. Booth was speaking with Shipman and Hillcrest.

"Listen, Booth, don't worry. I'm always here to help." Mr. Hillcrest sounded agitated. "We're happy with what you're doing, but we have to get football out of the basement."

"The problem is that chancellor of ours. That's the bottom line," demanded Mr. Shipman. "In my opinion, he flat out does not know how to help football, let alone the rest of the university. The president at Kansas State is kicking his butt. That president's been behind football since he took office, and look how they've soared. They're making tremendous progress in academics, too. I hate seeing the Purple ahead of us in anything."

Lance glanced over at the three men. He was sure they did not know that he was eavesdropping. The gentleman from Wichita, Mr. Hillcrest, scowled deeper than when he had heard Lance was visiting two other schools. Hillcrest said, "You are absolutely correct. What a mess."

Coach Booth stepped back and looked away from the group. "I've got to get back to my recruits. I'll leave this political stuff to you guys. You already know my views."

Booth called for everyone to gather around so he could say a few words. "Hope you boys got enough to eat. It's time for some football." Coach rubbed his hands together. "After the game, we'll have dinner at the Angus House, then at 8:00 sharp, we'll head over to Midnight Madness. Any questions?" None were asked.

Chapter 7

L ance followed the group as they headed for their stadium seats. He straggled behind so he could privately take in the fanfare. A little toddler with a Jayhawk painted on her right cheek was asking her mommy for another cookie. Five men, all dressed in KU blue, huddled around a grill, engaged in carefree laughter and sipping their favorite beverages. Next to them in a grassy area, three middle school boys were tossing a football, probably dreaming they would make a game-winning play for the Hawks one day. A couple in their late seventies sat happily, their picnic laid out on a folding table between them. Lance smiled and called out, "Are the Jayhawks going to win this one?"

The two elderly sweethearts cheerfully shouted back, "We got them this year. Go Jayhawks."

"Your first game?"

The couple laughed in unison. "Son, haven't missed a home game in forty-three years," the man replied.

Now that's loyalty, Lance thought. Walking away, he called back to the couple, "I hope y'all have a fantastic time today."

Lance climbed the steps to join John, Reggie, Sam, and J.C. They were seated right next to the student section. Lance estimated the students numbered at least six thousand strong, and they were fired up for this game. He focused on the teams. Kansas State was very impressive. Overall they looked much bigger and faster than Kansas, although their tailback was only about 5'7". "Hey, J.C., look at that little guy running at tailback."

"That kid's good," J.C. responded. "Really quick. Played for a team in my high school league and rushed for a bunch of yards. Wanted to come here, but the former KU coach didn't want to offer him a scholarship soon enough. Ran for 170 yards against the Hawks last year."

"Look at the size of purple 44. Is he the fullback?" Sam said. "No wonder their tailback runs so well. That 44 probably eats anyone who gets in his way."

"I think 44 is a transfer from a Big Ten school," said J.C. "Got in some trouble up north, but K-State had no problem giving him a second chance. And like Sam so eloquently puts it, he eats people."

Kansas was lined up in the south end zone for pre-game, running plays against the defense. The quarterback was about 6'1" with a cocky self-confidence about him. Lance noticed his handoffs were smooth, always faking afterwards, and his passing was crisp, very accurate. Lance couldn't wait to talk with Greg. He had seen enough. He knew his little brother was on the right track to master the skills to compete in the Big Twelve.

Kansas kicked one last practice extra point, huddled, then ran into the home locker room. The marching band took the field. They played several fight songs, and then stopped in formation for a special presentation. A voice over the loud speaker introduced the chancellor, athletic director, and an honored guest, Curtis McClinton.

The announcer said, "Mr. McClinton was a stand out running back for the Jayhawks. He has gone on to a stellar career with the Kansas City Chiefs. Today he is going into the K.U. Hall of fame."

Lance thought Mr. McClinton was a spectacular looking man. His face had the dignity of a Sioux Chief. His frame appeared capable of donning a uniform and starting with the Jayhawks today.

Mr. Henderson stood with an air of quiet dignity with the chancellor and Mr. McClinton. Lance appreciated the time that Henderson, so obviously busy, had taken with him when he first arrived on campus. Lance's glance fell upon the chancellor. He remembered the conversation he had overheard at the tailgate. The chancellor looked out of place, not the leader of a great university. Lance wondered what the stories were behind the vehement words against him coming from the boosters.

J.C. pointed to the scoreboard and said to the group, "Watch this, it's awesome."

Lance looked at the giant screen scoreboard, heard music, and saw a video flashing on the screen. The scoreboard displayed a jet in the shape of a giant Jayhawk flying towards campus. Eyes in the student section were glued to the screen. "Pretty cool." Big John smiled.

The video continued the jet's flight over campus and into the stadium, where it blew up a Wildcat football helmet. The crowd went wild with cheers from the Jayhawk fans and boos from everyone in purple.

With great fanfare, both teams' captains walked onto the field. Kansas State won the toss, but deferred to the second half. The Jayhawks would start on offense. Lance was hoping they might do well; the past twenty-four hours compelled him to be loyal to his hosts.

After running the kickoff back to the twenty-five yard line, the offense eagerly huddled for first down and ten. The tailback was stuffed at the line of scrimmage on the first play. Second down was a pass into the flats. Incomplete. Third and ten. Everyone in the stands knew the next play would be a pass, but as so often happens in life, everyone was wrong. A draw play helped the tailback gain nine yards. A great call, but the punting team was now required to perform. Lance was not surprised when the little K-State tailback lined up to receive the punt. The punt was caught on the thirty-two and in a flash, returned to the fifty-yard line. The Kansas defense was scrambling on to the field, when Lance heard J.C. shout, "Hello," welcoming Marla and Lisa.

"Hi, guys. Did we miss much?" asked Marla as she squeezed purposefully into their section.

"You're just in time to see the defense," Big John said in his best suave tone while making more room on his bleacher. "A lovely lady like you just might bring them some luck."

Simultaneously, Lance improved his own position as Lisa chose to settle in right next to him. She leaned over and asked, "How was your morning?"

Lance smiled. "Good. The morning went real fast. We had meetings with the academic counselor and head trainer, then went to the coach's tailgate. A great guy, John Mattington, drove us to the stadium. He works in Mr. Henderson's office."

"I've met Mattington. He's a grad student. Really sweet. A friend in the apartment next door has a huge crush on him." She took a deep breath and looked out at the field. "I'm sorry I didn't stop by the tailgate. Marla only got up an hour ago and I didn't want to barge in by myself."

He was going to tell her he was just glad she was with him now, when Sam stood up and hooted, "Big time play!" With a hard slap on Lance's shoulder, he shouted, "Did you see that linebacker stuff him?"

Lance focused back on the field realizing he had missed a few plays. The Hawks had forced a fourth down, the Wildcats would attempt a field goal. The scoreboard flashed the results: Kansas State 3 - Kansas 0.

Lance worked hard to keep an eye on the game while maintaining his conversation with Lisa. The Wildcats had little trouble building a seventeen-point lead by halftime, and happily sprinted to their locker room. Kansas State 20 ; Kansas 3.

The crowd moved like an army of ants, around and down the bleachers. Lisa and Lance followed, not stopping until they were at a concession stand. The couple continued out a gate and found a comfortable spot under a huge maple tree. The sounds of marching bands performing half time routines seeped out of the stadium. Sitting down, they shared a bucket of buttered popcorn, sipped on jumbo cokes, and lightly talked.

"About last night," Lisa said, changing the intensity. "I don't want you to think," she paused, then went on slowly, "that I help entertain all recruits when they visit campus. Marla quite often is in the mix, but I went last night only because J.C. asked me to come along. We've been friends forever. He called last week and said he had someone special he knew I would enjoy meeting."

Lance sensed the seriousness in her voice. "So my buddy J.C. was trying to fix us up?"

"No, I don't think that was his mission. J.C. really likes you. I felt I already knew you because ever since the two of you met in summer ball, he's talked about you. J.C. mostly talks about himself, not someone else." Her cheeks flushed pleasantly. "He speaks very highly of you. He thinks your parents are wonderful. I think he's looking forward to playing on the same team with you, big time!" She pushed his knee. "I just wanted to meet the guy J.C. thought was almost as great as J.C. himself."

"Well, you know how J.C. can exaggerate."

Lisa's voice softened. "I enjoyed last night. I didn't want you to get the wrong impression of me."

Lance sat up intently. "You don't have to explain why you came last night. I'm just glad you said 'yes' to J.C.'s invitation. I enjoyed every minute. I'm enjoying myself right now."

Lisa's greenish-brown eyes met Lance's. No words were spoken. The silence was intense. *She's beautiful.* The bands had stopped their routines. Lance stood, offering his hand to help Lisa up. "I have a sneaky suspicion that you're not a great fan of football, but shall we see what the damage will be in the second half?"

Many students were trickling out of the stadium, heading up the hill back to campus as Lance and Lisa started back to their seats. They walked slowly.

"Football's not really my favorite sport, basketball is," Lisa said. "I played on my middle school and high school teams. I averaged a respectable eight points per game."

When they arrived in their section, Lisa asked a depleted group, "Where's Sam and Reggie?"

"Those two said they were headed back to the hotel," explained John. "Can you believe they said they needed naps, or they wouldn't make it through Madness? Must have had a very interesting night."

Marla cut in. "Trust me, they did have one very interesting night, indeed. But don't tell Coach."

"You don't have to worry about Coach," said John. "He wants those two awful bad. You can see it in his face when he talks with them. But, so does every other Big Twelve team."

J.C. didn't acknowledge the group talk. He seemed to be growing impatient with what was happening on the field. "I'll give this game about ten more minutes, then I'm out of here." he snapped, with growing disgust. J.C. had known nothing except winning seasons. He had never experienced the agony of competing against a markedly advanced opponent.

Adjustments made by Kansas during half time had not made a difference. Kansas State received the kickoff, ran it back for thirty yards, then five plays later, easily found the end zone, adding six points to their side of the scoreboard. Crowd noise was owned by the Purple for the rest of the afternoon. Lance felt sorry for the Jayhawks' quarterback. He was obviously trying very hard to run the offense, but strong, fast weapons were not in his arsenal. Lance ached to suit up at tight end for the blue. In his mind, he would catch every perfect spiral thrown by the gutsy leader, dodge the purple gladiators, and then spark a Hawks comeback victory.

Suddenly, J.C. stood up. "That's it. I've had enough. I'm out of here. Lance, how about I give you a ride back to the hotel and I could change in your room, before dinner and Madness?"

"That'll work. What about Shane?"

"Coach asked me to bring you tonight. Shane's with his family."

J.C. asked Lisa and Marla if they needed a ride to their apartment. Lisa accepted readily, but Marla had been sitting next to John. She adamantly declined, being quite content to remain exactly where she was.

They walked through the dwindling student section. Passing the press box elevators, they saw the athletic director, Hugh Henderson, talking amicably with another man. Mr. Henderson motioned to them.

"Where do you three think you're going? The Hawks need all the help we can muster up in the fourth quarter. Come on over here. Meet Guy Melbourne, from Toledo, Ohio." Mr. Melbourne was probably in his late sixties, bald, with the stature of a former athlete. His tailored suit complemented an air of understood importance. "He represents what KU athletics is all about. Played both basketball and baseball for the Hawks. When you talk about character and integrity, the best example is this man right here."

Mr. Melbourne's face let it slip that he was extremely flattered. "What kind words. But I know your tricks, you devil. After another contribution, huh? The check will be in the mail next week." Then with mock seriousness, he said, "Make sure you young people watch your wallets after you graduate. This is a prince among men, but he can squeeze water out of a weathered desert cactus."

"Don't let them in on all my tricks." Henderson introduced Lance and J.C. J.C. introduced Lisa. Henderson quickly shared a few facts from Lance's bio, impressing Mr. Melbourne with the stats as well as impressing Lance with the fact that an AD obviously had taken quite some time perusing his file.

Henderson finished by saying, "Lance is a Kentucky thorough-bred. Nothing would make me happier than to have him commit to KU this weekend." The elevator doors opened. "Well, there's our ride. You guys be careful." Henderson gave the trio a goodbye wave.

Lance watched the door close. *If I could be surrounded each day with class people like the two inside that elevator, becoming a Jayhawks might be my destiny.* He turned to join another reason that becoming a Jayhawk might be his destiny: Lisa.

"Nice parking spot, J.C.," Lance ribbed. He opened the front passenger door for Lisa, then he climbed into the back seat.

"Got to have a place to park," J.C. showed a reluctant smile.

They drove a short distance to Lisa's apartment. She handed J.C. her entrance card to open the gate. The complex showcased well-manicured lawns and row after row of identical brick units. Lance thought that Lisa's parents must be doing all right if they could afford this for their girl. The Escalade stopped at number 106.

"Want to come in?" Lisa asked. "I've got pop and chips."

"No, we'd better get back to the hotel," said Lance. He walked her to the door. Lance noticed Lisa's face pull a slight pout. "I wish we could come in. But this is an official visit. I . . . better make sure we're ready and on time tonight."

She nodded. They agreed to meet during Midnight Madness. Lisa described exactly where she would be standing, making it easy for Lance to find her.

At the hotel, J.C. threw his stuff on one of the queen beds. "These rooms are nice. And what a view of the river. Huck and Tom would have loved floating along here."

Lance was more than a little surprised. "You never cease to amaze me. You've read a little Mark Twain?"

"God Bless my mom. Made all of us read. Don't understand how all you smart guys do it, but having Mom demand I read has made a difference."

"What do ya like to read?"

"Lots of sports books. Some history, too, especially about people's lives."

"Me, too."

Kicking off their shoes, they took two Cokes from the mini-fridge, then went out on the small balcony. Lance stretched his legs, crossed his feet on the banister, and took a long sip.

Lance hesitated before facing his doubts. "I'm not the only three-point shooter Kansas is recruiting. You think . . . they really want me?"

J.C. almost spit out his Coke. "They want you bad, Man. They know you committed to visit Ohio State and Kentucky, but they're afraid Duke and Louisville are going to jump back in the picture and try to swallow you up."

"Where do they get that stuff? I have no plans to visit Duke and my dad would disown me if I even looked cross-eyed at Louisville. Besides, I'm getting a feel for this Kansas-Kansas State rivalry. It reminds me of the Kentucky-Louisville showdowns. Most of the people have been terrific and make me feel welcome. I wonder about the coaches. I just wonder." It wasn't hard for J.C. to recognize that Lance really was scared. That he might actually think he's not talented enough for Kansas. "Am I good enough? Am I their first choice? I bet they really want Sam."

"Did I just stutter? You are good. You're *my* first choice. Ever since I met you last summer, I wanted to be your teammate. I know it was by accident we met, but my momma doesn't think so. When I talk to her about you, she says it's God's will we become teammates." J.C. leaned forward and stared at Lance. "She was impressed when you came home with me. You know, white country boys just never come to my neighborhood."

Lance recognized the sincere compliment, but used his wit to acknowledge. "It was an easy decision. Mom and Dad were heading to the malls, and you bragged and bragged about how your momma was frying up some of her chicken. All you had to do was ask me to take a break at your house." Lance took a long sip of his Coke. "You mean all this time you thought I went home with you just to see your autographed Michael Jordan photo? Naw, it was the chicken. It was as fantastic as you said. And your momma made me feel real welcome as soon as I stepped in the door."

Finishing off their Cokes, they continued to unwind, enjoying the view of the rushing river as the fiery sun faded in the West. Lance asked, "Why did you commit early? Was it the coach? You could've signed anywhere in America. Your pick."

"Hear me on this," J.C. was almost preaching. "It wasn't Booth. I hope he's a good coach, I really do. Have to get used to his style, though. When it gets right down to the bottom line, I thought of my family. You know we don't have a dad in the picture. My mom works her tail off for Mr. Graham and his company. There's my brother and two sisters to provide for. If I go to UCLA or Arizona, my family never gets to see me play, except on TV. Talk about your dad disowning you, my Mom would be lookin' for a new job the second Mr. Graham heard I may have even considered going somewhere else." J.C. stood up and gazed intently down at the river. "Couldn't even go to church on Sundays without two or three from the congregation pulling me aside." J.C. turned and leaned against the rail. "My choice was economics. I'm thankful the tradition at KU is so outstanding. It made my choice simple. I signed." A small tear escaped from J.C.'s right eye. "Momma got a big raise. Now we always have money for food… And Momma is able to make payments on my wheels."

Lance was silent. J.C. was speaking from the heart. His friend didn't need any more questions right now. Chances are he hadn't really figured out his mom, even with a promotion, couldn't afford to pay for an Escalade. Besides, Lance reckoned that from J.C.'s perspective, his decision was noble. Any benefits were deserved.

"Right now it's hard on my momma." J.C. wiped his eye with his sweater sleeve. "But I'm going to be one of the guys who makes it into the NBA. I know it's true, just as I know my next breath will fill my lungs with this good Kansas air. When I make it big, I'll repay her tenfold. She'll be set for life. It's my honest-to-God promise to her."

J.C. looked away from Lance, quickly gathering his composure. "Your mom and dad? Will they let you come here?"

"You met Dad. He always gives lots of advice, but he's strong enough to know ultimately that I must make my own life choices. Mom, she'll love me no matter where I end up, even though deep down, she's Bluegrass to the bone. Nothing would make her happier than watching me play for Kentucky."

"Man, the heat will be on for you to stay home. Why are you even considering Ohio State? Seems to me this should be a race between Kansas and Kentucky. The two K's."

"Have an uncle who lives outside Columbus. He's been pounding me and my parents about playing for Ohio State since he saw me make my first three-point shot. Everyone says the coach is a quality person up there. I'm a hoops man, but I love college football. I grew up loving Kentucky basketball and admiring Ohio State football because of my Uncle." Lance placed both hands on the rail, pulled himself up, then stretched. "It's complicated. Just like your situation." He noticed his watch. "Hey, go ahead and jump in the shower. I'll wait. Just make sure you leave me a clean towel and a little hot water, man."

The two were soon decked out with a few minutes to spare, so Lance turned on the TV. "Here we go. Alabama and LSU," Lance said happily.

"Alabama will kill them," J.C. predicted.

"No way. My high school football coach loves that LSU coach. Says he's a defensive genius."

"What's the score?"

Lance watched the corner of the screen. "There it is. LSU 10; Alabama 0. What did I tell you? That coach is gonna shut Alabama out." Lance sat down on the edge of the bed, trying to get closer to the screen.. "Look. Here come the scores."

They both watched the scores scroll across the bottom of the screen, Lance intently, J.C. leisurely.

"You have a favorite football team, J.C.?"

"Nope. Always liked Florida State. Never been to Florida. Just, they got an aggressive style. You?" J.C. chuckled. "Let me guess. Kentucky. And you said you always liked Ohio State. Right? Buckeyes? What's a Buckeye, anyways?"

"The nut from a Buckeye tree. Fans gather them when they fall off and string necklaces. Science hasn't found the cure for any mystery disease with the Buckeye yet; still tryin'. Fans carry one in their pockets for good luck."

"Miami's drilling West Virginia," said J.C. "Look at that score: 42 to 10."

"There's my Buckeyes. Yesss, no problem with Indiana; 28 to 3 at the start of the third quarter," said Lance.

"They're starting the SEC scores. Do you think your Kentucky Wildcats won?" asked J.C.

"They don't play South Carolina until later tonight," said Lance.

"Better duck. Here's the Big Twelve scores." J.C. watched the screen closely. "Oklahoma won, Nebraska won. My, oh, my. Must've gotten nasty in the fourth quarter. Kansas State 48 and Kansas 10. Ouch."

"That's too bad," Lance moaned. "I like the Kansas coach. He's brand new, but his players are trying. That coach called some pretty impressive plays, and the quarterback did all he could. Give him a couple of years and they'll be Bowl bound. Mark my words." *Greg might be one of the players the Hawks need to turn their luck around.*

Pointing a finger at Lance, J.C. teased, "How would you know about the plays the quarterback was trying to run? Looked to me like you were more interested in Lisa, my friend."

"You trying to set us up?" Lance let a grin pop up on his face.

"Not really." J.C. returned the grin. "Those girls are as tight as sisters. Marla's fun to be with. A little on the wild side, but she keeps a group laughing. Lisa's different -- great family, cheerleader, played basketball. Never any good at basketball, but she saw it through. Just thought you'd like to meet her." J.C. sat up on his bed. "Looks like you might fall in love, come to Kansas, play basketball with me then get married and become a lawyer. I'll go off to the NBA, hire you as my agent, and we'll all live happily ever after. How does that story sound to you, my man? Could be a best seller." He looked pleased with himself.

"Let's change that story just a smidgeon!" Lance countered. "Why can't I go to the NBA? You get married and start an insurance agency in Kansas City and I'll buy insurance on my home and fleet of cars from you."

"Dream on. I like my story better. Back to Lisa. Besides being one of the best looking girls from our school, she's also a merit scholar, student council rep, May queen court. You want me to go on? She's a prize. Handle her with care." J.C. wasn't looking at the TV any more. His voice had turned solemn. "Do I make my point?"

"I'm listening. Does Lisa know how lucky she is to have a friend like you? You're a good man. I'm lucky, too—I have a friend who thinks I'm almost worthy of such an all-around great girl." Lance stood up. "Before we come to blows or I give you a hug, isn't it about time to head over to the Angus House?" Lance grabbed his blue sweater and they were on the road again.

"What kind of gas mileage does this thing get?" Lance asked, shutting the passenger's door.

"Don't know. Mom fills it up."

Oh boy, Lance worried silently. *Black Beauty is a problem. A big problem.*

In less than five minutes, they were pulling into the Angus House parking lot. A faint odor of hickory coals embraced them as they entered the front door. A hostess immediately greeted them. "You must be part of Coach Booth's basketball party. Ya kind of stick out in a crowd." Laughing at her own joke, she started around the corner. "Follow me."

She led them down a staircase decorated with Western memorabilia. Pictures of Wyatt Earp, Wild Bill Hickock, and several nameless cowboys hung alongside weathered chaps, lassos, and saddles.

"Come on in," Booth greeted them as they entered a private room. "J.C., something wrong? You're actually early," Coach remarked dryly.

"Thank Lance. He's Mister Time Management. I'd probably still be enjoying the football scores on ESPN," J.C. answered confidently.

Booth frowned. "Let's not talk football. It was another tough day for the Hawks."

Lance peered down the hallway and noticed Big John trucking as fast has he could towards the room. "Marla and I stayed to the end of the game. Sorry if I'm late." He rushed to claim a seat.

"Don't be in a panic. You're right on time. They're just taking drink orders," Coach put him at ease.

Dinner conversation flowed easily. Coaches talked about some of the team's better games of last season. Each recruit listened as the staff offered glimpses of what it might be like to be part of even better games in the future. The menu suited Lance's appetite perfectly: big steak, bigger baked potato, endless salad, and the house specialty -- sizzling hot peach cobbler oozing with vanilla ice cream.

Booth closed the dinner. "I hope everyone is well fed and ready to head over to Allen Field House. It's time to have a little fun and get started with the real sport around here."

Lance felt fine. His sense of well being, however, wasn't just caused by the great dinner. Lisa would be in the house.

As the group left, Lance noticed stares and eager whispers from other diners. Sad faces, most probably created by the football game, began to brighten as they realized basketball would begin tonight.

"J.C., give me a second," Lance said. He slipped into the men's room. As he washed his hands, he looked up to see the face of the arrogant booster who he had met earlier at the tailgate suddenly beside him. "Mr. Hillcrest." Lance gathered himself. "Hello, sir. Sorry about the game."

"It was expected." Distaste was in his voice. "That doesn't happen in basketball. By the way, how's your grandmother?" Mr. Hillcrest wiped his hands, then forcefully threw the paper towel in the trash. Turning, he looked hard at Lance. "Keep in mind, we're prepared to help." He sounded like a TV commercial for life insurance.

"My grandmother? She's fine, sir." Lance was uneasy. "I've got to go. Coach will be mad if we're late."

Lance joined J.C. at the entrance. J.C. asked, "All set?"

"That was strange. Mr. Hillcrest from Coach's tailgate was in there. He gave me the creeps. Asked about my Nana."

"Questions. Boosters always asking questions," J.C. said. "Let's go."

Chapter 8

When they arrived at Allen Fieldhouse, they were quickly escorted to the locker room by Coach Mills. An attendant opened the doors and asked who the new managers were.

Lance noticed the toothy smile on the attendant's face. It was Joe, the parking attendant. *He must work at both football and basketball games. John Mattington had said he was great, but double duty?* This was someone who loved his school, and it showed.

J.C. and Lance took turns shaking Joe's hand. "Managers?" J.C. puffed, playfully squeezing hard.

The walls wore pictures of former and current players. Lance noticed a photo of Shane driving to the hole, finger rolling it in for a bucket. They passed a laundry room and small training room. Nothing fancy. The women's softball locker room was on the right and farther down was men's basketball. It wasn't a very big locker room, but it appeared to be functional. In the middle was a huge Jayhawk woven in the carpet. Wooden stools were placed alongside each locker. J.C. and Lance grabbed two and joined the other recruits already seated.

Booth came forward. "Gentlemen, this is our locker room. As you can see, it's cozy and has worked quite effectively. Some are fancier, but you'll not see any with a classier history."

Lance looked around the room, trying to picture all the great players who once sat in this special chamber; several of those Hawks were still playing in the NBA. Michael Lee would have spent hours listening to strategies for winning, maybe on the very stool where he now sat. Lance sensed the drama. He imagined players from the past coming out of the walls, silently cheering, "You tell them, Coach. There's nothing like being a Jayhawk. Nothing like putting on the Kansas uniform." Kansas tradition. It seemed to be reaching out, embracing his soul, saying, "Lance, take my hand."

Booth wrapped up his speech. Everyone stood and started into the Fieldhouse. "Lance, why don't you stay for a minute?" Booth asked. "You have an early flight tomorrow. Hoped I could start answering any questions you might have."

Lance pondered his thoughts as he watched the last recruit leave. "This has been an excellent trip. Your staff has been super." Coach appeared to be listening, but his expression was urging Lance to hurry up, as if he was anxious to say something rather than really answer questions. "Thank you for the opportunity to visit. Don't have any questions right now."

"Good." Booth put his hand on Lance's shoulder. "We want you to be a Jayhawk."

Those were the words that Lance had been waiting to hear. J.C. was right. They did want him. His heart skipped a beat. *I could be with Lisa. Focus, boy. You gotta focus. I've promised other coaches. I gave them my word. If this was my last visit, I could commit for sure*, he paused. "Whoa, that is awesome. But, Coach, it's not my last…"

"We all recognize that you got other visits." Booth cut him off, seeming to anticipate what he was about to say. "I hate for you to go back. You know . . . to those Wildcats." Booth put his foot on one of the stools. "It's good to get away. Going away to school -- and I mean away -- has helped many a young man mature."

"It's hard, right now, to figure all this out."

"Well, keep trying," Booth advised with a strong degree of forcefulness. "Kansas is the best thing that could happen to you, your family, and your future." He took his foot off the stool and said, "Go get a good seat. We'll talk more later."

"Thanks, Coach."

Perplexed, Lance walked back into the Fieldhouse. He decided that he would say nothing about his meeting with Booth to anyone until he could spend a little more time figuring things out.

He was suddenly surrounded by 17,000 fans, hungry for a reason to smile. His eyes tried to focus on the area where Lisa had promised to be. To his delight, there she stood, a tiny gem shining in the crowd. Approaching her side, he experienced a jolt of pleasure. The sensation lasted only a heartbeat, but it was real. Was this how all beautiful co-eds would made him feel or was this one awfully special?

During breaks in the entertainment, Lance and Lisa carried on bits of conversation.

"Will you be coming back to Kansas soon?" asked Lisa.

"If I commit, my parents plan on making a trip with me during the season. They haven't seen the campus."

"They'll love it," Lisa was enthusiastic. "If you let me know when, I could help show them around."

Lightly squeezing her hand, Lance said softly, "That would be awfully nice of you. I'd like that."

The team sprinted onto the court, ready for their long awaited scrimmage. Lance's concentration was totally on the floor. Mental notes accumulated in his brain.

As they shot, the nets kept swooshing. "I love that sound," he said happily.

"What sound?"

"Listen to those nets."

The scrimmage ended and the team left the floor. "I'll be right back," he said, almost as if he was asking for permission.

"I'll wait by the doors." Lisa's tone told him she understood his desire to go back into the locker room one last time.

In a room full of noise and activity, Lance made his way over to Shane. "Nice show. You guys are good. Thanks again for hosting me."

"No problem. My pleasure. Coach said you had an early flight. I probably won't see you tomorrow." Shane clasped Lance's hand. Their thumbs interlocked. "Good luck this season, and hit those threes." Shane's smile was genuine.

Lance released his hand and slowly turned away. Coach Holister had been watching them and motioned for Lance. "Coach Booth and I'll come by at about seven for breakfast, then I'll give you a ride to the airport. OK?"

Lance nodded.

Holister looked around the locker room. "Who's taking you back to your hotel? I'd be happy to drop you off."

"Thanks for offering. J.C. said he'd take me back."

When he heard his name, J.C. strolled towards them. "That's right, Coach. Doin' everything for him. Next thing, he'll be wantin' me to be settin' picks for him."

"You get him back safe and sound, now." Holister instructed.

They walked back through the arena to the court. The place looked different. Empty, except for a few stragglers and people cleaning up littered

Coke containers and popcorn boxes. Lance loved stepping into a gym after a great game. Families and friends waiting. Everyone beaming. The best feelings, surpassed only by Christmas morning.

Lisa was waiting, leaning against a row of bleachers. She didn't immediately see them. Lance relished the sight of her warm glow when she turned and noticed they were approaching. Grabbing their arms, she escorted the pair out the side door.

"I have my car. I'll give Lance a ride back, if that's OK," Lisa told J.C.

"What do you think, Mr. Stoler? Can I tell the limo driver to take the rest of the night off?" J.C. tried to jest, but gave Lance a searching look, as if to ask, "Are you sure you're ready for what could happen?"

"Sure," Lance said with a steady gaze.

J.C. turned to leave.

Lance called, "J.C., wait! I won't see you tomorrow." Lance recognized he had been given one of life's most precious gifts. A true friend. "I love you, man. Take care."

The friends exchanged a quick hug.

"Me, too, man. Tell your mom and dad that I took good care of their boy out here on the prairie." J.C. wiped his eye and quickly turned, running into the darkness.

Lance turned, catching a glimpse of Lisa's eyes. Slightly tearing, she took a deep breath.

"Boy, you two are something." Lisa took his arm and led him away from the parking garage. "It's only a short walk. I'm parked out back."

"I guess most freshmen don't get preferred parking passes, huh?"

"No, but the walking keeps us in good shape, so it evens out."

As the lights were shutting down in Allen Fieldhouse, they made their way to Lisa's car.

"A Honda, huh?"

"Yeah, I love it," Lisa said, starting the engine.

Within a few minutes, they were traveling down Naismith Drive. "Hey, you're a pretty good driver, for an old twenty-two-year-old."

"Don't bring that up. I only have the nerve to use that card when I'm with Marla." Lisa's expression hardened into a frown.

He had meant the remark to be cute. He hated that it might have hurt Lisa's feelings. He tried to make up for his mistake. "It was nice of you to drive me back to the hotel. You've really made this weekend special."

Lisa softened. "I had no idea it would be so nice for me, too."

The Honda turned into the hotel drive. The abundance of empty parking spots shouted that the purple-clad folks had deserted the area. Lisa pulled into a spot close to the entrance. The couple sat and enjoyed each other's company for several minutes until Lance reluctantly looked at his watch and said, "I better go on in. Have a meeting with the coaches early in the mornin'."

"I know, I know. I could go on talking to you for hours," Lisa spoke, sadly. "I've just met you and now you're going away. It's like our time together was just a sweet dream."

"That's one of the nicest things anyone's ever said to me," Lance could feel his throat tightening and words were hard coming. *What's wrong with me,* he thought. *Get yourself together.*

They sat looking at each other for a few seconds. Lisa then spoke, sounding like a little girl trying to think of another reason to be able to stay up a few more minutes at bedtime. "Before you leave, can we exchange e-mail addresses and phone numbers?" They exchanged information. "I'll e-mail you tomorrow," Her voice sang with excitement. "A message will be waiting when you arrive home. A little present from me."

Lance suddenly pulled her into his arms. They held each other tight. Reluctantly Lance did let go, and slowly climbed out of the car.

Lisa drove off quietly leaving him feeling empty and howling at the bright moon. "Why didn't I kiss her? Dang. Why didn't I kiss her?"

He walked slowly through the lobby. It was way after midnight. When he reached his room, he flicked on the lights, picked up the phone, and hit "0."

"May I help you?" A voice from the lobby desk quickly answered.

"Could I have a wake-up call at six?"

"Yes, Sir. Good night."

Lance took off his shirt and pants, then sprawled out on the bed. Sleep was not an immediate option.

Kansas?

Coach?

Loved those steaks.

J.C.'s a great guy.

Shane can really stroke it.

Wish I would've kissed Lisa.

Lance pondered until sleep caught the Kentucky kid off-guard.

At the hotel restaurant the next morning, a hostess led Lance to a reserved table. He was the first to arrive. Minutes later the coaches walked in. Lance watched them cross the room. *Coach looks tired.* He studied Holister. *I wonder if he'll get a head job.*

Everyone quickly ordered so Lance could get on his way to the airport and Booth could make early practice. They waited for their food. Booth crossed his arms on the table and with his best no-holds-barred attitude, picked up where he had left off in the locker room last night.

"Lance, here's an option. Sign with us right now. Play your senior year with no more recruiting hassles. No more phone calls. It would be all over. Signed, sealed, and delivered to Kansas."

"I appreciate that, Coach. I really do. It's just that I promised both Ohio State and Kentucky I'd visit. If I went back on my word, people would question my honesty and character. Isn't that right?" Lance hoped for words of approval.

"You just explain to them you're young and you changed your mind," Booth said. He rationalized, as if it were a jar of pickles that might be put back on the shelf, not a young man's integrity.

Lance was disappointed in Booth, but tried hard not to let it show. Lance didn't care how young or old he was, his word was his word. Gritting his teeth, he looked at Coach Holister, wishing he might jump in and say something. Holister looked back at Lance, but remained silent.

As the waitress finished pouring more coffee, Lance spoke up. "Coach, I can't go back on my word. I hope you understand."

"You haven't eliminated us, have you?" His voice sounded mean.

"No way. I really like Kansas. Just gotta' see my visits through."

"Will you visit Duke, or any other school if it comes into the picture?" He had softened his voice only slightly.

Lance remembered J.C. had told him Booth was concerned about other schools. "My plans are to stay on course with you and complete my visits to Ohio State and Kentucky."

"That's fair enough." He lashed his irritation on the waitress by curtly asking for the check. "I'm happy you could be with us this weekend. Coach

Holister, you had better get Lance to the airport." He extended his hand. "Have a safe trip home."

Lance excused himself to check his room one final time and get his suitcase. Coach might not feel too chipper right now, but Lance did. He had buried his doubts about Kansas. They wanted Milt and Helen's son.

The ride back to the airport was surprisingly pleasant. Holister was less reserved when he was away from Booth. He talked about his family and how much he liked Kansas. He shared that his only son recently joined the military. Lance said that he might enjoy the service, maybe the Air Force. His dad had served during the Vietnam War and Grandpa Stoler served in World War II as a tank driver for Patton. Lance enjoyed it when Grandpa would chat about his war experiences. During one of those rare conversations, the Stoler grandkids learned he had earned a bronze star and a purple heart. Lance was convinced there was something noble about the military. He was not prepared to give up his hoops career, but he would serve his country if life presented that expectation.

At the Kansas City airport, Lance thanked Coach Holister for the ride and told him how much he liked their conversations.

"Give my best to your mom and dad."

Lance gathered his suitcase from the trunk. "Tell your son I wish him the best."

He sat at the airport gate and waited for his section to be called. It had been a mere weekend, but so much had happened. He looked forward to seeing his family and giving them the Kansas updates. Greg would take pleasure in Lance's analysis of Big Twelve football. Cherie would want to know every last detail about Lisa, if she found out; and knowing Cherie, she probably would. Dad would quiz him about Coach Booth, and Mom would just be happy her eldest child had arrived home safely.

The plane launched from the runway, while Lance looked down one last time on the Kansas/Missouri landscape. He wondered if he would ever glimpse this scenery from the opposite direction. Would he be coming back?

Chapter 9

Lady Lexington was dressed in a gown of spectacular fall tones as the plane made its descent over her air space. Lance was eager to get home. Milt and Greg were waiting when he walked from the gate.

"Hi!" Lance gave them each a big Stoler bear hug. He said to Greg, "Hey, glad you guys won on Friday. Dad said you had a great game."

"We were really clicking again." Greg did a quick recap, sounding like sports on the six o'clock news. They made their way out of the terminal, found the family's Tahoe, loaded Lance's suitcase, and headed to the exit.

Milt paid the parking attendant, then pulled into Lexington traffic. "How's J.C. doing?" he asked.

"Looks great. It was super being with him again."

Greg quizzed, "Kansas recruiting any big guys? Someone's gotta rebound for you shooters."

"They are, in fact, little brother." Lance gave a lengthy description of his fellow recruits. "Kansas had four recruits in, plus J.C., who's already signed."

"Do you think they still want you? Or did you screw it up?" Lance knew he was trying to be playful, but was serious with his questions. He was positive his dad was thinking the same thing.

"I'm amazed, but they do. You won't believe what happened this morning. Coach Booth tried hard to force me to commit and turn down the other visits."

"You've got to be kidding me," Milt came close to swearing. "He wanted you to give up visiting Ohio State? Let alone Kentucky?"

"I told him I had promised those other coaches and couldn't commit to anyone yet."

"Good job," affirmed Milt. "Don't let someone pressure you into doing something until you're sure about it. It's wonderful that they really want you, but I'm delighted you stood firm and kept your word." Milt smirked. "Besides, if you don't visit Ohio State, you can forget about going to Columbus for the rest of your life. And come next spring, don't expect a graduation present from your Uncle Gary." they all chuckled.

Lance was glad his dad was driving. The wake-up call had been early. He was suddenly very tired. He had had little sleep during the visit and was excited about climbing into his own bed.

Milt let Lance rest his eyes a few minutes. After listening to the third song on Clint Black's new CD, Milt turned down the volume and asked, "Coach Booth? What was your read on him?"

Lance slowly sat up in his seat and rubbed his forehead. "That's still a hard one. Something isn't right. They have a successful program. But is it because of the coach or because of Kansas? Couldn't any halfway decent coach step into Allen Fieldhouse and carry on that winning tradition? Shane White made me believe he chose KU mostly because of the tradition." Lance looked out the passenger window, and then turned to his dad. "This seems like a small thing, but I never saw Coach wear Kansas stuff. You know, shirts and things that shouted, 'I'm from Kansas and proud of it!' And he was always talking about how things were done back home. I wondered why no one sat him down and said, 'Hey, Dude, this is Kansas.'"

Milt glanced at his son. "I'm sure we'll find out more over the next few weeks. You're making those other two visits." He paused. "How were the assistant coaches?"

"Coach Holister's real nice. He picked me up and dropped me off at the airport. We had some good conversations. I didn't get to be around Coach Mills that much. He seemed to always be running errands for Coach Booth. I did meet Michael Lee, though. He was with J.C. on Friday." Turning to the backseat, Lance said, "Greg, can you believe an NBA player carried my luggage?"

"Yeah, right. You mean you carried a bag for him."

"No, seriously. At the hotel, he took my suitcase inside for me when I was first checking in."

"Now that's impressive," said Milt.

"I think he'll probably work at Kansas when his career's over, which will probably be real soon," Lance predicted.

"Yeah, but he's making a million dollars a year," Greg said. "Kansas can't pay him that, can they?"

"Speaking of money," Lance almost shouted, "J.C. has an Escalade! A big black, Escalade with gorgeous leather interior."

"Like, as in a Cadillac?" Milt seemed more than a little surprised.

"Yes."

"Where in the world would he get the money for a Cadillac?" Milt asked.

"He told me that his mom got it for him."

"Come on, you went to J.C.'s house."

"Dad, I'm just telling you what J.C. told me. His Mom works for some big Kansas booster as a secretary. He said she got a promotion when he signed early with the Jayhawks."

"I could double promote every secretary we have at the school and they still couldn't afford a car like that. Do the coaches know?"

"I didn't ask them and no one said anything. Not even Michael and he was always riding around with J.C."

"Then they know." Milt's voice sounded upset.

"Great." called a voice from the back seat. "Will you get a black one or will yours be Jayhawk blue?"

Milt Stoler was sitting up straight now. Holding the wheel tightly, his posture stiffened. "Greg, this is some serious stuff."

"I think J.C. truly feels his mom got him the car. Or at least he wants to believe that." Lance positioned himself in the seat so he could hear his dad better. "How does that stuff happen?"

"People who think they're above the rules will find ways. A booster might have arranged something with a car dealer or figured out some other way to make it happen. J.C. and his mom might not even know the complete details."

"J.C. doesn't have to buy gas, either. He said his mom has the car filled up. I told him how you always complained about the forty bucks it took to fill this thirsty Tahoe." Lance looked out the front windshield. "It just doesn't add up."

"Did it occur to you how hard it would be for the Burbridges to turn down something like that?" Milt's voice deepened. "Remember what I've always told both of you -- work hard, be honest, have integrity, and honor the Lord. That will carry you through times when your values will be tempted.

And believe me, everyone is tempted and tested." Milt pushed against the steering wheel. "I'm not trying to judge J.C. and his mom. I know how hard it is for a mother to raise a family by herself."

They were only a few miles from home. Enough had been said. Each passenger sat in silence, watching the cornfields fly by. Shifting his attention from Kansas to home, Lance wondered what his mom was cooking for dinner and if Cherie had won her soccer game yesterday. If Nana was OK.

Gazing up at a periwinkle sky, he recalled his last contact with Mr. Hillcrest.

"Dad, everything alright with Nana?"

"Yeah, why do you ask?"

"Oh, nothing, just wonderin'."

He again shut his eyes and attempted to rest for a few minutes. A vivid picture of Lisa sitting in her car last night easily prevented him from dozing off. Should have kissed her. He left that mistake, then let his stomach pose a question.

"What's Mom fixin' for dinner?"

"Welcome home. I knew it wouldn't take you long to start thinking about food again." Milt laughed.

"Mom sure loves you," Greg blurted out. "Said she was gonna fix your favorite roast and mashed potatoes."

"Sounds good. Hey, did Cherie win her soccer game?"

"Sure did." Milt said.

"Yeah, our baby sister had several outstanding defensive plays," Greg bragged.

"Sorry I missed it."

The lazy, flowing water of the Big Sandy River was a welcome sight just before the Tahoe rolled up the driveway. "I think they call this home," Milt said.

Lance loved his home. His parents bought it when he was in seventh grade. It sat on two acres and had an awesome long driveway that curved up to a flat area across from the garage. There Milt had installed the best hoop in the county.

The house was white with green shutters which Helen insisted be added shortly after they moved in. She argued they made the house look happier. Shade trees softened the front, and out back the family had enough land to provide the Stoler version of a football field, soccer field, or golf course, depending upon the weather and which sibling got to the field first that day. There was a row of grapevines and various apple, peach, plum and cherry trees. Greg's favorite tree was an imposing oak, growing on the west edge of the property. Milt challenged his quarterback son that when he could stand on the opposite property line and throw a football over the top of that oak, it would be proof of a deadly, strong arm. Lance suspected Mother Nature's work on the oak would not be fast enough to prevent a future pigskin fly over.

Outside the play area was Helen's garden. Each year she fought raccoons for ownership. Rows of corn, carrots, beef steak tomatoes, and half-runner beans always survived, providing fresh, healthy nourishment to the summer dinner table. Marigolds shimmered around the perimeter, supposedly to keep out pests, but Helen claimed most of all they gave definition to her space.

Lance popped out of the car. The family's best friend was instantly there to give him a welcome lick.

"Bubba, how you doing, Boy? Did you miss me?" Lance gave the three-year-old Labrador retriever a big hug. The dog was exceptionally large for his breed. His coat was midnight black, and he had large, soulful eyes.

"Dignified," Helen often said of Bubba. "My sweetheart is dignified."

He was also the family bodyguard. The Stolers didn't have to worry about traveling salesmen coming to their door with Bubba on patrol. They would take one look at him and quickly decide to knock on a door further down the street.

Milt popped open the rear and said to Greg, "You're no NBA star, but why don't you grab your brother's suitcase?"

"Thanks, but I got it," said Lance. "Don't want to have to be carrying your bags when you're in the NFL."

The house smelled like Sunday. Helen threw her arms around Lance, barely reaching above his waist. Their height had reversed over the years, but her role remained constant. With unfailing love, she validated the good in each of her children. "It's wonderful to see you, Son."

"Glad to be home, Mom."

Pots were simmering on the stove, a beef roast was in the oven, and a good looking pumpkin pie sat invitingly on the table.

Cherie flew out of her room and flashed her brother a bright metal smile. He could see the beauty she was going to be when those braces finally were taken off. Her hugs, well, they were more like boxing punches.

"Hey, Girl. Greg told me that you won yesterday."

Lance savored the smells of the kitchen while he listened patiently to his sister's version of victory. She had grown up always a little cheerleader at Lance's games; now it was his pleasure to cheer for her.

"Coach had me in the whole game." Cherie stuck her finger into the pot of mashed potatoes, and brought out a dollop. "It was a big win." She stopped only long enough to place her finger and the attached dollop into her mouth. "I mean huge!"

"Man, I'm sorry I missed it." Lance opened the refrigerator door.

Helen and Cherie smiled at each other. They knew he found one of his favorites.

"Deviled eggs!" Before anyone could stop him, one disappeared. His speed slowed on his second attempt.

Helen's eyes proceeded to handcuff him. "Now stop that, Lance." She laughed. "You don't want to ruin your dinner."

Lance regrettably left the kitchen and made his way down the hallway, past Cherie's room. Nothing had changed. It looked like a big, pink dollhouse, with everything meticulously in its place.

He passed his brother's room. Greg's style of making a bed would be frowned on by any military academy. Three pairs of Nikes and a few wrinkled clothes were thrown haphazardly around.

Lance stepped into his own room. The walls were covered with tartan plaid paper. A picture of his championship shot was prominently displayed above his desk, and his trashcan -- with attached baby hoop -- was still in the corner. He sorted through his suitcase. The room was straightened, cleaned more than his standards, and he detected a scent of orange furniture polish. Undoubtedly, Helen had felt the urge to give it her blessing.

This is where Lance did his homework, studied his playbooks, listened to music, and dreamed about his future. After his clothes were put away, he jumped on the bed, contentedly closed his eyes, and drifted miles away.

"We've been waiting for this game," the announcer of his daydream radio began. "Kansas against UCLA". The Kansas fans were excited because they wanted to know if this kid from Kentucky can replace Shane White. "Our worries are over, folks. The new wonder just hit his fourth three. Look out Missouri. Look out Big Twelve. The Jayhawks will be deadly for four more years."

Lance must have floated off to sleep, because he was jolted awake by his dad's booming voice. "Lance! Greg! Cherie! Dinner's ready. Let's eat."

The family gathered around the table. Habit caused each to claim regular seats. Helen sat on the end, Milt at the head, Lance on one side, and Cherie and Greg shared the other.

Milt asked Lance, "Why don't you lead us in prayer?"

The family joined hands.

"Dear Lord, we glorify your name. Bless this food to our bodies and thanks for guiding me safely back home to my family. Help each of us have a good week. And if you could help the Bengals this afternoon that would also be appreciated. Amen."

"Your brother wants equal time for the Browns," Milt said to Lance as the family started to pass salad and cornbread.

"No problem, Dad. Browns don't need a prayer. They'll bury 'em." Greg looked across the table at his brother. "Browns-Bengals game is easy to figure out. What we need to know is what happened in that Kansas State game."

"Wait," Helen demonstrated her authority. "Sports questions come after Lance fills us in on what the campus looked like and something about the academic programs."

Lance went through a review of how beautiful the campus was and about his meeting with Miss Appleton. His descriptions made them all regret they hadn't made the trip along with him.

Cherie seemed tired of waiting her turn. "Do they have women's soccer?"

"Yes they do, Kiddo. I saw one of the soccer players in the training room, in fact. She was getting treated during our tour of the training facilities. Mr. Shaffer, the head trainer, was a great guy."

"Hey, what about the football game?" Greg asked, again.

"Wasn't pretty. Kansas State was much better and they love their purple. After they got ahead it was like a home game for them." He paused, then spoke seriously, "Greg, not because you're my brother, but I think you could play with those guys. I really do."

Greg laid down his cornbread and gave the table a loud, "That's me. Ready and waiting for their call."

"Lance," Helen scolded. "He's only a sophomore. Besides, he doesn't even know how to act at the dinner table."

Lance shifted focus to his sister. "When's your next game?" he asked.

"Wednesday. If we win, it'll be five in a row. Can you believe it?"

"After school or in the evening?" Lance asked.

"It's at 4:00."

"I hope our practice is later. I'd like to come over and watch Miss Master of Defense." He winked at his baby sister.

"Me too." Cherie flashed an adoring smile at her brother.

For casual family dinners, Helen left everything on the top of the stove so that everyone could serve his or her own main course. Lance got there first. He took a big piece of roast, piled his plate high with mashed potatoes, and covered both with a ladle of rich, brown gravy. There was little room for green beans, but he managed to place a serving in the corner. Soon everyone had returned to the table and conversation resumed.

Cherie asked, "What did you do on Friday night?"

"Dinner at Coach Booth's house. Then J.C. took me down to Massachusetts Street."

"What's that?"

"It's the main street in Lawrence. Lots of shops and restaurants." Lance thought that was a good way to describe the strip. No sense bringing up the numerous college bars.

"Did you meet anyone?" asked Cherie.

"Sure, there were a lot of people down there. After all, it was the night before a home football game."

"No, I mean did you meet anyone?" she demanded.

"J.C. did bring a couple of his high school friends with him."

Helen became interested. "Who?"

"Marla and Lisa."

"I knew it!" Cherie grinned her best Cheshire cat smile.

Lance shared a vague, condensed description of his encounters with Lisa and Marla. He wasn't ready to explain details.

"Is Lisa pretty?" His sister was a little lucky on that question. She could have asked the same about Marla.

"You're getting a little nosey there," Mom said. She stepped in when a family member needed help, and she had noticed her son starting to look like a beet.

"No, Mom, make him answer that one! I'd like to know, too," Greg showed great joy in seeing big brother squirm.

"By my standards, she was." Lance pushed away from the table. "I'm going to try some of that pie."

"Stay there," Helen said. "I'll get it. Want a scoop of ice cream, too?"

"That would be great."

"Who else wants some?" It was unanimous. The family also unanimously understood Helen had stepped in to help Lance, and further discussion about any girls in Kansas was closed. For a while, at least.

As always, everyone helped clear the table. Milt decided who would do dishes. "Cherie, why don't you and Lance finish this up?"

It was not a bad assignment. Helen already had the bigger pots and pans scrubbed and put away. And the dishwasher was working just fine.

Helen grabbed her gloves and headed to the garden. The two unassigned "boys" darted to the family room for TV. Cherie embraced her assignment -- Lance was cornered.

"Do you like this Lisa?" Cherie asked in a whisper.

"She was very nice." Lance said.

"So you like her."

"I've only known her for three days, Cherie. She told me she played basketball in high school. It was real easy for me to talk with her."

"I bet she e-mails you. Did you give her your e-mail address?"

"Boy, Mom was right. You are getting nosey."

"You're my brother. Did you give her your e-mail address?" she insisted.

"Well, what if I did?" He roughly forced the forks and spoons into their dishwasher compartments.

"Well, then she'll write." Cherie seemed content with her detective work. "All finished." She gave Lance one last look of satisfaction, then turned out of the kitchen.

Lance found his teammates in front of the TV. "Who's on?" he asked.

"Bears-Buffalo game," Greg didn't take his eyes from the screen as he answered.

"Bears winning?"

"They're ahead 17-10 in the fourth." Greg had a love affair with football. He analyzed every factor: players, coaches, blocking, passing, play-calling, crowd, even the officials. "Our game comes on right after this. Did you see that score? The Vikings are destroying Green Bay."

Milt dozed while his sons watched the Bears hang on to beat the Bills. Now it was time for some serious football. The boys loved watching the Browns vs. Bengals games. Not only was it two Ohio teams, but brother against brother. A little in-house rivalry.

"Well, your gals won the toss and elected to receive." Greg was in fine form. "Mistake. The Browns will stuff them and have excellent field position."

"Yeah. Watch this kickoff return."

"You boys should let the announcers do their jobs." Milt was now awake and ready to join in. "They actually get paid to broadcast the play-by-play, you know."

At half time, the game was tied 10-10. Neither brother could claim an advantage. "Go on out and see if your momma needs anything before the second half starts," Milt ordered. He then committed his full attention to school paperwork.

Greg and Lance slowly rose and shuffled out through the back porch, each praying their mom was content. They found her in the garden, looking happy as ever, humming to herself while working among the pumpkins. Bubba was sprawled on the ground beside her.

"Hi, Mom. The game's tied at halftime," Lance said. "We just came out to see if you need anything."

It seemed to Lance that minutes passed before she answered. He and Greg were sweating bullets to get back to the game. They had maybe six minutes before kick-off, and were missing all the halftime highlights.

Helen looked up, read their sheepish expressions and laughed. "No. My sweetheart Bubba and I are doing just fine, but thank you boys for asking. Y'all go on back to your game. I'm perfectly fine."

Helen insisted that working in her garden was joy, not drudgery. When asked what she loved most about working out there, she would say she prayed a little and generally navigated in a sea of calm where time and activity were second thought. She was at peace, with Bubba her constant sidekick.

The boys turned and sprinted back toward the house. They jumped up the back porch steps.

"Wait," Greg halted. He pulled out his Rawlings football from the equipment basket and ran back down the steps.

"Come on," he called.

Lance knew the drill. Greg positioned himself at the property line while Lance ran out by the oak tree. Greg cocked his arm, pumped three times, and let it rip. Lance ran up under the ball. The quarterback shook his head as he jogged over to Lance.

"Must be that pumpkin pie. I thought for sure I could get it there today."

"You will, little brother, you will. Let's get back to the game." Lance ruffled Greg's hair and walked him back into the house, an encouraging arm flung over his shoulder.

Milt had left for the bathroom, so the boys had the family room to themselves.

"Would you really go all the way out to Kansas for school?" asked Greg.

"I don't know. The basketball tradition's strong. It's like going to the very roots of something."

"I know. But it's still past Indiana, past Illinois, past Missouri," Greg made his point.

"Don't forget, I still have Ohio State and Kentucky to visit. Hey, I'm just glad to be home right now."

The brothers stretched out on the carpet, favorite pillows propped haphazardly under their heads. They had thanked their dad many times for finally breaking down and purchasing the big screen monster. Milt stressed reading over lazing in front of a TV, except for Sunday afternoon football or basketball games, of course. During those occasions the old twenty-inch screen had always suited him just fine. But that midget was not adequate for big games like this contest.

The Browns moved the ball down to the twenty-two yard line, but Lance's Bengals made them settle for a field goal and it was a draw for the rest of the third quarter. The score of 13-10 was not a commanding lead, but Lance knew Greg was starting to feel momentum switching to the Cincinnati bench. The phone rang.

Cherie raced to the phone before any of the family room crowd even blinked. At these times, the boys loved having a teenage sister.

"Dad, it's for you," Cherie called, obviously disappointed it wasn't for her.

"Thanks, Honey." He tweaked her nose as he took the receiver from her outstretched hand. "This is Milt."

"Hi. This is Donovan. How are you doing, Old Buddy?"

Mike Donovan and Milt went back many years. They had started teaching careers together and became great friends. The young teachers played on a softball team together and to this day enjoyed fierce competition while golfing. Donovan told great stories. His wonderful sense of humor caused Lance, Greg, and Cherie to look forward to any stop he made to Connsburg on his way to or from his Missouri home.

"It's good to hear from you," said Milt. "We're doing fine, thank you. Just got Lance back from his visit to Kansas."

"That's one of the reason I'm calling. It was in the papers over here that Lance was on the Lawrence campus. With the rivalry between Missouri and Kansas being like the War Between the States, they cover every little heart beat on both sides of the border."

"What did the article say?" asked Milt.

"They talked about Lance and three other kids Kansas is recruiting. They also pointed out the Tigers already lost J.C. Burbridge to the Jayhawks."

"Right. J.C. and Lance have been friends since summer ball."

"Have you met Booth?" The word "Booth" came out like a swear word.

"Only briefly, but we plan on going to a game this season, if that's where Lance commits. Helen and I had school obligations last Friday. You remember that stuff, don't you? Or was it just study hall you taught?"

"Thanks, smart butt. Here I am trying to help you and that kid I taught how to shoot. Seriously now, Milt, I know that I'm living in the heart of Missouri Tigerland, but you and Lance need to know what I've been hearing. They say that Booth has one huge ego. Tries to downplay it with his ole country boy act. Stories are circulating about how he doesn't like to be bossed by either his chancellor or AD. But he's won a lot of games, although some say it's not because of his coaching. You know, winning makes you mighty powerful. Word is, he's one malicious son-of-a-gun to those people who don't do things his way." Donovan slowed down. "He claims to be squeaky clean on NCAA rules. My guess is no one has really looked into his actions. Probably does a good job of diverting things away from himself."

Milt took a deep breath. His face tightened. "What else are they saying?"

"They also keep bringing up players from Kansas City. A few years back. It was some brothers. The oldest was getting recruited by everyone. Kansas wanted him. Missouri wanted him. It looked like some big time booster from KC was going to make sure he got delivered to the Jayhawks. The NCAA got involved and it seemed like there might be some recruiting irregularities. Booth had to back off of him even though the kid had pretty much committed to Kansas. If he had signed with Booth, it would have been interesting to see what the NCAA would've done. I believe the kid went out to one of the West Coast schools. His brother ended up playing for Missouri. Oh, yeah, and then there was that transfer from one of the Southeastern Conference schools. Few in Lawrence could believe that Booth let that kid play at KU. Questionable character. But Booth needed to win." Donovan paused. "Milt, you know I'm going to love watching Lance no matter where he goes. I just think you better be careful on this one."

"I know, I know." Milt rubbed his head in frustration.

"That kid of yours is going to Kentucky, anyway. You and Helen are just letting him go off and have a few life experiences. He's a Wildcat." Mike Donovan instinctively knew when to ease a conversation that drifted into the serious zone.

"That's what everyone around here hopes," Milt said. "You're a true friend. I'll have to share this with Lance. I hate maybe busting a bubble, but he had some questions about that guy already."

Milt promised to get together soon and hung up the receiver. He breathed in slowly, and returned to the family room, his face a mask of concern. The score was still 13-10. Unfortunately for Lance, Cleveland had the ball and was driving, with three minutes to go.

"How are your Bengals holding up?" Milt tried to sound lighthearted.

"They have all their time outs left. If they stop them on this drive, Greg will be crying like a little puppy taken from his momma!"

The two brothers started a mock wrestling match in the middle of the floor. Milt said nothing. He sat down, glanced at his sons, and then at the TV. The Bengals did stop the Browns. They were executing a well-prepared two-minute drill. The ball rested on the twenty yard line. It was third and six. The quarterback had a receiver wide open. However, the strong safety read his eyes and made a great break on the ball. Interception. Game over.

"Your Browns played some really good defense," Milt told Greg. "Now, you guys should go play some defense on that stuff you call homework."

Both would have preferred to watch ESPN Sportscenter. They started to get up, Milt spoke again, "Lance, let me see you a minute first."

He led his son into the kitchen. Helen was already there relaxing with a cup of tea, having finished her gardening. Milt sat down at the table while Lance leaned against the counter. "I need to share something with you two that Mike Donovan told me over the phone." Lance could tell his dad was upset about something.

"Like what, Dad?'

Milt described his conversation -- the stories circulating about Booth. NCAA concerns. Personality concerns. Helen seemed visibly surprised. Lance listened intently.

The three tried to make sense out of the stories. Lance explained that Booth had very little to do with the reasons he had liked his trip. He liked the people he met. The Fieldhouse was spectacular. The campus was beautiful. J.C. was his friend, and Lance kept thinking about Lisa, although she was left out of his explanation.

They agreed to not draw any conclusions yet. It was still too early. Milt simplified the situation. "You have two more recruiting trips."

Milt and Helen remained in the kitchen to share a cup of tea. Lance made his way down the hallway to his bedroom. Cherie's door was closed so it was difficult to tell what was brewing in her secret garden. Greg's door was wide open. No secrets there.

"Hey, the Cleveland coach is on the phone," Lance joked. "He wanted to say, 'Thanks for the help.'"

"Tell him, 'No problem.' He should try to hang in there until I'm through with high school and college, though. Then I'll really help." Greg was gleefully full of himself.

Lance grinned and continued to his room. One chapter in American Government and a half dozen calculus problems stared him in the face. Mr. Donovan's comments, J.C.'s situation, and Lisa weighed on his mind. He couldn't start his homework yet. After several minutes of lying on his bed gazing at the patterns on the plastered ceiling, he realized there were too many questions to resolve right now. He willed himself to escape into the tedium of homework.

Homework complete, he looked at the computer and pondered if he had the courage to turn the thing on. It had been only one day, but Lisa said there would be mail when he got home. "Maybe Cherie knows what she's talking about. No guts, no glory." He turned on the computer, then clicked his way to the inbox. He had mail.

Lance,

Hope you got home safe and sound. Did the flight take long? I am swamped. This week I have two major exams. I need to do well. Was your family happy to see you? You were in Sunday's paper. They said you were visiting with other recruits.

Have a nice week—Lisa

"Now what do I do?" Lance asked the computer. "Do I write back, or do I wait?"

Pushing away from the computer, he rose from the chair and found himself standing in front of Cherie's door. He knocked gently.

"Yeah, who's that 'a knocking at my door?" she sang out.

"You got a minute?"

"I'm busy," she called. "What do you want?"

"Never mind. Coulda' used your help, though." He whispered loudly, "I got an e-mail."

Before Lance could take a step back toward his room, the door flew open and the Love Doctor was ready to operate.

"What did she say?" she hissed, happily.

"Come on. I'll let you read it."

Cherie jumped into his chair and eyeballed the screen. She offered her best professional advice. "Lance, you've got to e-mail her back right now."

"You sure? Shouldn't I wait?"

"Gotta show you care."

"But isn't it too soon?"

"Nah. Can't you read between the lines? She's a nice person. Asked about your trip home and wanted to know about your family. Those are always good signs. Anyway, she'll be able to study better if you e-mail her. She'll stop worrying whether you care enough to write back."

"Do you think she's really just sitting at her desk in Lawrence waiting for me to write back?"

"Were you wondering if she'd e-mail you? Did you hope she would?"

Lance looked out his window. *She's good. How'd she know exactly what I'd been thinking?*

"All right, Counselor," Lance conceded. "What should I say?"

Cherie sat up straight, fingers on the keyboard, and clicked on the reply button. Lance welcomed her help. And he felt confident her assistance would be filed under a code of silence.

"Let's try this," Cherie suggested. She typed.

Lisa,

It was very kind of you to write. I love you . . .

"Cherie, what are you doing?" Lance choked. "I can't say that!"

"OK, OK. I was just kidding. I wanted to see if you were paying attention." Cherie laughed at her brother's sudden pale complexion. "How 'bout this?"

Lisa,

I got home safely and it was good to see my family. Thanks for asking. Good luck with your exams and write again when you get a chance. It was nice of you to e-mail me.

Lance.

"That OK? It's short, shows you actually read the e-mail, and encourages her to stay in contact."

"I like that. No obligations," Lance agreed. "Hit the send button."

Cherie sent it off. She jumped out of the chair, gave her brother a little wink, and was off to her room. Lance smiled contentedly. He headed to the kitchen to get a glass of ice water. His mom was sitting at the table working on her lesson plans. Helen had been teaching for a long time and her students loved her. Lance felt it was because of the great effort she put into each day of teaching. Her lesson plans were well thought out and she always provided special activities. Every other week, Lance would stop by her classroom with some of the guys from the football or basketball team, and Helen would have them read with the class. The kids called them their "Big Buddies." In return, Helen would bring the class to one game a year. Her students didn't know much about the games or who the Green Bears were playing, but they loved seeing their big buddies in action.

Lance rubbed his mom's shoulders gently. "Whatcha doing?"

"Finishing up. Will you be coming by on Tuesday? My kids love seeing their buddies."

"We have study hall third period. We'll be there."

"Great. A new order of books should be delivered tomorrow." Helen started clearing her work from the table, organizing it in her tote bag.

"You and Dad are still going to make the trip to Ohio State, right?" Lance asked.

"Absolutely. We'll drive to Portsmouth after Greg's game and meet you there on Saturday." Helen set her cup in the sink. "Your dad's looking forward to the OSU football game almost as much as talking to the basketball coaches."

"He'll like the game. Iowa won on Saturday. They'll be ranked in the top ten with the Buckeyes."

"Wish we could go with you on Friday. You know your dad. If he possibly could go up on Friday morning, he would. So I could go shopping, of course." Helen smiled. "Yeah, right," she puffed. "He'd be golfing. What's that golf course he likes to play up there?"

"Muirfield?"

"Yes, in Dublin." Helen appreciated her son's help.

"Mom, any golfer in their right mind would love to play Muirfield. Did you know Muirfield is one of the top courses in the world? Maybe top twenty-five." Lance had a mischievous thought. "Greg better hope Dad doesn't get a golf invitation. There'd be a change of plans."

"No." Helen gladly defended her husband. "Your dad would rather watch you kids play than enjoy a round of golf. He wouldn't stiff Greg on Friday night for 18 holes."

Lance could not give up his smile. "You're right. Greg's safe, but Dad'd be tempted."

Milt called from the family room, "What are you two talking about? Did I hear you mention golf?"

"Mom said you were playing Muirfield this Friday."

"Just a minute," he snapped back getting out of his chair. "You two are bad. All I'd have to do is call Chuck." Milt stepped into the kitchen. "I'd be breaking the course record. Wait. Who's Greg playing Friday night? If they're sure to beat them by 30, I won't be needed, will I?"

"Mom, I knew it. He's tempted."

"Sure, I'm tempted," Milt reached into the cupboard for his favorite coffee cup. "I'm human, but I wouldn't give up watching Greg, Cherie, or you for any golf game. Well, maybe one of your games." He poured a cup of coffee, then pulled out his chair to join Helen at the table

Lance knew he was kidding. "You really like playing Muirfield, don't you?"

"I've been lucky. I've played a number of top-notch courses and I still rank Muirfield as my number one favorite." Lance knew that expression on his dad's face. A story was on the way.

"I still remember as if it were yesterday when Chuck Carlson invited me to play that course for the very first time. What a day." Lance had heard the story several times, but that didn't prevent him from wanting to hear the latest version.

Milt started to reminisce. "It was early May, just before the big tournament Muirfield hosts around Memorial Day. We were playing with two of Chuck's customers. The greens keeper was already making preparations for the tournament, so the rough was high, and the greens were lightening quick. That didn't scare me -- had plenty of golf balls."

Lance took a long, slow sip of water as Milt enthusiastically continued his tale. "Walking into that lobby and then to the locker room was an experience for anyone, let alone a new, green principal visiting from Kentucky. The carpet was plush, the chairs -- mostly leather backs -- and trophies were everywhere. Did I mention the steam room, jacuzzi, and bar area? Nothing but the best. It was sweet. Jack Nicklaus knows what he's doing."

The storyteller yawned but didn't slow down. "I was the first to arrive. An attendant was waiting. Asked if I needed anything before giving me one of those dark wood visitor's lockers. After putting on my golf shoes, I poured a cup of coffee -- not as good as this your momma just made -- slid into one of those luxurious chairs, and started to read the morning paper. Chuck Carlson showed up next. Everyone said hello and asked how he was doing. One member asked who he would be robbing today. "Some easy mark from the Bluegrass State," he answered. "Gave me a big wink, before I could stand up and defend myself."

Milt's animation grew as he described just about every hole on the course. His favorites were 12 and 18. "Twelve's a par three over water -- a spectacular looking hole. A non-golfer could stand on that tee and marvel all day about the work required to design it." He turned to Helen. "Remember, Honey, that was the hole I showed you when we walked out on the course the last time we visited Gary."

Helen smiled to appease him. "Yes, Darlin', it was beautiful." She went back to her lesson plans.

"Eighteen... was a long par four." Lance always liked this part. "Son, I'm telling you, danger lurked in every direction. Hostile fairway traps were carved out of the earth on the right. A creek, a wide sucker, flowed on the left -- extremely unsociable to stray golf balls. This baby," Milt hesitated for effect. "This baby was designed to challenge the best golfers and at the same time provide spectacular viewing. People in the clubhouse, the pavilion, or along the fairways could watch, without difficulty, as golfers try to finish strong." Milt gave his son the steady stare of a pirate. "That was my intention. Finish strong."

"I was sitting on 85, mind you. Played seventeen marvelous holes. Only hope of breaking 90 was a par. A pleasant ride back to Connsburg depended on it."

"Right down the middle. That's where my tee shot landed." Milt's voice first bragged, then apologized. "Maybe a little to the right." He continued, "Yes, I had a chance at par. I was 170 out. Five iron." Milt acted like he was gripping a club. "Checked my alignment then let it rip. It felt good, it looked good."

"Chuck gave me the bad news - sand trap."

"Dang, if it wasn't a semi-buried lie, making things even worse. I stepped into that steep bunker and prepared to fight my way out. My wedge flew through the sand and caused the ball to land fifteen feet from the hole. Gravity. Beautiful stuff. Would you believe my Titleist red three rolled and rolled, stopped about six inches from the hole." Lance couldn't stop from grinning. Milt neither. "Didn't mind losing four bucks to Carlson. The 89 was worth it."

Moving down the hallway to his room, it occurred to Lance that it had been a long water break, but worth the trip. It was a grand story. *Someday, I'll play Muirfield. Eighty-eight. Got to shoot 88.*

Lance shimmied under his soft down comforter. He stared at his four walls, thinking about next week. He'd get to see friends, recap his stay in Lawrence, help his Mom with her first graders, and, hopefully, get to see Cherie in action on Wednesday. A moment of regret captured his attention. Once again he would miss watching, in his opinion, the best quarterback in the state. The only thing better than watching Greg throw was being on the receiving end of one of his passes. Sleep came easily for Lance that night.

Chapter 10

Monday morning came with little fanfare. As usual, everyone in the Stoler family was on their own. Tempers could be short, and space, which seemed perfectly adequate during other times of the day, now seemed limited. Each sibling had a bathroom game plan to avoid having to wait in line. Lance followed his regular routine. He arose early, allowing Greg and Cherie to battle for the shower and the last of the hot water.

During weekdays, the kitchen was methodical. There was no big breakfast. It was cereal, fruit, toast, and always plenty of orange juice. The family should have been on the Florida Orange Growers' Christmas card list.

This morning, there was only enough Wheaties for one generous portion. Lance arrived in the kitchen after Greg, and his options were slim. He had to suffer through some of his dad's Special K.

The weekday kitchen was not the place for major conversations. It was a time to be polite, but to stay out of each other's way. They all knew where the dishwasher was, how to wipe up crumbs, and by eight o'clock everyone had departed for school.

Normally, Greg and Lance would stroll up to the high school together. He came to appreciate the variety of houses along the way, seeing something special in each dwelling. One was a tiny gray cottage with white gingerbread trim. The owners ran the corner Hallmark gift shop in town. The yard was flawless, manicured impeccably, and the survival time of a fallen leaf could be counted in minutes, not days. The wife would often be picking up the newspaper as Greg and Lance walked by. Lance thought that she probably couldn't remember their first names, because she would normally stoop a little bit, then say, "Good morning, Stolers."

His favorite house was on the corner of Canterbury Court halfway to Akers High. Lance guessed the large two-story English Tudor had been built at least seventy years ago. In front was a huge bay window, allowing walkers-by a privileged view of the spectacular living room. Without trying to be a window peeker, Lance could see the cathedral ceiling with large beams matching the outside trim. A curved fireplace extending across the far wall was likely a vibrant participant in many fine occasions. The front door was sturdy, very thick, and looked like it could hold out an attack by most armies. Although the windows seemed rather old and probably let in a few drafts, they were impressive frames for the life within. On the front lawn, a small wooden bench found a resting spot among a tall row of lilacs, probably planted when the house was first constructed. In the spring, their thick, gnarled branches were always covered with the sweet smell of purple blossoms. Set back from the house, an unattached one-car garage reflected older times when few people had one car, let alone two.

The Stoler brothers arrived at school. Akers High was an impressive red brick facility with a row of tall pillars stretching across the entrance. Lounging against the wall by the front door were Terry Dickerson and Dale Zellers, two of Lance's best friends. The three had played basketball together since the seventh grade. They were all guards. Not by choice. The good Lord had not blessed either of them with the height to play forward or center. Terry was about 5'10" when he stood perfectly straight. Coach Hunter brought him off the bench if the team needed Terry's gift of constant hustle. Dale was the other starting guard. Only a few schools were after him. Lance hoped more of those college coaches would figure out what he already knew. Dale could play.

Dale nodded at Lance and Greg, coolly. "Mornin', Wheatman."

Terry didn't wait for Lance to respond. "How was Kansas? Tell us 'bout those college girls."

Greg grinned. "You got it. Make him talk about the babes, the important stuff."

After a couple of customary hand slaps around the group, Lance asked Dale, "How did you know about The Wheat?"

"Your Mom taught me how to read in first grade, remember?"

Lance dipped his shoulders and grinned slightly. "Well, boys, I liked Kansas. I told ya'll about J.C. after summer ball. He was there. We had a great time."

"J.C. Burbridge?" Terry seemed a little jealous of sharing Lance's friendship with any newcomer. "What kind of trouble did you get into?" Terry's voice made it obvious he was eager for some outlandish stories.

"You'd like J.C. if you met him." Lance read Terry's voice. "If he was standing right here."

"Yeah right," Dale butted in. "With him, you'd shoot a bunch of threes. The other team would be chasing him. All you'd have to do is wait for a pass. That's why you like him."

"That thought did occur to me," Lance said. "J.C. is a good guy, though. I'm telling ya. I got no problem with the fact that if we played his team, Coach Hunter wouldn't let you guard him. We couldn't afford to give up the fifty points."

"Enough of him," Terry had finished his laugh. "Give us the real lowdown about Kansas."

"I'll give you the quickie version because homeroom starts in about seven minutes." His words led them through Allen Field House, up Massachusetts Street, and over to Memorial Stadium. In the course of his descriptions they met Coach Booth, Director Henderson, Michael Lee, Ms. Appleton, Dayle Jarrett, and other Kansans he had been introduced to during his short weekend stay. Mr. Melbourne was mentioned, but not Hillcrest. The gang especially liked his portrayal of Big John, Reggie and Sam. It was a fun journey, lasting but a few minutes. Lisa was not mentioned. Greg clearly took notice.

The bell was about to ring, and they started on their separate ways to homerooms. Greg caught his brother. He whispered, "Good move. Terry would have wanted you to get him a date with Lisa." He slapped Lance on the back and ran off laughing.

During third period study hall, Lance was paid a visit by Coach Hunter.

"Got a minute?"

"Sure, Coach."

"Come on down to my office, we need to talk."

The study hall teacher was also the assistant football coach. He had no problem with Lance's packing up and departing.

Coach Hunter didn't wait for the confines of his office to start the inquiry.

"How was Booth? One of his assistants, said his name was Holister, called to let me know about your trip. Those sons of guns want you real bad," Hunter blurted out as they stepped into his office.

"They were real friendly."

"No kidding. I suspected they would roll out the red carpet for you."

Lance sat down in a chair next to the desk. "I don't think you're too high on Coach Booth's list, either. He asked about you, but I could tell by his expression it was only a courtesy comment."

Hunter barked back, "He knows my ties to UK. I bet he's scared stiff I'm going to steer you to the Wildcats. And he should be. Now, don't get me wrong. I know the decision is yours. But Son, you're a Kentucky boy. Personally, I don't give a hoot about Jayhawks or Buckeyes," Hunter hissed, fighting to lower his voice. "But I respect your need to visit other schools."

Coach was obviously fired up. He stood up and slapped his hand sharply on the windowsill. "Somethin's not right about Booth. The sucker wins, but . . . " Hunter turned and looked directly into Lance's eyes. "Napoleon complex! You know, a little man with a great big ego, who wants every darn light shining on *him* and all the power in *his* hands." Lance watched his coach shake his head. "That's what Booth's got—a Napoleon complex. It's just a dirty, dang hunch, but you're one of the best." Hunter sat back down and folded both hands on the desk as if in a prayer. "Best this ole boy's ever coached. Don't want things to . . . you know, get messed up for you."

Lance had waited, nervously scratching the back of his head. When Coach hesitated, or at least stopped for air, he seized a chance to speak.

"Thanks. That means an awful lot to me, and you haven't hidden your love of the University of Kentucky. I could've visited more schools, but I picked out three. Three good ones. I've grown up a Wildcat. It's just, just . . . " Lance fidgeted, pushing back the empty coffee cup perched on the edge of the desk. "The thought of going out of state to school keeps calling to me."

Before Hunter could reply, Lance went on, knowing his coach's love of basketball. "Let me tell you about Kansas."

Lance walked him through his visit. Hunter's eyes let Lance know he hit a nerve when he mentioned Naismith, Wilt the Stilt, and Allen Fieldhouse. The bell rang.

Hunter dismissed Lance. "See you at practice, son," he said softly, understanding, reluctantly evident in his voice.

Mini-conversations about his trip before and after each class period, made the rest of the day fly by. The best was with his friend Bruce, who had arrived late and had missed the usual morning gathering on the school steps. Bruce Miskowski was now the starting tight-end for Akers High and the best picker on the Green Bears basketball team. His barrel chest and spirited attitude was ideal for starting at forward and banging under the boards for Coach Hunter's team.

After school, Lance trotted home and made a peanut butter and strawberry jelly sandwich. He had only a little homework, but it could wait. Within seconds, he was out the back door and running down the driveway. His practice was at six. He could catch a little of Greg's.

In a few heartbeats, he arrived at the football fields. The team was going through drills. Coaches intensely barked out instructions and corrections that people up the road in Pikeville could easily hear. There was no letup at Akers High; the coaches wanted a win - not just last Friday, but every Friday. The managers blew a horn, signaling specialty team's practice.

Besides starting at quarterback, Greg performed as team punter. Of the two Stoler boys, Greg was probably the better all-around athlete. The sophomore was bigger, faster and taller, but Lance was stronger. He loved to watch Greg punt. The center snapped the ball. It had what seemed like a minute's worth of hang time before being caught by the punt returner, fifty yards down field. Lance marveled. *This boy is good.* He had seen enough. It was time to start running again.

Back at the house, Helen greeted him. She had just arrived home from school. "Hi. How was your day?" It was her usual compassionate welcome. "How many times did you have to talk about Kansas?"

"No less than a hundred. Even Coach Hunter had me down to his office. What's for dinner?"

"Your dad said he would be home early tonight. How does barbequed chicken sound?"

Helen was eating a piece of leftover cornbread from Sunday's dinner. She loved cornbread broken up into a cup of milk, cherishing its nourishment most after a hard day.

Lance interpreted the signs. "Tough one today, Mom?"

"The kids were a little feisty," She looked tired. "I love them, but I was glad to see the afternoon end." She took another bite of crumbled cornbread.

"Anything you need me to do?" Lance offered. "I don't have practice until six."

"No thanks, Honey." She looked up at him and sat down her spoon. "You'll miss dinner again."

"Save me something. Don't worry about saving any of that cornbread. Looks like you enjoyed it for the both of us." Helen smiled into her empty cup.

That evening after practice Lance bounded into the house.

"Did you save me any chicken?" He called out to the house, grabbing a plate from the cupboard.

"Snooze, you lose," Milt responded from his chair in the family room.

Lance suspected his dad was kidding. Still, he was relieved when he opened the refrigerator and found two chicken breasts and three drumsticks on a plate. He looked up as Helen entered the kitchen. Carrying a stack of neatly folded bath towels that were headed for the hallway closet, she stopped and asked, "Do you want me to heat that up for you?"

"No, Mom, it looks great."

"There's a salad on the lower shelf. I even saved you a big piece of cornbread. I made another pan." She laughed at herself as she walked by.

By this time, Milt had given up his favorite chair and ESPN.

"Good day in school?" he joined Lance at the table.

"I was bombarded by everyone wanting to know about my recruiting trip. It was cool."

"That's only natural," Milt told him. "It's a big deal, you visiting Kansas. Wait till you get back from Ohio State!

Lance picked up a chicken leg.

"Just remember, it's gonna get harder," said Milt. He got up and grabbed a glass from the cupboard. "People will be watching and following your every move." He turned on the faucet. "Don't worry about us. If you sign with Kansas or Ohio State, folks around here will understand." Milt took a big slug of water. Wiped his mouth. "Naw. They'll probably shoot you and we'll have to move."

Lance stopped eating to laugh with his dad

"You go through anything like this?" Lance asked.

"Not even close." Milt said humbly. He sat down next to Lance and placed a hand on Lance's forearm. "Don't worry, son. The Lord won't put anything on you he feels you can't handle."

"You're probably right." Lance picked up another drumstick. "It was nice of you and Greg to leave me a few pieces of chicken."

"We didn't. Your mother made us." Milt stood, squeezed Lance's shoulder, and strolled off. "The Lord will guide you, son. Lord will guide you."

Lance finished his dinner, cleaned up his dishes, and started to his room. He tapped on the queen's door and waited for a response.

"Who goes there?" the queen replied. "I'm studying."

"I was just looking for an e-mail reader." Lance said.

The door opened instantly. Cherie was raring to help, homework no longer top priority.

"Would you check my e-mails? I don't want to face the screen if I don't have any. You know what I mean."

"What's a sister for if she can't help in a time of need?" The two entered Lance's room and Cherie turned on the Dell. Lance kicked off his shoes. Cherie made the clicks. She was first to see the bad news.

"Kansas is an hour behind us so it's probably too early to expect Lisa to write." It was Cherie's best attempt at consoling her brother.

"You're probably right. I have a lot of homework to do, anyways." Lance tried to sound nonchalant.

"Do you want to check later or wait a couple of days?"

"I'm in no hurry. We can wait. Maybe Wednesday."

Waiting was all that could be done. Cherie got up, gave her brother a hug, and returned to her room.

Lance buried himself in schoolwork. He was an hour into his calculus when the phone rang. Again, Cherie was the fastest in the house.

Cherie called in a pleasant voice, "Lance, it's for you. It's J.C."

He took the phone from his sister. "Hi. What's going on?"

"Hey, man." J.C. sounded different. "Did you hear about Sam?"

"Sam? You mean Sam Wilson?"

"Yeah. I just heard the NCAA is looking into him. Seems that when Sam had to re-take the SAT, he had a jump of something like 600 points in his score. That's how he got qualified. The newspaper's saying he took it the second time in a different state."

"How could that happen? Sam lives in Texas."

"I know, I know. Just telling you what I heard. Word is he'll lose his eligibility."

"His eligibility?" Lance was stunned.

"Yeah, the dude's cooked." J.C.'s voice tried to be sympathetic. "Probably kissing his full ride good-bye." Lance remembered how defensive Sam was about academic stuff. "I'll let you know if I hear anything else." He paused. Lance could tell something else was on his mind. "I have a question -- what did you do to Lisa, Man? Marla said she won't stop talking about some Kentucky Shooter."

Lance wanted to play it cool. "I didn't do anything. We just talked."

"Well, you did something," J.C. was unyielding. "Marla and I plan to keep our eyes on you two."

J.C. started to bombard him with questions. "Have ya had time to think about your visit? I hope your parents keep an open mind. Did you cancel that Ohio State trip yet?"

"Man, slow down." Lance switched the phone from his right ear to his left. "I'm leaving for Columbus on Friday. I could call the Buckeye coaches and ask if you could come along."

"Don't you be getting me in trouble,"J.C. protested. "Come on. Tell me what your parents think."

"Like I said on Saturday, they're fine, they want what's best for me. It's too early. Got two more trips."

"I'm not worried." J.C. spoke like he had a secret weapon. "You had a good time, right?"

Lance stalled a few seconds. "Sure."

"I'm positive Lisa's part of the equation." Lance let J.C.'s comment die without a comment.

"Hey, I got to go." He was not about to promote any conversation about Lisa.

"Me too."

"Don't forget to let me know if you hear anything else about Sam," Lance remembered the purpose of the call. "Tell your mom I said 'hi' and that I'm missin' her fried chicken."

Lance hung up the phone. How could that stuff happen on a SAT test? Did the coaches know? He walked into the kitchen where he found his mom and dad sitting at the table browsing through some magazines and brochures.

"What are you two doing?" he asked, trying to conceal his anxiousness.

"Your dad got this information on Jackson Hole, Wyoming. He might be a good guy and take us all there next July for our vacation.

"Sorry kid," Milt snickered. "The postman didn't drop off literature on places in Kansas."

Lance took a moment to inspect the brochures. "These look nice. The Grand Tetons seem just a tad bigger than our hills, don't they?" He couldn't wait any longer. "Dad, that was J.C. on the phone. He had some information about one of the recruits I was with in Lawrence."

"Which one?" Milt put aside a Yellowstone Park brochure.

"Sam Wilson, the shooting guard from Dallas. J.C. said the NCAA is looking into his SAT scores. He had a huge jump the second time he took it. Dad, he took it the second time in a different state."

Milt's face tightened. "In my job, I know more than a little bit about standardized tests. This isn't the first time I've heard of something like this -- a coach or a student so eager for eligibility that they do things improperly. What did J.C. say happened?"

Lance shared J.C.'s information.

"Getting a jump like that in the SAT is highly improbable," Milt said with disgust. "You don't increase 600 points overnight. And it's very unusual for someone from Texas to take his second test in another state." Milt took a sip of Helen's iced tea. "Son, I believe Sam won't become eligible if the NCAA is pursuing this. I hope they find out who helped him if he did do something wrong. If it was a college coach who arranged this, they should fry him."

"Should I do anything?" Lance asked.

"No, the NCAA should handle it."

Helen remained an observer. Milt was more knowledgeable in these matters and she felt he would be the best shepherd for Lance. She did not know Sam, but her son had said he liked him and that was enough for her. Lance was halfway down the hall when he heard his mom's soft but forceful voice.

"I feel sorry for the Wilson boy," she said to Milt. "But I'll tell you what; I'm going to keep my eye on that Kansas coach."

Chapter 11

Next morning, everyone was on their way before eight. The Hallmark lady was watering two huge clay pots of brilliant rust mums as Lance and Greg walked by.

"Hi, Stolers," she called.

"Mornin', Ma'am," they answered in unison.

Third period study hall came fast. Lance once again asked Dale, Terry, and Bruce to go with him to his mom's classroom. While these visits counted toward Akers High's required community service hours, going to the elementary school was just plain fun. Each time they entered that mini-world, they were made to feel like rock stars. The class would gather around, all innocent smiles and adoring eyes, asking only for a few minutes of the giants' undivided attention. Mrs. Stoler would step in after she had given her class enough time to greet their "Buddies," and break the class into four groups. She provided a well-chosen book for each buddy and they would start their readings. Today would be no different.

"Hi, boys, come on in," Helen said. "Class, now give our reading buddies some air, or they won't visit us anymore." She seemed as enthused as the class.

Nancy, one of Helen's tiniest students, was well acquainted with Bruce since she lived a few houses away from him. Before Helen had finished her request, Nancy had already started her move.

"Mrs. Stoler, can I be in Bruce's group again?" With pink-ribboned pig-tails flying, she ran over to her huge tight-end neighbor and hugged him around the knees.

"You sure can, Darlin'," Helen responded, lovingly.

Bruce smiled at his little fan.

They spent a fulfilling thirty minutes. The buddies finished their readings, said good-bye, and walked back to the high school.

"Thanks guys, Mom always appreciates your help," said Lance.

"No problem," said Bruce. "We enjoy it."

Lance was back in his groove. Happy with his friends. Happy with his hometown routine. Happy to be with his family. Football, basketball, and soccer practices were all right after school. Milt wasn't scheduled for any evening assignments. That guaranteed something really important - all five Stolers would sit down together, at the same time, on a weeknight, for dinner.

Arriving home about four, Helen immediately started chopping onions and green peppers for spaghetti sauce and meatballs, a family favorite. While the meatballs slowly simmered in thick, spicy sauce, she prepared a fantastic salad.

Helen was extremely skilled at kitchen tasks. She picked up many cooking tips during her travels and in magazines such as her favorite, *Southern Living.* But she was an artist in the kitchen before she ever heard of *Southern Living* or *Martha Stewart.* She inherited her cooking finesse from generations of Kentucky women who had learned to prepare whatever the land was good enough to provide. Her grandmother and aunts never used cookbooks. Recipes were shared like oral histories, and committed to memory. Family reunions would have tables stockpiled with such Southern delights as chicken and dumplings, mustard greens, shuck beans, corn bread, fried chicken, and always, slow cooked green beans that melted like butter in a Kentuckian's mouth.

About 5:30, the rest of the troops started to return home. Cherie was the first. She said hello to her mom and was headed straight to the shower, but stopped to offer her services.

"Do you need any help?"

"No, Honey, I have a handle on dinner. When you get out of the shower you can help set the table, though. Even your brothers will be here tonight."

Next in was Lance. "Hi Mom," he said, heading for the stove. He had smelled the sauce's aroma as he walked up the driveway. "That smells like spaghetti. How did you know I was really hungry for some red sauce?"

"The kids were beaming this afternoon. Thanks for bringing the boys over today."

"No problem. I'd enjoy a little taste of that sauce as payment, though. Can I have a sample?" Lance got a spoon out of the drawer, anticipating Helen's answer.

"Yes, but not too much. You don't want to spoil your dinner."

After a second spoonful, Lance said, "Oooohh, this is good."

"That's enough. Get out of here," she ordered.

Greg came home from football practice, leaving no doubt he was related to Lance. He worked his way right into the kitchen. Helen was at the table reading the mail. Like Lance, Greg felt obligated to sample his mom's work. After two spoonfuls he got the same treatment.

"Get out of here! You're as bad as your brother. We'll eat when your dad gets home," she pretended to be angry.

With a happy grin, Greg hugged her then headed to his room.

His school chores finished, Milt walked in, set his briefcase down, and demonstrated where the Stoler boys picked up their habits. He slid right over to the stove, picked up the spoon, and proceeded to have his two samples.

"Oooohh,' he gushed. "This is good,"

The kitchen sheriff was still on duty. "You're no better than those other two varmits I ran out of here. Wipe your face off, you've got sauce all over it. We can eat as soon as you get cleaned up." Helen grabbed a napkin, wiped his chin, then gave him a quick kiss.

Cherie had finished her shower. She entered the kitchen, prepared to set the table.

"I see you beat me to it, Mom." The table was set for five, just like Sunday. "Anything else I can do?" Cherie put her arms around Helen's neck.

"You can set out the salad dressings if you like, 'cause here they come."

One by one, the Stoler men advanced into the kitchen. Everyone fixed a salad and found their regular seat at the dining room table.

Milt asked Greg, "Why don't you give us one of your best efforts tonight?"

"Dear Lord, thank you that we could all be together tonight. Bless this food we are prepared to eat. Please take care of Nana. And if possible let me have the biggest meatball. Amen."

"You're too late." Helen chuckled. "Your dad already ate it for an appetizer."

Milt grinned. He jabbed his fork into a cucumber. "Cherie, how was school today?"

"Fine. Art class was fantastic. We started to work with clay. Ms. Simons said we could make whatever we wanted to later on." She looked up at Helen. "I might make you a nice pot for your plants and if dad is real lucky, I'll make him something for his desk."

"What about me?" Greg asked.

"Oh, by that time I'm sure we'll be out of clay," She answered with glee.

Lance glanced around the dining room table. *Next year at this time, I'll be sitting around a table with a bunch of people I don't even know yet.* In his time remaining at home, he wanted to make sure he remembered that fact. He wanted to savor the time he had left with his family.

Enjoying hearty table discussions, he asked his Dad, "Will the school levy pass in November?"

"It's no secret that your mom and I have been working hard to make certain it will. But who knows?" Milt pointed with his fork. A clear sign more was to come. "It's like trying to guess who will win a big game. You thought the Bengals would win on Sunday and the meatball man liked the Browns. What ticks me off is that education is one of the most precious things we can give children, and voters keep trying to shortchange the funding for good schools."

"You're right," Helen agreed. "Everybody wants their children to get a good education, but they aren't prepared to pay for it."

"It seems self serving, but the truth is we need to pay excellent teachers more and we needn't be bashful about providing dollars for a sound education," said Milt. He didn't let the last bite of his salad stop him from continuing. "But who knows, maybe the school district will get a break this year and the voters will do what they know is right."

Everyone had finished their salads. It was time to head to the kitchen to fill their plates with some of Helen's spaghetti and meatballs. Lance got there first and kept everyone waiting while he squeezed the tongs and took one big scoop of pasta and then another. He performed the same drill with the sauce. His creation looked superb and was ready to take it to the table with one exception - garlic bread.

There were only eight pieces. Lance knew his math. Two people would get only one piece. Once again, speed was important in the Stoler family. Lance figured since he was fast enough to be first in line, he deserved two. He would let the rest of the clan fight it out. Sort of like musical chairs with garlic bread. But his conscience wouldn't let him swipe two.

"Mom, is it OK if I take two pieces of bread?"

Helen laughed. "Go ahead. I only want one and your dad only needs one."

Within a few moments, everyone was back in their respective seats savoring what had to be the best spaghetti in the whole Commonwealth of Kentucky. Greg started the second round of dinner dialogue.

"Dad, did you see that Iowa moved up to eighth in the nation on Monday? You guys are going to see a big-time game on Saturday."

Lance didn't wait for his dad to answer. He boasted, "The Buckeyes are still ranked number two."

"The way I see it, I'll watch the big-time game on Friday night and go watch the junior varsity on Saturday," Milt said, twirling spaghetti around his fork.

"What time are you leaving?" Cherie asked, cutting her meatballs into tiny portions. Her brothers and dad ate them in one bite.

"About eight."

"Nana is taking Lance over to the airport," Helen added.

"I wish I didn't have school. I'd like to ride with you and Nana to the airport," Cherie said.

"That'd be great. I'd have two of my favorite women driving me to the airport. But you probably just want to go shopping with Nana in Lexington, don't you?"

Cherie looked up. "No. Nana hasn't taken me shoppin' in a long time." She was serious.

"She will." Helen noticed her daughter's expression. "Anyway, she's probably just waitin' for the time when you're old enough to drive *her* around."

The Stolers finished their meal with walnut brownies and vanilla ice cream. The rest of Tuesday night remained peaceful. Everyone went to bed early, having the deep sense of well-being that comes from a full stomach and a loving family.

The early morning walk to school on Wednesday produced the same response as the boys passed the Hallmark house.

"Good Morning, Stolers."

Before third period study hall, Lance saw Coach Hunter in the hallway.

"Got another phone call," Hunter barked. "This time it was the Ohio State boys. They wanted to know if you would be backing out of your visit this weekend. I wasn't going to tell them anything. Let them sweat." Hunter hurriedly continued. "But I didn't. Told Meadors not to worry. Told him that he didn't understand he was dealing with a Stoler."

"Coach, I said I'd visit." Lance could not hide the confusion on his face. "I'm getting on a plane Friday morning."

"I know that. Somebody must have called them. Gave them reason to worry. There are a lot of coaches who use negative recruiting. They use every trick in the book to land the kid they want." Hunter slapped Lance on the arm. "I'm not accusing anyone. Just know it happens."

"I appreciate your setting the record straight with Coach Meadors and his staff. Better get to study hall now."

Lance was welcomed into study hall by three teammates, every one of them trying to get a preferred seat in the back of the room so the teacher would have to hurt his neck to try to discover if sleep happened upon them. Being quick today, Lance secured a desired back seat. He leaned over with his elbows on the desk, and soon found himself deeply involved in a daydream about Lisa. *Would she e-mail again? What would she say? What should he write back? Should've kissed her.*

As the school day ended, Milt worked in his office, Helen escorted her little wonders to the school bus stand, Greg headed to football practice, and Lance ran home to change for the big game. Cherie was in the locker room preparing for her team's match against the school from Hazard. She made no secret that she loved her uniform. The pants were dark green with a white stripe, and she described them as looking "sweet." At first, the jersey was too big, but after Nana's sewing machine magic the family jewel wore a number "11" that fit perfectly.

Both teams were still warming up when Lance arrived at the field. Yesterday it had rained for at least an hour, but this Wednesday afternoon saw one of the best Kentucky skies October could possibly produce. The sparkling bright sun caused the temperature to hover close to 70 degrees. Its warmth had dried out the field, so all conditions were a "go" for a very entertaining skirmish.

Lance stood along the side of the field next to the bleachers. This was not a football stadium. There were only enough seats for the moms and a sprinkling of dads. Everyone else made do with standing room only. The crowds did not compare in size to those who watched the Stoler boys, but they were just as enthusiastic for the Cubs. When Milt was in the house, they became even more so.

Lance watched his sister. He turned when he heard his mom's familiar warm voice. Helen was talking with two other moms as she approached him.

"Hey, Lance, how does Cherie look? Are those little ruffians from Hazard any good?"

"This is going to be a tough game, but Cherie looks ready." He put his arm around her shoulder.

Helen gave Lance a hug before she headed for a bleacher seat. As the game began, the local team was holding its own but neither team was able to score. The Hazard team, decked out in their yellow uniforms, was having problems because every time they tried to move in for a score, number 11 went into action. Lance ignored the game for a moment and just watched his sister. She moved with great ease, her red hair and well conditioned, teenage body always in fluid motion. Like a beautiful lioness, she prowled about the field. Her speed and grace was on constant display. A Hazard striker approached the Cubs net. Cherie's hazel eyes focused in determined concentration. She rapidly moved toward the intruder, attacked, and her right foot sent the ball sailing to one of her teammates on the left wing. The crowd gave a cheer.

During the first half, neither team was able to penetrate its opponent's goal, but the second half started with a fury. The green team moved down the field, a player shot, but the ball hit the left post and ricocheted wide left, leaving Cherie and her teammates disappointed. A poor pass by a Hazard forward allowed the Cubs to be on the move again. Two quick passes and they were in position to score. One of the forwards was prepared to strike. She was tripped. No call was made.

"You have got to be kidding me! That's tripping!" roared a new voice on the scene.

Milt had left his office, now primed to properly support his baby girl. He was no bleachers guy; he preferred to roam the sidelines. He tried to behave to the best of his ability, but this was his daughter, and safeguarding her could, on occasion, cause some interesting statements to sprinkle toward the officials

With five minutes to go, the contest remained at a standstill. A new commotion occurred that was not part of the game on the field. Lance looked up and saw his brother running across the far field. Football practice must have just ended.

As Greg rounded the south end of the soccer complex, several eyes turned to stare. One of Kentucky's finest thoroughbreds was approaching. He wore his white, grass stained practice pants and a gray cut-off tee shirt. Well-proportioned muscles, hardened by relentless conditioning, powered his arms and legs in complete harmony. His biceps curved just enough to foretell the future -- a football sailing over a certain towering oak tree. He trotted behind the Cub's bench. Those girls not in the game took notice.

"Woooah, is that my knight in shining armor?" Lance heard the shortest one say.

"What's going on, Lance? I leave you to handle one little soccer game and you can't score?" The stallion snorted as he drew near the sidelines.

"Hey, I'm in charge of the defense and my responsibility is well under control thanks to my superior coaching of Number 11," snapped back the stallion's big brother.

"How are the officials holding up? Have they been able to handle the scrutiny of Eleven's dad?"

"Been pretty good so far. He hasn't strangled any of them yet." Lance shook his head, laughing.

Cherie continued to do a stellar job defending her goal. Then, with a minute thirty to go, the Cubs got the break they had been waiting for. A Hazard girl made a bad kick. It was intercepted. The green team made three great passes. Suddenly, the ball was in the visitors' net. The crowd roared as the game ended in a 1 - 0 victory for the happy Cubs.

Coaches shook hands, the teams paid their respects, and it was time for the families to get involved. Each of the players headed to their loyal followers. Those who didn't have followers of their own found welcome arms in a teammate's family. A jovial Cherie jumped on her oldest brother and Lance gave her a winner's whirl. Milt, Helen, and Greg were just a step behind. They all shared high fives and hugs.

"I've got to get to practice," Lance gave her one last hug. "Great job. I'll see you at home."

"Thanks. I was just trying to act like a relative." Cherie flashed him the biggest smile her braces allowed.

Greg sprinted back to the showers, Lance ran over to the gym, and Milt walked Cherie to the car for a victory ride home, a proud arm stretched around her shoulder. Helen strolled behind, soaking up the view of her precious daughter in the arms of the love of her life.

Lance missed the family's celebration dinner. When he arrived home, Greg and Cherie were back to the reality of tackling homework. Helen and Milt had moved to the family room to see if anything worthwhile was on TV.

"Mom, Dad, I'm home," called Lance.

Milt had clicked to the History Channel. Helen got up and headed for the kitchen.

"Honey, there are a couple of bratwurst in the oven. Get some milk and I'll heat up the beans."

"Sounds great, Mom. I'm starved."

Lance devoured his dinner. When he was finished, he navigated to his room. He popped his head into Greg's room.

"I saw those girls on the bench look at you. They think you're one cute hunk."

"Get out of here. Can't you see that Pythagoras and I are working on something?" Greg acted like it meant nothing. His smile told Lance otherwise.

Next was a stop by the soccer player's room. The door had been left open, which was not the custom. Tonight was different. Lance walked in and sat down on the corner of her bed.

"Nice game, Kid. Super stop in the first half. I would've knocked the ball away and dribbled through ten defenders and scored a goal, but you're only in middle school." Lance now watched his sister smile. He pulled one of her braids.

Cherie rubbed her knee, "I'm still sore from that one. She caught me with her spike when I slid to get the ball." Cherie paused. Her face was serious. "Do you need me?"

"What do you mean, do I need you?"

"You know, do you need me?" she asked, slowing emphasizing each word.

"Yeah, sure." He realized what she meant. "Come on over and let's check it out."

She was off her bed and in Lance's computer chair clicking the mouse before big brother knew what was happening.

"You got mail!" She was almost as pleased as Lance.

He peered over her shoulder. "Who from?"

"Well, one is from Uncle Gary."

"Great. Who else? Is one from Lisa?" He stood behind the chair, nervously wiped his crew cut hair and stared at the screen with hopeful eyes. There it was. He saw the KU e-mail address.

Cherie proudly broadcasted, "Live, from the Lawrence campus."

His face brightened. Knowing for certain he had mail from Lisa made it easier to be a caring nephew.

"Let's read Uncle Gary's first."

Dear Lance,

Greetings, Nephew. This is a big weekend. We're delighted you will be visiting the Buckeyes. The Iowa football game is going to be on ESPN. It'll be a head knocker. Those corn boys are actually ranked eighth. No problem for the Scarlet and Gray. Can't wait to see you. I have already alerted the sheriff that your dad will be visiting Columbus. Best to your mom, Greg and Cherie.

Love, Uncle Gary

"Oh, that Uncle Gary. He loves jabbin' Dad." Cherie laughed.

"He sure does, but Dad likes to jab him, too. I wonder how Grandma stood it?" Lance shook his head. "Naw, she probably loved every minute she had them together. Let's open the next one."

Lance,

Hope all is well with you. School is fine. One exam down and one to go. I'm going home this weekend. My mom and dad are restless to see me. I have not been home for all of six weeks. But you know parents. When my dad called last night I told him I met you. He reads a lot of sports and dad said he read a college recruiting magazine about you and it said you couldn't hit the broad side of a barn. Remember, he is a Missouri grad. Oh, well, got to go. Hope you have a good week.

Lisa

P.S. Actually, Dad whispered to me that you are really good. He wants you to visit Mizzou.

"Lance, this is very good." Cherie diagnosed, enthusiastically. "She really likes you, I can tell."

"How can you tell? It's just an e-mail."

"A girl knows." She looked up at him incredulously. "Just trust me."

"All right, all right, out of the chair. I need to answer."

"Don't you want me to help you?" she offered eagerly.

"No, you coached me well last time. Better handle this one in private, but thanks for the help, Madam Counselor."

Cherie didn't argue. He could tell she was pleased to have the inside scoop on this development. Lance jumped in the driver's seat, pondered what to type for a few seconds, then his hands were on the keyboard.

Dear Lisa,

Thanks for writing. Cherie won her soccer game tonight. I truly love watching her.

I'm glad school is going well. Hope you enjoy being with your parents. Please tell your dad that I am sorry, but it might be a little hard to make a trip to the University of Missouri. I visit Ohio State this weekend.

As ever,

Lance

Lance hit the *Send* button, finished his homework, and was off to bed. Another great day.

Chapter 12

Early morning light sprayed glory over front-page news clippings hanging on Lance's bedroom wall. Last spring, Helen proudly framed and hung them without her son's knowledge. The bottom of Lance's bedspread lay softly around his ankles. He rolled over peacefully, until he remembered it was a school day. As he slid out of bed, the sound of running water caught his attention. He entered the bathroom.

"Hey, Boy, what are you doing in my shower?"

"Since when is this your shower?" Greg argued through the steam. "Gotta leave early. Offensive starters are the guest of Rotary for breakfast."

Lance remembered having to get up in front of the Rotary Club after his state championship. He had worried endlessly the night before. Dad had encouraged him to calm his nerves when he began speaking by squeezing the sides of the podium hard. "You'll do fine," Milt had said. After President Clinton Kidd introduced him, he stood up, stared at the suits, gripped the podium, and ripped a five-minute speech that had Milt beaming and Greg proud to be a relative.

"Reckon' you can be first under those circumstances. If you have to speak, don't forget to squeeze that podium."

Milt and Greg were preparing to leave when Lance entered the kitchen. His dad was wearing his favorite dark blazer, blue striped tie, and penny loafers. Milt gave the impression he was prepared to have a good day. Greg was spiffed up in a starched button down, rather than his usual tee shirt. His brother always looked as if he would be having a good day.

"Don't you guys have to get going?" Lance asked.

"We just wanted to see your pretty face before we left. Today's menu is cereal, Boy, but tomorrow will be special. Nana's fixin' breakfast for all of us." Milt set his cup in the sink. "C'mon, Greg, don't want to be late. See you tonight, son"

Lance finished his Wheaties, rubbed Bubba's head, then slipped out the back door. Brisk morning breezes invigorated him as he walked through autumn leaves that swirled with each gust of wind. Approaching the Hallmark house, he received the standard greeting from the lady of the house.

"Good morning, Stoler."

"Mornin', Ma'am."

Lance detected disappointment. Could a missing brother be the cause? He felt compelled to explain. "Greg went to Rotary with my dad."

She smiled curtly, morning paper in hand.

The first part of the school day was amazingly quiet. Lunch was different. Bruce was hungry for information about the upcoming Ohio State trip. He sat hunched over, nibbling on a bologna sandwich. Questions flowed like a beat writer for a big city newspaper. Who would he talk to? Would he meet the whole basketball team? Would they take him to the football game?

"I'm gonna watch it on TV," Bruce said, devouring the last bite of sandwich. "Sorry, sorry. You're just going up there for basketball. I forgot football's not your game anymore."

Lance retaliated by throwing a hastily formed Saran Wrap ball. It grazed off Bruce's head as a friendly reminder he wasn't the only tight end at the table. Terry and Dale took pleasure watching their friends' mock fight. Lance agreed he was going for basketball, but he couldn't wait to be in the Horseshoe, "Singin' *Hang on Sloopy* 'with the rest of em."

"Ohio Stadium. Hundred thousand people. Yeah, as if anyone's gonna hear you." Bruce seemed almost jealous.

Lance shrugged his shoulders. "Yeah, just wish my Uncle Gary could come, though."

"I thought you said he lives in Columbus. Why wouldn't he go?" Bruce seemed puzzled.

"Can't get tickets. Sold out."

"All sold out? Amazing." Bruce was jealous.

"Hey guys, we'd better get going." The group continued to talk about Ohio State as they walked to class.

After school, Lance headed home to start packing. He stepped through the back door and eased down the hallway. He set his books on his desktop and went back to the kitchen to get a Pepsi. No smells drifted from the kitchen and he didn't have a desire for his usual peanut butter sandwich. Standing there alone, he peered through the kitchen window and saw Greg's oak tree, Helen's garden, and the barren row of grapevines. In less than ten months, he wouldn't live here anymore. It was a sobering thought. At times like these, sports had taught him to take a deep breath and to forge on. Shutting his eyes, he breathed deeply, then returned to his room. The blue sweater Lisa had told him to wear was the first item packed. He reached for his dress shoes as a voice floated down the hallway.

"I'm home. Anybody here?"

That voice had a history of providing Lance warmth and comfort, as if someone just threw another log on a fire.

"Yeah, Mom. Back here packing."

Helen placed her school bag on the kitchen table and walked quietly toward her son's room. She stopped in the doorway, watching the boy in Levi jeans, Nike tee shirt, and neatly trimmed crew cut with his head bent intently over his suitcase. She marveled at what a man he was becoming. Helen felt the sudden, forceful grip of change. It wouldn't be long before this one flew away. At times like these, struggles of raising a family had taught her to take a deep breath and to forge on. She walked in, put both arms around her son's waist, and gave a gentle hug meant to be imprinted on her own heart.

"Honey, do you need any help?"

"Pretty well set."

Helen sat down by the open suitcase.

"Don't need to take much with me."

Helen noticed the blue sweater. "They hate Blue in Columbus. Hate Michigan," she teased.

"You're right. But that sweater's making the trip." No explanation was given.

"Your Nana will be here early tomorrow. She's excited to be going with you to the airport."

"Me, too," Lance asked softly. "Is everything alright with Nana?"

"Sure, Honey - why?" Helen refolded one of his shirts.

"Oh, nothing. Just that a booster in Lawrence asked me about her"

"That's the Heartland, honey. Probably just trying to be thoughtful, askin' about Nana. You kids sure have one to be proud of."

Nana was extraordinary. A strong woman who grew up during the Depression, she hadn't allowed her lack of worldly goods to diminish her spunk or wisdom one bit. In seventy-plus years of living in eastern Kentucky's hills, she was no stranger to change. Dirt roads had become paved roads. Swinging bridges, once made of wood, were now concrete structures. She had traveled by foot, by horse, by car, by bus, and, sparingly, by plane. Her mail on Prater Creek was first picked up at Clyde's Grocery Store, then delivered to a mail box across the creek, and now was delivered electronically to a PC screen on her bedroom desk. Nana liked to say she had survived six bad Presidents and gotten pleasure from six good ones.

The most essential qualities in her life were her faith, her deep love for Hoover, grounded southern values, meaningful friendships, and a loving family. These essentials continued to burn brightly, no matter how many times people or events tried to snuff them out.

"When Dad gets home, we're ordering pizza." Lance watched his mom's face brighten. "Can't promise there'll be some left when you get home from practice, but I'll try." She stood up and automatically straightened the bed. "Gonna take Bubba for a walk down by the river." She rubbed her hand tenderly across Lance's back.

"Thanks, Mom." Helen left and Lance finished his packing.

Practice ended on time. When Lance turned up the drive, Bubba came bounding out of the backyard. The black lab had a way of making all the Stolers feel like royalty. Lance skimmed his hand along Bubba's neck. "Come on, Boy. Let's go see if there's any pizza left. I'm starved."

Milt was sitting in his favorite chair, a brown leather recliner that frequently encouraged its customer to get heavy eyes. Greg and Cherie were sitting on the floor around the pizza-laden coffee table while Helen relaxed in a rocking chair beside Milt.

"Save me any?"

"There's plenty," Cherie assured him.

"I talked to Nana," Helen said as Lance joined Greg and Cherie around the table. "She'll be here at six."

"Why didn't she come tonight and sleep over?" Lance asked.

"She had a church meeting at Aunt Norma's house," said Helen. "Said she didn't want to drive up the Big Sandy late tonight."

Lance accepted the reason, but it still seemed strange. She frequently drove to their house in the dark. He switched questions to the weekend plans.

"You and Dad are stopping in Portsmouth tomorrow night?"

Milt sat up in the recliner and answered for Helen. "We'll leave right after Greg has thrown, let's see, maybe his third touchdown pass."

Lance and Greg shared smiles.

"Good. I'll see you at the brunch. You have all of the directions and time?"

"You ever see me miss a meal?" Milt grabbed the last piece of pizza.

"Don't worry, honey, we'll be there," Helen tried to comfort her son. "You know your dad. He's never late."

Lance didn't have to say anything. He did know his dad.

After finishing his pizza, Lance completed his homework, finished packing his bag, and was going to hit the sack. *Wait. E-mails?*

He tapped on Cherie's door. "You in there?" He could hear her singing along with the radio.

"Yes." She turned down the music.

"Want to do some more e-mail work?"

"Not right now, I'm busy." The door opened hastily. "Gottcha!" she crowed.

Cherie jumped in the driver's seat. Within seconds, she was moving the arrow to the mail symbol and clicked. They were both pleased.

Dear Lance,

Finished my exams and all seems well. Surprisingly, I'm now looking forward to going home. Dad said you can transfer to Missouri after one season at KU or UK, whichever. You would just have to sit out a year. I told him no way. Hope you have a good time in Columbus. Write if you can.

Yours truly,

Lisa

Lance dictated as Cherie quickly typed:

Lisa,

Please tell your dad I appreciate his advice. Glad you did well on your exams. Thanks for writing again. It was nice to hear from you. Have a good weekend.

As ever,

Lance....

"How does that sound?"

Cherie's face twinkled, "You just got rid of your training wheels, big brother. I like it."

"Thanks, Little Sis. Wish you could go with me to the airport."

"Me, too. Night, Lance."

I thank you, Lord, for such a precious relative.

The next morning something woke Lance up. He rolled over. His nose detected the faint smell of . . . bacon. Dressed in his favorite pajamas -- an old pair of basketball shorts and a white tee shirt -- he quickly moved bare feet across the cold floor. Aromas grew stronger.

"Good Morning, Nana." Lance wiped sleep from his eyes and swallowed her in a hug."

"Good morning, Darlin'. Did you sleep well? Hope you're hungry."

"Sure smells good. Been here long? Didn't want you to get up early just for me. How was the church meeting?"

"What?" Nana had a strange look on her face, but seemed to quickly adjust herself. "Oh, fine . . . Looking forward to takin' you to the airport."

Lance grabbed a piece of crisp bacon. Nana didn't stop him. She probably would have let him eat as many pieces as he could handle, then turn around and fry up some more. She had been preparing biscuits, the kind he and Grandad had devoured many a morning on their farm.

Wiping his hands on a paper towel, he couldn't help but notice how well Nana carried herself. She always dressed to perfection. Today was no exception. Her silver hair was beautifully arranged, no doubt from careful instructions given to some beauty shop attendant yesterday. She was wearing a Kentucky blue pullover sweater, white pants, and her tiny feet looked extremely comfortable in a pair of running shoes. *My Nana's cool.*

"I'll be right back. If Dad gets here before I do, please make sure he stays out of the biscuits and gravy."

Getting dressed took less time than usual. Conscious of his mom's advice, he picked out a red button-down shirt, slipped on his best tan Dockers, and tied his size twelve Nikes. A quick look in the mirror and he was ready for Nana's good cooking.

"Ya cleaned up swell, Sweetheart."

"Thanks. You're lookin' great this morning, too, Nana."

"Fetch a plate and get started. I'll keep everything warm for the rest of the family."

Lance needed no arm twisting. He piled on three eggs, several pieces of bacon, then poured gravy over two browned biscuits he selected as best of the perfect bunch. He poured a tall glass of orange juice and sat down.

Milt walked in eager to load his plate, too. "Mornin."

"This food is for the kids," said Nana. "Your cereal's in the cupboard."

Lance watched the playfulness on Nana's face. Grinning, he encouraged his dad to go for a biscuit, as if to say he'd protect him.

Milt answered the grin. "Son, you've got it a lot easier. You were born into your Nana's family, but I have to get up each day and prove myself worthy again."

Nana stepped over to her son-in-law and kissed him on the cheek. "Alright, Milt. I talked to Helen. She said you've been a good boy this week. Get yourself a plate and join us. I'll get your coffee."

Lance was not a coffee drinker, but he appreciated the aroma from the freshly brewed pot of French roast. Nana filled up his dad's favorite cup, the one Helen had brought back from a bed and breakfast they had visited out in California. He'd miss watching his dad catch a little morning pick-me-up.

Helen joined them, dressed in her regular Fun Friday spirit t-shirt.

"Morning, all." Helen said, looking at all the food. "Mom, you spoil us."

"Ready for your first graders?"

"I bet they're ready for me." Helen poured her first cup. "I hope these boys have been no problem for you."

"Been a pleasure."

Greg and Cherie joined the table a few minutes later. Greg sported a Cleveland Browns tee shirt while Cherie had chosen to wear her favorite hot pink blouse. Breakfast met everyone's hearty approval; the lack of leftovers was more than enough evidence. Lance started to help clear the dishes as his parents headed off to school. Greg and Cherie were not far behind.

"Nana, if you give me the keys, I'll put my suitcase in the trunk."

"They're by my purse. I'm going to freshen up."

Nana's car was perfect. Old, but perfect. It was a squeaky clean Buick LeSabre that always ran great and had a trunk large enough to swallow several sets of luggage. It devoured Lance's small bag.

As he stepped away from the car, Bubba greeted him with a wagging tail. He patted Bubba on the head. The dog followed him inside and to his room where he checked to make certain he hadn't forgotten anything. Bubba rubbed against his Dockers. Lance kneeled down and took time hugging and petting the massive animal.

"Hey, Boy, I'm going to miss you."

Bubba's eyes seemed to answer back, "Me too."

He released his pet when he heard, "Better get going. Why don't you drive?"

Lance was delighted to drive. Nana was a grand passenger. She wouldn't second-guess him like some other family members were quite capable of doing. He lent a hand with her door.

"Thanks, Honey."

Lance jumped into the driver's seat and turned the key. Nothing. He turned it again. Nothing. The third time it reluctantly started. He had never known the Buick to act like this.

"When was the last time you had this baby tuned up, Nana?"

She was quick to respond. "I'll have to try and do that when I get back."

Lance figured the tightness in her voice was concern for the car.

They drove along silently to the outskirts of town. Lance saw the city limits of Connsburg in the rear view mirror. There were no tall buildings or an abundance of traffic lights, but it was home and he was proud of where his roots were planted. Nana was the first to speak again. "So it's between Kansas, Ohio State, and Kentucky, I hear."

Lanced hesitated. "All good schools, Nana. The people in Kansas were very nice to me."

"You could get along with anyone. It'd be easy for them Midwestern-ers to take up with someone like you. Who else visited?"

Lance told her about the other recruits and his friend from Kansas City. He mentioned that J.C. already had committed to Kansas.

"How does that work? Could you just tell the University of Kentucky that you're coming like that boy, J.C., did at Kansas?"

"I could, Nana." Lance said gently. "But I'm trying to figure out which school is best for me."

He snuck a peek at his precious passenger. In her eyes, blue was best. Kentucky Blue. Lance admired that she didn't bully, persuade, or demand he make a decision based on her desires for him. She seemed to be content to let him grow on his own. Although every time he looked through the rear window, it probably pleased her that the Wildcat decal reminded him of her undying loyalty.

Lance figured he would have plenty of time when he finished his visits to talk with Nana, to let her voice what she thought was best for him. He was more concerned about her situation. Hillcrest's question was eating at him. He had run it by his dad and his mom. Why not go to the source?

"Nana, everything all right with you?"

"Sure, Honey. Why?"

"A guy in Kansas asked how you were doing. Said he could help. Really didn't make sense to me."

Nana was silent for a moment. "That was real nice. People asking about your family. Very thoughtful." She stared out the passenger window.

Nana offered no more insight and Lance didn't challenge her explanation. They drove on for a few miles, each viewing the state they loved. The rolling hills provided a natural boundary that encouraged people to know their neighbors well, but little about people living on the other side. Lance thought of Lisa and how little he knew about her. However, he did know that whatever it was that she had, he wanted more of it.

"Tell me about Grandad. How did you two meet?" Lance wondered if it was anything like his meeting Lisa.

She turned towards Lance, suddenly animated. "Oh, that was a long, long time ago."

"I know. Tell me."

The driver sat back quietly and let the lady he adored reminisce.

Nana sighed as she looked over the dashboard. "Oh, he was a handsome, sturdy man. Young and full of energy." She tapped Lance on the arm, gently. "We grew up together you know." Putting her hands together, she went on. "When I was about in the eighth grade, Hoover saw me trip while I ran across the schoolyard with a friend. Got knocked out. As I woke up, he was staring down at me with such concern written all over his face. My love was true from that moment. Never looked back, I guess."

"He became an exceptionally good carpenter, didn't he?"

"Very much in demand, too." She looked at Lance's hands. "Big, strong hands like yours. Powerful with the hammer. A master with the saw. Became more of a supervisor his last twenty or so years." Helen sighed. "I always had the notion Hoover missed just being a carpenter, though. Working magic with his tools."

Lance followed the signs to the airport and steered the Buick toward the departing gates. He parked at the drop-off curb, removed his suitcase from the big trunk, and set it on the pavement. Nana was standing, elevated by the curb, her eyes noticeably red. The conversation about Grandad had taken its toll.

"Thanks for letting me drive." Lance wrapped both arms around her tiny shoulders. "I love you, Nana."

"I love you, too, Darlin'. See you Sunday. Be safe up there with them Buckeyes."

Chapter 13

Lance had been a little nervous about recognizing Assistant Coach Clermont. He shouldn't have worried. When he arrived in Columbus, he instantly spotted a tall man with a shaved head wearing a red Ohio State Basketball shirt waiting at the gate. If he was trying not to be seen, Jim Clermont was poorly camouflaged.

Lance had read a website bio on Coach Clermont. He was walking down the ramp with one of the Buckeye's best from the early seventies. Jim had a nice career in the NBA and like Lance, had helped win a state championship in high school. Lance liked him immediately.

"Your first time to Columbus?"

"First time flying in, but I've driven up many times. Have family here. My Uncle Gary lives in Dublin. Big fan of the Buckeyes."

"We have a few of those in this town." Coach Clermont's laugh sounded like a light melody. "They'll all be fired up tomorrow."

In the parking garage, Clermont unlocked a shiny red Lexus. Lance placed his suitcase in the back seat and they were off. Since last week, he was paying closer attention to transportation.

"Nice car, Coach. New?"

"It's a year old. A gift." Clermont seemed to like answering Lance's first question. "Gave it to myself for having handled my money matters well when I was playing pro ball."

"Which pro teams did you play for?" Lance asked next, even though he knew the answer. It just made him feel better asking something.

"I made a living with the Lakers, then later on with the Cavaliers. Money was good, but those road trips were long. Politics weren't easy. Coaching suits me just fine-these days."

Clermont turned the Lexus onto Route 315, heading north. Lance saw a sprawling campus through the passenger's window.

"Look at all of those buildings!" He felt almost overwhelmed.

"That's the medical school and farther up is the dental school. That big red thing is the biological sciences building." Clermont pointed to his right. "See those two structures with the white stripes that look like twins? One is Morrill Tower and the other's Lincoln Tower." He pointed at another structure. "I guess you know what that is."

Lance was staring at Ohio Stadium. "Uncle Gary just about worships the Horseshoe. Look at the size of that thing. I bet you could fit Kansas and Kentucky's football stadiums inside of it at the same time."

"The place will be humming tomorrow," There was that melodious laugh again. They turned onto the Lane Avenue exit and started eastward. "Check that out!" Pride was in every word.

"Schottenstein."

"You bet. The home of Buckeye basketball."

"Uncle Gary brought us by here when they were building it." Lance's voice showed his excitement. "Can't wait to go inside."

It took a while to pass the gigantic Schottenstein Center. Lance maintained continuous surveillance. He envisioned running up and down the court, competing against the best from Michigan, Indiana, and Illinois. All the Big Ten schools. The Voice of the Buckeyes would be screaming to the radio fans, "There are only four seconds left. We're down two. It doesn't look good, folks. Wait! Stoler stole the ball. He's dribbling down the right side. Just across midcourt, he stops, he pops . . . It's GOOD! Unbelievable! Stoler just hit a three! We beat Michigan State!" Lance slid back into reality and looked quickly at Coach, hoping he wasn't a mind reader. He looked at another building.

"Now, I know what that is. I've been in there. My dad loves golf, so there's no way Uncle Gary brings us this close to Jack's Museum and we don't check it out."

"This Uncle Gary; I take it he's a favorite uncle?"

Lance described the great relationship his dad had with his uncle. "Uncle Gary likes all sports, especially football. It's a shame he can't come to the game tomorrow."

"That's a tough one for us," said Clermont. "Our football games are sold out. It's against NCAA rules to provide you, a recruit, extra tickets. I hope you understand."

"Sure, Coach. Even though it would be special for Uncle Gary, it means a ton to me that you're honest about it."

The Lexus crossed the Olentangy River. Lance gazed at another structure. "Been in there. St. John Arena."

"That charming lady was my college basketball home." Clermont confessed like he was describing his first true love. "She also hosted the state championships my senior year. I admire the Schott, but my heart still aches for the hard wood in that sweetheart."

Lance was savvy enough to know exactly what Jim Clermont was saying. He harbored those exact feelings about Rupp Arena, the site of his state championship.

They turned left, away from St. John. Clermont pulled up in front of the Holiday Inn and shut off the Lexus.

Clermont waited in the lobby while Lance registered and entered an elevator that could have passed for a twin to the one in Lawrence. Six dings later and Lance arrived at his floor. The room was very modest. Nothing fancy. Being so close to campus, it needed no extra features to be booked solidly throughout the year. He pulled the drapes and Coach Clermont's heartthrob, St John Arena, was staring right back at him. An old gray fence surrounded its outer perimeter. Several parking lots and a few green spots of grass provided sparse landscaping. It was not an architectural masterpiece, but its charismatic, strong, rugged appearance was quite charming to Lance.

The sidewalk in front of the hotel was alive with pedestrians on their way to High Street or some other Friday afternoon delight. Lance remembered hearing Uncle Gary describe High Street as a place where many of the popular college bars conducted business. Of course, Uncle Gary was speaking from hearsay, not first-hand experience. At least, that's what he said if he thought Helen or Aunt Carolyn were listening. Lance left the drapes open, then turned to unpack. Within minutes, he was ready to go.

Lance met Clermont downstairs where he had been relaxing in a comfortable high back lobby chair. Lance was almost reluctant to interrupt his peace.

"All set," he announced happily.

"Great. Let's get you over to the Schott." Clermont slowly pulled his tall frame from the soft, sunken cavity.

The Lexus stopped before crossing the Olentangy River Bridge once more. Lance looked out the passenger side where the Schottenstein Center blocked all of his vision, and then his head swiveled around sharply.

"I missed seeing that on our drive in."

"You mean the Woody Hayes complex?" Clermont asked. "How could you miss that?"

"I know, I know. I've even been in there. It just hits you -- how big it is!"

"Don't tell me. Uncle Gary made sure you saw it," Clermont guessed. "He does know you're being recruited for basketball, not football, right?"

"Doesn't know yet. He thinks I'm up here for a visit as a tight-end." Lance smiled, checking Jim's reaction. "He knows. Uncle Gary is a basketball fan, too. It's like pumpkin pie and apple pie. A lot of people love 'em both."

"Nice analogy. You must be hungry. We'll get a bite to eat after our visit to the offices."

Lance peered back over at the Woody Hayes facility and recalled his visit with his uncle last spring. The Stolers had driven up to Dublin for Uncle Gary's fiftieth birthday party. The party was on a Friday, and Milt and Helen brought the family to spend the weekend. Saturday morning, the boys, including Cousin Andy, jumped into Gary's Jeep and headed for a campus tour. They had gone only two miles when the Jeep veered into a little hole-in-the-wall breakfast joint Uncle Gary and Andy loved. It was owned by a couple of Greek gentlemen who cooked scrumptious food. Five colossal omelets, a loaf of whole wheat toast, and several pounds of home fries later, the Jeep resumed its trip with five happy passengers.

They headed south, taking the Ackerman exit. Gary weaved the vehicle around a few turns. They were soon moving parallel to what Andy described as a huge aircraft hangar where the Bucks practiced football. The Jeep settled into a parking spot and the driver told everyone to get out.

Gary was prepared to just walk in, but Lance's dad asked a man walking out if it was OK to go inside. The man was a stately gentleman, about Lance's height. He had burly black hair with a thick, black mustache proudly running across his entire upper lip and well-developed hands strong enough to squash a fully inflated football. His red hat and white Ohio State shirt gave the hint he was a coach, or used to be.

The man's deep, mellow voice answered. "Go on in, guys. You're more than welcome to look around."

"Thank you," Milt responded for the group. "You know how long this building has been opened?"

"Oh, about since six o'clock this morning." The big gentleman presented a slow, teasing half-smile. "We opened it several years ago. The athletic director back then, Rick Bay, was very forward thinking. He knew this would be a great recruiting tool and would help the Bucks stay powerful in football. He was right. He and his staff had to raise a bunch of money, and I mean a bunch. But they did. If you're a Buckeye, you won't be disappointed when you walk out."

They all thanked the gentleman and walked through the north entrance. The group marveled at the All-American photos, Heisman trophies, and team pictures showcased in scarlet and gray hallways. They visited a gigantic weight room and a spectacular training room. Everything made quite an impression on Lance. Andy had seen it before, but he seemed to take immense pleasure in his second visit. The group walked by the equipment room, but the doors were locked. Everyone except Greg had walked on. Greg knocked. Within a few seconds, a small man with a stern face answered the knock.

"What do you want?" he asked gruffly.

Before Greg could think, his manners kicked in. "Sorry, Sir, I was just wondering what was in there."

"Well why don't you come in and find out?," the man said sharply.

"Can the rest of my family come in, too?"

"Yes, but if just one of them acts up, I'm holding you responsible." Greg searched his face. The stearn look disappeared into a pleasant grin. The man held the door open, now giving the impression that the group had better hurry—he had things to do.

The family quickly backtracked and accepted the invitation. Lance could not believe what he saw before him: countless jerseys, huge shoulder pads, hundreds of Buckeye football helmets, and rows upon rows of football shoes. The equipment room manager introduced himself as John. He picked up a pair of size seventeen shoes. Even the dads in this exploration party gawked at how large those shoes were.

"Gentlemen, these belong to one of our little offensive linemen," John offered. "By the time he's a senior we'll probably have to get him a bigger pair."

John's gruff voice took on a softer rhythm in his words and his smile grew with each explanation of his neighborhood. Lance suspected someone could travel to many campus equipment rooms and never find another person this talented and this devoted to his job.

Filled with excitement, the Stolers left the equipment room. Each found a special joy in what they had just experienced. Only Santa's elves could probably be able to claim a better moment. Next, they wandered into the main attraction of the gigantic facility --the indoor artificial turf football field. It was surrounded by soaring walls and a roof which appeared to be so high that the local weatherman might predict rain from clouds that gathered below the roof. At this time in the morning, only three people occupied the area. The three became more visible as the Stoler group walked farther into the structure.

"They have to be players," Lance said. The tallest one was about six-five and weighed at least 300 pounds. The shortest was not much more than five-ten but was very sleek looking. The last had piled-up biceps, thundering thighs, and no neck.

Uncle Gary immediately identified them. "An offensive lineman, wide receiver, and linebacker."

"Gee, you must be a genius. How did you figure that out?" asked Milt with a fake snarl. Their body builds had given each away.

"It's a gift, little brother. I just know these things,"

Greg walked right up to the three strangers. "Hey, Guys, you all play here?"

The three hundred-pound giant answered, "No, but we used to." Then he looked the short one right in the eyes. "Well, I'm not sure about the squirt. He's too petite to have played here." The "squirt" gave a jovial forearm to the giant and all three laughed.

Chatting with the group, they found out the three were former Buckeyes now under NFL contracts. They were using the weight room to go through workouts. The lineman was playing for the St. Louis Rams, the wide receiver for the Dallas Cowboys, and the linebacker was a New England Patriot.

Coach Clermont accelerated through the green light. Lance turned his attention back to basketball. "Coach, I know you like St. John's, but this baby looks mighty nice."

"Hey, no one is complaining. Goin' to create a bunch of memories in this Lady also."

The Schott was state of the art. Its red exterior was the perfect hue for Ohio State. The landscaped grounds gave the building a sense of elegance. Lance was teeming with emotions, the same he had experienced when he first visited Rupp as a middle school kid.

Parking next to the building, they entered and headed down a long hallway.

"Can we take a quick look at the floor?"

"Sure we can." Coach seemed to understand his urge to visit the floor first. "Cut through this way."

Lance let his eyes wander. Thousands of seats surrounded a shining hardwood floor. He had seen the arena on television over the years, when the Buckeyes were showcased on ESPN or another national TV game. Standing on the floor and breathing the air inside the Schott made Lance dizzy with excitement. Slowly he looked up and saw a bounty of hospitality suites.

"Who gets to sit up there?" he asked.

"You have got to be a big dog to have one of those. I think they go for about $50,000," replied Coach Clermont. "And that is per year."

"Man, that's a lot of money," Lance said, shaking his head. "What does this place seat?"

"For hoops, it's over 19,000, and a couple thousand less for hockey. I think for concerts they try to jam 21,000 or more in here."

"Amazing." Lance mentally compared Allen Fieldhouse, which was smaller and the Rupp Arena, which was a bit bigger.

They moved on and entered an office.

"Well, this must be Lance Stoler. We have been expecting you. I'm Coach's secretary. We're so delighted to have you in Columbus." She was a small woman with charcoal hair and a beautiful smile. Her welcoming voice had a slight Southern accent, which only enhanced Lance's admiration.

"Nice meeting you, Ma'am."

She led him the few steps to the doorway of the head coach's office, knocked, then walked in. "Coach, got a wonderful package from Kentucky. I thought you might want to see it."

"Well, yes, I do. Thank you." A cheerful looking man swirled his desk chair around, immediately got up, and started towards the doorway. "Good to see you," Homer Meadors said, looking Lance squarely in the eyes. He shook Lance's hand. "I've got to tell you, we've been sweating bullets. Thought we might not get you to visit. Rumors have been flying all over the Midwest about you."

"Gosh Coach, I'm sorry. I never had any intentions of not coming. When I told you that I would visit, it was non-debatable."

Lance was upset the Buckeye staff had been given wrong information about him and more upset at whoever had spread the wrong impression of him.

"Please sit down. I understand even more, now, what Coach Hunter has been trying to explain about you. He said you come with a little old-time honesty and integrity, along with a halfway decent three-point shot." Homer's words were not phony. Something created just to make a sale. Lance accepted the compliment with inherited modesty.

Coach Meadors began a review of several recruiting items and the weekend schedule. Silently Lance gauged the man in front of him. Meadors' dark brown hair was combed over to the side, thinning enough to let a hint of future baldness shine through. His tailored pants were neatly pressed, and his shirt left no doubt that Ohio State was his team. His hands moved about him, emphasizing points as he spoke, but they always returned to the same position: fingers touching at their tips and thumbs pointed to his chin. In Lance's mind, Coach Meadors was clearly a man of quality.

It was pleasing to hear that the evening meal would be downtown at Morton's with two other recruits. Uncle Gary had mentioned Morton's Steak House as a place Lance might get to visit while on his recruiting trip. His Uncle raved about their thick, juicy steaks.

While Coach Meadors finished his review, Lance scrutinized the plush office. The bookshelf behind the desk exhibited an assortment of pictures. Lance suspected most were family. Along the far wall, a collection of photos, from all eras of Buckeye basketball, were flawlessly displayed.

"That's about it. Any questions?" Coach Meadors followed Lance's eyes to the photo wall.

"Those are some interesting pictures. They all Buckeyes?"

"Indeed." Homer nodded. "Many are All-Americans, but some are not. They're here to remind me each day of our great tradition. I take great pleasure when recruits see these pictures. Gives you a feel for what it means to be a Buckeye." He rose from his chair and motioned for Lance to follow him. "Come here, take a closer look."

Meadors started with a picture of Dr. Jimmy Hull. "This guy was on the 1939 team that lost to Oregon in the first NCAA tournament. Back then, the tournament wasn't what it is today. There was no CBS coverage and no big money for your school if you made it to the national championship. Jimmy loved the hook shot. We've had more than our fair share of great people. However, I would have to say Dr. Hull might be the classiest of them all. He ended up becoming a dentist and a leading citizen in this community. When you look up Buckeye in the dictionary it says, 'see Jimmy Hull.'"

"He sounds like one of those guys I wished I would have had a chance to meet," Lance said as he peered at three players grinning proudly with their arms around each other. "Who are those guys?"

"The 1960 team. Won the national championship." Meadors pointed at three players. "Lucas, Havilcek, and Nowell." He shook his head. "Coach Taylor, the coach back then, was fortunate to have recruited those three." He pointed at the next picture. "Now this guy, Gary Bradds, was a young gun who came in a few years later, but he did get to play some with those other three. Gary was bony: an awkward looking player, but he could really stroke it." Meadors rubbed his chin, chuckling. "Floor burns were a constant problem for him, if you know what I mean."

"Sure do," Lance quickly responded, resisting the urge to brag to Coach that he was no stranger to floor burns, either. "What's he doing now?"

"Unfortunately, he passed away several years ago. After a short time in the pros, he returned to Ohio and coached near where he grew up. He taught and was an assistant basketball coach at a high school called Tecumseh. A great person. A real gentle giant."

Meadors stepped towards a larger picture. "This guy look familiar to you? I don't know what happened to him. He's probably a lot fatter now with no hair."

Lance knew who it was right away. "Isn't that the limo driver who picked me up at the airport?"

"Well, good. At least the guy has a job," Meadors said. "In all seriousness, Jim Clermont was a keeper. And I say that not just because he's my assistant. His left-handed jump shot was automatic."

"Who is that tall skinny guy?" Lance asked.

"That's Luke Witte." Another story surfaced. "He was the center on a team in the seventies that went to Minnesota for a game where all hell broke loose. There was a big fight. He took a real beating. Coach Taylor and the athletic director, Ed Weaver, never enjoyed each other's company after that incident. Mr. Weaver was one of the old guard athletic directors: a big, silver-haired powerful man. He worked with Wayne Duke, the Big Ten Commissioner at the time, to resolve what happened and to figure out who should be disciplined." Meadors shook his head. "Mr. Duke was one of the best commissioners ever. He had been a graduate of the University of Iowa, worked at the NCAA in Kansas City, and served as the Big Eight commissioner for several years before coming over to the Big Ten. Weaver and Duke never did get the incident handled to Coach Taylor's satisfaction. I suspect Coach Taylor was bothered significantly by the incident, because his coaching was never the same." Homer hesitated. "Unfortunately, the record books show his last Buckeye teams really struggled."

"Sorry to hear that, Coach."

"I guess we all are." Meadors returned to his desk. "We're very proud of our winning tradition. We want it to continue. But we care even more about integrity and what becomes of a man after he wears the scarlet and gray. This weekend my job is to convince you that hanging your picture with these gentlemen could make both of us very proud." Homer's face and words exhibited unrehearsed honesty.

Lance nodded his appreciation.

Meadors replaced his seriousness with a lighter subject. "We need to get you something to eat. Coach Clermont is prepared to take you for a bite and then bring you back here to watch practice. We have two other recruits coming in later today. Melvin Howard is a center from Chicago and Chris Anderson's from Toledo. You'll meet them at practice."

"Sounds great." Lance followed Meadors into the reception area where Clermont was waiting patiently.

"See if you can't find a good sandwich in this town for Lance," Homer good-naturedly handed Lance over to his assistant.

"Not a problem, Boss."

They were soon swerving through traffic on Route 315. Lance reflected privately. His visit with Coach Meadors had gone much easier than he had imagined. Meadors had put him at ease and his stories about former players were fascinating. He looked over at Jim. "Where we headed?"

"Bumpers. It's a small sports bar. They've got excellent sandwiches and the owner always makes sure we get fast, excellent service. His son played football for the University of Toledo, but he loves the Buckeyes."

Bumpers' parking lot had few open spaces. A huge indoor athletic club sat behind it and a quaint restaurant housed in a former church building occupied the neighboring property. They walked inside. The walls were covered with Ohio State mementos and various other sports memorabilia.

A yellow and blue pennant hung over the bar. *What are Michigan colors doing in here?* After closer review, Lance saw the pennant was from the University of Toledo. The Rockets. *Oh yeah, the owner's son.*

The lights were turned down low. A man approached them, calling to Clermont. "You slumming again?"

"No. We just happened to be in the neighborhood and we asked the gas station attendant down the road if he knew of a good place to eat around here. He said no, but if we could make our way another five miles, there were plenty of places." Clermont chuckled. "If we had more gas, we wouldn't be here." He slapped the man on the back. "How you doing?" They grabbed each other's hands. "This is the owner of this shack," Clermont said to Lance. "Meet Lance Stoler from Kentucky. Word on the street is he made a few threes in a basketball game and now everyone thinks he can play. His uncle lives in Dublin. Paid me a hundred bucks if we'd recruit him. I needed the money; what can I say?"

The owner spoke with a gleam in his eye. "In this establishment, we welcome the best three point shooter from the state of Kentucky when we meet him. Just follow me. I have a table waiting for you."

They followed him to a booth situated perfectly for watching games. No games were on at the moment, but Lance could tell it was a preferred location.

"Everything on the menu is good. If you like hamburgers, we have the best in town," he boasted. "And the biggest."

"You have buffalo wings?"

"We do, and they're good. If you like 'em hot, we can light your fire."

"Mild works for me."

"We can handle that." He said setting two menus on the table. "It was my pleasure meeting you, Lance. You're with a great one. We love Coach Clermont."

"Thank you; I appreciate that," Clermont said kindly. The bar owner smiled and walked away. "I didn't pay him to say that, but it was nice. Have you decided what you want to order?"

"I'm easy." Lance folded the menu. "The wings and one of those big burgers will do me fine."

"Burger sounds good to me, too."

When the wings were served, Lance took a bite. He immediately knew that the chef was no rookie; these were worthy of the Stolers' chicken wings stamp of approval. The Stoler boys were experts on buffalo wings. Greg could eat them really hot, but Lance and Milt preferred theirs on the mild side. Lance finished the last one and was wiping his hands when two huge burgers were delivered to their table.

"Now, that's a burger," Lance said.

The meat extended over the bun and was generously thick. Crisp lettuce and juicy tomato slices complemented the burger, but there was an intruder -- an onion. Lance had never figured out how to like them. He quickly discarded it to the plate piled high with chicken bones. The fries were perfect. The owner must have known his customers preferred big Idaho cut fries, not the pencil midgets some places served. They finished their meal and headed for the front door. Jim had left a nice tip for the waitress. Lance took notice.

Coach Meadors saw them coming as soon as they stepped out onto the Schott's hardwood floor, and waved Lance over. "Lance, come here. I want you to meet a couple of people."

He introduced Melvin Howard, Chris Anderson, and the tallest of the three. "This guy is Brad Byers, our starting point guard." Homer waited to see the expression on Lance's face before he continued. "Well, maybe we use him at center, but he's always trying to get open twenty-five feet from the hoop when that big ugly center from Michigan State is guarding him."

Coach Meadors called the team together to give a few instructions about practice, then proceeded to launch a description of each recruit to the team. Starting with Melvin, Coach explained he was considered the best big man in Chicago, perhaps one of the top ten in the nation. Melvin's height and wingspan allowed him to nearly touch the rim without jumping. Meadors assured the team that if Melvin would commit to the Buckeyes he could teach him to dunk in no time. Big Melvin rolled his head as the team snickered good naturedly.

Next he described the recruit from Toledo. "Can you believe Michigan and Indiana want this kid to play for them?" Coach shook his head. "I guess it's because he was the leading scorer in the state last year, as a junior. He averaged 29 per game. If I was coaching him, his opponents would have been happy. My coaching, no doubt, would have held him to twenty." There was immediate laughter.

Homer started slowly with the Kentuckian. "Now this fellow wouldn't make a half bad tight end." Lance shyly lowered his head. "Reports coming out of the Bluegrass state say that he can." He paused. "Hit the broad side of a barn. But we really want him as an investment." Meadors winked towards Lance. "If we land this guy, we then get a shot at having the true athletes in the Stoler family becoming Buckeyes: his bother and sister." Lance was overjoyed with Coach's light-hearted remarks. He could tell he wasn't the only recruit feeling at ease and welcome.

"Time to go to work," Coach Meadors directed. "You guys can sit right over there."

The three young men accepted their orders. Sitting in the first row, Lance watched the team and believed they looked very similar to Kansas. They appeared to be quite talented. Appearances only made you feel good at tip-off time, though. Shooting ability and conditioning separated teams during competition. If Ohio State played Kansas right now, who would win was the question Lance privately mused. *I would have to go with the Jayhawks,* he answered himself. *All things being equal, Shane would be a ten-point differential.*

Lance was curious about the Buckeye's other two guests. "When did you guys get in?"

"Landed about two and they drove me straight to the hotel and then here," Melvin answered. "How about you?"

"Came in this morning,"answered Lance.

Chris joined in. "Toledo isn't that far. I drove down with my parents. Took us two hours."

"You guys been here before?" Lance took a crack at another question.

"Not me," Melvin said.

"Been here a lot," Chris said. He seemed pleased to report that he was no rookie. "But not as a recruit. My Mom's a teacher. She graduated from Ohio State."

"Hey, my Mom teaches first grade."

"Get out of here. Are you kidding?" Chris responded. "My Mom teaches first grade, too. Small world." They laughed at the play on words.

"My mom and dad will be here tomorrow. We've got to make sure our moms meet each other. I'm sure they'd love to compare war stories."

"Super," Chris answered.

Melvin broke in, "Hey, Kentucky, who you looking at besides the Bucks?"

Lance had to look up. Melvin was a big person. He liked the way Melvin asked the question, though. The warmth in his face and calm, deep voice made Lance feel at ease. "Can't be from Kentucky and not consider the Wildcats, if you are invited to visit. Last weekend I visited the University of Kansas. Those two and the Buckeyes. That's it for me . . . How about you, Big Man? Who has your interest besides Ohio State?"

Lance watched the giant swivel in his seat and rub his chin with a larger than normal golden brown hand and long slender fingers. "Visited Illinois, and last week had an unpaid visit to DePaul. Told the coaches at Marquette and Fresno State I'd visit."

Chris asked, "How did Fresno State get into your mix?"

"Ever heard of Rod Higgins? He was from my neighborhood. Several years back, he played for Fresno. He was one of the best players ever out there."

Before Chris could reply, Lance shot back, "I met Mr. Higgins last summer at a basketball camp. He was in management or something with one of the NBA teams. Wizards, I think. He gave a speech and was very good. Wasn't he Michael Jordon's roommate with the Bulls?"

"Kentucky man, you're good. That's Rod. He's my man. Respected back where I come from. Know what I mean? Gonna visit Fresno 'cause of him."

"Where is Fresno?" Chris asked.

"Coaches told me it's right in the middle of the San Joaquin Valley in between Sacramento and Bakersfield," Melvin said. "Tell me it's beautiful. The Sierra-Nevada Mountains are real close."

Lance smiled at Melvin. "Does that mean you'd become a California surfer?"

"Be a big one, wouldn't I?" His laughter thundered.

"How about you, Chris?" Lance asked. "You really looking at Michigan and Indiana like Coach said?"

"Gotta keep my options open," Chris said. He told them that Michigan is in Ann Arbor, only forty miles north of his hometown of Toledo. "The Wolverines have a big influence in my town."

"Indiana, they have great basketball tradition," Melvin affirmed.

"I want to check them out, too," Chris leaned over. "Also considering the University of Toledo. You know, stay put and play for the home town team. Their coach is pretty nice. I really like him." Chris sat up in his seat, "Boy, talking about all these schools sure makes you realize how tough it is to decide."

"Got that right," Melvin moaned.

"Isn't going to be easy for any of us," Lance agreed. "But my dad says we should be awfully thankful we're being recruited."

"Your dad's right. I'm thankful." Melvin shrugged. "But . . . my high school coach wants me to go to Marquette, my mom wants me to go to Illinois, and I want to go to Fresno."

"It sounds to me like you might want to get away," Chris suggested.

Melvin's voice became even deeper. "What's wrong with getting away? I don't want to have to join the Navy to see the world."

The big man's words struck a nerve with Lance. "Got all those feelings. The love for Kentucky is so powerful in my town. I feel almost guilty I liked Kansas." Lance looked at Melvin with a grin. "It's not California, but it's a long way out there to the Heartland when you haven't traveled much."

"I hear ya." Melvin looked back onto the court. "Can't solve it today."

"Yeah," Lance accepted the big man's opinion. "Let's concentrate on the Buckeyes."

They turned their attention back to practice. They hadn't solved any problems, but Lance was certain all three felt better for having aired a few emotions about the powerful personal decision each would soon make.

Homer was providing instructions as he worked with the post players under the near basket. There was no shouting and screaming, no belittling any of the men he was coaching. Homer Meadors was like a teacher in the classroom. His students displayed respect and appreciation while he offered words of advice. As he was breaking down a particular move and demonstrating in a fashion so everyone could learn, Lance thought of his mom: how she instructed her first grade classroom and how eager her students were to listen to most every word. Her classroom was a safe harbor for her little ones. They could feel secure as she nurtured their minds and strengthened their souls. Meadors seemed to be very much the same.

Having finished with the players, Homer headed their way. He stopped in front of them. "We always work hard on the fundamentals. The sounder we get with the fundamentals, the more it guarantees in game time, during crunch time, our reactions will become automatic. End up doing those things that usually helps the team win. And then, by golly, even I look good." Lance was pleased that Homer kept revealing his character. He was a teacher, big on integrity, a stickler for the fundamentals, and possessed a fun wit.

Before turning back to his team, Homer made an additional proclamation. "After they finish shooting some free throws and I check their conditioning, we'll get you back to the hotel and then see if there's still anything good to eat in this town."

"Check their conditioning. Check their conditioning. I know that teaching method," Chris said once Homer was out of hearing range. "After they shoot some free throws, he's going to run their rear ends off."

"You're right," Lance and Melvin said in unison.

Free throws. Lance's style of play afforded him plenty of chances to step to the line. He drifted back to younger days when Milt would have him on the driveway, perfecting form and consistency. To weekends in the school gym. Normally, no one else would be there. *Not bad, having a relative who had a master key to the school.* In that privacy, he polished not only his free throws, but all of his skills. Sometimes Greg would come. Sometimes Cherie. Sometimes Milt just left them alone in the gym while he shuffled off to the office to catch up on paperwork.

During those times, Lance seldom considered dribbling and shooting as practice. He felt pleasure navigating with a ball - moving in any direction, controlling with either hand, magically having it return to his ready fingertips.

With one fluid motion, he would stop and move the ball above his head. Elbow down. Wrist cocked. Eyes focused. Then firing.

After hours upon hours, then years upon years, on driveways, and in gyms, basketball grew from play to practice, then to outright work. Nevertheless, Lance never lost interest. The music would not let him -- basketball music -- *swish, swish, swish.*

The Buckeyes were working on their free throw shooting, doing quite well. But this was practice. Game conditions are a different matter. Lance learned that lesson well from his dad. Milt would say, "You can't miss in practice. To make one free throw in a game, you have to make a bundle in practice without a miss . . . The pressure of a live crowd can mess up all bodily functions. When a player steps to the line, he'd better react with exact precision."

His mind wandered to a possible future game . . . The Buckeyes needed to get the ball in play. Only five seconds remained. Ohio State up by three. TV personality, Clark Kellogg, is commenting on the game. "Indiana has to steal the ball or foul immediately. They better not foul Stoler or this game is over . . ."

The other TV announcer starts the play-by-play. "Stoler comes off of a pick." His voice rises. "He's open." His voice switches to astonishment. "The Hoosiers foul Stoler! Wait, there's still three ticks on the clock. A miss and Indiana will have a chance at a three to tie the game."

"I don't think so," Kellogg quickly predicts.

The referee hands the ball to Lance. His toe sets up just in front of the line. He eyes the rim, his knees bend, his fingers flex, his wrist snaps. The crowd watches the ball track towards the backboard. It rises up over the front of the rim and gravity pulls it to the floor. But no one, not even Lance, hears the swoosh. The noise becomes deafening before the ball travels half way down the dangling white net. The second one seems just as easy and the Buckeyes win another Big Ten Championship.

"You daydreaming on me, Boy?" Melvin nudged Lance. "Coach wants us. Let's go."

"Just thinking," Lance started to follow Melvin. *Melvin would have grabbed the rebound if I'd have missed.*

The guests gathered around Coach Meadors. Three Buckeye players stood at his side. One was Brad Byers. Meadors introduced the other two. "This is John Hollis and Jay Buxton. Along with Brad, they volunteered to be hosts this weekend. I'm sure you noticed how I took it easy on them in the sprints because of their volunteering spirits."

Standing in soaking wet practice jerseys, John and Jay looked at each other. "Yeah, right, Coach," Jay quipped. "Easy?" He wiped their faces with a towel.

John Hollis was a reserve point guard from Vermilion, a little town on Lake Erie. He'd signed with Ohio State after being named all-state and probably was the best player to ever come out of Vermilion High School. He could have been a starter at any other university in the state. His lack of playing time was nothing more than a reflection of how severe the competition was at this level of college basketball. He was tall and handsome, with slick dark hair. Lance suspected he just might be a big hit with coeds.

Jay was the starting point guard. He walked and ran with an aggressive, roadrunner-type gate and his slender body resembled a tightly wound bundle of wire. Like John Hollis, Jay was from Ohio and had earned first team All-state both his junior and senior years. Lance had watched him play on television several times and thought he was a fierce competitor. Television announcers described him as more of a scorer than a shooter. He averaged nearly twenty points a game.

Brad gazed at the group and said, "Melvin, my first piece of advice is that you watch your step around these little people so you don't step on them. We'd have no one to pass us the ball."

Jay grinned at his friend. "You better be nice to your point guard or the rest of your passes will be coming off of the rim."

John was first to act as a sincere host. "Good to have you guys here. We're happy to help out, and especially when we know how it benefits the program and Coach Meadors. There's not one of us who doesn't know Coach has our best interests at heart. That's every day, all the time."

Coach Meadors appeared pleased to hear such kind words – very special coming from John, a non-starter. "Obviously, John will get more playing time this season," A smiling Meadors teased. "Let's get out of here. Coach Clermont will take you guys back to the hotel and these three intellectuals will meet us at Morton's."

Clermont dropped them off and they strolled through the hotel lobby. Scarlet and gray was everywhere. Anyone dressed in different colors easily stood out. Lance was pleased he had picked out a red shirt for this trip. Chris was either coached by his mom or lucked out because he had on a pair of tan slacks and a multi-colored shirt sporting plenty of red. Big Melvin didn't have a clue. His green polyester sweater was tucked into long, well-worn blue jeans. Melvin seemed not to care.

One Buckeye fan, holding his favorite "Bud" in his right hand, advanced towards them. "Hey, you guys players?" Lance could tell by the manner in which his words came stumbling out that he and his friends had been working hard at getting his cheeks rosy. Lance answered for the group. "We're just up here visiting."

"Yooou sure? You sure look like players."

"Sir, we're in high school." Chris tried to help. "Visiting for the weekend."

"Then yooou're recruits. See? I knew yoou was players." The fan tried to focus, delighted with himself.

"You bet," Melvin replied. The three tried to walk by him towards the elevator.

The fan's voice turned up a few decibels. "Well yooou guys are welcome here. We kick butt in football and we're going to do the same in basketball."

Melvin pushed the elevator button and the doors opened. They got on and playfully waved goodbye, trying not to laugh until the doors closed securely.

"That man's feeling no pain," Chris cracked up.

"What was your first clue?" Melvin deadpanned as the doors opened on the sixth floor. They all got off and headed to their respective rooms. "See you guys at six."

Chris nodded. "Don't leave without me."

A dry, sterile hotel smell hit Lance's nostrils as he entered the room. He quickly opened a window to let in a little fresh air. He looked down. Traffic had picked up on Lane Avenue. The number of pedestrians seemed to have doubled since he had checked in. Across the way, St John arena looked even more majestic as the afternoon sun reflected off her silver exterior.

His thoughts wandered back home. He hoped Greg would play well tonight. No doubt, Milt would review every play of the game with Helen on their ride to Portsmouth. His mom would hear in excruciating detail how Greg got the pass off in spite of a poor snap, a missed block, and the receiver being well covered. Helen's love for her husband would orchestrate a caring smile, even though her hearing might be turned down a notch or two.

Nana would be beaming. She would have Greg and Cherie to herself for the whole weekend. Those two would be experiencing a little Christmas cooking in October.

Nana's got to get her car tuned up next week. Why had Hillcrest asked about her?

Lance decided he'd better take a quick shower. He stripped, jumped in, and shivered until the hot water finally kicked in. It was a first-rate shower.

He took a moment to place both hands against the tiled wall, letting water flow over his shoulders and down his back, gently relaxing stiff muscles from the day's travel. Slowly, his thoughts drifted to Lisa. He wondered who she would be with tonight. *I'm happy she's going home for the weekend. Marla will have less of an impact.*

Reluctantly, he turned off the shower and reached for a towel. It was dinky and hardly big enough to wrap around his waist. After a needless shave, he picked up the red shirt he had worn since early this morning. His evaluation: "This shirt looks fine."

His Dockers, on the other hand, needed an iron's touch. He peeked into the closet and found one hanging on the wall. Helen had trained all of her children on the finer procedures of using this weapon. Lance pulled the board out of its rack, grabbed the iron, and stooped over to place the plug in a wall socket.

"Where the heck is it? Why don't these hotels put extra outlets in these rooms?"

He gave up his search. The bathroom outlet would have to do. He hated having a cord hanging around the sink, but those Dockers needed some attention. Lance laid the pants on the board and firmly pressed one leg before he flipped them over and finished the task. His mom was not there, but he swore that he heard her voice. Respectfully, he picked up the shirt and gave it a serious dose of heat. After putting the iron back into the closet, he went to the suitcase and picked up his blue sweater. He slipped it over the freshly ironed shirt and pulled the red collar out. *Even a little red in this town would take the attention away from a blue sweater.* A peek in the mirror hanging over the chest of drawers guaranteed him he was presentable.

Chapter 14

As the elevator doors opened, Lance stared in amazement. The color red had become even more dominant, intensifying the gaiety. The weekend was beginning. Fans were forgetting about any problems at work or at home. They were happily immersing themselves in a temporary world where the anticipation of victory was real and comforting.

Lance casually watched one group of people in their early fifties. He suspected they were close friends who probably had attended Ohio State together and were now reminiscing about their younger days when Woody was coaching, when they studied hard, and partied even harder.

One couple in the group especially caught Lance's attention. They seemed to be oblivious of the crowd. She was an elegant woman, dressed in a gray skirt. A scarlet turtleneck sweater proudly displayed her sleek dimensions. The man sat guarding her attention, admiring a long strand of buckeyes hanging from her shoulders. Lance could not hear their conversation, but he noticed something. *No rings!* Had they been sweethearts at OSU, but after graduation, pursued different life paths? Had fate caused them to run into each other again here, in this crowd? Lance wished them well, no matter what their story might be.

Lance steered his way through the lobby to the front entry. There he could wait for his fellow recruits and watch for Coach Clermont. His eyes scanned the room and stopped at a man surrounded by a small crowd. The man and his admirers were no farther away than the length of a free throw lane. It was easy for Lance to hear bits and pieces of their conversation.

"Rex, you look great," said a fan near the back.

Rex was probably a former player, still trim with a sturdy face - a model of strength and determination.

"Tell us how you beat Michigan in '68," a man shouted as he straightened his black cap embroidered with a scarlet block "O."

Rex's eyes gleamed, showing he welcomed the question and he began to speak. At that moment, in that corner of the lobby, anyone could hear a pin drop. Laughter cut their silence when Rex stopped after a humorous statement. He held them in the palm of his hand. Lance wondered if he might become someone admired like Rex someday.

Melvin and Chris arrived. Melvin pointed to the parking lot where a Lexus had just arrived.

Big Melvin shouted out, "Taxi. Taxi!" His mammoth right hand flagged an imaginary cab.

"Get in," Coach Clermont said, his smile bright as ever. "I'll give you a taxi ride."

"Hey, Coach," Lance asked as the so-called taxi pulled out, "how long does it take to get to Morton's?"

"You must be hungry again. It's downtown. We'll be there in less than twenty minutes."

"Coach Clermont," Melvin spoke slowly. "Have you ever had to deal with any sports agents?" from the anxious tone of his voice, Lance suspected that Melvin may have been waiting quite some time to ask that question. "You know, guys wanting to help you."

"Yes, I've dealt with them. When I was in the NBA -- when it was appropriate. Never in college." Clermont steered the car into the right hand lane. "I would only talk to agents who were of solid character and who would be more interested in my well being than their making money for themselves." His smile evaporated. "Are you involved with an agent?" His voice became deeper, more serious. "You know your NCAA eligibility can be severely hindered if you are."

The Chicago kid responded immediately. "No, Sir." he glanced quickly over at the driver. His face was blank.

Clermont peered through the rearview mirror. "How about you two? Have you had any contact with an agent?"

Chris' voice overrode Lance's. "No, Coach."

"Me neither, Coach," said Lance. "My dad thinks many of those guys are pretty sneaky."

Clermont was sitting up straight in the driver's seat, concentrating intently on the road, but ready to interject some of his own beliefs. "Your dad is right. None of you should ever let yourselves get hooked by a dirty sports agent. Don't let them buy you anything. And for God's sake, don't let their runners buy you anything."

"What do you mean by runners?" Chris asked.

"Those are the guys who do the dirty work for agents. They might pretend to become your friend, or they may be someone you have known in your past. The agent uses them to get to you."

Clermont charged on with emotion. "Runners might buy you an airplane ticket, give you money, buy you expensive meals, buy you clothes, and yes, provide you with women. A runner is someone who is breaking the NCAA rules, and someone who can mess up your lives. They have their own interest at heart, not yours. Your integrity hinges on defending yourself against their tactics."

"Let me get to the point." Clermont cleared his throat. "Melvin, don't tell me if someone comes up to you and gives you a couple of hundred dollars that bells won't go off, sounding a warning that something is not right. Chris, don't tell me if someone offers you a free flight and all-expenses-paid weekend to Vegas, that something illegal is not happening. Lance, if someone offers you five hundred dollars' worth of new clothes, it better be your mom. Wait, even that could be a problem. If there's no way she has that kind of money, something's going on."

The three recruits' heads were nodding in agreement.

"You guys need to be the ones saying no," he said. "I hope I'm not the first one to explain this. What really happens is these sharks get their teeth into a player and will not let go. Once they have you, because you've taken something you shouldn't have, they really have you. They own you."

Clermont stopped for a red light, giving him the chance to stare boldly into the eyes of each passenger. "They're betting a player will not say anything because of his eligibility. If you turn on them, then they turn you in and your life gets ruined. Trust me. Your life was already ruined the moment you made the wrong decision. If you cross the line, your conscience will be a monkey on your back. It will gnaw at you like a man cheating on his wife. You'll always be frightened that you'll get caught."

Clermont accelerated through the intersection. "It burns me when I read about the NCAA investigating some school and a player comes out two or three years later and says he took money or something. In most cases the coach didn't even know, and for sure, the athletic director and president wouldn't know because the agents, the boosters and the athletes who cheat are too devious. If I had my way, I would burn those athletes who cheated. I would make them pay the school back if their university went on probation because of them. They are the ones who made bad choices. They are the ones who should suffer some significant consequences."

Clermont kept venting. "And don't give me that ghetto stuff: that, 'oh, how poor we are' stuff. Income and money have nothing to do with your character and integrity. Someone dirt poor can have superior values." Not a word was spoken by any of the passengers. "I pray some of what I just said sinks into all three of you. No matter what school you commit to. Don't get me wrong, I'm hell-bent on making sure all of you recognize Ohio State is your best choice. I just don't want to see any of you have your life destroyed."

The car sounded like a hearse. Jim had given a powerful sermon. It was apparent by the silence and facial expressions that the preacher had struck a nerve.

As the Lexus pounded the freeway towards downtown Columbus, Lance's mind drifted back to his friend in Kansas City. He fervently hoped J.C. hadn't done anything he would later regret; that he hadn't crossed the line.

A valet was waiting as they pulled in front of the restaurant.

"I like this place already," Melvin said.

"It only gets better." Clermont took the valet ticket and pushed it into his pocket.

Lance got out and peered down the long city street. It was definitely not eastern Kentucky, and for sure not Connsburg. Early evening sunlight was bouncing off the windows of each gigantic building. The sidewalks were crowded. The pedestrians seemed to all have similar ambitions -- get home or get to a place where the Friday night fun could begin. Lance was no different. He was ready to have a pleasant evening.

The entrance to Morton's was not well lit, but Lance was still able to observe the fine furnishings and dark wood trim masterfully constructed on each interior wall. The hostess stood behind a tall walnut podium. A young, attractive brunette, she left no doubt that Clermont was no stranger.

"Good evening, Coach." Her sparkling white teeth became completely exposed in a smile after her last word. "We have the private room all set up for you. No one else is here yet, but I'll take you back, if you like."

"These are a couple of our recruits. I was hoping you would help us feed them tonight."

"No problem. If they like great steaks and delicious seafood, we can surely handle that." She smiled at them. "Please follow me, Gentlemen."

They followed the hostess's short black skirt, long graceful legs, and spiked heels as she slowly crossed the room towards the back of the restaurant. Melvin softly said to Lance, "Oh, yeah. I really like this place."

A cheerful greeting from a table near the door of their private room stopped Jim and his recruits. "Hey Coach. Working late tonight?" inquired a friendly voice.

"Hey, Denny. Our work is never done." Jim stopped. "I found a couple of strays that haven't had a good feeding in a long time. Chef said we could let them graze in the private room for awhile."

"No way! These boys look much better than strays."

Clermont motioned to the hostess that they would be right in.

"Gentlemen, this is Mr. Tishman." Clermont introduced him to the recruits. "The Buckeyes have a wealth of supporters and friends, but none better than this man."

Mr. Tishman stood to shake hands, saying words of welcome to each. "That was nice of you to say coach. My family and I appreciate your kind words." Tishman presented his family. He walked with stately composure around the table, slowly laying his hands on each family member as he introduced two sons, a daughter, and his striking wife.

Mr. Tishman had strong shoulders, a firm chin, and the thickest black wavy hair Lance had ever seen. His gray suit and scarlet tie looked custom made. The cufflinks on his striped shirt confirmed distinction.

His wife was a beautiful woman. She remained seated, but as Lance stared down at her perfectly fashioned brown hair and compassionate warm face, he saw a lady he suspected possessed the same kindness and compassion he had been privileged to experience throughout his life from his own mother and Nana back home.

The three children looked like their parents. The two boys had their father's handsome ruggedness and the daughter, like her mother, was extremely pleasing to the eye. Melvin and Chris had hardly taken their eyes off her since they had arrived at the table.

Lance could tell by the body language that they must be enjoying a wonderful family dinner. Were their conversations akin to Stoler exchanges? When their dinner was over, would the whole family have experienced a variety of stories told, lessons preached, or confessions made? Would Mr. Tishman go to bed a happy man because he, his wife, and children had shared another moment in time that allowed them to grow closer as a family? Lance beleived so.

Mr. Tishman turned to the recruits. "It's good to have you gentlemen in Columbus. We would be honored for you to become part of the Ohio State family."

Lance stood closest to Mr. Tishman and offered a response for the recruits as he held out his hand. "Thanks. So far we have had a wonderful time. It was very nice to meet you and your family." The Kentuckian was not surprised by the Ohioan's handshake. It was firm and powerful like the grip of a heavyweight fighter about to enter the ring. As Lance released Mr. Tishman's hand, he snuck one more peek at his charming family and his mind traveled all the way to Kansas City.

The daughter reminded him how beautiful Lisa looked last Friday night when J.C. brought her and Marla to his room. His emotions were running fast and furious with the thoughts. He wished Lisa could be here to show him around Columbus. *How stupid. Lisa probably has never been to Columbus.*

He was warmed by the remembrance of holding her warm body in his arms. Even though it was for only a few moments, her sweet smell and sparkling eyes were vivid in his mind as he entered the private dining room. His last Kansas City thought was wishing Lisa would stay home or go out to dinner with her parents. He sent up a passionate prayer. *Please don't let Marla take her out partying.*

The hostess was waiting for them. A dark cherry dining table set for twelve occupied the center of the room. Against the far wall, a counter displayed a large bowl of shrimp and a bountiful tray loaded with cheeses and vegetables.

"Gentleman, the chef has brought in some specialties of the house for you to munch on while you wait for Coach Meadors. Please enjoy your stay with us here at Morton's."

"Thanks," Clermont responded courteously. "Your kindness is appreciated."

A dazzling waitress with an awesome mane of thick, auburn curls walked through the doors and approached Melvin. Lance could tell Melvin was not losing his satisfaction with this steakhouse.

"What can we get you to drink, Big Guy?" she asked

"Coke would be great."

"Me too," said both Lance and Chris. They headed toward the shrimp bowl.

"Coach Clermont?" she asked.

"A tonic water with a slice of lemon would be super."

Lance looked around the room. The place was much fancier than any back home.

"You got any of these back in Kentucky?" Chris asked as he dipped his first shrimp into the Buckeye red cocktail sauce.

"The room, or the shrimp?" Lance asked.

"The shrimp, Fool." Chris laughed.

"We have shrimp, but these look like they've been in the weight room."

Melvin had stopped to gaze after the waitress as she left the room, and was now making his way to the shrimp bowl.

Chris became a defender. "No way, Big Guy. Go get your own shrimp."

"Al Capone mean anything to you?" the king-sized Chicagoan answered. "Get out of the way or I'll send one of his grandkids to Toledo. They'll have a little talk with your kneecaps."

The trio did some serious damage to the shrimp bowl before Coach Meadors walked through the doors with his wife and the three Buckeye hosts, Brad, John, and Jay.

"Glad to see you could find this place," said Meadors. "It looks like the shrimp's agreeing with you."

"Oh, this is the best I've ever had," Chris responded happily.

Meadors put his hand softly around his wife. "Gentleman, this is the woman I answer to."

Janet Meadors looked like a Coach's wife, well dressed in a light gray skirt and sweater. A beautiful scarlet pennant proudly hung from a gold chain around her graceful neck. She was a tiny woman, but seemed full of energy and grace -- it was clear that she could be an exceptional ambassador for the basketball program.

"Hi, Mrs. Meadors. Nice to meet you," Melvin declared as he swallowed another helping of shellfish.

"Nice to meet you, Ma'am," Lance said. He appreciated seeing a coach and his wife wearing school colors with such obvious pride. "That's a beautiful necklace"

"Thank you. Homer got it for me when we were in the Final Four a few years back. If you three boys decide to let my husband coach you, I'm sure I'll get another one."

Homer gently squeezed her hand in appreciation then requested politely, "Let's all grab a seat. Coach Barnhart and his wife were parking their car. They'll be right in."

Coach Barnhart came through the doorway with a bright smile on his handsome face. His wife hung on his right arm like it was their first date. Ricky Barnhart had no inhibitions. He walked around the table stopping to greet Melvin and Chris. His friendliness was abundant and he had Future Head Coach written all over him. When he got to Lance, Barnhart extended his right hand which was dominated by a ring.

"Coach, you been working out? You have to be awfully strong to carry that rock around."

Barnhart's gleeful response was immediate. "I'll work out even more if you will help me win another one of these. It's the Big Ten Championship ring. My head coach said I better be helping him get a new one to replace this beauty awfully soon."

Barnhart looked over at the hors d'oeuvres and the half-empty shrimp bowl. "What happened to all of the shrimp? The chef promised me a full bowl of his very best."

A grin appeared on Melvin's face. Chris and Lance had smiles that could not be held back.

"Lance and Melvin made me do it," Chris whined. "I was only going to have one. Honest."

Ricky chuckled and moved to the shrimp bowl. He graciously loaded up a plate of the remaining seafood before sitting down. The seating was not arranged by accident. Each recruit had a coach at his side. Coach Meadors by Melvin, Coach Clermont by Chris, and stationed on the Kentuckian's right elbow -- probably the best college basketball recruiter in the nation.

The waitress returned, her beautiful auburn hair falling gracefully down her back. She followed up on drink orders and detailed the specials of the evening. Lance gave the impression of being a good listener but had already made up his mind. He would have his regular big salad and the New York strip. Bumper's big burger was long forgotten.

Lance watched Melvin and Chris as the hard-working waitress went through her script. He was skeptical if they were truly listening to her words; they seemed to be paying more attention with their eyes than their ears. She finished her presentation and confirmed she would be back in a few moments to take everyone's order.

As they waited, Coach Meadors took the opportunity to make a formal welcoming speech and offer a toast to the visitors. "Here is to the three seniors visiting the Buckeyes this weekend. We hope they enjoy this trip so much they'll become teammates and win that Big Ten ring for Coach Barnhart."

Glasses clinked and Lance set his Coke back on the table. He began to feel he was truly wanted in Columbus. It was a good feeling. He turned to

Coach Barnhart's wife and asked her, "How long have you and Coach been married?"

"He asked me five years ago, but my daddy made him go through two years of probation before that."

Lance loved the sound of her voice. It had a charming Southern cadence. She continued her yarn about her noble husband.

"He was an assistant coach at Alabama at the time. My daddy thought he wouldn't last long. Daddy was more of an Auburn fan. Thought he was nothing more than a plowboy." She giggled. "Mom encouraged him. He survived." She moved her water glass, hesitating for a moment. "Oh, and did I mention Ricky got my daddy two tickets to the Auburn–Alabama football game and arranged for Auburn to win?" Her eyes twinkled. "Well, he did get the tickets at least. That Sunday, Daddy approved Mr. Charming's giving me an engagement ring."

Barnhart's face shone as he listened to his bride tell the story she had probably repeated a hundred times. His affectionate expression could not deny that each telling was a delightful moment in his life. It was easy to see they made a great team.

Lance turned his focus to the other table discussions. Melvin was expressing to Homer and Janet his wish to play power forward rather than being relegated to the center position. Chris appeared unconcerned about basketball; he was describing his favorite steakhouse in Toledo to Coach Clermont, a place called Mancy's, on the north side of town, and that his mom and dad would take the family there on special occasions like birthdays and big victories.

Lance's thoughts drifted away again. He had harbored the idea of being fortunate enough to be accepted into law school someday. But his first choice, his dream, would be to coach. Would Lisa be like Coach Barnhart's wife? Help him handle the stress of coaching after he finished playing ball?

Not only might he help these Buckeyes get a few rings as a player, but he would move into coaching and keep getting more. Probably run out of fingers. What about Lisa's Dad? Mrs. Barnhart had said her daddy loved Auburn tickets. He would have to get Mr. Gosline tickets to the Kansas-Missouri football game. No problem. They don't sell out. What if he wanted Kansas-Missouri basketball tickets? That'd be a problem.

He jumped back to reality. What was he doing? Already marrying Lisa? For some strange reason, that thought actually comforted him. But Lisa was probably out partying, not even thinking about some guy she had met a mere week ago. Besides, he would have to play college ball in Lawrence to make those dreams come true.

Clermont interrupted his private deliberations. "Lance, tell us about your Uncle Gary."

Lance sat up straight. "He's my dad's older brother. Lives in Dublin, but most of his relatives are in Kentucky. You Buckeyes have converted him and his whole family. They're scarlet and gray." He leaned over to gain eye contact with Coach Meadors. "He lives and dies with you guys."

"Now that's what I call a great uncle," Coach Meadors emphasized great. "We need more fans like him."

"Uncle Gary will love to know you said that. Thanks." Lance explained that his uncle moved to Dublin about thirty years ago, when it was only a small town. "There used to be only one high school back then."

"Golf and Muirfield helped changed a lot of small communities on both sides of the Scioto River in that area," Mrs. Meadors said. "What type of business is your Uncle in?"

"Owns a small trucking company. Real small. Carries scrap metal all over Ohio, mainly. If he gets a trip to Kentucky, he always stops to see us."

Mrs. Meadors nodded. "I understand the need to be with family."

"My parents hope to have dinner with him after the game tomorrow. Mom and Dad are watching my brother's football game tonight. They'll get here in the morning."

Lance would have enjoyed talking more about Uncle Gary, but the main attraction of the evening had just arrived and the Stoler boy was not disappointed in the size of the sizzling New York strip steak placed before him. Green asparagus smothered in hollandaise sauce only made the chef's dinner presentation more succulent.

When all had been served, the discussions continued. Melvin and Chris were invited to share stories about their families. Melvin boasted his sister could also play the hoops game and Chris talked about his mom's teaching. Homer kept the table entertained with stories about how he and his wife had met and jokingly of how he was trying to train his "puppies", Coaches Clermont and Barnhart, to grow up. Someday to be head coaches.

During dessert, Mrs. Meadors stole the show. She clearly wanted the three prospects to know how caring her husband was and that the quality of his assistants was no accident.

"All of you can go to about any school you want, and I know there are a lot of good programs and coaches out there." She stopped to look at each recruit. "My husband carefully handpicked his staff and he chose people with values and character, not just people who know basketball. He's a friend, a darn good teacher, and mighty fortunate the good Lord blessed him with great coaching ability." She placed her hand on top of her husband's. "The Man up above forgot to give him a lesson in home mechanics and yard work, but we're trying to live with that." There was a jovial buzz at the table. "I guess what I am trying to say is . . . you will never be just a basketball player for my husband. You will be family."

Lance didn't know if this was the first time Mrs. Meadors had said anything that powerful. It didn't matter. He felt it was sincere and came from her heart. The expressions on the faces of each coach were powerful proof of the genuineness of her forthright words. It was clear the three host players felt the same way. Brad Byers nodded his head. Lance turned to John Hollis and Jay Buxton. Their heads nodded in agreement and they gave a silent applause to her wonderful speech.

"Mrs. Meadors," Jay said softly, "I have never heard you say that before. Your husband has us locked up all the time." He stopped for the laughter. "Seriously, every player would endorse your feelings, and it's not for show. We know Coach Meadors and the assistants care about us."

Homer looked at his wife with pride. "Honey, it was nice of you to say those things. I can't thank you enough for speaking such kind words. It's a given. We care today and we'll care tomorrow." He paused, turned his eyes away from her, and looked around the table. "Your hosts are prepared to show you some of the campus nightlife. Everyone, be aware we don't need anyone doing anything stupid tonight." Meadors became a teacher again. "Pull out a can of your best behavior and use it. Besides, tomorrow's football game might be worth watching."

Meadors reminded them about the brunch in the basketball offices at nine and that all of their parents were welcome. "Afterwards, we'll walk over to St. John Arena and listen to the Best Darn Band in the Land warm up. Then we'll watch Coach Baxter handle those Hawkeyes from Iowa."

As the group prepared to leave, Lance stood, offered to help Mrs. Barnhart with her chair. She gave him a hug and wished him well.

"You guys know where you're going and who is taking care of whom?" asked Coach Barnhart.

"We've got you covered, Coach." Brad said. "You go home and relax. Don't worry about these recruits."

Lance walked out with Jay, and a thought suddenly occurred to him.

"Hey, my dad was a Beta. Is there any chance we could take a look at the Beta Theta Pi house tonight?" asked Lance.

"Absolutely," said Jay. "It's at the corner of Fifteenth and Indianola. Won't be out of the way. I have a couple of friends who are Betas. It's a great house."

The valets had brought Meador's car in mere seconds. It appeared Morton's had given the coach's car a preferred parking spot. The two assistant coaches' vehicles were brought up next, leaving the six hoopsters standing on the gray pavement as they waited for their cars to be brought around.

The night was clear and the crisp air pierced Lance's lungs, reviving him after the lengthy dinner. Columbus was an attractive contrast to the beauty of standing on the farm beside Nana's backyard fence. Lance recalled how the black country nights made the stars appear bigger and brighter. He listened for the cricket's chirp or a lonesome dog's cry. There was none. Instead, the city whistled to its own beat of horns and brakes. Lance mused to himself. In Connsburg, lights were being turned off. They were rolling up the streets. *Not this town. They'd be swinging way past bedtime.*

Jay took over as the leader of the group. "Lance wants to go to the Beta House. I can take him there if you guys want to go on up to High Street. We can catch up with you later."

"That'll work," said Brad. "OK with you guys?"

"OK by me," said Chris. "What about you, Big Man?"

"No problem," said Melvin. "Let's check out High Street."

The valet brought up Jay's vehicle first. A Camaro. "Jump in," Jay told Lance. "See you guys later."

Lance powered down his window and shouted, "Later, guys." Jay's tires squealed for a second and they were headed north.

"What year is this baby?" Lance asked.

"Three years old. Got it working summer jobs. I love it. Especially the color."

Lance was sitting in a comfortable bucket seat and could see the bright red color of the hood shining in the street lights. "Didn't have one in blue, did they?"

"You're catching on. A Michigan blue car in this town has a sign all over it: "PLEASE THROW ROCKS AT ME." Jay smiled. "Where was your dad a Beta?"

"Eastern Kentucky," Lance proudly answered. "You in a fraternity?"

"No, but I would consider the Betas if I was. They're a good group of guys and they actually try hard to do well academically, if you know what I mean. Some fraternities are always getting into trouble or they are close to it. Others, like the Betas, get involved in campus activities and are proud of their house grade point average."

"You mean some fraternities drink a lot and love to party?" Lance grinned.

"Should've known you're not some naïve country boy. Don't get me wrong, Lance. I came from a small town like you and I like to have a good time. But I think basketball has helped me keep balance in my life. I don't have to attend a drinking party every weekend to have fun. What am I doing? You're a big boy. You can make your own decisions. I'm just trying to explain all fraternities aren't *Animal House.*"

"I appreciate what you're saying. So Coach Meadors would let you join a fraternity if you wanted to?"

"He isn't encouraging or discouraging. My guess is that basketball, school, and a fraternity are a bit much for most of the team."

Jay talked about two of the players who were in fraternities. One was a walk-on, who will be going on to medical school. "He's so bright he could probably juggle five things at one time and still get a four point. Got the smarts, but isn't quick enough to start in the Big Ten. The other guy is a Sigma Chi. It hasn't been a problem for him or the coaching staff. He doesn't start, though. Good student, a business major."

"Hey, you got a girl?" Lance asked. "I mean, are you dating anyone?"

"Sherry Boyd. We grew up together, since the second grade. She's a cute little blonde and you'll get to meet her tomorrow at the brunch. We both came to Ohio State. She's majoring in international studies."

"What kind of job does she want to have with that major?"

"You can ask Sherry tomorrow. Be prepared. She explains her major with passion. You got anyone back home?" Jay waited more than enough time for an answer. "Come on, I told you about Sherry."

"Dated several girls, but haven't found someone like your Sherry." Lance's conscience twinged. He did not mention Lisa. Lance thought Jay would think him foolish if he told him how he felt about a girl with whom he had spent so little time.

"Don't worry, if you come to Ohio State there are only about 25,000 female students. You'll get your chance." Jay pulled the Camaro next to the curb. "Well, we're here. This is 165 East Fifteenth Avenue."

"Now that's a fraternity," Lance was impressed. The Colonial house was supported by four enormous white pillars stretched across its front. An enormous green front door provided further elegance. Jumping out of the car, Lance leaped up nine steps, turned back, and saw Jay getting out. "I know I said I just wanted to see the house, but it's spectacular. Could we go inside?"

"It's nine o'clock. Friday night before a home football game. They're probably all in bed or at least off to their rooms studying." Jay was toying with Lance. There was lots of noise coming from behind the closed door.

"Come on," Lance pleaded.

"Alright, but we shouldn't stay long."

Lance started to knock on the front door.

"What are you doing, Rookie? This isn't trick or treat. You walk right in at a fraternity house," Jay instructed. The big door swung wide and the two walked over the threshold, right into a thunderous Beta toga party. A six-foot Julius Caesar approached the intruders and offered some assistance. "You guys Betas?"

Before either of them could spit out an answer, Julius was joined by two more toga buddies. One said, "You're Jay Buxton."

"Sure is," Lance bragged.

Jay grinned. "We were on our way to High Street, but stopped here first because Lance asked to see the house. He's here on a recruiting trip and his dad was a Beta."

Several brothers and their dates started to gather around the newcomers. "Where was your dad a Beta?" Julius asked.

"Eastern Kentucky. I'm from Kentucky."

"Sweet," replied one of the brothers. "That means you can play."

"He sure can," Jay bragged now.

Lance felt happy. "This place is awesome. You guys must love living here."

A small guy quickly gathered up the bottom of his toga so he could move closer. "You bet, man. This is the best house at Ohio State. It's an easy walk to campus and well, you know, it's a chick magnet." While everyone laughed, Lance glanced at the little dude and bet Jay was probably thinking the same thing. His date was four inches taller and quite attractive. *It had to be the house.*

"Let's let Jay and Lance get a look at the house," Julius said, taking control. "Everyone back downstairs. Back to the party." Grabbing Lance by the arm, he escorted the guest into a large room on their right. "I'm Bill Goodline from Maumee," Julius officially introduced himself. "Everyone'll go back to partying so you two can have a look around. If you come to Ohio State, we'd enjoy having you pledge Betas."

"Thanks, I'd like that."

Lance allowed himself a few moments to check the room out. Spectacular. It was a study with the feel of a classic conversation room. At a private club in any large city, this room would be where fine gentlemen, sitting in leather-backed chairs sipped cocktails and smoked expensive cigars while enjoying conversations on world politics. In Lexington, the whiskey would be Wild Turkey and the conversation wouldn't be world politics. The exchange would focus on the Wildcats. The last game.

"Follow me," Bill said. "Take a look at this room. It's our library." The three young men walked into the next room, and Lance walked to the rear and peered out the window. It gave a clear view of the back of the Beta House. It had the ambiance of what he had always imagined college would be like. Lance could live here.

Turning around, he saw three guys enter the library. One was a skinny kid with black hair, dressed head to toe in Abercrombie's best. "Are you the recruit? Is Chris Anderson with you?'

Jay helped. "No. He's up on High Street."

"Shoot, we're all Betas from the University of Toledo and we heard a recruit was here. We knew Chris was supposed to visit this weekend," the Abercrombie model moaned. "Chris is from Toledo. And guys, let me tell you, he can play."

"We know," Lance acknowledged.

"Where you from, Man?" the second Toledan asked. He was a tall blonde and reminded Lance of one of those young professional golfers he saw on television.

"Kentucky. And this is Jay Buxton, he plays for . . ."

"Right," the golfer turned toward Jay. "I thought you looked familiar. You had twenty-five against Michigan last year. I watched that game."

Mr. Abercrombie asked, "You liking Ohio State? Isn't this a neat house?" he didn't wait for a reply. "Ours at UT is nice, but nothing like this. Rob's dad got us tickets for the Iowa game so we made a road trip and the rent is real good here when you're a Beta." He stopped. "Hey, I'm sorry. This is Rob Beers and the big guy is Andy Gladwell. I'm Keith Dasbach."

"Lance Stoler. Nice to meet you guys. He's my host." Jay nodded a friendly greeting.

"Been here before?" Keith asked Lance.

"Not the Beta house, but I've been in Columbus lots. My uncle lives in Dublin."

"No kidding," said Rob. "I'm from Dublin. Where does he live?"

"Place called River Forest. Out by Muirfield."

"Know it well."

"You know Andy Stoler? He's my cousin."

"Yeah! Andy's a really good football and baseball player. I played on the golf team," said Rob.

Knew he was a golfer. "Have you ever played Muirfield?"

"All the time. It's a great course."

"My dad has played it and says there's none better."

"He's probably right." Rob seemed pleased.

Changing the subject, Jay asked, "You guys play hoops?"

Keith was eager to answer. "We sure do. Last year the three of us played on the same basketball team and nearly won the intramural championship. We used Andy for rebounding and not shooting."

Andy Gladwell, the biggest of the three, ignored the jestful slam and asked Jay how the Buckeyes would be in basketball this year. Attention now removed from him, Lance began to analyze the three Betas from Toledo. They looked like very good friends and reminded him of his buddies back in Connsburg.

Jay entertained the three with the inside scoop on his teammates, then turned to Lance. "We better get going or my teammates are going to send out a search party."

"It was nice to meet you guys," said Lance. "Hope you win that championship this year."

Jay and Lance turned towards the front door and were headed that way when Lance made a suggestion. "Are you sure we don't want to see what's going on in the basement?"

"Coach Meadors will run me to death if I let you get into any trouble. There'll be kegs and women down there." Jay pulled on his belt and buttoned the top of his shirt. "Besides, Sherry would give me a hard time if she knew I was snooping around too much." He stopped, tapped Lance's bicep. "Wait, I could use you as the excuse. I was just showing you around and all of a sudden we were in the basement." Jay shook his head. "No, let's go before we do something stupid."

They were back to the Camaro in seconds. Jay started the engine and they were moving on to their next stop. "We were in there for a long time." Jay mapped out a new plan. "Let's go straight to the Varsity Club. That's probably where John and Brad took Chris and Melvin after a few stops on High Street." Jay looked over at Lance. "It's right by the hotel. If that's OK with you?"

"Sure, that's fine by me. Ya know, that Maumee guy was nice."

Jay nodded as he spun the Camaro around the corner. In less than five minutes, he pulled the car into a parking stall on the east side of St. John arena. "My parking sticker works here tonight, but I don't want to leave my car overnight. On game days the tow trucks come by and tow anyone with out a football parking permit. Including basketball players. We get no parking perks." The two started walking. "This is a prime-time parking lot. Wait till you see the tailgaters in here tomorrow."

"I can imagine."

The big sign hanging outside boldly let customers know they were about to enter the Varsity Club. The place was hopping. It was dark, bursting with music, and smelled like Budweiser. Fortunately, Brad and Melvin would stand out in any crowd. Brad's seven-foot frame was leaning against a wall in the back next to a bartender who was surrounded by cases of Bud Light. There was a line formed in front of him to buy beers. The bartender's line never diminished. He was forced to just keep twisting off tops and taking money. Lance assumed this kind of activity was a ritual before every home football game. Or maybe it was a ritual every Friday night, game or no game.

Jay and Lance squeezed their way to the back "How long you guys been here?" Jay asked.

"We just got here," Brad spoke up. "Where you guys been? We figured you'd end up down here."

"Lance couldn't get out of the Beta House." Jay offered.

"Must have been some babes up there," a lighthearted John Hollis suggested.

"Just talked to some of the brothers. They were having a toga party." Jay looked at Chris. "There were three Betas from Toledo who wanted to meet you. They were kind of disappointed they had to settle for a kid from Kentucky."

"Did you guys get down to the basement?" John asked. "It can get a little wild down there."

"No, we were only on the first floor," Jay said defensively, as if Sherry was listening. He then turned to the bar. "Lance, I'll get us a couple of Cokes."

"Thanks."

The five hoopsters lined against the wall picked up a conversation on who should be number one in football. John thought Ohio State was getting screwed because they were undefeated and could beat anyone in the nation. Chris was supportive of John's emotions, but reminded him that Oklahoma and Miami had not lost to anyone yet. They all agreed those three teams could beat anybody on a given Saturday afternoon, and the Buckeyes would be tested tomorrow and again in November against Michigan.

Lance let his eyes wander around the room. The low lights and simple, dark wood walls reminded him a little of The Wheel in Lawrence where he had visited last Friday night.

The customers' voices were operating at thunderous levels as alcohol dampened normal behavior. The setting of the sun did not change the color of the day. Ohio State Red and Buckeyes were printed or displayed on shirts, hats, glasses, napkins, and all the walls. Anyone foolish enough to walk in here with a yellow Iowa shirt would be punished severely. Wear Michigan Blue and the bartender might as well call 911.

Who are these people? Are they all college students? No way. Many of them were undoubtedly students, but a fair share had to be alumni coming back to their favorite watering hole. Some of them were probably the same people he saw in the hotel lobby earlier. Sitting in the booth right next to Lance were two couples. On the near side, a guy and his date were cuddling. He looked to be in his early twenties and she must have been a few years younger. He had dark black hair like the Beta from Toledo, was slender in build and because he was sitting, it was hard to estimate his exact height. Lance guessed at about five-seven, maybe five-eight. His face was covered with a warm glow, more from the redheaded coed sitting next to him than the Coors he was drinking. She was just as tall as he, and her smile and flowing hair made many of the men around the booth continue to gaze back in her direction. Her face was sprinkled with cute freckles that surrounded her perfect nose and exquisite eyes.

The couple across from them seemed to be enjoying the evening. Her name was Allie. Lance had heard the redhead call her by that name. Allie sat next to her date, a man much taller wearing a number 45 jersey. The man with the dark hair had pulled out a large envelope that contained several black-and-white pictures. Leaning over, Lance could see them perfectly from where he was standing. The top picture was of Allie and it looked like she was singing. He listened to the red head say, "Mike took these at Allie's performance and thought she might like to have them." The pictures were much better than the instamatic pictures regularly taken in the Stoler home. These were by a profes-sional.

When Jay returned from the bar with a couple of Cokes, the eavesdropper returned his focus to his host. "Thanks, Jay." Lance took a big sip from the glass.

"This place is like this every Friday night. It's always packed." Jay looked around the room. "I wonder what they say about me in here after one of our games."

"Knowing you, I bet most of the comments are very good. But there are always one or two jerks who don't have a clue. Ya know, the kind thinking they could hit the game winner every time."

"You're probably right, but you better get used to it. This isn't high school. In high school, they love us no matter what. Here they love you win or tie. A few drinks and the people in here will be critics of your entire game. If you lose, be prepared for the worst." Jay took a sip of his Coke. "The media is just as bad. Win or lose, they have a story. Everyone likes the story when we're doing well. It's when the media wants to make you the goat, the cause of the blunder or the team's loss that it becomes quite challenging. I've been lucky. They've only burnt me a few times." He took another sip. "It's easier on me than on my family. It really hurts my mom and dad when a writer prints a crummy article of my performance." Jay let escape an uncharacteristic groan. "I can go out the next night and if we win and I score twenty, they'll be praising the same guy they were ripping the day before."

"You're so right." Lance appreciated Jay's mini-confession. He started to wonder whether Greg's picture would be in the *Floyd County Times* tomorrow praising a big win. That sure would keep the Akers High playoff dreams alive.

Lance and Jay turned an ear to the rest of the group. Their debates bounced back and forth like a ball being passed during warm-ups. Topics emerged without any clear direction: college football, NFL football, three girls walking ever so seductively past them, college hoops, the girl with the short skirt sitting at the bar, and what's the best brand of hoop shoes. Everyone but Lance was an active participant, throwing out opinions and expertise on each subject.

Lance was content to remain silent. His mom and dad should be pulling into Portsmouth by now. Lisa entered his thoughts. *Was she out, or asleep at her parent's home?*

Lance began to feel the effects of the long day. He leaned over toward Jay and said, "This has been a fine night. Thanks for hosting me. It's getting late, so I'm going to walk back to the hotel."

"You know what? It is getting late," Jay agreed. "We start early tomorrow with the brunch. Hey, guys, Lance and I are out of here. We'll see everyone in the morning."

"Hey, Man, it's still early," said John Hollis.

Jay was not bashful. "Midnight is early for you, but for us country boys it's time to hit the sack."

John had probably spent enough time with Jay to know that arguing was pointless. "OK, we'll see you guys who need your beauty sleep in the morning."

Jay walked Lance out.

"See you at the brunch," said Lance, as he watched his host fade into the night. Walking the few steps to the hotel, he became thankful that the coaches had provided such a good host. Jay reminded him of last weekend's shepherd, Shane White.

Lance was ready for some sleep, but the people in the lobby were not. Moving silently through the festive atmosphere, he proceeded to his sixth floor room. He pulled off his blue sweater, threw it onto the bed, and kicked off his penny loafers. He was about to slip on his Akers basketball shorts when he noticed the red message light was blinking. He pushed the message button. Lance was delighted to hear his dad's voice.

"Hey, Big Guy, what's going on? Guess you're still out to dinner, but we wanted you to know the good news. Greg won. 49-0. Our Akers quarterback had a good night. He threw three touchdown passes. One to Bruce. Last year's tight end would've had two. Your mom and I are on our way to Portsmouth. We'll see you in the morning at brunch. Your mother said to say she loves you, but you already know that, don't you? Pleasant dreams."

It was only one-way communication, but it sounded mighty fine. Sleep came easily.

Chapter 15

Milt and Helen had enjoyed every second of Greg's game. Afterwards, they positioned themselves just outside the locker room entrance to make sure they could celebrate with Greg before they had to leave for Ohio. As the team came running towards them, Helen was the first to grab Greg into her proud arms.

Then it was Milt's turn. "Great game. East Ridge High is dreading the fact they will have to see you for two more years."

"Nice pass. Thanks for tossing it my way," Bruce shouted as he walked by. "Mr. Stoler, tell Lance I'm going to be looking for him on ESPN tomorrow."

"Forget about Lance," Milt called back cheerfully. "You just watch for me and Mrs. Stoler."

Helen was now walking with an arm around her boy. "Your Nana is staying with you and Cherie so you should be all set, Sweetheart."

"We'll be fine, Mom. Have a good time and tell Lance those Buckeyes better win, I'll be watching."

Cherie and Nana joined the scene outside the locker room. "You two better get on down the road," Nana said, replacing Helen's arms around Greg with her own. "Don't worry about us. We'll be fine."

"You and Dad can go have a fabulous time," Cherie assured them. "Greg will mind his manners," she teased as she jumped on her brother's back.

"I want your Nana in one piece when we get back, so both of you act like relatives," Milt ordered.

Helen and Milt relaxed as they finally headed north on Route 23. "Honey, why don't you put in a CD?" Milt urged.

"Sure. Anything special?" Helen smiled. She pulled the tray of CDs from the back seat and started to flip through the options.

"Whatever you like."

Patsy Cline? *No, Milt only tolerates Patsy because he knows I love her voice. Crr-a-zy . . . Crr-a-zy for feelin' so lonely . . .* She put Patsy back into the tray and picked up the CD from *The Big Chill,* placing it at the front. *We'll listen to that in a few minutes,* she quietly decided.

She considered K.T. Oslin and Bruce Springsteen. *Kenny G and Jim Brickman might put Milt to sleep.* Helen pulled out *Notting Hill,* the score from the movie. She slipped it into the player and settled back.

"Nice choice," Milt said. He shook his head. "Amazing. Can you believe our quarterback is only a sophomore?"

"You're kidding. I thought he was a senior." Helen grinned. She glanced out the window. "Where's the cell phone? I'd better check in with Mom." Milt pulled the phone out of his pocket and handed it over. "Hate these things," She grumbled as she figured out which buttons to push.

"Stolers," said a cheerful voice.

"Hello, Honey, this is Mom."

"Hi, Mom. Nana's fixing us hot chocolate. Greg has his buddies over and Sarah's with me. If Nana says it's alright, can she spend the night?"

Sarah was a good friend from school and on the soccer team with Cherie. Sarah hardly ever got to play in games, but playing time meant very little to these girls who still slept with baby blankets and teddy bears while proudly experimenting with training bras and make-up.

Helen happily gave her permission. "Fine, but make sure you're no trouble for Nana."

"Thanks, Mom. Here's Nana."

"Are they behaving?" asked Helen.

"Everything's fine back here. Greg and his friends haven't cleaned out the refrigerator yet."

The two women chatted for a few minutes. "I love you. See you Sunday." Helen hung up the phone.

"Is everything okay?" Milt asked.

"You know, she has them actually enjoying being home and not out running around. She's gifted that way."

"She's alright, isn't she?" Milt shifted his weight and bent forward into the steering wheel. "Lance said some guy in Kansas was asking about her."

"He mentioned the same thing to me. Other than some regular aches and pains, I'm sure she's doing fine."

Helen had noticed no signs of any problem with her. She was sure the people in Kansas were just trying to be extra thoughtful to Lance. "You think Lance is ready for college?"

"He is as ready as any senior. What do you mean?"

"I don't know. I just wonder about the people he'll meet and what influence they'll have on him."

"Like who?"

"You know. It's college. He'll be around people using drugs, drinking, and who knows what else."

"Excuse me. You can't shield them from the world. A kid who can't say 'no' is in for some hard times." The caffeine in the coffee Milt had picked up on his way out of Connsberg must have kicked in. He was fired up. "It's not just drugs. Drinking's a problem. So's gambling. We tell kids not to gamble, and then we see commercials about Las Vegas."

Helen tried to slow her husband down. "Kentucky's lottery was up to fifteen million. Mom bought me a ticket." She waited for his reaction.

"See what I mean? Even we want to win the lottery."

"I was just kidding, Honey. Calm down and watch the road."

"Drinking." Milt wasn't about to stop. "I've been known to enjoy a cold Bud Light, so I'm not a purist. College students. Drinking. It's a big problem."

"It sure is," Helen whispered. "Don't have to go to college for that training. I don't think Faulkner, Fitzgerald, Hemingway, or a few other writers picked up their drinking problems at college. Look what happened to your dad."

Milt took a quick peek at Helen. "That was war."

"Makes no difference."

"You're right. It only helps explain it. Dad and others who served in World War II watched their friends get shot or killed. Had to deal with being away from loved ones. I can't say that I'm surprised they drank when they had time to rest." Milt shrugged. "After the war, they'd end up at the VFW hall. More drinking." He pushed his hand through his hair. "The guys who served in Vietnam, those who came home with drinking or drug problems, were probably not much different. We don't know what hell they endured."

Helen remained silent and so did Milt as the Tahoe moved on down the highway. They had started the evening with joy and happiness over Greg's football game and now both lumbered with concern. Helen sliced the stillness. "It isn't just Lance," she said softly. "I worry about all three of our children. It's more pressing with Lance. He'll be gone in a few months." She hesitated, then sighed. "Milt, what do we do?"

"I hope we've done a lot already. We certainly have tried."

Milt placed his hand on his wife's. The warmth of his grip and faith that the Lord's love surrounded her family caused Helen's emotional seas to calm.

"I love you," she said, gently squeezing back hard.

Chapter 16

Lance had no problems getting up after his 7:00 A.M. wake-up call. He was eager to know more about the school, the basketball program, and at the moment, he was anticipating a great football game. Pleased to find a *Columbus Dispatch* delivered outside his room, he picked up the paper and flipped through what seemed like a hundred pages of advertisements before finally securing the sports section. The headlines were no surprise. **The Buckeyes Will Battle The Hawkeyes Today.** Glancing through the rest of the sports pages, he noticed Ohio State was favored by seven. He skimmed down to find Kansas was playing Oklahoma and they were a 24-point underdog. He was thrilled that he would be able to contrast Big Ten football with the Big Twelve, compare Greg with two other top level quarterbacks, and even sneak a few peeks at the tight-ends. A quick glance at the clock alerted him to fold the paper and start getting ready for a great day.

He stepped over to the window and looked down at Lane Avenue while buttoning his shirt. Even this early in the morning, people were milling around the parking lots, setting up for pre-game festivities. He noticed the gray cloud cover. That didn't bode well for a warm, sunny day. The phone rang.

"Hey, Lance," a shaky voice greeted him. "This is Melvin. Can I come over and talk to you?"

"Sure, what's wrong?"

"I'll be right over." Melvin hung up the phone.

Lance wondered what had happened. There was a quick knock. Melvin stood in the doorway, visibly shaken.

"I didn't know who to talk to," his voice so deep his whispers seemed to echo.

"What's wrong?"

"It's about last night. Had some trouble."

"What kind of trouble?"

"You won't tell anyone if I tell you? I just met you yesterday, but I figured you were a good guy."

"What is it? How can I help?" Lance made Melvin sit down. He began to speak hurriedly.

"It was about an hour after you left the Varsity Club. These girls come over to us and we started talking. Chris took off with one and another kept talking with me. She got real friendly and about ten minutes later she said she wanted to leave with me. I was feeling good. I said, 'Why not?' We ended up in my room and we talked for a while. Listened to some music, you know, just having a good time."

"So what's the problem?"

"Well, when I asked her to leave, she didn't want to go. She got really upset. Must have thought she was spending the night." Melvin sat slumped forward, elbows resting on his knees, hands gently supporting his head as if he had a migraine that wouldn't go away. "She was different. Feisty. Don't think she was use to being told what to do."

"And what happened?" Lance asked anxiously.

"I grabbed her by the arm and as I closed the door on her, she said I'd be really sorry for this. She was pissed."

Lance didn't want to jump to any conclusions, but he had heard plenty about guys beating up girlfriends. "Did you hit her?" He had to ask.

"No, Man, I swear. I grabbed her by the arm, and that's it."

Lance was trying to be helpful, but he had a lot of questions and was not sure of Melvin's honesty. Lance had known him only since yesterday. He sensed Melvin wasn't telling the whole story.

Lance looked him full in the eyes. "I need you to be honest with me."

"I am, Man. That's why I didn't sleep a bit last night. Kept thinking of what she meant. Waited until I thought you would be up, so I could come in here."

Lance was trying to sound calm, but he could feel his heart racing. *What questions should I ask? I don't really want to know the answers. I'm feeling sick.*

He finally spit out. "Did you sleep with her?"

Melvin hesitated before he moved his lips. He looked at the floor.

"Yeah," he whispered.

"Will she say you forced her?" Lance was gaining strength.

"No way, Man. She was all over me."

Lance's mind was racing. "Did she say 'no' at any time?"

"You're starting to sound like those cops back in Chicago."

"I'm trying to help," Lance was loosing patience. "Did she say no?" he demanded.

"It wasn't that way. She was . . . easy. We just did it."

"Did she say 'no'?"

"No. Never, not once!" Melvin replied as he tried to work his voice back down to a whisper. "She was fine until I said she couldn't be there in the morning and she needed to leave.

"So what's the problem?"

"You should've seen the look on her face, Man, when I told her to leave. She said I would be sorry." He hesitated. "It was like she was going to show me. Like she could destroy me. What if she would go and tell a bunch of lies about what we did?"

"Have the police called your room?" Lance asked.

"No, no one has."

"Do you have her phone number?"

"She gave it to me in the bar. Should I call her now?"

"No, let's think." Lance took a deep breath. "You probably need to let things settle down."

"What if she calls the coaches just to spite me and they stop recruiting me?"

"You can't control what she does. You didn't hit her and you didn't force yourself on her, right?"

"Right. Absolutely," Melvin pushed his head harder into his hands. "Wish I'd have left when you did last night."

"My dad always says, 'Nothing good happens after midnight'."

"I didn't think there'd be any trouble. Everything was goin' fine."

"I understand what you're saying." Lance took another deep breath. He thought for a minute then suggested, "Let's do this: I'll come over to your room and you can give her a call. I'll listen then we can decide what your next move should be."

The two recruits walked down the hall. Melvin looked more scared with each step. "What if she goes crazy on me?"

"Right now, you don't know much. Make the call and let's take it from there."

Melvin picked up a napkin with numbers scribbled on it and dialed. Lance took a seat and waited. The phone seemed to ring for a very long time. Melvin appeared discouraged and was about to hang up when someone answered.

"Cheryl? This is Melvin. I was just calling to check up on you."

The next few seconds seemed quite long. Melvin sat hunched over the phone. Lance could not hear Cheryl's voice, but he liked the change in Melvin's expression. He listened.

"I do. It's just that it was late and I had to get some sleep. Can I see you tonight?"

Lance jerked up straight in his chair and wondered what in the heck Melvin was doing? He said he was worried to death about this girl and now he was going to see her again?

"I'll see you tonight, then. Go back to sleep. Bye."

Melvin slid down in his chair. Two swipes of his brow didn't take care of all the sweat.

"Mel!" Lance barked in disbelief. "You're going to see her again after what you just went through?" He was shouting, now, and didn't care who heard him.

"I didn't know what to do, Man. I couldn't call a time-out and ask to talk to you in the huddle, could I? She was purring like a pussycat. She let me know she was pissed last night, but was glad I called this morning." The giant was near tears. "I guessed seeing her would let me make sure she's OK."

"What do you mean, OK?" Lance demanded, walking back and forth in front of Mel. "I thought you said you didn't hurt her or anything." Lance was in the big guy's face.

"I didn't, Man." Melvin stood up, walked across the room, then turned back. "I mean, I could see if she's okay with her feelings and not going to do something stupid to hurt me. She wants to see me, Man."

Lance was trying hard to understand Melvin. Really hard.

"It's just that this reminds me of my buddy who went to Minnesota to play ball," Melvin tried to explain. "When he tried to break it off with his girl-friend, she got all bent out of shape. She called the police. Said he assaulted her. He didn't do anything to that girl. The guy was innocent, but the media found out about it and it was all over the Minnesota papers. The coach suspended him until they had time to investigate. He missed three games. Three games."

Lance understood that his role now was to simply listen.

"Rafer, that's his name. He was guilty in the public's eye. Everyone looked at him differently. Later, the girlfriend confessed. Says she was just hurt he was breaking up with her, that he never assaulted her. She thought he was her ticket out of the old neighborhood, hoping he'd take her along if he made it in the NBA. Rafer was innocent, but he was always defending himself to reporters after that. Some of those reporters printed that they thought the coaches got him off. Rafer has to carry that load all his life, now."

Melvin sat down on the corner of the bed, covering his face in his hands. "I just don't want that to happen to me." He sounded ready to cry.

Lance pulled up his chair in front of Melvin. "That stinks about your friend, Mel. I sure don't have all the answers. Something like that could happen to any one of us." Lance leaned forward. "Maybe you should take it one step at a time. If you see her tonight, be careful." He looked hard into Melvin's face. "Just treat her like she was your sister. You know what I mean?"

"Hey, Man, Cheryl is definitely not my sister. She is one sweet lookin' lady." Melvin grinned sheepishly, even though he obviously knew this was no joking matter.

"Do whatever you want to," Lance replied. "I'm just saying a fire is burning, and you're the one who can get burnt the most."

"I hear ya, I hear ya. I'll be on my best behavior tonight."

Lance had intended to get over to the Schott early, so he could look around again. Arenas and stadiums held special fascination for him. As things worked out, though, he was glad he hadn't departed early.

"Come on, let's get out of here." Lance grabbed his jacket. He didn't know if Melvin's problems were over, but he had helped ease his mind for a while. They headed over to the Schott, together.

Clouds covered the sun. Lance was apprehensive about the cheerless sky. He could only hope the rain would be gracious enough to wait until later in the afternoon. "Gonna rain."

"Doesn't seem to bother these tailgaters," observed Melvin, as they walked slowly through the crowd.

"They worship their football around here."

"Do you think they really care that much about basketball, Lance?"

"My Uncle Gary says they do. Remember, they won a national championship in basketball here and they have been to the Final Four several times," Lance said. "Football and basketball aren't at odds here. It's interesting. When I was at Kansas last week, I sensed friction between the two."

"You mean the players from football didn't like the basketball players."

"No, it's more about the basketball coach. He had a tailgate for his players as if he were supporting football. But he acted like a king watching serfs clearing a field, rather than an enthusiastic fan supporting his school's team." Lance stopped to look as they crossed the Olentangy intersection. "It's different here. These scarlet and gray fans would cheer and support any Buckeye team, especially the basketball squad."

Chapter 17

Homer was waiting. "Morning, Coach," Lance smiled as he greeted Coach Meadors. "Any luck on holding off the rain?

"It's not looking good," Homer said. "Football." He stretched the word out. "If it rains, they play. If it snows, they play. If it's two below zero, they play. See that thermostat over there? That's how we control the climate of a basketball game."

"Melvin," Coach Clermont called from across the room. "How'd you sleep last night?"

Lance immediately perked up. Did Clermont know about Cheryl? Lance could see an awkward expression creep on the big man's face. "He slept like a baby," Lance jumped in quickly. "He said he didn't have all that Chicago traffic to listen to."

"Yeah, Coach, I slept like a baby." Melvin gave a thankful glance at Lance. Both recruits seemed to wait with anxiety.

Coach Clermont did not ask about Cheryl. "Well, that doesn't surprise me. Where's Chris?"

"We thought he would already be over here," Melvin said. Lance and Melvin looked at each other.

Having spent the last hour troubleshooting, they had totally forgotten about Chris. "I should have knocked on his door." Lance frowned.

"Me too," Melvin added.

"We should have all planned to walk over together." Lance sat down and was immediately tapped on the shoulder.

"Are you Lance?"

"Yes Ma'am."

"I'm Chris Anderson's mom and this is his dad, Cal Anderson."

"You're a first grade teacher. Chris was telling me about you yesterday," Lance said, standing back up. "Nice to meet both of you."

"Chris said your mom teaches, too."

"Yes, ma'am. She's been teaching first grade as long as I can remember. Mom and Dad should be here any time. My mom will really like meeting you."

Mrs. Anderson had schoolteacher written all over her. She had a caring smile, rosy cheeks, and eyes that made you feel comfortable. Those qualities encouraged Lance to ignore the fact that she was a very robust woman. Chris's dad was quite dapper. He wore a tweed sport coat with a fair share of yellow in it, gray slacks, and a blue turtleneck. No one must have warned him about mixing yellow and blue in this town. Before the day was out, Mr. Anderson would undoubtedly have a few people reminding him of this unwritten law. Lance was sure of it.

Mr. Anderson was a large man who had lost the hair of his youth. His size and frame left no doubt -- this man had played some hoops in his life. Lance asked, "Mr. Anderson, can you still take Chris on the driveway?"

"In my day, I owned that boy. Now he's just a little too quick for me."

"Did you play in college?"

"Played a little at Toledo, then I hurt my knee and was relegated to the milder sports like tennis and golf."

Lance looked across the room. Chris was coming through the door and headed towards them. "We thought you were already over here," Lance said, trying to make up for not checking on him.

"Got in late last night, needed my beauty sleep. I suspected you guys would already be here." Chris reached over, gave his mom a hug, and bumped his dad on the shoulder. "So, you met my mom and dad, I see. Are your parents here yet?"

"Not yet, but they should be shortly."

Pre-game festivities had a way of invigorating people. Lance was trying to be upbeat, but he began to be concerned he hadn't seen his parents yet. *What if Dad was speeding, got stopped? A wreck? Five minutes passed. Something's wrong. Dad is never late.*

Lance tried to maintain a jovial appearance. Fifteen minutes ahead of schedule was late for Milt. Something must have happened. Lance kept a nervous eye on the door.

His host, Jay, walked in accompanied by a gorgeous companion, a tiny blonde with slender hips and gorgeous legs. Her Ohio State sweater fit snugly against her frame, pleasingly revealing important body parts. Lance hoped that Jay didn't notice that he noticed.

"This is my girlfriend, Sherry Boyd."

"Hi, Sherry. Jay told me a lot about you last night."

"I hope some of it was the truth," she said, possessively holding Jay's arm.

Lance and Jay talked about the previous night, and the upcoming game. Jay interspersed a few stories about his high school days to make Sherry feel included. Lance detected a sparkle in her eye when she listened to Jay share stories about their courtship. Lance tried to stay focused on the conversation, but it was well after nine. *Where are they?* If he didn't see them in ten minutes, he would ask to use a phone.

"You all right?" asked Jay.

"It's my parents. They should have been here by now."

"I'm sure they will get here," Sherry tried to console him.

Suddenly, as if by magic, they appeared. Helen could have passed as a stunning coed. Her honey blonde hair fell softly around her face, as if she had just left the hairdresser's chair. She wore a new red sweater and perfectly matched plaid skirt that stopped right above her knees. Lance had never seen this outfit. Milt was right behind her. He walked with a rush, knowing all too well that he was past due. They were safe and sound, and Lance was relieved. After a silent, *Thanks, Lord,* he excused himself from Sherry and Jay.

Homer was greeting them. "Glad you could make this visit. We're happy when the whole family is involved."

"We're pleased to support Lance." Milt meant it.

"Enjoy your visit," Homer said cordially as he rotated to the next group. Lance could tell from the expressions on their faces that Coach Meadors had started off well.

"Hi!" said Lance as his arms swallowed his mother. The warmth of her hands on his back helped to relieve any lingering worry.

Lance released his mom and put out his hand. Milt grabbed it, pulled his son into his arms, and said, "Sorry we're late. The traffic was unbeliev-able." Milt stepped back and took a quick look around the room. "Started to get bad thirty miles south of Columbus. Something going on in this town you didn't tell me about?"

"I knew something had to be wrong."

"Hope we didn't worry you too much, Honey," Helen soothed him.

"Not much. And now you're here." He gently squeezed his mom's hand. "Come with me. I want you and dad to meet Chris Anderson's parents."

After introductions, Vicki politely said, "Lance told me you teach first grade."

"So that's what she does," Milt teased.

Vicki and Cal smiled as Helen gave her husband an "I can't take you anywhere" look before answering.

"Been my pleasure to teach for many years. You teach, also?"

"Cal told me I'd better use my Ohio State education." Vicki laughed. "I've been teaching for twenty years."

Milt and Cal instantly started a discussion about the big game, each predicting the Bucks would win. Lance did his best to stay interested in the men's conversation, but was drawn to the teacher's voices. The two women became instant friends. It was as if they were two travelers in a foreign country where each finally found someone who could speak their native language.

"You knew Charlotte Huck at Ohio State?" Helen said with amazement.

"What a great professor. I had her for at least three classes. That woman taught me how to get kids turned on to literature."

The Kentucky teacher would share a story, then the Ohio teacher shared. Each nodded their agreement. They discussed first graders, how important it is to help them get an early, strong foundation. They blasted standardized testing. It took little time before learning centers, science projects, good books, and special authors were all appraised. Lance had the notion that if the two were left alone, they would talk until dinnertime. If anyone asked them how the game went, they would say in harmony, "What game?"

Homer brought the social time to a halt when he asked for everyone's attention. This part of the recruiting process seemed to resemble a classic church service. The service began slowly with Coach Clermont earnestly declaring his strong feelings for this great university. He drove home his fervent conviction that playing for Coach Meadors is a uniquely special gift. "The best thing that could possibly happen to any recruit."

Lance thought the Kansas service had been similar, but not as emotional, and suspected the Kentucky service would be spoken in modern Wildcat.

Lance became engrossed. He enjoyed each speaker: the trainer, the equipment people and two professors. He sensed that the professors had wit enough to keep students thoroughly engaged.

The last person to make a presentation was Larry Roemer, the academic counselor for the athletic department. He knew the university well and his unassuming, honest demeanor gave Lance the impression that he would be comfortable seeking Larry's assistance.

"Enough of our sales pitch," Homer looked over at the recruits. "I think we'll lose Melvin, Chris, and Lance if we don't feed them soon."

Milt and Helen had stopped only for coffee and Lance's morning had afforded no time for food. Lance and his dad piled scrambled eggs, sausage, bacon, biscuits, fruit, and cinnamon rolls on their plates. Helen was much more modest. They sat down. Mr. Roemer took a seat right next to them.

"I really liked your talk," Lance moved over to make more room at the table.

Larry used a nod to express his thanks. "We're pleased you're here."

"Glad you guys have to feed him this weekend." Milt stuck a fork in a piece of sausage.

"No question, that's one of the nicest things about recruiting. There's always plenty of food. Good food." Larry turned to Lance, appearing eager to speak directly to him. "You given any thought to a major yet?"

"No, Sir. My dad and I were talking about that last week. Got any suggestions?"

"I encourage students to take their time. Find something they can be devoted to. Most students change majors at least once before they find one that is right."

Lance looked at his dad and smiled. No words were necessary. He had heard Milt use the exact words on several occasions.

Coach Clermont moved to the front of the room. "We're going to head over to the stadium now," he informed the group. "We'll stop at St. John Arena first. The marching band warms up there. The band's good, but I also like stepping into that arena for personal reasons." The room chuckled. Lance was positive everyone in this gathering knew Clermont earned All-American honors in St. John Arena.

Homer walked along with the Stolers and Andersons, Clermont right beside with Melvin. Traffic was backed up in all directions. Police officers were doing their best to keep cars flowing, but they seemed to be losing the battle.

Overhead, the sky was gloomy. Homer ignored the potential for bad weather. "Only a few years ago, before the Schott was built, this land was a pasture. Cattle roamed here during the week. On football Saturdays, it was loaded with cars. Those state troopers you're looking at would be directing cars in here to park, as I speak."

"What'd they do if it rained?" someone in the group called out.

"University makes hundreds of thousands of dollars off of football parking," Homer said, smiling. "They parked the cars in the mud. They'd hire tow trucks and hope the cows didn't sprain an ankle walking through the ruts when they were finally let loose on Sunday." Coach stopped and pointed. "See back there?" Everyone turned towards where he pointed. "They've added a lot of parking, farther from the horseshoe, but people just grit their teeth and walk the extra distance. After a win, the walk is quite satisfying. After a loss, the walk turns out to be a dismal hike."

Entering the arena hallway, Homer's parade saw trophy cases displaying hardware from numerous championships, pictures of former athletic greats, and cement floors that Buckeye fans had walked on for over forty years. Lance completely understood why Clermont so loved it here.

Inside the arena, they stared at 13,000 seats. Banners hung proudly from the ceiling. The floor, once the sight of spectacular Big Ten basketball games, was now filled with over two hundred members of the Ohio State Marching Band. They wore black military-style uniforms wonderfully enhanced by white straps that crisscrossed over their neatly pressed jackets.

"Let's sit here for a while," Homer said. "I think you might enjoy this."

Helen had played in the Connsburg High School marching band. She was overjoyed with the surprise. The band performed their signature routine to *Hang on Sloopy* while thousands of people in the stands enthusiastically clapped overhead to the music.

"They are fantastic," said Helen.

"This is really something. They are really good." Milt surveyed the crowd. "Can you believe this many people are in here?" He continued his survey. "What do you think, Lance?"

Lance stared at the highest seats. "It's not packed, but there's more than ten thousand in here."

The conductor introduced a few band members then announced, "The next number, for those of you new to Ohio State, is our alma mater, *Carmen Ohio*. Please rise."

Within seconds the largest choir Lance had ever seen assembled began in unison: "Oh, come and sing Ohio's praise . . . " The song finished with a massive "O-HI-O." then a roar. The visitors from Chicago, Toledo, and Kentucky could feel the electricity.

"It's time," said Meadors. "Don't want to miss any of the pre-game festivities."

Out the south entrance down a wide concrete path they walked until coming to Woody Hayes Drive, which separated the parking lots of St. John Arena and Ohio Stadium. To the right was a large lot filled with tailgaters. Grills were glowing and tables were loaded with assorted pre-game provisions. Lance's eyes caught sight of burgers, brats, ribs, and chicken. He wondered what was wrong with him. He had stuffed himself at the Schott, but all this food was tantalizing. Turning to his dad, he knew by his wicked little smile that he, too, was having the same guilty feelings.

"I say we mosey into that lot and act like we are guests," teased Milt. "We eat maybe two burgers, a brat, and by the time they figure us out, we'll have satisfied our cravings." Lance didn't get to answer.

"You two are bad," scolded the first grade teacher, moving in between, taking hold of their arms. "You just ate, for gosh sakes."

Crossing the road, they walked into a mall area containing a statue honoring Jesse Owens. "This is the Jesse Owens Plaza," Homer explained. "Jesse ran track for the Buckeyes. He went on to become one of the most famous Olympians of all times. He was mighty fast for his time. Mighty fast. Well, let me correct that. He was mighty fast for any time."

"Did he play hoops?" asked Melvin.

"Don't think so. Back then basketball wasn't as big as it is today," Coach replied. "The Final Four didn't start until 1939. I might add the Buckeyes were in that first Final Four. We lost in the finals to a bunch of Ducks from Oregon. Let me say this about Jesse: if he would have been a basketball player, you would not have wanted to guard him. Michael Jordon wouldn't have. The man was fast."

Entering Ohio Stadium, everyone was captivated by its beauty and enormous size. Lance stopped and gazed at the light gray exterior walls, then upwards to a massive rotunda containing blue flower clusters. "The architect on this sucker was no apprentice. He knew what he was doing."

"You're right," Milt stood back. "This place is spectacular."

Homer directed them to their seats. Helen sat comfortably down between her husband and son. Jay and Sherry took the next two seats.

Lance began an extensive examination, appreciating the ambiance of the Buckeyes' stadium. The south end zone scoreboard was the largest he had ever seen. The field was handsomely decorated with pristine white yard lines while in the north end zone, a flagpole, standing ready for the American flag, sprouted straight up like a Georgia pine. The upper levels of the stadium contained a press box and bountiful skyboxes. These luxurious viewing rooms for the media and wealthy people of influence gave the stadium an added sense of splendor.

Scarlet and gray clothing glowed brightly under ESPN lights. Tucked away in one corner were Iowa fans, proudly adorned in their black and yellow; however, this little drop of mustard was no more than a small stain on an extra-large scarlet tee shirt.

Hundreds of police officers patrolled outside the stadium. Inside, the number did not diminish. Two officers stood atop the north wall of the stadium. Their view could only be enhanced by climbing into a helicopter. Through binoculars the stadium was completely patrolled.

The entries into the seating sections employed centurions dressed in red coats. Each assisted fans searching for seats, and re-routing those trying to sit in a wrong location.

Team locker rooms were located in the corners of the south end zone. Iowa personnel were moving in and out of the southwest corner while the Buckeye workforce kept coming in and out of the southeast.

The Hawkeyes were running some pre-game plays that caught Lance's eager attention. The field general for Iowa, a powerful looking quarterback, was graceful as he handed the ball off to his running backs. He seemed to be in control of his offensive unit. The tight end was huge. A true corn fed monster.

On the other end of the field, the Buckeyes were completing position drills with military precision. Lance immediately focused on the quarterbacks. Each threw perfectly spiraled bullets to uncovered receivers. Lance mentally began to grade the line-ups, so he could make a complete report to his brother.

"Isn't 15 the starter?"

"Mike Thomas," Milt said. "Uncle Gary says he's a player."

"Hey, did Uncle Gary get any tickets?"

"I called him when we were backed up in traffic. He hadn't had any luck." Milt's frown showed his disappointment. "This game's too big. No one wanted to give up their tickets."

"Dang. He would have loved being here."

"Your dad will have a tough time at dinner tonight if the Buckeyes lose," said Helen knowingly.

"Mom's right," Milt confirmed. "Gary will be all over me if that happens." His mood suddenly changed. "He's taking us to LaScala."

Lance groaned. "That great Italian restaurant? Shoot. I love that place."

"Me, too." Helen winked.

Lance turned his full attention back to the Buckeyes. Like the Iowa quarterback, Thomas had great presence. He wasn't as big, maybe six-one, but his passes were right on the money. "I think Uncle Gary was right. Fifteen seems to be mighty good. Who is the starter at tight end?"

"Don't know," Milt replied. "Hey, Jay, you know who's the starting tight-end?"

Sherry answered for him. "Steve Rossi, number 86."

"Thanks. He isn't as big as the Iowa guy."

"Yeah, but on third down, if the ball is anywhere near his territory, he'll catch it." Her voice was completely confident.

"That's my kind of tight-end. Who in the heck is number 72? Look at the size of that guy."

Milt read down the player roster in his program, trying to find number 72. Before he could finish his task, Sherry, once again rose to the occasion.

"That would be Orlando Ward. He's one of the biggest offensive linemen we have ever had." Sherry leaned against Jay. "Pretty boy here wants him to come out for the basketball team. Thinks Orlando would set some awesome picks."

"Dad, even you could get open off of one of his picks," Lance joked.

"Watch it boy." Milt stuck out his chest. "I can tell Sherry and Jay think I'm an athlete. Don't blow my cover."

"Honey, I think you lost your cover a while back." Helen watched Milt give her a friendly *I get no respect* look.

The crowd started a vibrant roar as the Buckeyes gathered and jogged towards their locker room. As the team disappeared, the Buckeye Marching Band entered through the north tunnel. Raving fans listened to drumsticks. "Click-Click-Click." Then bass drums. "Boom-Boom-Boom." The sounds caused hair to rise on one hundred thousand spectators.

"Whoa," Helen loved the spectacle.

"Wait till you see the halftime show," Sherry warned. "They'll do Script Ohio."

Captains started to come out of their respective locker rooms. An official escorted each to the fifty-yard line for the coin toss. Lance wasn't surprised when number 15 showed up as a captain. A big linebacker wearing number 46 accompanied the quarterback. Sewn on the back of his jersey was the name Mossberg. He walked with a bowlegged cadence, shoulders leaning forward, his arms dropping from a jersey more fitting for a grizzly bear than a college student. His feet stomped the turf, waiting for the official to throw the coin into the air. His body language screamed, "If I could just hit one of the enemy captains, I'd probably settle down."

Fifteen was cool. He showed no signs of agitation. His walk was that of an accomplished gladiator. After the head official acknowledged Iowa had won the toss and had elected to defer until the second half, he confirmed with a crisp and sure voice, "We'll receive." The visitors elected to defend the north goal, taking advantage of a brisk wind blowing in their favor.

Numbering less than one hundred, the Hawkeyes flew onto the field. Greeting them was a chorus of "Bo-o-o-o-o-s." They advanced into the red valley. There would be no reinforcements. From the southeast, like Huns sacking Rome, the Bucks stormed onto the field desiring to once again taste sweet victory.

The Iowa kicker held a new pigskin. His hands massaged it vigorously as if to warm it and himself. After placing the ball on a tee, he stared out at eleven scarlet jerseys. His teammates were preparing to run at top speed down the green meadow and smash whoever had the audacity to run the leather object back at them. He looked at the sidelines. Everyone on the team was clapping their hands, trying to give him encouragement. The coach's lips moved, but Buckeye fans made it impossible to hear.

At the official's whistle, he approached the ball and let it sail. His teammates were as explosive as if shot from a cannon. Bodies began to collide with enormous impact. The kicker held to the rear, apparently feeling his services rendered. The ball flew down from the gray sky with the beauty of an eagle flying into a stream to catch its daily meal.

Scarlet number 33 had captured hundreds, maybe thousands of these leather birds. This one he secured two yards deep in the south end zone. His knees buckled slightly, causing him to hesitate for a moment.

Suddenly, he bolted up the east sideline. He met his first intruder at the fifteen-yard line. One swivel of the hips and the intruder was tackling air. Next came a backup free safety. He had eluded two Buckeye blockers and was prepared to shatter 33's left hip when a second-string tight end caught him on his blind side and delivered him like a UPS package towards the sidelines.

Thirty-three cut to the left off that superb block, and headed towards the center of the field. He dodged another would-be tackler at the thirty. His feet carried him with the grace of the swiftest lion in the jungle. Two more Hawkeyes made insignificant stabs at his right side as he swiveled past them on his way to the far sideline. Turning back to the north, he was prepared to finish his journey unscathed.

The kicker was clearly disappointed when 33 didn't down the football in the end zone. His disappointment must have grown when his first two teammates failed their kickoff assignments. He started to move to the west sidelines, appearing to get weak in the stomach. When 33 passed four more Iowa barricades, his lips formed his thoughts, "Oh shoot!" He frantically moved faster and closer to the sideline. His body prepared for impact with the ball carrier at the forty-yard line.

It was more like a gym class somersault than an impact. The kicker desperately grabbed hold of the runner's right shoe just as it was about to fly by. Thirty-three had beaten ten Hawkeyes. The eleventh did him in.

"Wow," Sherry shouted. "He almost went all the way."

"That kid is fast," praised Milt.

The first offensive play of the game had been called on the sideline. Number 15, Mike Thomas, ran up to the line of scrimmage where his center and offensive lineman had already established a straight line of attack.

The ball was snapped into the soft, flexible hands of the quarterback. Mike and his center had performed this hundreds of times. There was little reason for concern, even though millions of people were watching. People prepared to verbally make the signal caller a hero or a goat in the next few hours.

Mike snatched the ball and backed away from his center, then spun clockwise as 24 removed his hands from his knees and stepped towards the line of scrimmage. The running back placed his right arm above his left creating a secure resting spot. Mike firmly placed the ball into its nest, and the exchange was complete.

Everything was designed for the ball carrier to run between his left guard and left tackle. Unfortunately, some big, ugly Iowan had lined up across from the left tackle and at the snap of the ball exploded into the gap between the two offensive linemen. The Lord had clearly gifted number 24. Superb agility and balance steered him further left. Steve Rossi, the tight end Lance had asked about during the warm-ups, was demonstrating why he might not get all the glory but was more than worthy of his starting assignment.

He had pushed the defensive end to the inside and was slipping off to check whether the outside linebacker was having a good day. The linebacker made a sudden change in direction. Steve seemed to recognize exactly what this meant. His running back had bumped the play outside.

The Iowa linebacker was about to have a bad day. Eighty-six took one step and popped the Iowan at the bottom of his shoulder pads. His cleats flew off the green turf. Wind appeared to gush out of his lungs. The whole stadium imagined his pain as his body became airborne like a bail of hay pitched up into a wagon.

Twenty-four took advantage of this gift and was now scampering around the left edge of the line of scrimmage. He advanced to the thirty-five yard line where his wide receiver was in a dogfight with a Hawkeye corner-back. The receiver's effort secured another five yards, but trouble was approaching. The defensive free safety had been sucked up towards the line of scrimmage with the original intent of the play and was now making his angry adjustments.

Clearly having received excellent coaching, the safety did not sprint directly at 24. His pursuit angle was designed to nail the runner at the twenty-five yard line. Lowering his shoulder pads, he thrust forward, a mountain lion pouncing on its lunch. His arms grabbed for the hips and thighs of his prey. Twenty-four's legs snapped together. What must have been budding jubilation disappeared in a heartbeat. The running back's legs -- lean, powerful rockets, burst from the free safety's grasp and leaped to the twenty-three yard line. The Iowan lay with his helmet face up, claws empty, reading the back of a fast moving jersey. Everyone wearing scarlet and gray knew the name he was reading. Archie Tait was gliding over the five yard line and into the end zone.

"Did you see that?" Milt gloated. "Unbelievable."

The crowd noise was the loudest the Stolers had ever encountered. Even the loyal fans in small Kentucky gyms and Rupp Arena were no match for generating the decibels these happy campers were manufacturing. The band amplified the situation as they blasted the University fight song.

Sherry screamed, "The kid is only a sophomore. Perhaps a Heisman in the future? It isn't like we haven't had a few before."

"The best was Archie Griffin," Milt added. "He won two of them."

Milt and Lance had listened to Gary gush about Archie many times. Milt explained to Jay that his brother heard Archie speak a few times and was always impressed. Gary had said, "Griffin always talks about values and isn't afraid to state publicly he has wonderful faith in the Lord."

Ohio State kicked off. Despite the wind, the football sailed deep into the back of the north end zone. Iowa made two first downs, but then failed and had to punt. The Buckeye offense trotted back out onto the field and after two running plays then one pass, the coaches and team faced fourth and three. The logical thing to do was to punt. They did.

The first quarter ended with similar action -- thunderous tackling and little offense. The beauty of the game's first play was not repeated. One hundred thousand people took a breather and waited for the second quarter to begin with the score still locked on seven to nothing. Lance thought about Coach Meador's comments. About Jesse Owens. He looked for signs that a track had been moated around the football field.

"You sure a track was inside this stadium?" Lance asked Jay and Sherry. "It doesn't look like it."

"It was beautiful," answered Jay "Red, perfectly lined, and boy, was it soft."

"Jay is modest," Sherry said. "He ran on it in high school. His senior year he made it to State in the 400 meters."

"My man has some wheels." Lance was impressed.

Jay calmly confessed, "That track, I loved it. But the stadium needed remodeling." He explained that the stadium had been built in the early 1920s by L.W. St. John, who was the AD at that time. "Can you believe St. John had the bravado to build a stadium this big back then? They put the track in, but it was history when fans kept complaining they wanted to be closer to the field. Michigan doesn't have a track in their stadium. Notre Dame doesn't either. Most big-time football schools don't. So Jesse's track's gone." Jay sighed and looked away. "I'm a track guy, too. Learning to live with it being gone . . . miss it."

The suspense picked up in the second quarter. Iowa managed to kick a thirty-yard field goal and with one minute remaining, the Buckeyes manufactured a twenty-five yard field goal of their own. The halftime score was ten to three.

"Don't go anywhere," Sherry ordered the Stolers, as they stood up to stretch. "This is what I wanted you to see. This is Script Ohio."

The crowd started clapping loudly to the beat of the drums. Cheering grew louder and more powerful. The band weaved like a pied piper parade, stopping only when it had created a human script of Ohio. The final touch was a masterpiece. One tuba player, chest expanded, sprinted from the sidelines and dotted the "i."

Helen turned to Sherry. "You're right. That's fantastic." Sherry just smiled and squeezed Jay's hand.

Iowa received the second half kickoff and advanced the ball to their twenty-eight yard line. Nine plays later they were sitting on the two yard line, at third and goal. Lance watched intently as the Hawkeye quarterback faked a handoff to his tailback, primed to pass into the end zone.

On the other side of the line of scrimmage, Mossberg had not changed his bullish attitude. He was blitzing. The fake handoff had little effect. A safe landing was all the quarterback could hope for. Iowa settled for a second field goal. Ohio State, ten; Iowa, six. The teams entered the fourth quarter with the same score.

Milt asked Jay, "You getting a little tight over there?"

"Dang, we should've had this game over with," Jay complained. "They've been able to hang around too long. It's like hoops. When you're better than another team, you pour it on so you don't have to make free throws at the end to win. I guess that's a long answer for yes." Jay tried to smile. "I'm getting tight."

Sherry could not hide the strain: feet fidgeting, eyes glaring, teeth grinding, and her hands pressing against each other, as if in prayer. Helen was no stranger to Sherry's anxiety. Place her at one of her children's contests and her demeanor would mirror the young coed's. But today, Helen was a visitor. She didn't have a personal investment over a win or loss. Ohio State was nice, but to her, it wasn't Kentucky. In fact, at this moment, it wasn't the game she thought about, but her family. She thought she had it pretty darn good. Nana was shepherding her two children back home, she sat happily between two hunks, and tonight's dinner with Gary's family would be enjoyable. Yet, Helen knew her manners. She and her men were guests of Coach Meadors and he was a Buckeye. She would give Ohio State her complete support during the fourth quarter.

"I like 15. He seems to be very confident," Helen commented. "He reminds me of Greg."

"He's good, Honey," Milt said, his eyes focused on the next play. "But Iowa has a pretty darn good defense."

"You're right, but we'll break them," Sherry exhaled with fingers crossed.

Eyes were watching. Hearts were thumping. Then it happened. The outside linebacker's holding grip on Steve Rossi gave way and he headed up the seam. The wide receiver was on a go route, leading his defender deep down the sideline. Fifteen was faking a handoff to Tait. The Iowa defense bit. Mike Thomas read the situation. He floated the football over the linebacker who had realized his mistake and was now chasing after the tight end. Rossi's competent hands caught the pigskin and pulled it carefully to his breast like a father holding his firstborn.

Lance was already shouting, "Yes! Yes!!" He loved that pass. Greg and he had completed hundreds of them in practice. Last year the same pass had resulted in two touchdowns for the Green Bears.

The strong safety for the Hawkeyes threw his two hundred pounds at the Ohio State tight end's right knee. A well-timed leap prevented collision. Eighty-six was still running. Sherry, Jay, Lance, the Stolers, every Buckeye in the stadium, and Ohio Staters around the country viewing on television watched with delight as Rossi headed closer towards the end zone.

Mike Thomas watched from his front row seat. He had been knocked down, but by lifting his head quickly, he easily could see the cornerback break away from his coverage and move into action. Like a cowboy competing in a Western rodeo, the defender lassoed his prized steer. The two adversaries landed with a thud on the nine yard line. Milt threw up his arms and shouted something, but the crowd noise overwhelmed any conversation.

"Throw to the tight end again! Throw to the tight end again!" Lance demanded as if the coaches could hear him and might comply with his wishes. Now, holding their breath, the entire row of fans listened to Lance beg.

Thomas, waving his arms, encouraged the crowd to quiet down even more. "Blue twenty-two." He growled. "Blue twenty-two. Hut, Hut, Hut."

Lance stood up with the whole stadium. The ball was snapped. Most thought 24 had received a handoff, which would give him another chance at glory. The line was blocking for a running play to the right side, similar to the play that started the game. Lance was disappointed. He really wanted to see a pass to the tight end. He was about to switch his focus to the tailback when Mike Thomas spun and Steve Rossi slipped off of his block. They ran to the left in complete harmony. No Hawkeye was within ten yards of the tight end. The motion of the football official stretching both arms straight above his head brought joy to the Buckeye fans and complete satisfaction to an ex-tight end from Kentucky sitting in the stands with his parents.

Iowa was unsuccessful in their last two possessions and the dancing started as Mike Thomas took a knee, watching the clock tick down to 0:00. The Stolers' first experience in Ohio Stadium had been wonderful. The rain had held off, the band had been superb, and the Buckeyes, once again, left the field as conquerors.

As triumphant fans started for the gates, Coach Meadors happily gathered his troops. "Everyone enjoy the game?" Smiles were unanimous. "Coach Clermont will be by the hotel at six to pick up those who need a ride to my home for dinner. Parents are invited. We'll have a great evening talking basketball now that we've assured our football teammates are happy. Does anyone need directions?"

"Coach, we won't be able to make it for dinner," said Milt.

"Thanks, Milt. Lance gave us a heads up that you would be with his favorite Uncle. A Buckeye uncle, I understand." Homer shook Milt's hand, then winked at Lance.

The basketball group weaved their way through the sea of Ohio State fans. Celebration was everywhere. Lance reveled in the Buckeye's excitement. He thought it was indeed a special occassion when people can leave a stadium on the winning side.

"It's time we leave for Gary's, Boys." Helen said. "You two aren't going to have me listen to you analyze the entire game and tell me Greg would have blown out those Hawkeyes." Helen hesitated, her cheeks blushed. "Well, maybe he would have. He's my son." She wrapped her arms lovingly around Lance. "How about a hug from my firstborn?"

"You and Dad have a great dinner," Lance shut her door. "Tell Uncle Gary I wish I could be with you. Tell him I took care of him. That last touchdown was a tight end special."

Chapter 18

Milt and Helen arrived at Gary's house by four-thirty. Andy was at the door to greet them before they could knock. "I was watching for you, Uncle Milt. How about those Buckeyes?"

Milt was cut short by sounds from the kitchen. "Wasn't that a great game?" Carolyn came out to welcome them with hugs. She had the biggest heart in the whole family. Her nickname was "Mellie" because she was so much like the character in *Gone With The Wind*.

"Tremendous." Milt picked Carolyn up, twirling her around. "Where's that brother of mine? That was a nail biter."

"Put me down, you nut." Carolyn laughed as two hair pins fell out of her neatly styled French twist. "Gary's not here."

"What do you mean?" Gary never missed watching a Buck's game.

"It was unbelievable." Carolyn began pushing the pins back into her hair. "About half an hour before kickoff, the phone rang. It was one of the guys Gary hauls scrap iron for. He said his client from Ashland had car trouble and couldn't make it to the game. So, Gary asked, "Why are you telling me this? You want me to go pick him up? Tell him I'll be there right after the game!!" The guy explained to Gary that he'd already arranged to get the car towed. He wanted to know if Gary could use the extra ticket. Your brother flew out of the house like a little boy running towards presents under the Christmas tree. I don't even know if he was properly dressed! We haven't seen him since."

They all laughed. Unexpectedly, the front door flew open.

"How about them Buckeyes!" A second shout was louder. "HOW ABOUT THEM BUCKEYES!" Gary's big frame wobbled towards his brother, a big stupid grin plastered all over his face. "Can you believe it?" He slapped his brother into a bear hug. "I was in the Horseshoe. What a big game." He gathered Helen into a gentler embrace and planted a stinky smooch on her cheek. A faint scent of beer testified to the fact that Gary hadn't been an innocent bystander at the tailgates.

"I'm so happy you were at the game," Milt grinned at his big brother. The two were identical except Gary had never lost his hefty bulk from playing football, years ago.

"Forty-five yard line! Twenty rows up. I might as well have been calling the plays." Gary was just about singing his good news.

"I told them how you got the tickets, Honey. I still can't believe it either." Carolyn ruffled his hair.

"Looked all over for you guys. I scrutinized at least 100,000 people through my binoculars. Gave up hope and concentrated on helping my Bucks. Did you see the first play by Archie Tait? That boy will be an All-American, or my name ain't Gary Allen Stoler."

"Helen and I missed it. We were reading some poetry during the first play of the game. Heck, yes, we saw it. Tait is good."

"How about that last touchdown? Wait till you see the replay tonight." Andy joined the merriment. "The tight-end was wide open."

Milt remembered Lance's request. "Your favorite tight end told us to tell you he was responsible for that play."

"How is Lance doing? Enjoying his visit?" Gary asked. "Carolyn, get Milt a Bud Light. My brother's going to dehydrate right in front of me."

"Thanks, but I'll get it. You didn't move the refrigerator, did you?" He slipped into the kitchen, opened the refrigerator, grabbed a bottle, and took a long drink before reappearing. "He likes the coaches and we met his host Jay Buxton and his girlfriend, Sherry, today. They seem to be great kids."

"Come on Helen, let's go have a glass of wine," urged Carolyn. "These boys are goners. They'll be talking ball until dinner."

"Sounds wonderful." Helen hooked arms with her sister-in-law.

Milt, Gary, and Andy didn't notice the girls had left the room. They quickly moved in front of the family room TV for an update of all the games. Between ESPN scores and highlights, the trio completed a thorough assessment of the Ohio State game. They analyzed each player, each major coaching decision, and every penalty. Although they had not attended any college practices last week, or any week for that matter, and didn't personally know players 15, 24, 86, or anyone else on the team, that didn't prevent them from feeling comfortable making an in-depth appraisal. They were duplicating a practice that was happening in thousands of family rooms across America. They were after-the-game experts.

When they finally exhausted their analysis, Milt asked, "The basketball coaches seemed like really good guys, don't they?"

Gary was still deep into Buckeye football therapy, watching for additional scores, trying to understand why ABC was broadcasting a Pac -Ten game in Columbus, Ohio. "Why are they showing this minor league college football in my town?" his voice sound dumbfounded.

"Basketball! Think basketball, Old Man," Milt pressed his brother.

"The coaches? I like'em. Buxton, the kid you met, he's all right too. Will fight you for every point. Got to be honest, though; they're struggling. It doesn't look like this year's team will be any better than last year." Gary turned back to the TV. "Look at that score." His attention clamped back on the screen. "Notre Dame got beat by Air Force . . . Is it 6:30 yet? Our reservations at LaScala's are for seven."

"It's six-fifteen, Dad," said Andy.

"You better get your act together, Milt." Gary barked out orders. "We got to go."

"Hey, I stay ready," Milt stretched. "What's your excuse?"

Gary ignored him. "Andy, go see if your mom and Aunt Helen are ready."

"Tell them we're ready," Carolyn called sweetly from the kitchen before Andy rose out of his chair.

LaScala's was only a short drive down the West River Road, over the Scioto River bridge, up a small bluff, and into their parking lot. Gary pulled his Jeep Cherokee under the front entrance porch and let his passengers out.

"Milt, why don't you entertain the ladies? Andy and I will park the bus."

"My pleasure."

The place had not changed. A coat room was on the right at the entrance. To the left was a huge banquet hall. Straight ahead was a lively bar and main dining room decorated with Roman statues and a glimmering marble floor. A painting of the owner's family prominently occupied the far wall of the waiting area. It quietly peered at incoming customers. Lights were low, creating an atmosphere perfect for romance or a relaxed evening of unhurried conversation. Distinctive aromas of incredible Italian sauces filled the air.

Gary joined them as the hostess asked everyone to follow her. Their table provided a view of the bar, a small dance floor, and a grand piano. Tonight an older gentleman was tickling the ivories. He was wearing a bowtie, brown scholarly glasses, and a neatly trimmed white mustache. Milt didn't know the name of the song he was playing but liked the melody.

"Honey, what's the name of that song?" he asked Helen.

"Cast Your Fate to the Wind. Lovely, isn't it?"

"I like it. I like you, too." Milt leaned over and kissed her cheek softly.

"Hey," Gary was watching the two lovebirds. "Cut out that smoochin' in public." Milt acted like he didn't hear his brother, then looked across the room. "Wasn't there a bocce ball court over there?" Milt pointed before leaning back in his chair. "I remember. I kicked your butt in a game of bocce ball right over there."

"Helen, how long has he been like this? Poor memory." Gary huffed. "You're right. There was a bocce ball court, but I kicked your butt. You can look it up in the *Columbus Dispatch* if you want to. They reported you were an emotional wreck for two weeks after you got thumped."

"Carolyn, if these two boys are going to fight, we should get our own table," Helen acted as if she had two first graders in need of time-out.

"You're in public," Carolyn reprimanded. "Act like adults or we'll have Andy march you to the car."

"What did I do?" Gary playfully tried to defend himself. "I can't help it if my brother's losing it."

A waiter came to the table, took drink orders, and tried to get everyone's attention to explain the evening's specials. His words had little impact on Milt. When in an Italian restaurant, Milt ordered chicken parmesan, period. He would order it again tonight no matter what the specials might be. The waiter finished then walked to the bar to collect their drink order.

"Who will be able to make it tomorrow?" Helen asked.

Gary and Carolyn had arranged for more of the family to come for Sunday dinner, if Milt, Helen, and Lance could stay. Milt had agreed, but said they had to be on the road early. Monday was a school day and all three had obligations.

Carolyn provided the update. "Marlene's coming and so is Patty."

Marlene and her husband, Ron, were cousins from Haysville, Ohio. Patty was Carolyn's sister from Cincinnati. Helen's bright smile confirmed her delight in this news. Marlene was a wonderful woman who had happily survived three decades of farming with Ron and Patty was just special. Having suffered the loss of her small son and a brutal divorce didn't stop her from bringing joy to every family gathering.

The waiter returned with a Bud Light, two Merlots, a regular Pepsi, and a Diet Pepsi. He courteously asked, "May I take your order?" Helen and Andy ordered spaghetti and meatballs, Carolyn opted for spinach ravioli, Gary decided on the veal parmesan, and Milt didn't flinch. "I'll have the chicken parmesan. That comes with a side of spaghetti?"

"Yes, sir, and lots of marinara sauce."

"Oh, yes," Milt sang out happily. "I love this place."

Dinner was served, everyone was delighted with their meals, and a lively conversation resumed. They discussed the game, mixed in some politics, and even found room to talk a little basketball. Gary lectured in more detail about the Ohio State basketball team, the coaches, and his professional opinion of the total program.

Sitting at the table next to the Stolers was a group of eight people who must have been at the Ohio State game. They were dressed in scarlet. One of the women proudly wore a university sweater that read "Ohio State Mom" on the front. Sitting closest to Milt was a man with an intelligent, stately appearance. He could easily pass as a U.S. senator. He had been listening to his own table's dialogue, but was apparently eavesdropping in on Milt and Gary's exchange. Milt watched the man as he pulled away from his own table and stepped over to theirs.

"Excuse me. I couldn't help hearing you talking about Ohio State and Kansas?"

Milt replied, "Yes we were."

"I'm Frank Davenport from Dayton. We love the Buckeyes as you can probably tell." He laughed. "My niece is on the rowing team at Kansas and works as an intern in the athletic department."

"My nephew is thinking about playing basketball at Kansas or here." Gary had no inhibitions about bragging. He saw the expression on Helen's face. "Kentucky is in the mix too."

Both tables became an audience for Milt and Frank. Milt explained that Lance was here for his recruiting visit, had been at Kansas last week, and next week he would visit the University of Kentucky.

"Wait a minute, I've read about your son," Frank said. "He's good. A lot of people are talking about your boy. The recruiting services say he's one of the best high school three point shooters in the nation."

"He's not bad." Helen liked the way Milt's face shone when he answered.

Helen said nothing. She folded her hands on the table, taking extreme pleasure in listening to someone speak so kindly about her son. Andy looked astonished. By the way the Dayton man had described him, Lance was a celebrity. To Andy, Lance was the cousin he golfed with during his summer visits in Kentucky and could always beat in rook and gin rummy. "You sure you're talking about my cousin?"

"Sure am," Frank said. He then asked Milt, "Did he like his trip to Kansas?"

"He seemed to enjoy it," the father acknowledged.

"I'm a Buckeye," Frank stated. "Not trying to badmouth anyone, but that coach out there is different."

"What do you mean?" Helen perked up. She was through being just a listener.

"Well, my niece Amanda had me out to a game in September. You know Kansas isn't very good in football and they were trying to do everything possible to fill up their stadium. So the athletic director had his marketing people bring in an American eagle. It flew down on the field during pre-game and gave quite a performance. The bird probably brought a few more people to the stadium than normal. Maybe 40,000 in attendance that day. You know, the equivalent of one end zone in the Horseshoe." Both tables laughed, enjoying Frank's story.

"At halftime, Amanda took me up into the press box to show me around. That part of their stadium was very nice. They had two floors of suites. The third floor held the press, the athletic director's suite, and right next to it was the basketball coach's suite, with just a glass wall dividing the two. They were real hospitality jewels with lots of dark wood trimming, plenty of seats, a bar, televisions, and several dining tables. Amanda wanted me to meet the AD and his wife." Frank peeked down at Helen. "She really likes them and he's giving her some great opportunities to work on a variety of projects for the department." He took a quick timeout for a sip of his scotch. "We were in the AD's suite and could look right through the window into the coach's suite. That's when it got interesting." He took another quick sip. "That eagle. They brought it right into the AD's suite. The director's wife, a superb hostess, presented the majestic bird, perched on its trainer's arm, to a guest to see it firsthand." Frank hesitated, as if to build up suspense. "Well, I couldn't help but spot the basketball coach staring at them. He was not a happy camper." Frank's eyes got wider. "It was like he thought the AD and his wife were trying to show him up. Everyone knows that coach thinks he's the big man on campus. He appeared to be livid. The thing is, the AD and his wife were only trying to be good hosts. They wanted their guests to enjoy the game." Davenport shook his head. "I'll never forget the ugly glare on that coach's face."

"Thanks for sharing your story," Helen reacted graciously. The rest of her table was quiet as they pondered Frank's words.

"Hey, let me buy you all a round of drinks. We can show you some good old Ohio State hospitality. You won't find any ugly glares here!"

Milt was quick to reply. "Normally I'd take you up on a Bud Light, but I'm not the best on the NCAA rules. Might be considered an extra benefit. Thank you, though."

"Sure. That's right," Frank said, in agreement. "Tell your son we'd love to be in the Schott cheering for him next year."

Frank returned to his group and both tables resumed their bantering, fueled by fine food and good company. Helen struggled to focus on the conversation because of a mother's natural instinct to worry. She drifted in and out of thoughts about her son. Was Lance enjoying his trip this weekend? Was he having a nice diner at Coach Meadors house? She wished he could have heard Frank Davenport's story. Her thoughts shifted to Nana. Was she having a good time with Cherie and Greg? Might something be wrong with her? She willed herself to ask more pleasant questions. Would there be any food left in the house when she got back? Milt's voice stopped her questioning.

"Check please," he said to the waiter.

Chapter 19

Mrs. Meadors was making last minute arrangements for dinner and Homer was busy orchestrating interaction between the recruits and current players. He clearly was looking for team chemistry, besides basketball skills. Most of the chemistry lesson took place in their comfortable family room. A stone fireplace with a hickory mantel separated two bookshelves on the far wall. Lance gazed at a few of the titles. Homer noticed. "I like to read."

"What's your favorite book up there, Coach?" Lance asked.

"Oh, I like a lot of them, but I would say that my favorite basketball book is *The MBA* by Red Auerbach." Homer seemed to relish the question. "Red tries to use basketball to help people understand sound business principles." He scanned the bookshelves. "There's a lot of fiction up there, too. I'd probably put Hemingway's *The Sun Also Rises* at the top of that list." He pondered some more. "My favorite of all, though, might be the biography of Robert E. Lee. Gained some interesting insight from reading how the general tried to lead." Homer noticed that the whole room was listening. He raised his voice. "He wasn't a basketball coach, but Lee had to drill and train some pretty interesting characters in his day. Would've been a formidable foe to compete against."

Lance couldn't wait to tell his dad about Homer's favorite. He also hadn't expected such a long answer, but he understood the coach's point. Homer was working a lot of hours, making a living with hoops, but his interest in reading demonstrated that balance in life was mighty important to him.

After dinner, Coach Meadors went over a few more recruiting matters then focused on his approach to academics.

"You will be going to class. It would be a dereliction of my duty if I let you miss class." Homer's voice slowed. "I may not convince you to become a

Buckeye, but what I say is doggone important." Every basketball player in the room sat up straighter. "No matter what school you choose, don't be afraid to learn." Meadors' eyes captured the entire group. "Get an education. It's the key to your future."

Homer reminded everyone it was "a jungle out there," and told the recruits to "be extra careful and responsible tonight."

The head coach and his wife stood by their front door and wished everyone a safe and pleasurable evening. Lance walked out with Coach Clermont and met Jay, who was standing with Sherry and Brad Byers.

"Coach C., we can give these guys a ride," Jay offered.

"You sure? It's no problem for me to drop them off."

"It's easier this way."

"Works for me, then," Clermont said, relinquishing his duty. "Behave yourselves."

Lance was scheduled to have a private breakfast with Clermont and Coach Meadors in the morning. Melvin and Chris, undoubtedly, had private meetings set up also. As Clermont approached his car Lance called to him, "Good-night, Coach. See ya at eight."

Lance had not forgotten that Melvin had some problems to work out before the night was over. He was curious about the rest of the evening's agenda. "What's the deal? What's next?" he asked Brad.

"Jay and I were talking. One of the football players who lives two houses down from me is having a party. Thought we'd take you guys over there. Should be a good time."

"Count me in," said Chris. His parents had just pulled away, headed back to the hotel.

"Where is it?" Lance asked.

Sherry answered, "It's only a few blocks from the Holiday Inn."

"Jay, why don't you take Chris and Lance? I'll let Melvin stretch out in my Blazer. We big guys need room," Brad offered jovially. "We'll meet you at Eddie's."

"Let's do it," Lance said to Jay, thinking it would be easy to help Melvin under the camouflage of a party.

Jay started the car.

"You'll like Eddie," Sherry explained to Lance and Chris. "Remember Tait's score on the first play? The wide receiver who made a great block? That's Eddie. He loves to have a good time."

Eddie's house was a three-story home, at least eighty years old, and showing its age. The original owners of the house had to be quite wealthy, but now the house had been turned into a multi-suite student residence. The front porch was filled with people. Lance noticed four people on the porch smoking. He hated smoking with a passion. He wasn't trying to be judgmental, but he had lost Grandad Hoover and Grandmother Stoler to lung cancer. Both had been smokers.

One of the smokers called out as the group walked up the steps, "Hi, Sherry! Hi Jay, who do you have with you?"

"Some of the basketball recruits," Sherry answered the girl. "You guys been here long?"

"My, oh my, who's the one with the crew cut?" the girl appeared not to have heard the question.

Sherry smiled, as did Lance.

"That would be Lance Stoler," Sherry replied. "Missy Reed, meet Lance Stoler."

Missy lowered thick black eyelashes. She softly blew smoke towards Lance's face. Moving slowly forward, dark brown hair curled around her stunning face, she seemed proud to let her generous breasts lead the way. Missy sniffed him out like two dogs on a walking trail. She left little doubt that she had taken an immediate liking to the newcomer. Smoke irritated Lance's eyes, but he felt compelled not to move as she came closer. A large hand squeezed the top of his arm. It was Melvin.

"Hey, Man, I got to talk to you." Melvin pulled Lance towards him.

"Sure." Lance quickly accepted this lifesaver. "Let's go to the other side of the porch." He made his apologies to Missy, noticing the sour expression on her face as he turned his attention to Melvin.

"What should I . . . Cheryl . . . told her I would see her. You heard me this morning. Don't want her to freak out on me like she did last night." He was blubbering.

"You still have her number?"

"Yeah, right here."

"Let's go see if we can borrow a phone. Call her and tell her that you're with me." Lance tapped Melvin gently on the shoulder. "Maybe, just maybe, she'll tell you to have a good time and you won't have to see her. You won't have to worry about her anymore."

"You lead the way." Melvin pushed Lance towards the front door. "I don't know any of these people," he said stubbornly.

Lance didn't know any of these people either, but Melvin was agitated. His priority was to help Melvin settle down. They worked their way inside. Lance spotted Jay, and headed towards him.

"You guys enjoying yourselves?" Jay asked.

"Sure, but Melvin needs to use a phone."

Jay scrutinized the room, then raised his voice. "Yo, Eddie! Over here." Eddie began swerving through the crowd. He repeated the gracefulness employed earlier in the day to catch six passes in the Horseshoe. Jay and Eddie locked their hands together.

"What's up?"

"Wanted you to meet these guys. They're recruits. Lance Stoler from Kentucky --Melvin Howard out of Chicago."

"Glad you guys are here. I loved to play hoops, but my dad said I should stick with catching footballs."

Lance had to raise his voice. The party was heating up. "You had a nice game. The block you had on the first play was awesome."

"Thanks, man. Just doin' my job." He clearly enjoyed the compliment.

Lance eyeballed the crowd. Eddie was popular. The number of coeds in the house was easy enough verification. Lance was reminded of his mission by a sharp nudge in the back.

"Excuse me, Eddie, but Mel needs to make a local call. Could we borrow your phone?"

"Got my cell right here. . . hold on, don't want any recruiting violations. Use the phone in the kitchen." Eddie hesitated again. "It's local, right?"

"Absolutely," Lance looked like he was saying 'Scouts Honor!' "Thanks, Man."

Melvin hadn't said a word. They mixed their way towards the back of the house and into the kitchen. Lance picked up the phone, then set it back down. He sensed that Melvin could use a little coaching.

"Let her know you're with me. You've had a great day. Try to encourage her to go have a good time with her friends. Got it?"

"Yeah, Man, I got it."

Lance handed the phone over, stepped back, leaned against the far counter, and watched Melvin anxiously punch in numbers. Melvin looked up and stared into Lance's eyes like a sad puppy.

Seconds passed as they waited for someone to answer. Finally, Melvin was talking, "Hi, is Cheryl in?"

Lance could hear only Melvin's words, but Melvin was doing quite well, sticking to their game plan. Then the conversation turned south. Lance was becoming alarmed by the change in expression on his new friend's face.

"I'll see you in about ten minutes." Melvin hung up.

"See you in ten minutes? What the heck was that?" Lance shouted his disbelief.

"What could I do? She wants to see me!"

"Where are you meeting her?"

Melvin's eyes expanded like boiled eggs. "She's coming here. Said she lives only a couple blocks away. Said she knows Eddie and several of the football players."

"Come on, we'd better wait for her on the front porch."

They headed back through the house and found a spot were they could watch from the porch. Missy saw Lance and Melvin waiting. She threw her cigarette on the old wooden planks, twisted the butt under the toe of her black high-heeled shoe, and casually kicked it into the front lawn.

Lance watched her approach clutching a Coors Light, her long brown curls gently dancing around her face in the cool October breeze. She wore three-quarter-length pants slightly tighter than her sweater. Lance and Melvin each took pleasure admiring Missy as she strolled towards them.

"Now what are you two gentlemen doing out here all by yourselves?" she slowly purred.

"Hello, again," Lance answered quickly. "We're waiting for someone." To have her standing so close made him uneasy.

"Is she cute?" Missy laughed softly, moving closer.

Lance was caught off-guard by Missy's directness, but mustered up a response. "Melvin thinks so."

Lance had no more than answered when a tall lanky girl with jet-black hair walked up the porch steps.

"Hello, Missy, how are you doing?" she asked sharply, looking questioningly at Melvin. "I see you've been keeping Melvin company for me."

Missy didn't comment. She just stood, unflinching. Melvin awkwardly gave the new arrival a quick hug.

"Cheryl, this is Lance Stoler. Talked to you about him on the phone." Melvin's introduction was cumbersome. "Seems you already know Missy."

"Yes. Missy and I have been to a few parties together," she said, returning Missy's gaze. "Has she been behaving herself?"

"Lance would have to answer that," Melvin said innocently. "I've just been standing here watching for you."

Melvin melted. Cheryl's long runner's legs and swaying black hair probably had the same effect on quite a few Columbus boys. Lance kept silent. Missy and Cheryl made some small talk, then Cheryl grabbed Melvin by the hand.

"Come on, Melvin. Let's go inside. I need a beer."

Melvin was not about to say no. Lance knew it was probably not good to leave his recruiting buddy alone with Cheryl, but he reckoned there were a lot of people at the party and things should be fine.

"How old is she?" Lance asked Missy, when they were alone.

Missy crossed slowly behind Lance, teasingly brushing her firm chest against his back. She leaned against the porch railing beside him.

"She's twenty-three. Why? How old is Melvin?"

"Don't know. Maybe eighteen."

"Cheryl's on the six or seven year program at OSU. I know that. I'm in my senior year and she was here at least a year before me. Her parents are wealthy. I don't think she has any sense of urgency to graduate. She loves college life, especially the ballplayers and parties."

"She won't be any trouble for Melvin? Will she?"

"Oh, I think Melvin's going to enjoy every minute of his time with Cheryl." Missy snickered softly, inching even closer. "You're quite protective of your buddy. How old are you, anyway?"

He was mesmerized by Missy's beauty. He finally choked out, "I'm a senior."

Lance wasn't convinced Melvin could keep away from disaster. He was beginning to worry the same about himself. He listened to Missy, willing his eyes to watch her lips, not her body. She talked. She told Lance she was a business major from Cincinnati and had gone to the same high school as their host, Eddie. She made it clear she liked football better than basketball. She brushed his cheek with her soft lips.

"Maybe I could be persuaded to change my mind by the right basketball player, though," she whispered.

Lisa suddenly flashed through his mind. She wouldn't approve of this front porch fascination.

They talked softly for about ten minutes. Missy took the last sip of her Coors Light and placed her hand on top of Lance's, which was grasping the porch railing hard enough to whiten his knuckles. She had no clue this was how Lance was able to disguise his confusion.

Before another word could be spoken between them, Missy pulled her hand away and greeted a young man storming up the steps.

"Bobby. What's the matter?"

"Where is she?" he demanded.

"She went inside Bobby. This is..." Missy could not finish her sentence as the young man bounded through the door, looking as if he was on a secret mission for the navy seals. Lance assumed the navy seal must play football. He had a thick neck, thundering biceps, and a chest that looked like a refrigerator.

"Who was that?" Lance asked.

"You saw him play today. That was Bobby Jackson, number 56."

"He's an outside linebacker. I did see him. He's pretty good."

"You're right, and all you have to do is ask him," Missy sneered. "He'll tell you just how good he is. It really bothers him that he makes big plays, but Daryl Mossberg, the middle linebacker, gets all the credit."

"Wait a minute, Daryl is pretty darn good."

"We all know that. It's Bobby that doesn't know. And did I mention that Bobby is Cheryl's boyfriend?"

"What do you mean he's Cheryl's boyfriend?!"

"Cheryl recently broke up with him because he got crazy jealous too often. Every time another guy would so much as look at her when they were together, he got redneck angry."

"Got to check on Melvin!" Lance quickly ran through the door. Missy followed right behind. Eddie was slow dancing with a coed he obviously knew extremely well.

Lance stopped them and asked, "Have you seen Cheryl and Melvin?"

Eddie looked like he did not appreciate the disturbance. He turned reluctantly from his partner. "Last time I saw Melvin, he had a big grin on his face and Cheryl was giving him a tour of the house, including the upstairs bedrooms. If you know what I mean, my man."

"Thanks," Lance said under his breath. He turned toward the steps. Missy was two steps behind. He wasn't certain where to go, but needed to find Melvin, praying he hadn't done anything stupid.

He was too late.

A girl screamed. The noise came from the far bedroom. Lance ran and stopped in the doorway. Cheryl was on the bed, her skirt around her waist, her sweater lying on the floor.

Bobby had pulled Melvin roughly off the bed. Lance and Missy watched the linebacker's first hard blow land in Melvin's gut. The next was planted squarely on Melvin's jaw, causing blood to gush out of lips which moments earlier may have been sampling the sweet taste of Cheryl's body.

Bobby's left forearm was cocked, loaded to deliver another blow when Lance grabbed Bobby's wrist. Lance was surprised by the strength in his hand. Although country strong, he had never had to demonstrate his might in this fashion before. An inner strength beyond his comprehension aided him, stopping Bobby's swing in mid-air.

The jealous attacker turned his pained face towards Lance, and let a right hook fly toward his left ear. Lance ducked as the fist missed its target, spinning the linebacker around. Lance didn't hesitate. He pushed Bobby to the floor and spread on top of him like a Florida gator holding its prey. Holding firmly, he smelled alcohol on the breath of the discontented boyfriend. In this situation, alcohol had become an ally. Beer had drained much of his opponent's strength.

"Let me go, you son of a gun, or I'm going to kick your butt, too," Bobby growled.

"You got to settle down, Man," Lance growled back, holding him down with all his might.

"Maybe you didn't hear me. Get your fat butt off me or you're dead meat."

"Someone call the cops," Lance shouted.

"No one's calling the cops," Missy said calmly. She pulled the bedspread over Cheryl, who was wiggling back into her clothes.

"No way. This jerk might have broken Melvin's jaw." Lance was determined.

"Let him go." Missy grabbed Lance by the shoulders, helping him stand up, allowing Bobby to roll over onto his back. She planted her high heel firmly in his ribs. "He won't hit anyone again. Right, Bobby? I said, right Bobby? Or I will let someone call the police and you can forget about playing in the Michigan game."

Cheryl was now sitting up on the side of the bed, buttoning her sweater. Melvin was on the floor, mopping his bloody lips with a pillowcase. Missy was, amazingly, in complete control of everyone in the room. Bobby pushed back his hair.

"I want to talk to Cheryl!" Bobby said with arrogance.

"No way am I leaving you alone with Cheryl," said Missy. She gazed at Melvin, "How's your jaw?"

"Just a little blood. But if that wimp comes after me again, I'll take a two by four to his head."

"Come on, Melvin. We should leave," Lance said. "Coach doesn't need this kind of trouble from us."

"You mean just because of that creep, my night has to be ruined?"

Bobby lurched up, stumbling towards him. "You want me to finish your pansy butt right now?"

"That's it!" Lance stepped between them. "I'm calling the police right now."

"Settle down!" Missy shouted. Everyone looked at her. "All right. Lance, you take Melvin back to the hotel, and let me make sure Bobby and Cheryl have a conversation. I'll stay with them. They'll be fine. Trust me."

Melvin glanced at Cheryl. He wiped more blood on the bed sheet. "Are you fine with that?"

"Maybe it's better this way," Cheryl answered. She looked suddenly tired. "No one call the cops."

Missy turned to Lance with regret in her eyes. "Maybe we'll hook up on your next trip to Columbus."

"Thanks, Missy." The whole scene had Lance completely bewildered.

Bobby slouched back down on the floor, while Cheryl fell weeping into Missy's arms. She caught Lance's gaze.

Softly, Lance said, "Missy, I did enjoy meeting you." He quietly escorted Melvin out of the bedroom.

The noise of the party had been so rowdy, the upstairs incident had gone undetected. Lance peered out over the crowded living room and dining room. He searched for Sherry and Jay. They couldn't leave without telling someone of their departure. Lance saw no sign of them.

Lance grabbed Melvin by his right shoulder. "You see Jay or Sherry? We need to tell them we're going."

"Hey, Man," Melvin snipped, "let's just get the heck out of here."

"Find Jay. We've got to tell them we're leaving. Otherwise they'll come searching for us. Start asking all kinds of questions. Everyone saw you with Cheryl. You don't want them interrogating her. You don't know what she'll say. Besides, if no one knows where we are, they might call the cops."

"I see him." Melvin's height made the discovery. "He's in the kitchen."

"You keep your mouth shut and let me do the talking."

"No kidding, little man. I can handle that real well," Melvin responded, rubbing the side of his face.

Lance and Melvin made their way to their host. "Jay, we're taking off. Back to the hotel. It's only three blocks. We'll walk back so you don't have to leave."

"You sure? It's early—even for us."

"We both have headaches." Lance made up the lame excuse. He thanked Jay and Sherry for being so kind. Like a big sister putting her little brothers to bed for the night, Sherry hugged the two recruits. When Melvin turned, she noticed the blood.

"What happened? You have blood on your shirt."

Lance saw the scared expression on Melvin's face and acted. "That's nothing. The big guy bumped his head going up the steps. He's fine."

Melvin nodded.

Lance and Melvin walked silently out the back door, around the side of the house, and down the sidewalk towards Neil Avenue. Melvin massaged his jaw.

"You know, I would have handled that son-of-a-gun if he didn't blind-side me. I was right in the middle of something, if you know what I mean." It apparently hurt Melvin to grin. "He sure was a big sucker. Wasn't he?"

"He was a good-sized boy, Melvin."

"You sure are something, Kentucky. Why'd you come upstairs anyways?"

"I was with Missy on the front porch when I saw Bobby. He looked pissed off before he even went into the house. Then Missy told me he was Cheryl's former boyfriend. Former, as in last week. I didn't have to be Dick Tracy to figure that one out."

"I know you, what? Two days? And man, you treat me like I've been your friend since elementary school." He gave Lance a push sideways. "You must be strong, too. He was going to give me another one of those Mike Tyson blows when you stopped him right in his tracks. I loved watching you nail his butt to the floor."

"You would have done the same for me."

The recruits went another twenty yards to the intersection of Lane and Neil.

"You feel like some pizza?" Melvin asked as they approached Tommy's Pizza Parlor.

Lance didn't need his arm to be twisted. "You expect me to turn down that offer? If they have a large pepperoni, I'll fight you for the last piece."

"After what I saw tonight," Melvin said, "I'll give it to you right now." It didn't hurt Lance to grin.

They sat eating pizza for over an hour, just rambling on about life and sports. Lance liked Melvin. He just hoped his tall friend didn't have to take a punch every time he had to learn one of life's lessons.

Heading back to the hotel, they crossed in front of the Varsity Club. Lance wondered if Melvin had an urge to go inside. The music and noise coming out was tempting, but the giant didn't hesitate. He walked right by without even looking in that direction.

Melvin declared. "Last night was enough for me in there." He flinched in pain.

"Me too."

The lobby showed no signs of letting down. Scarlet and Gray fans were in their glory. The Buckeyes had beaten a top ten opponent and for them life was good. Melvin's height again drew attention from the fans, but the recruits kept marching toward the elevators. They climbed on and Melvin pushed the sixth floor button.

Melvin turned to Lance, "You're special, man. Needed a friend and you were there. I guess I won't see you tomorrow."

"Probably not. I have to meet with the coaches and then my dad's picking me up." Lance studied his new friends face. "I've enjoyed being with you." He searched through his heart for more assuring words "What happened tonight . . . what happened tonight is history. As far as I'm concerned, it never happened. No one'll ever hear about it from me." Lance was sure the incident had little chance of being repeated. Melvin would not talk. Bobby Jackson wasn't about to tell his buddies some high school kid knocked him down. Cheryl had to be embarrassed. Missy seemed to understand best. "Yes, I'm sure --it's history."

Lance saw relief wash over Melvin's face as if a migraine had finally melted away. He had undoubtedly been wondering if Lance would share the incident with the Ohio State coaches. Now he knew. A handshake would not do. Melvin wrapped his big lanky arms around his friend and held on tight.

"Hey, Kentucky, wouldn't it be great if the next time I see you, we'd be teammates?"

"It would, Melvin. It would be great."

Melvin unlocked his room and Lance did the same. They nodded towards each other then each closed his door.

Tired from the long day but not sleepy, Lance pulled off his blue sweater, slid into his Green Bears shorts, then fell onto the bed. He gazed out the window and thought of Lisa. It was probably Lisa who sent Bobby up the front porch steps. Just when Missy touched my hand. *It was Lisa's way of protecting me.* A happy warmth slowly spread through Lance's body. He closed his eyes and dreamed.

Chapter 20

J im Clermont pulled up at exactly seven forty-five. Lance was waiting. Within minutes the Lexus pulled into the Ohio State golf course. The weather was a great deal better than the day before. Warmer temperatures and sunny skies brought out a few extra golfers and the football victory probably didn't hurt the brightness of the day either. Tradition was harbored everywhere. The likes of Jack Nicklaus, Tom Weiskoph, Ed Sneed, Joey Sindelar, and many other worthy linksmen called this home during their collegiate days.

"The breakfast is awesome here," Jim pointed Lance to the entrance.

Coach Meadors was sitting at a table looking out on the eighteenth green. He rose, extended his hand, and greeted his guest, "You had a good time last night, I hope?"

Lance made sure a warm smile appeared as he shook Homer's hand. Melvin's affair would not be revealed.

"Sure did. Thanks again for dinner. You and Mrs. Meadors have a beautiful home."

"As you could probably tell, I have little to do with it. I just know that I love going home," Homer replied.

Lance took a brief moment to stare out at the eighteenth green. A foursome was on the green. Lance speculated they were playing for money because the gentleman putting had walked on both sides of his ball and was eyeing it over pretty hard. The ball was about ten feet from the hole and looked like a level putt from Lance's dining room angle. Everyone else was in the hole. No more balls were on the green. The gentleman lined himself up, brought his putter straight back, moved it forward, and the ball rolled off of the face and followed a straight line. With about two feet to go, the ball seemed to slow down, as if running out of gas. But it just kept on going and going and stopped its journey with a slight fade to the right, disappearing into the hole. Four hands went up in celebration and two heads dipped. Homer had been watching the same drama.

"You figure that guy knows this whole restaurant is watching him dance?"

The three spectators chuckled, then turned their attention to breakfast. They spent twenty minutes eating and chatting with no significant conversation. Homer was ready for significance. "Well, what are your thoughts?" he asked. "Have you been able to get a good enough feel for Ohio State?"

Lance told them he had the greatest respect for the coaching staff. They had made him feel wanted and that they believed he would make a difference. But, he still had to visit Kentucky. "Don't you agree that I shouldn't be premature? Follow my plan and give myself the benefit of being able to honestly compare the three programs?"

"No way. You should tell us right now you'll be coming to Ohio State. So I can cheer like that guy on the eighteenth green!" Coach paused and smiled good-naturedly.

"Lance, I haven't sheltered my emotions. Our basketball program needs you desperately. We need your character as much as your athletic talent. But I can't, in good faith, sit here and tell you not to wait. You have to visit Kentucky. It's your home, for God's sake. I know about the wonderful tradition at Kansas. I wouldn't want to be in your shoes. Hundreds of schools would love to announce Lance Stoler will be playing for them. You narrowed it down to three. Knowing you and your family, Jim and I are taking it as a great compliment we made your final list."

Jim added support. "Lance, I want to coach you. Coach Barnhart wants to coach you."

Lance's voice trembled, showing the impact of their words. "Thanks, Coach, that's very kind of you to say." He took a deep breath.

"This is the deal. Visit your home state school. Consult with your family. Talk with Coach Hunter." Homer paused. "Then look in the mirror. This is a decision that will follow you the rest of your life. In the end, just do what you think is right." he stared into Lance's eyes. "We'll be here. We'll sit in the corner hoping, anticipating, praying that you might just see a Buckeye in your future and ask her to dance."

"It means a lot to me that you understand my situation." He took another deep breath. "I'll do my best to look hard into that mirror."

The Lexus stopped in front of the Holiday Inn lobby. "Your parents are all set to pick you up?" asked Jim.

"Dad said he would be here at eleven."

Lance started to open the car door, but Clermont grabbed his left arm. Lance's brain froze for a few seconds in fear. Was Coach going to ask him about Melvin and the incident last night? Clermont did not.

"That's where my dreams came alive." Clermont stared across Lane Avenue focusing on St. John Arena. He looked back at Lance. "Just as I did years ago… you have to figure out how to spread your wings and fly. You can make a difference here." Jim's face expressed sincerity. "I wish you the best. God speed."

Lance clenched Jim's hand, sending his signal of appreciation. "Thanks, Coach."

The crowds were gone, the elevator empty. On his floor, he passed a cleaning lady's cart. The door was wide open. She was running the vacuum. The guests were probably traveling home, making plans to return for the next game. Lance pondered, *Would he return?*

He quietly packed his small luggage bag. A good throwing technique was all that was required. The last thing he threw into the suitcase was his blue sweater. Lance had second thoughts and retrieved it from the top of the bag. It deserved special attention. The touch of it made him feel like Lisa was near him, making him eager to get home. See if he had any e-mails.

He stood and waited by the main entrance to the Holiday Inn. No one disturbed him there. On this Sunday morning, Lance was an ordinary young man standing on the corner, watching the cars pull in and out. It was still a few minutes before eleven so he patiently waited for the Tahoe. Through a few fluffy clouds, the sun warmed his forehead. He thought of home. Nana would just be getting ready for Sunday service. This was the second week in a row that he had not been in church. He actually missed not being there.

It wasn't the Tahoe, but Lance immediately recognized that Jeep and the big guy driving it.

"Hey Boy, you looking for the limo to the airport?" Gary shouted as he jumped out the driver's door.

"Hey, Uncle Gary, thanks for coming." Lance was swallowed in a bear hug.

Gary chuckled deeply. "Give me that suitcase."

"Hey Son, you been behaving yourself?" Milt said from his front passenger seat as Lance opened the side door.

"Sure have, Dad. But it's good to be going home."

Andy was clearly excited to see his Kentucky relative. "Hey, Lance."

"Hi, Andy. Neither of those guys would let you drive?"

"Offered, but Dad said he was the Dale Earnhardt of Dublin. We only left the house fifteen minutes ago." Andy rushed on to be the first with news. "Dad got tickets! To the game!"

" Uncle Gary, you were at the game?" Lance almost shouted.

The driver gloated. "Boy. I was so close to Coach Baxter that he kept turning around asking me what play to run next."

Stories about Gary's adventure in the Horseshoe and Lance's recap of his visit kept the four passengers enthralled. Twenty-five minutes later they were pulling onto River Forest Road.

Dinner conversation was lively. Too soon Milt said it was time they gathered their things and loaded the Tahoe. Best wishes and good-byes were passed around like candy. Hugs were just as plentiful. Milt pulled out the car keys and threw them to his son.

"Why don't you drive the first leg of the trip home?"

Lance didn't need to be asked twice. They waved at their family as Lance backed out of the driveway. It had been an extraordinary weekend.

Chapter 21

"What do you think you are doing?" Milt watched Lance put a CD into the player.

"I thought we'd listen to a little OutKast vibrations."

"You've got to be kidding me. I'm not listening to any of that hippity-hop rap stuff."

"Mom, Dad forgot the rules again. The driver picks the music. Right?"

Helen, as usual, didn't have a chance to answer.

"It is obvious, Young Man, that you didn't read the fine print. Let me get the rules out." Milt faked opening the glove compartment. "Here they are. Let me read something to you, son. Driver gets to pick the music." He hesitated. "Wait, there's an asterisk. Let's see what it says. "Driver gets to pick the music unless Milt Stoler is planted in the passenger seat and he disapproves.""

Resting quietly in the back seat, Helen listened, waited, and hoped her two boys would solve their musical problem. The teacher in her made for a short wait. "Milt, it won't hurt you to listen to something different for a change. You might even learn to enjoy it."

"Fat chance. Did Hoover end up liking the Beatles? The Rolling Stones?" Milt rolled his eyes. He got nothing but silence from the back seat. "Boy, this is your lucky day. Let those choirboys sing."

The CD began to play. Lance was content. Helen returned to viewing the Ohio landscape. They passed by Grove City, Circle-ville, and Chillicothe on rustic Route 23. The countryside flourished with rich farmlands, brown hills, and golden trees that sparkled in the afternoon sun. The hills were not as large as those surrounding Connsburg, but their charm was nonetheless quite comforting.

Helen suspected people growing up along this road nurtured roots that drew them back if they traveled too far away. She knew the feeling well. She gazed up at the driver's seat. Where would he go? Did Lance feel as strongly about the Kentucky hills as she did? Had she carefully watered his roots?"

If Lance would have glanced into the rear view mirror, he would have seen the conflict registered on Helen's face. Would have seen lips that wanted to speak, but couldn't. *How do I help him?* She didn't want to tell her son what to do and she definitely didn't want to be an overbearing mother. Where he went to college was his choice. It was his life. She and Milt had pioneered their own lives. Each of their children needed to do the same.

Her roots dug deeper and caused her to smile. *That all sounds good, but you know what? I want my boy to be a Wildcat.*

They had traveled quietly for some time when Helen felt compelled to bring up Mr. Davenport. "Milt, you'd better talk with Lance about our dinner on Saturday night."

"Thought you guys ate at LaScala with Uncle Gary."

"We did. The chicken parmesan was outstanding. Your mom's referring to a gentleman we met."

"Who?"

"Man from Dayton. Frank Davenport. Nice guy. Big Buckeye fan. Sat at the table next to us and overheard when we were talking about Kansas."

"His niece is on the rowing team at Kansas," Helen added.

"No kidding. Does she like Kansas?"

"I think so, but that's not why I asked your dad to share something with you. Mr. Davenport told us an interesting story. We thought you should know."

Lance knew his mom was rarely that blunt. His hands pressed harder against the steering wheel. "What did he say?"

Milt retold the eagle story and the suspicions Frank had about Coach Booth. Lance would have preferred positive feedback, but it didn't matter. Lisa and J.C. made Kansas attractive to him. He liked J.C. and had been thinking more and more about Lisa. Time with her was different from time he'd spent with any other girl, including Wanda. Nothing could replace the magic he had felt a week ago.

Lance twisted his hands on the steering wheel, signifying he needed to say something. But what? He wasn't prepared to discuss Lisa. Dodging the coaching situation also seemed best. "Wish you could have made the trip to Lawrence. It's a nice town and the campus is beautiful. I really like Burbridge."

"How'd it compare to Ohio State?" Helen asked.

"They're different. Strange, but if truth be told, I liked both of them," Lance paused because the past two days had been fantastic, even with Melvin's episode. The only thing missing -- J.C. and Lisa. "This weekend was first-class. Got along with all the coaches." He lowered the volume on his CD. "Coach Meadors is exceptional, and wait till you can spend more time with Coach Clermont. You could trust your wallet with that guy. Know what I mean, Dad?"

Milt nodded.

"And Coach Barnhart. That man has head coach written all over him." Lance thought for a second and released a slight giggle. "It's not too shabby having the fantastic football program the Buckeyes have, either. In three years, what if big Greg was recruited as a Buckeye freshman?"

Lance lifted his voice with the sole purpose of assuring his parents that a third option wasn't forgotten. "It'll be nice going to Lexington next Friday. You know how I love Rupp Arena."

"Rupp's seen a few good games." By the slight movement of Milt's head, he hinted his thoughts were replaying last year's championship. "After next week, you should have a good feel for how all three schools match up."

Helen said nothing more. The Tahoe kept moving south. Lance turned off the CD. The whistling of northbound traffic was now the only sound. Silence had captured the three passengers crowding the air with private thoughts.

Just outside Lucasville, Milt checked with Lance. "Can you make it to Portsmouth before we switch?"

"I could drive the whole way."

"Probably so, but it's best if we switch. Once we cross the Ohio River, we'll need to find a gas station. Might as well buy some Kentucky gas."

Chapter 22

Milt pulled into their driveway. "I hope the place is still in one piece," he yawned. "Honey, you go on in. Lance and I will get the luggage."

Bubba was just walking up as Helen opened the back door. He raced to happily greet her, and then ran to Lance demanding his attention.

"Hey, Bubba. Was Nana good to you? I bet you'd like to go for a run. Let me get this stuff put away and we'll take off." Lance rubbed Bubba's head and watched his tail swirl in excitement.

Milt and Lance lugged everything inside and sat down to chat with Nana, Greg, and Cherie. Lance started to share his weekend stories. Nana loved that her grandson was home, so she listened, but not very enthusiastically. He wasn't talking about her Wildcats.

Greg described his football game and the drudgery of raking leaves Saturday morning before watching the Buckeyes.

"Cherie wanted to help, but I was told the soccer coach strangely called for a special practice."

Cherie giggled.

Nana stood up, gave Lance a squeeze around the waist.

"Could have handled Milt being gone even longer, but we really missed you and your mom." Nana's giggle was Cherie's echo. "It's getting late. I'm heading home."

"It's not late," Lance pleaded as each family member lined up for a hug.

"Got some work to do before a few meetings tomorrow."

"Who are you meeting with, Mom?" Helen asked.

"Nobody special. Just meetings." The lifting of her chin made it clear she was not inclined to explain further. She looked at Milt. "Quit pouting. I was kidding about not missing you." She gave him a little peck on the cheek. Milt's eyes could not conceal his pleasure.

After Nana drove off, the family dispersed. Helen steered herself to the laundry room, Milt headed to his computer, Greg went back to the NFL game, and Cherie was almost in her room when Lance caught up with her.

"Goin' to take Bubba for a run. Got no exercise all weekend. When I get back, want to do a little checking with me?"

"What makes you think I haven't already checked?"

"Well did I, you know, did I get anything?" Lance asked.

"Start smiling. You can see when you get back. It'll be dark in a little bit. You better get going."

After unpacking and quickly putting on his running gear, Lance carried his dirty clothes to the laundry room. Helen was preparing to put in a load.

"I'll take those. I know you and Bubba are itching to get going," Helen insisted, taking his clothes.

Lance placed a kiss on her cheek. "Thanks for coming this weekend."

"My pleasure. Are those other two speedsters going with you."

"Goin' to find out right now." He shouted down the hallway. "Dad, Greg, I'm taking Bubba for a run. Wanna come?"

"Sorry son, I got a dozen e-mails so I'm a no-go."

"How far you going?" Greg yelled.

"Our regular two miles."

"Yeah, sure, give me two seconds. Got some football to play, but I better start thinking about getting in basketball shape. You might need me for a pick again this year."

The three had made this trip many times, usually at a decent clip. Bubba never had a problem keeping up, but things slowed down pretty good if Milt decided to tag along. A brisk breeze whistled out of the Northeast causing both boys to pull up their hoods. Their path took them past the Hallmark house, up Canterbury for almost a mile, then east on Evergreen before bringing them back about half a mile from their home.

Greg ran smoothly with no traceable signs of effort. He glided along the blacktop with the ease of a Rusty Wallace Dodge on the NASCAR circuit, seeming never to need a pit stop. Lance's stride was more akin to an old Ford pickup. It wasn't flashy, but it always got the job done. As the three finished, Greg had hardly worked up a sweat, Lance was puffing, and Bubba's tongue was hanging out. They walked up the driveway. Lance put his hand behind his friend's ear, giving the Lab several gentle pats to let him know he had done well. Bubba returned the compliment with a rub of his damp coat against Lance's leg and a wag of his tail.

Lance showered, filled with anticipation. *Lisa e-mailed me. What did she write?* He shut off the water, quickly dried, and headed to his room. He was pulling his Green Bear tee shirt over his head when he heard a knock on the door.

"Already turned on the computer. Want me to get your e-mails?" Cherie asked outside the door.

"What do you mean e-mails? That's plural."

"You're right. You have two."

Lanced threw his towel into the hamper. "Let's get them," he said, swinging the door open.

Cherie sat down in the chair. Lance hunched calmly over her shoulder, eyes twinkling. She made the required number of clicks and two e-mails from Lisa appeared.

Dear Lance,

I know you are in Columbus, but I didn't know if you would be able to check your e-mails or have time to when you are on a recruiting trip. I hope you do. I just wanted you to know I watched the Ohio State-Iowa football game. My dad thought something was wrong with me. He never saw me watch a football game before. I don't think I've watched too many games on TV. I watched the whole game. I thought I might see you in the crowd. Pretty dumb, huh? Well, you were nowhere to be found in all those Buckeye fans. Dad's taking us out to dinner tonight. Missouri won their football game and he thought we should celebrate. He said he was a considerate dad since he might even be persuaded to feed a Kansas student.

Saw J.C. and Marla last night. They said to make sure I told you hello.

Hope your trip goes well.

Lisa

"Dang. Should have tried to use the hotel's computer."

"Read the next one, Big Brother."

Dear Lance,

It's Sunday and I'm certain you probably did not get a chance to read my e-mail from Saturday. I hope you enjoyed your trip, but not as much as the one to Lawrence. Nothing against Ohio State, but the only way I get to go to school with you is if you become a Jayhawk. J.C. called me last night. He seems to be hurting about something. If you can, call me. I could explain. Good luck in school this week.

Lisa

"Better call her now."

"Probably best," Cherie agreed. "It's only seven back in Kansas City."

"Thanks, Sis." Lance squeezed her shoulder, then moved quickly down the hallway.

"Dad, is it OK if I make a long distance phone call in the kitchen?"

Milt looked up from his computer. "What's wrong?"

"Nothing, well . . . Lisa e-mailed me. She's the friend of J.C.'s I met in Lawrence. Said J.C. is hurting about something."

"Sure, let me know if you need anything."

Lance was alone in the kitchen. He dialed the number and waited for someone to pick up in Kansas City.

It was a man's voice. "Hello, Gosline's." The deep voice had a cheerful ring to it.

"Hello, this is Lance Stoler. Is Lisa in?"

"Is this the Lance Stoler who's going to transfer to Missouri?" the voice asked.

This has to be her dad. What do I say to that question?

"Sir, I won't have to transfer if I go there in the first place."

"Now you're talking. This is Lisa's dad. You were at Ohio State this weekend, weren't you?"

"Yes, Sir."

"My daughter watched that whole football game on T.V. I've never known her to do that."

"She saw a good game. I understand your Missouri Tigers won, too."

"That they did! Well, let me get her. And don't waste your time going to that junior college in Lawrence. Lisa's going there just to aggravate me. You need to get a good education."

"Thanks for the advice, Sir."

Lance could hear Lisa's voice in the background. "Daddy, what are you saying to him? Give me the phone, please."

"Hello, Lance." Her voice was like honey.

"Hi, Lisa. Hope you weren't busy. I got your e-mails."

"I was hoping you'd call. Sorry about my dad." There was a pause. Lance suspected Lisa was trying to motion for her father to leave the room. "I'm alone now."

"He seems to be a neat guy. I don't think he likes you going to Kansas."

"He'll get over it."

"Tell me about J.C. What's going on?"

"I don't know what you or someone else said to him, but he's all upset about his car."

Lance thought the worst. No one in J.C.'s financial situation could legitimately pay for that car. Maybe the NCAA found out. "What happened?"

"Don't know. You should call him. He really respects you. He called me late last night. We talked for over an hour. He wouldn't completely explain. Said he wished he never got that car."

Lance didn't feel comfortable sharing his suspicions about the car with her. "At least it wasn't an accident or something like that?"

"No, he's a really good driver."

"I'll call him tonight."

"Thanks. I knew you'd help."

"No problem."

Lisa hesitated, then asked, "Did you like Ohio State?"

Lance rubbed the back of his head. "It was like my Kansas trip. Very enjoyable." He paused. "I can't believe you watched the whole football game."

"I was eager to see if those Hawkeyes could beat a bunch of Buckeyes. Well . . . not really. Thought maybe I'd see you. Say, what is a Buckeye anyway?"

He remembered J.C. asking the same question. "It's a nut from the buckeye tree." Lance softened his voice. "It was kind of you to watch."

"So, it was like Kansas? Did you meet someone there? You know, like you met me?" Her voice sounded like a small child almost in tears.

Lance was indecisive. What if someone told her he had been with Missy? Misrepresented what really happened. Didn't explain how he gripped the porch when Missy made her advances. She'd be ticked. She'd probably say she watched that whole darn football game for nothing. He broke the silence. "Met a lot of people in Columbus, but no one like you."

"That's sweet of you to say." She sounded grown-up.

Now it was Lance's turn to do a little investigation. *Did Lisa meet someone Friday night when she was out with Marla?* His brain clogged his thoughts with doubts. *Is she interested in me? I'm just some other recruit who might not even go to Kansas. Why should she be interested in me? There's no good reason. None.*

"What'd you guys do Friday night?" Lance asked, trying to get a grip on his emotions.

"Marla took us to a place on the Plaza."

"What kind of place is the Plaza?" Lance visualized some nightclubs where Lisa would have danced. Some jerk holding her who didn't even know who she was or how special she is. *She probably had so much fun that I would have been the last thing on her mind.*

Lance was getting anxious. If she was with Marla, they had been drinking. *Drinking gives false courage. Did something happen? Did that jerk she was dancing with buy her a bunch of drinks and want to take her home? Or worse, to his place??*

"It's neat. Only a few miles from my parent's home and it has a bunch of restaurants, shops, and, you know, night life.

"This might surprise you, but I didn't feel like being out. I enjoyed being with you so much last weekend, it wasn't much fun. I asked J.C. to give me a ride home. He said, 'Lisa. It's only nine o'clock!' But he's a friend. He brought me home, then I watched a movie by myself."

Lance danced. He looked around the corner. If Dad or Greg saw him, they would wonder what the heck was wrong with him and if they found out he was talking to Lisa, the harassment would be unmerciful. His voice helped him out. It tried to sound mature. "What movie did you watch?"

"A chick flick. *Steel Magnolias.*"

"My mom loves that movie. It's the one with Julia Roberts and Sally Fields, right?"

"My Mom loves it, too. I watched it with her when she first bought the tape. It's sad, but I enjoy it. What else did you do on your trip?"

"Not much, the usual stuff."

Lance held back. Melvin's situation was dead. No one else needed to know, not even Lisa.

"I really liked my host, Jay Buxton. He's their starting point guard and his girlfriend was real nice too. On Friday, Jay took me to the Beta house. My Dad was a Beta so that was kind of neat. I saw the Horseshoe and the Schottenstein Center, where the Buckeyes play hoops. How'd the football stadium look on television?"

"That's a lot of people in one place. Looked different than a Jayhawks game. Wish I'd have seen you. You weren't the one with no shirt and the lettering on your chest, were you? Maybe I did see you."

"No. You'd have been able to pick me out. I was wearing the same blue sweater you told me to wear in Lawrence."

"I liked that sweater. It was so soft . . . Lance, I'd better go. Have some studying and my first class is at nine in the morning. You'll call J.C., right?"

"You bet. Thanks for the e-mails. Great talking to you."

"Wait. You still have my apartment number and cell phone number? Please call me this week to let me know what J.C. says."

"I will. I'm looking right at them."

Lisa called out both numbers, then she had him recite her home telephone number as good measure.

"Guess I'll talk to ya later," Lance quivered. He felt a strange sensation. It was that missing puzzle piece feeling again. Speaking to her, the piece locked firmer into place. "Good night."

"Good night, Lance."

Sliding back in the kitchen chair, he folded his arms over the top of his head and breathed deeply. Happiness surged through his body. After a minute, he got up, and with rapid strides returned to his room so he could look up Burbridge's phone number.

A voice so pleasant any church choir would adore having it as a soloist answered. "Burbridge's."

"Mrs. Burbridge?"

"Yes, may I help you?"

"Mrs. Burbridge, this is Lance Stoler, from Kentucky."

"Lord's sake, it's good to hear your voice, Lance. How you doing?"

"Fine."

"How's your Momma and Daddy?"

"They're doing great. Thanks for asking. How about you?"

"Honey, I'm doing well." She stopped. Lance could hear her take a deep breath. "It's J.C." Her voice trembled. "Let me get him for you. He was hoping you'd call."

Lance sat waiting with dread in the stillness of his mother's kitchen. He nervously ran his hand over a cupboard door. The counter tops were spotlessly clean. Nana must have treated Greg and Cherie to biscuits and gravy before church since a pan of leftover biscuits sat invitingly on the stove. Fresh flowers from the garden brightened the corner by the sink and the pictures on the refrigerator door exhibited a variety of family photos, but mostly of a playful black lab and the parents' three kids. A calendar, opened to the month of October, was held in place by two red clothespin magnets Cherie had proudly made in kindergarten.

There was silence. Lance breathed deeply, not knowing what lay ahead.

A voice interrupted the silence. "Lance, how you doing?"

"How **you** dooing?" Their routine had begun.

"No, How **you** doooing?"

Both friends shared a little chuckle, then Lance got serious.

"Had a good visit with the Buckeyes, but when I got back Lisa said I should give you a call. What's up?"

J.C. seemed to gather himself and coughed. "So you and Lisa are talking on the phone together now, not just e-mailing?"

"How'd you know about the e-mailing?"

"I've got my private eyes I employ, My Man."

"Well." Lance figured he could get back to J.C.'s curiosity about Lisa. "That's not as important as telling me what's wrong."

"It's the car." J.C. spoke like he was trapped.

"What do you mean?" Different scenarios raced through Lance's mind.

"Don't tell me you don't know what I mean. I saw the look on your face. The questions."

"Give me a break." Lance raised his voice just enough that J.C. easily knew that Lance wasn't arguing -- just right. "I did wonder. A black Escalade?" His voice mellowed, alerting J.C. that a friend was speaking. "How many high school seniors have wheels like that?"

"You should've seen the heads turn, Man." J.C. sighed. "We never had anything so nice. Remember, it's legit. Mom feels so, too."

Lance didn't try to stop his rationalizing.

"She don't quite understand how Mr. Graham made it happen. Me neither."

"I hear ya, Man."

"Sam Wilson's situation gave me a wake-up call. Scared the crap out of me." his words sounded like raw emotions. "NCAA problems. Don't want any. Can't have any. Give me a great senior year and then I go and get my college education." Now, the Kansas City voice rose. "Listen Kentucky, my family needs me not to screw up." He sniffled, "Want my degree." Lance could tell he was trying to control himself, willing his voice to be lighthearted. "It'll come in handy when I've played, say, twelve years in the NBA."

"Listen, I'll get my degree in four years, not five like you, and I'll be signing a five year contract extension with the Boston Celtics when you retire after your twelfth season," Lance couldn't sustain any joyfulness. "Seriously, what are your options?"

"That's why I wanted to talk to you. You know me. You understand me. I haven't talked to anyone about this except my mom. What should I do, Man?"

"Does Booth know you feel this way?"

"He's hard to figure out. Never said anything. Never given me any advice."

"Consider this. Keep the car and continue to feel like ya do. Or, give it back and hope for the best. Better yet, how about talking to someone who knows and understands this stuff?"

"Like who?"

Lance had been talking from the gut and hadn't prepared for this type of conversation. He slid down semi-horizontally in the chair. Searching his brain like a computer, he kept producing a blank page. Nothing. No names. No suggestions.

"Hey, you still there, Man? You didn't fall asleep on me, did you?"

"No, I'm here." Lance reported. "Just thinking."

"Man, there has got to be someone." J.C. sounded desperate.

The computer connected. "What about Mr. Henderson, the Athletic Director? Remember when we met him in his office?"

"Yeah."

"Why not see him?" Lance thought for a second about his idea. "I liked him. Seemed solid. He'd be a good one to bounce this off of."

"He's always nice when I talk with him." J.C. seemed to warm up to the suggestion "How . . . how do I do that?"

"Dayle. Call Dayle. You know, the lady we met in his office Ask her for a time to meet him. Bet he'll have you into his office right away."

"I'll call her tomorrow." Enthusiasm seeped back in Burbridge's voice.

"Great. You do that."

"I will, Man."

"Your mom have any other ideas?" Lance was still searching for the best things to help.

"I love Mom and she would do anything to help me, but she's not been schooled in this stuff... got real scared when I told her the car might not be totally legal. She was really relieved when I told her I'd ask you for help."

Lance measured that as a tall compliment. "Well, we're not veterans in these things by any means, but who knows? Maybe this'll work."

"I sure hope so."

"Call me and let me know what happens. Hey Man," Lance paused, "Proud of you."

"Shoot." J.C. sniffled again. "You're the first, you know, real friend I've ever had."

"Forget it," Lance was touched. "You make it easy."

There was another lumbering silence before J.C. went on. "Be nice if... if we get to play ball together."

Lance was going to Lexington on Friday, but still he let his heart answer. "Sure would. It sure would."

The phone clicked. Lance slid down in his chair again. After a moment, he bent over and leaned on the table, elbows squarely planted for support. Someone coming in the back door would be staring at the top of his crew cut. His eyes were closed. It soothed him to ask Jesus to set a pick for his friend.

Pushing his chair back, he was about to get up when Helen walked through the hallway door.

"Hey there. Finally got you some clean clothes." Helen placed her hand on Lance's shoulder. "Who were you talking to?"

Having made both phone calls, it was now easier to share. "Remember me talking about the girl I met in Lawrence?"

Helen smiled. "Moms remember things like that."

"Well, she e-mailed me. Said I should call J.C. So I called her first."

"And?" She picked up 'her' was spoken with a degree of affection. "Is something wrong, Honey?"

"Lisa -- she's the girl from Lawrence -- Lisa said that J.C. had a problem with his car.

"The Cadillac?"

"Hard to forget an Escalade. So I called him. Neither he nor his mom knows the complete financing behind it. My guess is they were rationalizing that the man Mrs. Burbridge works for got them a good deal. Mom, he's a good kid. Says the car's legit."

"Laaance." She drew out his name as if he were three again, in need of a reprimand. "You don't even have a car."

"I know. I know. He hasn't felt comfortable about the car, although he loves it. Who wouldn't? But deep down something's fishy."

"So, what's he going to do?"

"He's calling Dayle, that's the lady in the AD's office. Remember, I said you'd really like her?"

"I remember your telling me about her."

"She'll get him an appointment with the athletic director. He'll ask the director to help. Make sure he does the right thing."

"Don't know how you two guys came up with that idea, but I'm proud of both of you. It seems like a good plan." Helen placed her lips on her son's forehead and gave him a mother's kiss. Nothing else was said.

Later, in their bedroom Milt would have normally been reading, but was exhausted from his computer work and had already conveniently tucked himself in. Helen turned off the light and quietly slipped under the sheets. In the dark, she reached for her husband's hand and told him about the conversation with Lance. He squeezed her hand three times, their signal for "I love you." Helen squeezed back twice, "Me too."

Chapter 23

Monday morning Lance was up early, sitting on the edge of his bed, tying his favorite Nikes, when he heard a light knock. Milt pushed the door wide open and propped himself against the frame.

"Your mom told me about the phone calls last night. J.C.'s doing the right thing. I think you're accurate about him. I deal with all types of kids in my job. He is showing some real courage."

"Thanks, Dad."

"I'm proud of you." Milt finished knotting his tie. The look on his face made it perfectly clear to anyone seeing him at that moment that he was filled with pride.

After breakfast, Lance and Greg meandered down the street towards school. In front of the Hallmark residence they heard, "Good morning, Boys." The lady of the house was sitting on her front yard bench. She set down the flowers she was trimming. "Hi, Greg."

"Told you the first one was for you," Greg quickly called back to the normally reserved lady.

A robin chirped in the tree above, then suddenly flew off. A weak breeze was slowly pushing a layer of milky clouds across the sky. A brief break in their coverage occurred, allowing several beams of sunshine to escape through. They bounced off the brothers' shoulders. "Hey Boy, I bet Ms. Hallmark thinks we're two knights, heading out to do the king's work."

"Yeah. Right." Greg lifted his eyebrows, rejecting his brother's stab at humor.

"By the way, Sir Gregory, what was that all about? How did she know your name?"

"Don't know. Last Friday when I walked by, she said, "Hi, Greg Stoler." I said, "Good mornin'," and told her about Friday's game. Said you were out of town. Promised my first touchdown pass was for her."

Lance recalled he had told her Greg's name last week. He was pleased she had remembered. "Do you think she would have said something if you hadn't thrown a touchdown pass?"

The boys shared a laugh and trotted on to school. The gang was waiting on the steps. Terry and Dale started asking about the Ohio State babes. Bruce wanted to know about the football game, especially the Horseshoe. Lance told of his adventures, enthusiastically holding the eager ear of each friend. He easily could have been Mark Twain spouting about Tom and Huck, rather than a plain Kentucky boy telling stories about, "them Buckeyes".

"So the Beta house was loaded with babes?" Terry grinned mischievously.

" 'Suspect so, Terry, but Jay and I had to go to the Varsity Club. Never got an official count."

Not one word was mentioned about Melvin's episode. Lance was staying the course. The incident was buried, where it belonged. He doubted that anything had changed. No big, feisty, jealous Ohio State linebacker was going to speak about it. He still had to be thoroughly embarrassed. A kid from Kentucky, a basketball player for gosh sake, flat-out got the best of him.

As expected, at the beginning of third period, Coach Hunter walked into the study hall. Mr. Harley, the study hall teacher, gave him the "OK, you can take him" sign, and Coach Hunter walked back to Lance.

"How's my shooting guard doing? The rest of the boys missed you at their running exercise on Saturday." Coach loved to run his players. Said he always wanted to have the best-conditioned team on the court.

"Sorry, Coach, I was eating donuts in the Ohio State basketball arena at that time. Was that OK?" Lance joked back. "Greg and I ran last night, right after I got home. I know the drill."

"Good," Hunter barked. "You know that brother of yours should give up that pansy sport and concentrate on basketball." Coach was evidently in a good mood this morning. "What you got going? Come on down to the office. Let me get the update."

Hunter didn't want to be left out of the loop. Kansas would be calling, Ohio State would be calling, and Kentucky had already made it clear, it was not an option for them to lose the Stoler kid.

"I'm all caught up." Lance picked up his books.

The head coach and the young senior walked easily in each other's company. Lance had traveled down this hallway thousands of times. Today, he seemed to be in slow motion, noticing everything, as if it were his last walk. The green lockers, dim ceiling lights, worn gray paint on the interior walls. The only sound was the rhythmic clicking of their heels. A hint of ammonia still lingered from the nightly floor scrubbing.

Akers High School was the pride of the county when it was opened, but now, the wear and tear of time and neglect was capturing its distinction. Recent school budgets had put delays in even routine maintenance. Nonetheless, the halls were precious to Lance. They oozed warmth and fond memories. For over three years, he had walked them, kissed a few girls in them, and participated in some pranks he sure couldn't embellish at home. Last spring, on his way to a rally before the state championships he marched these identical steps.

At the rally, Coach Hunter had wanted his All-Stater, Chet Johnson, to speak for the team. Hunter did not understand that Big Chet was too nervous to speak in front of the whole student body. Chet grabbed Lance before they walked through the gym doors and said, "Lance, you gotta do it. You gotta do it."

"Gotta do what? What are you talking about?"

"Can't speak. I'll mess up. Stutter or something. Right in front of all of them. They'll laugh all night at me."

"Nobody's going to laugh at you, Chet. You're the MVP of the team."

"They will. Man, I tell ya they will." His voice squeaked as his forehead developed one new bead of sweat for each urgent word he spoke.

They would be on the stage in less than two minutes. "OK, OK," Lance complained. His brain knew better than to whine. It started to improvise. He conjectured a plan. *No time for permission from Coach Hunter. If I screw up, I'll ask for forgiveness later.*

"Chet, listen up." Lance rushed his words. "Get up there and just say, 'We're going to beat 'em. You watch, we're going to beat'em.' Tell them you've asked me to tell them something." Lance thought for another second and said, "Then, say 'Go Bears'. And sit down."

He looked into his big center's eyes and asked, "You got it? You got it? Can you do that?"

"I can."

His teammate's color returned. They entered the gym. For two seasons, Lance and Chet had never let the Connsburg fans down on this home court.

During that time, every visiting team started the bus early and most visiting coaches probably moaned all the way home.

The pep band lit up the crowd and the students were going wild. Cheerleaders led a few "Go Bears" cheers and Coach Hunter introduced All-State Chet Johnson. Chet got up, looked at his fellow students, and said, "We are going to beat 'em. You watch, we are going to beat 'em. I've asked Lance to tell ya' something . . . and, oh yeah, Go Bears."

Chet sat down with a thump as Lance approached the podium. Lance coached himself. *This should be fine. I've had all of two minutes to prepare.*

He took a deep breath, looked at the cheerleaders, looked at the pep band, and looked into the crowd. Standing in the far doorway was the principal. The principal was holding out his right hand and his fist was closed and cocked with the thumb up, giving his son all the encouragement he needed.

"How bout those Green Bears?" he yelled. "I said how bout those Green Bears?"

The Bleachers erupted with screams. Hundreds of feet stomped up and down.

"We've got the best coach in the State of Kentucky. Coach Hunter!"

Lance attempted to continue, but no one heard him. He waited, winked at Wanda, who had positioned herself in the first row, then tried again. "You're the best fans. We won't let you down. Get ready to bring a trophy back to Connsburg. Go Bears." Lance needed to say no more. The crowd went bananas again as he sat down and Coach Hunter took over the show.

Lance and Hunter arrived at their destination. "Have a seat."

"Sure, Coach."

"Well, how'd those Buckeyes treat you? Coach Meadors sure is a nice guy, isn't he?"

"He's great. Super trip. Just like Kansas, the people were all very kind. Really liked the basketball arena."

"I've seen the Schottenstein Center on television," Hunter said. "Looks big."

"Has a bunch of ritzy suites, too," Lance added.

"Ya think Ohio State's really interested in you?"

"They made it pretty clear. Said they needed me. They aren't like Kansas or UK. They've been good in basketball, but football is their trump suit. Coaches said they wanted me to help them get hoops going again. Said I could make a difference."

Hunter gave Lance a hard glare as if to say, "Oh shoot, this kid liked the Buckeyes. I knew Meadors was good, but this is a Kentucky boy, and we're not goin' to lose him to some other sorry state."

He composed himself before his lips finally moved. "Well, Lance, that's good to hear. I like those coaches."

"Me too."

"But you're visiting Kentucky this weekend, aren't you Son? What a tradition. You've been in Rupp, and that place was awful good to us last spring. If you haven't screwed up your three-point shooting, might be good to us again." Coach's sudden smile exposed coffee-stained teeth.

"I love Kentucky." Lance searched for the right words, knowing his coach's deep affection for the University and their basketball program. "Coach Jones has been very nice to our family. He's maintained the Wildcats as one of the top programs in the nation. And of course his devotion to beating Louisville has made a few Stolers mighty happy."

"Good." Hunter leaned back in his chair. He seemed to relax. "Then you haven't made up your mind yet."

"No way. But I'm still determined to commit during the early signing." Lance showed more boldness than usual. "Don't want recruiting to mess up our repeat."

"I like your team attitude, always have. Early signing is the second Wednesday in November. We're getting close."

"Couple of weeks." Lance didn't want the comment about his shot to go unchallenged. "You want to go in the gym right now? I'll relieve any bad feelings you've got about my three pointer. By the way, Dad says even he could coach our team back to Rupp." Lance displayed his best *gotcha* smile.

Milt Stoler and Dick Hunter were best of friends. "Your dad wouldn't say that." He looked like a hurt puppy, but quickly regained his composure. "Get your butt to class, before I decide to make you run extra tonight. Don't forget, practice is at six . . . There's a volleyball game at four."

After school Lance was glad to find his dog waiting for him at home. "Hey Bubba, you have a good day?" he patted the black lab, feeling the warmth of his soft pelt. "I bet you need some more water. Let's check it out."

He watched as Bubba soaked up the liquid with his long red tongue, his tail wagging back and forth in delight. Lance threw his arms around the dog's neck, then held him close feeling his strong heartbeats. Lance couldn't imagine loving another dog more.

He threw his books on the kitchen table then made his favorite sandwich. Peanut butter and strawberry jelly oozed between two fresh pieces of whole wheat bread. Contentment happened quickly. He wiped off the table and gazed out the back window. His intentions were to hop right into his homework, but another idea was more appealing.

Dear Lisa,

I talked with J.C. last night. He's going to talk to the athletic director about the car. Let's hope everything turns out OK. Did you have a good day in school? I sure would like to talk to you about my next visit, if that's OK. Just let me know when I should call. Thanks for caring about J.C., as much as I do.

As ever,

Lance

Lance leaned back in the chair as he re-read the letter. It would serve the purpose. He clicked on *spell-check*. It needed to be perfect, when beautiful greenish-brown eyes found his message waiting.

Bubba and Lance were masters of the Stoler house for at least another hour before Helen came home. Greg and Cherie had practice. Milt, no doubt, would be dealing with school problems until six. He considered running back over to school to watch the volleyball game. Two weeks ago, it would have been a no brainier. Wanda Akers was one of their star players.

He was dancing with change. Lance and Wanda had been an item, on and off, since grade school. She was considered one of the best-looking girls in the county. That's high praise, since Floyd County girls have a reputation for being unusually beautiful. Her grandad, Wincie Allen Akers, was the person for whom the high school had been named. Thinking of Wanda did not move him to the door. His homework tried hard to get his attention, make him feel guilty. It faired no better than the volleyball game. More than anything, he needed solitude. He needed to reflect.

The house was empty, but Lance could have sworn he heard something calling from the back porch. It was a whisper, "I'm here if you need me." He changed into his favorite Green Bears tee shirt and quietly followed the whisper.

The hardwood floor in the hallway creaked as feet met the cool surface. Late October weather in the hills wasn't the perfect condition for bare feet, but his size twelves prized themselves on being confined by nothing except pure air penetrating their most sensitive spots.

He stepped onto the porch and eased into the swing. Was this the source of the whisper? His thoughts soon drifted off. Where would he go to school? Kentucky? Ohio State? Kansas? *Where do I belong?*

As he pushed slowly, the swing picked up pace. His mind shifted. He thought of Lisa. Had she read his e-mail yet? *No, it's only been a few minutes.* The fact that he was content on the swing and not watching Wanda play volleyball was interesting.

In a perfect cradle he leaned back, moving with the swing's rhythm. Sparrows flew into Greg's oak tree. The smell of a neighbor's burning leaves blew gently through the late afternoon air. His hand embraced the swing's chain while toes continued to push effortlessly. The comforting motion had just begun to work its magic when Bubba appeared, staring amiably at his friend. Lance bent over to gently stroke his back. Bubba perched on the edge of the porch, head over his paws piercing Lance with tender, soulful eyes.

"You're a good friend, Boy."

Lance looked up into the hills. They gave him a sense of security. Moving leisurely back and forth, memories of the swing began to voyage through his mind. This hanging seat was where Lance sat with friends gazing at the hills, talking about nothin', giggling about somethin'. More than a few of those friends were -- girl friends. When he thought no one was looking, he had even kissed a few -- one was Wanda Akers.

Helen loved the swing. She had insisted Milt install it, explaining, "Front porch swings are more for company. Here it would provide a spot for solitude, for private dreaming." This is where the family found her on warm afternoons, sitting with a glass of iced tea, Bubba contentedly at her feet as she read a magazine, or planned a new lesson. Often, she would just sit aimlessly. After a few precious moments of gentle swaying, tension or grief usually searched for a new home.

Uncle Gary regularly occupied the swing on his trips to Connsburg. Lance loved sitting here with Greg and his uncle, talking about any subject that entered their minds, but mostly sports. This is where he fostered his affection for the Cincinnati Bengals and he was led to firmly believe Paul Brown was nothing short of "a great football man."

Gary would say, "Forget about those guys playing basketball today. Bob Cousy was the best point guard ever." Lance and Greg would always smile in agreement although they knew little about Cousy. Baseball was never left out. Especially Joe Morgan. "Best second baseman the game ever saw," Gary would boast. And, yes, if people wanted to watch real college football, "They had to visit The Ohio State University. The Horseshoe. Amen."

Sundays provided special memories on the back porch swing. After church, Lance and Greg would share the swing leisurely reading the newspaper, sports pages of course. From this prime location, kitchen aromas always played tantalizing games with their appetites while they waited impatiently to be called to the dinner table.

Evening found the swing a peaceful oasis. No Stoler was a stranger to this refuge. Each might stop for a few minutes reflecting on the week past, speculating on what the next might have in store. It was always inviting, and, when used properly, it was a master at swinging away problems.

Lance remembered sitting with Grandad on the farm's front porch swing, talking about loose teeth that would soon fall out, his next math test, an upcoming game, his current girlfriend, or secretly planning to raid Nana's kitchen for another piece of apple butter stack cake. He cherished the recollection of a big hand slipping candy into his tiny palm, then looking up to see a little wink coming from the corner of the carpenter's eye, as if to say, "Now this is between the two of us. Your Nana doesn't need to know."

His memory wandered all the way back to his fifth birthday. How high that basket was. How small his hands. How loving and powerful were Hoover's.

His mind was slowly drifting to a new thought when Bubba barked casually at a movement in the back yard. The lab seemed to be saying, "Beat it. My friend's thinking."

Lance looked again at the oak tree and thought of Greg. Friday was a big game for him. A win in the Green Bears' last regular season football game would propel them into the state playoffs. He wasn't sure if Greg as a sophomore could lead them to the finals, but in his mind it was a foregone conclusion that his brother would before he graduated. Football aside, Greg was the best brother a boy could hope for.

Cherie. A sense of guilt enveloped Lance. With everything else going on, he hadn't thought about his baby sister. He loved Greg, but had felt protective of Cherie from the moment his mom laid her in his arms when she was brought home from the hospital. Watching her totally absorbed in a soccer match was a treasure. She would do well in basketball, too. Her grades consistently proved without a doubt she was the brightest of the Stoler kids.

He worried about J.C.'s situation. *Had he arranged his appointment with Mr. Henderson? Would his friend be in trouble with the NCAA? Why had Booth not done something?* A car pulling into the driveway diverted his attention. He suspected it was his mom.

"Anybody home?" A soft voice questioned with a hint of tiredness.

There was no debating who came first in the family dog's life. Bubba shot like a slingshot to the back door, anxiously awaiting a hug from the queen of the house.

"Hi, Mom. I'm out here," Lance called.

Helen walked to the back door and peered out at Lance, still slowly swinging back and forth.

"Everything OK, Honey?"

"Sure Mom, just thinking." He talked to the porch ceiling, head leaning back. "Don't have practice until six."

Helen turned towards the kitchen. She slipped into the bathroom and wiped her face and hands, then added a spray of White Shoulders, the scent of choice for many Kentucky ladies. Normally, she would have started dinner, but Helen appeared to also hear a whisper.

Joining Lance, she stroked her hand lightly across his back, then softly massaged his neck. Her hands felt good to Lance, but it also seemed to help relieve some of Helen's tension built up from caring for energetic first graders all day.

"I love this swing. If I could, I'd sit here all day." Helen squeezed his neck one more time and gazed towards her garden, and then into the hills. "How was your day?"

"Everybody keeps asking me where I'm going. I smile back and just tell them to stay tuned. We'll know in November."

"Kansas, Ohio State, Kentucky. You sure didn't make it easy on yourself. They're all good schools. I think a degree from any one of the three would be extremely valuable."

"Mom...Where do you think I should go?"

"It's not my choice, Honey. You're going to Lexington this weekend, so why worry over the decision today?" Helen watched in delight as a cardinal flew away from the oak tree towards the river. "When you come home, you'll have a week to figure it all out."

"Biggest decision I'll ever have to make."

"I don't know about that. You might find one bigger later on." Helen placed her hand on one of the white planks, hesitated, gathered herself, and spoke. "I do know that if you put your faith in the Lord he'll show you some light. He'll pick you up, right off this swing, and carry you wherever you are supposed to land. Do you remember the words from 'Footprints' hanging in your Dad's office?"

"Kind of, not all of them."

"The last paragraph goes something like this." Helen repeated the words. "The Lord replied, my precious child, I love you and would never leave you. During your times of trial and suffering, when you see only one set of footprints, it was then that I carried you."

She shifted her weight on the swing before going on. "Lance, use the power of your faith. You'll do just fine."

"Thanks," Lance said, cherishing the love he saw in his mom's caring eyes. "When He picks me up." He stopped for a moment. A tiny smile gathered on his face, "You suspect the Lord might wear a school jersey or something to give me a clue?"

Helen tried not to smile. "No, Son. Sorry," she consoled. "But the angel with him, she'll be sporting a mighty fine 'Go Cats' hat."

Helen's hand made a few pleasant swirls on her son's back, then embraced him gently. "Guess I better go fix this family something to eat."

"What are we having?"

"How's baked pork chops sound to you? I set them in the fridge to defrost this morning. There's a dozen. Should be enough."

They both got up. Helen stopped at the kitchen sink and Lance prepared to change for practice. What if Lisa had been on her computer and saw his e-mail?

Click, click.

There it was. Lisa had already e-mailed him back. He read eagerly.

Lance,

Thanks for getting back to me. I am thankful you talked to J.C. Are you sure everything will be all right? I have a class at six. You could call me after nine. I'll be in the apartment.

Yours truly,

Lisa

"'Yours truly. Yours truly'. She keeps using 'Yours Truly'. Yes, sir. I think she likes me. I'll call her at nine sharp."

He pulled on his sweatshirt, clutched his jacket, and bounced down the hallway into the kitchen. He kissed his mom on the back of the head and leaped out the back door. "See you after practice!"

Helen was breading the last of the pork chops, her hands covered with crumbs. She rubbed her nose with a shoulder to relieve an itch. "Have fun, I love you!"

She couldn't help but notice the glow on her son's face and the extra bounce in his step. Must have been an easy night of homework, she guessed.

Chapter 24

Basketball conditioning went on forever. Lance could only think of getting home, devouring a few pork chops, and calling Lisa.

It was past eight when Bubba greeted him at the door. The dog was looking more than happy, and it wasn't because Lance was home.

"Hi, Boy. You get a few of those pork chop bones? Did you?"

He opened the fridge door. To his delight, three prime chops were waiting.

Helen had already set a place for him at the kitchen table. "I'll put these potatoes into the microwave," she said as he grabbed the milk. "The pot of beans is still warm on the stove."

"That'll be great."

Lance poured himself a big glass of milk and sat down at the table. He had forty minutes to eat, take a shower, and get ready for his Kansas call. Two bites into the first chop, Greg strolled into the kitchen.

"You guys have a good workout?" he asked.

"You know Hunter. That guy loves to run us."

"Wait till you see this new play we put in for Friday's game." Greg was excited.

"What is it?"

Greg bent over with his hands down, as if taking a snap from center. "I hand the ball off to the tailback. He hands if off to the wide receiver on a reverse. Well, what looks like a reverse. I run a banana route into the left flat. I'm wide open. Touchdown!" Greg ended up in the utility room for the touchdown.

"Excuse me. You caught the ball?" Lance said with a brotherly smile.

"Yeah, I caught it." Greg rubbed the top of Lance's head. "Oh by the way, some guy named Burbridge called."

"You know that was J.C. Burbridge? How long ago did he call?" Lance's face tightened. His voice became demanding. "What did he say?"

"Easy, man. Cherie wasn't home yet. I'm only the backup receptionist." Greg voice was sharp at first, but softened. "Seemed to be fine. Said he would be out until about nine. He wanted you to call. Something about an appointment he has."

"I'm sorry." Lance apologized for snarling at Cherie's replacement. "I talked to him last night and he has a sensitive situation going on."

"You mean the car?"

Lance nodded a yes.

"Will he get in trouble?"

"I pray not, but don't know for sure."

Greg grabbed a glass of water and returned to his room. Lance cleared off the table. His mind became completely occupied with a calling strategy. *I'll call J.C. first, then I can give Lisa a complete update. Yes, that's the best plan.*

Milt was working on the computer when Lance finished his shower. "Got any good e-mails, Dad?'

"I'm not convinced if e-mail is all that good. People can send e-mails and say what they want to without any conscience. I get them from teachers, parents, students, and even some locals who think they know heaps more about education than I do. And they aren't a bit bashful about telling me so."

"You answer all of them?"

"Every one of them," Milt grumbled. "Some get a quick, easy response. Nothing complicated. If they take the time to contact me, I want them to know I care. That's part of my job." Milt spoke as if he wanted his son to know that he took his work seriously and wanted to do a good job. "The trick is to listen, then turn around and do what is right. People want to be heard. You might not do what they suggest, but they get more ticked off if they think you won't listen to them."

"Got an easy one for you, Dad. Can I make another long distance phone call?"

"You mean like the kind to Kansas?"

Lance hesitated for a moment. "Yeah, to Kansas."

"You falling in love on me, Boy?" Milt teased.

"No-oo." It was a long no. One that tried to deny.

"Did you call last night?" Milt asked his question like an attorney who knew the witness was hiding something.

"Yes sir."

"You want to call tonight?"

"Yes sir."

"Interesting." Milt's full attention was now on his son.

"Dad, it's not what you think. I talked to J.C. and Lisa last night. J.C. called when I was at practice today and asked if I'd give him a ring. Need to give Lisa a call because she e-mailed, saying she needed to talk. Something's going on out there."

It was convenient for Lance to leave out that he had e-mailed Lisa and asked to call her, and how much he really wanted to call her, but he could not bring himself to explain all this to his dad. Not yet. How could he explain to his dad that whenever he thought about holding Lisa he heated up inside and craved to hear her voice on the phone? For right now, he would shelter his emotions.

"Now I'm in a tough spot," Milt declared to his son.

"It's just a couple of phone calls."

"It's not the phone calls. It's your Nana I'm worried about. She finds out I'm an accomplice to your becoming a Jayhawk, you know what happens to me?"

"Dad," Lance grinned. "I'll testify you had nothing to do with it. Besides, I visit Kentucky this weekend and I never said I was going to Kansas. Yet."

"No, but I know you really like Burbridge. And this blonde girl must be something."

"Daaad," was the only thing Lance could say.

"Make your call. But I'm keeping the phone bills. You go to Kansas, I'm going to make you reimburse me for all the calls to Dorothy and the Scarecrow. Now, get out of here." He lovingly waved his hand. "Let me do some work."

Using the phone in the kitchen, Lance leaned on the counter as he dialed the Burbridge's number and let it ring.

No answer.

Lanced waited a minute then hit the redial button.

No answer. "Come on, where are you?" he muttered.

Lance pushed the redial button. After what seemed like an eternity, he heard a winded voice. "Hello?"

"Where you been, Man?"

"Hey, just ran in the door. Had conditioning practice tonight. Out here in the wilderness we try to keep in shape." J.C.'s breathing became a little slower. "Got my message?"

"Yeah. What happened?"

"Dayle is awesome. Said she would get me an appointment to see the AD."

"So when are you going?"

"Thursday, right after school. It's set. Four o'clock."

"That's great. Mr. Henderson's got to be the best person to help."

"That thing is sweet. I'll miss it." Lance didn't have to be a genius to know that his friend was referring to the black beauty. "Remember to write one of those in my NBA contract when you become my lawyer."

"Consider it done." Lance answered with pleasure. He could tell his friend was feeling better. Helen's words from the swing came flying back to him. *Maybe that only one set of footprints in the sand stuff really happens.*

"So what's up with you and Lisa?"

"What do you mean, what's up?" Lance's protective shield engaged. "Nothing is up."

"OK, I can tell you're sensitive. But Marla says you're all Lisa talks about. You must be saying something to her."

Lance didn't want anyone to know what he was feeling. He didn't want his family or even his friend to know about his innermost thoughts. Cherie knew, but it wasn't because Lance had to explain anything to her. He wasn't going to tell J.C. that as soon as he got finished with this conversation, he was making another call.

"We have e-mailed a few times. Nothing serious."

"Fine, don't fill me in. You still visiting Kentucky?"

"Are ya crazy? If I don't, might as well move in with you right now."

"Hey, Mom! We need to make up the extra bed. Lance's moving in."

"You're a piece of work." Lance chuckled. "Next week, you know I'll need your help. My visits will be finished. Have to get off the fence."

"You don't want my advice."

"Sure do." Lance said earnestly. J.C.'s opinion was extremely important to him.

"You know where I want you to go. We know where your parents want you to go."

"Wait a minute. They're letting me make the decision."

"OK, but what about that coach of yours? What's his name?"

"Hunter."

"How about him? Where's he want you to go?"

"Sorry, Man, I don't think he likes Booth, and he loves the Wildcats."

"Well, is KU hanging in there?'

"Come on. You know they are."

"It's getting late. We have homework out here. Something you Kentucky boys haven't heard of." It was easy for Lance to take a little ribbing. The cheer returning to his friend's voice was worth it. "Have a good week. I'll say 'hi' to Lisa for you when I go over to Lawrence on Thursday."

"Good luck. Tell Ms. Dayle I said hello."

Lance hung up the phone and breathed a few seconds before dialing Lisa's number. He was happy for J.C. and liked what Marla had said about Lisa. Maybe Lisa was having some of the same feelings he was.

"Ring . . . Ring . . . Ring."

No answer. What's going on? Lisa said she would be in her apartment. It's after nine.

"Ring . . . Ring . . . Ring."

"Does she have an answering machine?"

"Ring . . . Ring . . . Ring."

Lance's mind raced. *Why doesn't she have an answering machine? Dang. I stayed on the phone too long with Burbridge. She probably left to go out with Marla, or something. It's only fifteen minutes after nine. Did she give up on me after fifteen minutes? Dang. I should have called Lisa first. I would've told her I was going to call J.C. right after I was finished talking to her. Why didn't I call Lisa first?*

"Ring . . . Ring."

"Hello."

What a sweet voice. Lance forgot his last three minutes of worry. He was just grateful Lisa had answered.

"Hi, Lisa. This is Lance."

"I know."

"You don't have an answering machine?"

"Broke. Last weekend. Have you been trying to call? Marla called from her cell phone about nine and I couldn't get her off the phone. Finally she had another call coming in and I told her to take it." Lisa paused. "I was hoping you might call."

"It was no problem. I just waited."

"Marla. She's a hard one to get off the phone."

"That's OK. If I miss a jump shot, I don't stop shooting. I just kept dialing. It sure is nice to talk to you. Talked to J.C."

"What did he say?"

"Sees Mr. Henderson on Thursday."

"It's real sweet of you to help."

"J.C. has a big heart and he's a good person," Lance responded. "Things will work out for him."

"Good," Lisa said with the speed that clearly revealed she had another matter to discuss. "So you liked Ohio State and now Kentucky's getting its shot. Is Kansas still on the radar screen?"

She questioned him just like J.C.

"You bet. I'm staying the course."

"I guess everyone back there's pushing you to stay home. I mean, go to Kentucky." Sadness slipped into her voice.

Lance committed a turnover, let his guard down, his feelings traveled tenderly through the phone lines. "They haven't visited Kansas like I have. And they didn't meet you."

"That was nice of you to say," Lisa answered warmly. "What'll you do on your visit this weekend?"

"It'll be like the other two," he said. "I meet with the coaches and other university people. Have some good dinners. Not going to complain about having a good steak anywhere. Kentucky plays Mississippi State at home, so we'll go to the game. I love the football games."

"Kansas hasn't been doing much better since you left town. Oklahoma beat us last weekend. Oklahoma's football team must be awfully, awfully good."

"I saw that score. It probably got out of hand early on."

"I didn't see it. It was at Oklahoma. It was on TV, but I didn't watch it. Remember, I watched another game last Saturday? Never watched two football games in one day."

"It's easy. Bet I can teach you how."

"Why do you like football so much? I thought you loved basketball."

"I do. I love basketball very much. But I'll never give up on football. Maybe you would have to catch one of my brother's passes to understand what I mean. Greg will play major college football. The kid is only a sophomore but trust me, he'll have our high school in the state playoffs this year."

"That's great... I trust you," Lisa said softly and with a gentleness that let Lance know she wasn't referring to football. "How's Cherie doing?"

"This is her last week of soccer, then she starts basketball. My sis is going to be the Lisa Gosline of Kentucky girls' basketball." Lance had a boastful quality to his voice.

"Get out of here. She's probably really good." Lisa's laugh revealed some blushing was probably taking place in her apartment, then she asked, "Where does Cherie want you to go to school?"

"Kentucky, of course. But she understands my wanting to look at Ohio State and Kansas. That little squirt seems to always guess what I am feeling." Lance stood up from his chair and looked out the window. "I love my state. I really do. But what makes people move? What made people leave this part of the country and move out West? Daniel Boone is probably one of the biggest heroes of this state. He left and moved to Missouri."

"You got any Boone blood in you?" Lisa laughed. "That would be a good sign."

"Don't think we have any Boone relatives, but it might still be a good sign."

"Indeed."

"How's school?" asked Lance. "Is this a busy week?"

"No exams this week, so that's good. Should do pretty well this semester. The adjustment from high school to college hasn't been too much of a problem for me. I took a lot of college prep courses in high school. How about you? What courses are you taking?"

"I'm taking a lot of college prep courses, too. The NCAA has helped high school athletes plan. They have these things called core curriculum courses you have to take. So many math classes, so many science classes, so many English classes -- you know, stuff like that. I'm over a B average and I did OK on my SATs so I should be ready." He switched the phone to his other ear. "What do you think? Is there something I should try to take so I'm better prepared? Only have half a year. Just half a year away."

"Sounds to me like you're doing just fine. What about a foreign language?"

"Been taking Spanish."

"Me too," Lisa said. "My Dad thinks we can't take enough Spanish. He says look at what is happening in California, Texas, and Florida. I'm taking another Spanish class next semester."

"He's probably right. Your dad seems to be really smart."

Lance didn't want to hang up, but manners told him he had talked long enough. He wanted to ask permission to call her again, but could only come up with saying he liked her e-mails.

"I like getting your e-mails too," Lisa said, not being able to see the joy her words spread on Lance's face. "I study in my bedroom a lot. If you get a chance and could call again, it would be real nice."

"I will, if it's not an inconvenience for you." After the words were out of his mouth, he thought, *Couldn't you come up with something better than that?* He was embarrassed.

"Not at all, Lance." She wiped away his unwarranted humiliation. "You have a nice week."

"You too, Lisa."

He hung up the phone and replayed Lisa's good-bye. When she spoke his name, it sounded extra special. He could picture her perfectly trimmed hair swirling around the phone as she said, "You have a nice week."

Her effect on him was causing some of the dirt to loosen around his Kentucky roots. The one person who would understand had just walked into the kitchen.

"Hey, Big Brother. Who have you been talking with?" Cherie asked.

"J.C. and Lisa."

"And Lisa? This is going to get interesting."

"What do you mean, interesting?"

"Is J.C. all right?" Cherie said nothing about Lisa, apparently to badger her brother.

"He's fine. What do you mean, interesting?"

"Listen to your voice. I'm on your side, remember? I haven't been talking about you-know-who to anyone."

"What about leaking e-mail stuff to Dad? Did you leak anything?"

"You know Dad has to have a little information. He's lord and master of this house, for goodness sake. I only told him you got an e-mail. He doesn't know how serious this is getting."

"It's not getting serious."

"Oh yeah?" She said with determination. "You're lucky Dad and Mom are in their bedroom and Greg is working on some new plays. Do you see what time it is? It's nine forty-five. Dad will have a fit when he gets the phone bill!"

Lance looked up at the clock. Cherie was right. He had been on the phone for almost an hour. Most of that time with Lisa.

"So, I was on the phone for a little bit."

"A little bit, my eye. I've never known you to be on the phone for even ten minutes. Wanda Akers got no more than seven minutes, if that."

"What's your point?" Lance knew when to surrender. Cherie was gifted in the art of sniffing out information. He might as well open up. He liked talking about Lisa, and Cherie was the only one he felt comfortable talking with right now.

"My point is you've got a thing for Lisa," Cherie informed her big brother.

"A thing?! A thing?"

"Yeah a thing."

"Amazing," he said. "Don't know how you do it. So now what do I do, since I have this 'thing'?"

"Well first . . . This is going to be complicated. She lives in Kansas. You're only considering the possibility of living in Kansas."

Lance gawked at her puckered-up face. "What kind of expression is that? You just bite into a lemon?"

"Feeling some pain for you." She told him that she had a dream about him, all dirty and dehydrated, trying to walk to Kansas. "Nobody here would talk to you or even think about giving you a ride when you declared your intention to sign with Kansas. Dad broke down and was going to take you, but then Nana stabbed all four tires of the Tahoe with her Wildcat knife. As you walked along, barefoot -- Mom kept all your Nikes -- your feet were bleeding a little. And Lance," She slowed down for more drama. "You were wearing some old blue sweater and it looked weird because the sun was cranking down hard and you were sweatin' like a pig at a pig roast, but you refused to take off that sweater." She gasped, mockingly. "It was a nightmare."

"Enough. Enough. I got the picture. What do I do?"

"You might as well start praying, Boy."

"Come on, Cherie. Help me. I'm drowning here. What do I do?"

"OK. As I said, this is complicated. Take it one day at a time. If you feel about Lisa like I think you do, then you've got to keep in contact. Daily. Seeing her right now is out of the question. That's what I mean by being complicated. You don't have the money to buy an airplane ticket, plus Mom and Dad won't be buying any of us a car in our lifetimes. You could take the Tahoe, but I suspect the next morning Dad would sort of miss it. Taking Mom's car is not an option. We wouldn't want our sweet little mother having to walk back and forth to school, would we?"

"Whoa. Slow down. Should I be taking notes or something?" he grinned, just happy to talk about Lisa out loud.

"Hey, I'm not charging you for this stuff. Listen up. Keep in contact with her and let things fall into place."

"You're probably right. Makes sense, and I've no better ideas."

"Never know what might happen. Can't you hear Dad saying," Cherie tried her best Milt imitation, "One day at time. Take it one day at a time, and you'll be fine, Boy."

She was right and Lance knew it. "Thanks, Sis. No leaks on this. Even to Dad or Mom, OK?"

"I got your backside." She was radiant.

Staring at the sparkling braces, he thought, She's growing up. When did our roles reverse? She would always toddle to me for advice. Now she's my counselor. Lance pulled Cherie into a well-deserved hug, then ruffled her hair. "Say, when do you start basketball practice?"

"Our last soccer game is Wednesday. I could start practicing on Thursday. Some of the girls not playing soccer or volleyball have already been practicing. What would you do? Can I wait till next week?"

"I would wait till next week. Unless the coaches have a practice on Saturday." Lance laughed. "You might want to keep that practice in the back of your hat just in case Dad wants some leaves raked."

"Yeah. See you got my backside, too." She waved in appreciation as she left the room.

"Always." He meant that with all his heart.

Lance let Bubba out for a few minutes and then as he passed his parents' room, he tapped on the door. He found them sitting in bed reading.

"Just wanted to say good night," he called softly.

"Everything all right?" Milt asked.

Lance hastily discussed the conversation with J.C. but didn't bring up his talk with Lisa. His parents needed their rest and he wasn't ready to share his love life with them. One relative at a time was enough.

"Sounds good, Son. See you in the morning." Milt turned over to shut off his light.

"I'll fill up your mom's Camaro on Thursday so you'll be all set for your trip," he called after Lance.

"Thanks, Dad."

"Good night, Honey," Helen said gently. "Your rowdy friends are going to stop by and read with my rowdy young-uns tomorrow?"

"You bet, Mom. Good night."

Chapter 25

The rest of the week went smoothly in Connsburg. Lance had basketball practice every night while Greg and his coaches were preparing to win the last regular season football game. It continued to disappoint Lance that he'd miss it. The good news was that he would get to watch his brother in the playoffs if they won on Friday, and he had every confidence they would.

Wednesday, Cherie was the pride of the Stoler family when her team won their last game. She had several awesome defensive plays and continued to show signs of becoming a talented player. Keeping her word, she didn't say a peep about Lisa to a soul, not even Bubba.

Helen had a good week in school. Her kids enjoyed the reading visit on Tuesday. Little Nancy, Bruce's neighbor, went home from school crowned with happiness because Mrs. Stoler had allowed her to be in her favorite Big Buddy's group again.

Helen loved her classroom and its occupants, but she loved going home the most. Home was a cherished place. Even in the midst of a complex lesson, a thought about home, her family, or her roots would appear and disappear in a flitter of time. She was on the playground with her kids when a cool breeze swept through her hair. Helen had one of those reflections. She was pleased Cherie had won, was nervous about Greg's game, had an uneasy feeling about her mother, and prayed Lance's visit to the University of Kentucky would be the best ever.

Thursday was a special night. Nana came over for dinner. Once the dishes were put away, the two ladies retired to the back porch swing. They didn't try to solve any world problems, but they did enjoy catching up on a wide range of topics. Lance's future was only one of them. Helen explained she and Milt would go to Greg's game Friday night, then drive over to Lexington the next morning. The big difference with this trip was -- it was The Trip! Lance was visiting their Wildcats. Both women believed UK was the best option of the three. Hands down.

Nana kept the swing moving slowly back and forth, comforting her daughter, assuring Helen she could handle two weekends in a row watching over the house and this time she would guard the refrigerator a little better when Greg's gang snuck in. She didn't tell Helen, but she planned to start baking Friday morning to stock up with more snacks this time. Greg and Cherie had already slipped her their secret wish lists for favorite cookies.

"You sure you're OK, Mom? Anything you need to talk about?"

"I'm fine," Nana answered. Her eyes betrayed her.

"What is it? Tell me."

"Helen, I . . . " They both heard the screen door open. "It's nothing." Nana took advantage of a visitor walking out on the porch. "Hello, Milt."

"What's nothing?" Milt asked.

"I have to get your wife to stop worrying over me." Nana said. "How was your day?"

"I'm just happy to be home tonight." His week had been demanding. Besides the usual problems, a few students needed some extra discipline and a new teacher he had been trying to mentor was still struggling in the classroom. Cherie's win was a big deal to him. By three o'clock on Thursday every secretary, teacher, and staff member knew which team had won and who the star of the game had been. Greg's upcoming game made him a little uptight. He wanted the team to win for three big reasons: his son, the school, and selfishly, he didn't want his visit to Lexington spoiled by a sour taste in his mouth from a Friday night loss.

The Stoler phone rang. Cherie was back on duty. Everyone heard her call, "Lance, it's J.C."

Lance sprinted to the phone. "Thanks," he mouthed to her. Into the phone, he spoke, "What's going on in Kansas City?"

"A bunch." He told Lance everything.

J.C. said he worried about the meeting with the athletic director all week. He made it to Thursday and felt some relief when he saw Dayle Jarrett's smiling face. Mr. Henderson was waiting. After formalities, he explained the whole situation to the director then asked for help. Mr. Henderson listened intently, all the while making him feel relieved for having come forward.

Henderson hoped there was no NCAA violation, but they'd have to investigate and report it to the proper authorities. Speaking directly with the athletic director had made him feel better about turning in the car. "It was uplifting, Man." J.C. said. "And by the way, Dayle said 'hello right back to you' and wanted to know what dorm you wanted to stay in your freshman year."

Lance let that slip by with no comment. He was happy for his friend. The two potential teammates chattered for a few minutes. Lance said he would call next week and they hung up, both in good spirits.

Next he dialed a number now memorized. The phone rang only once. Lance heard the voice he had missed since Monday.

"Hello?"

It was a sweet, sweet sound to his ear.

"Hi. This is Lance. That was quick."

"I remembered your comment about no answering machine." Lisa laughed. "Told Marla not to call, either."

The call lasted for over thirty minutes. It started with joy for their friend J.C., but rapidly moved to talk about the two of them. They agreed he'd call after he returned on Sunday. Lance let Lisa know he planned on wearing the same blue sweater she told him to wear in Lawrence. He had worn it in Columbus, and would in Lexington. Good-byes were now an even bigger obstacle. Each hung up with reluctance.

Lance returned to his room. The phone calls made packing an effortless task and he relished the thought of a weekend in Lexington. He was throwing in the last few things when one reoccurring predicament kept creeping into his thoughts. *Can't be in two places at the same time.* He went to his brother's room.

"Hey, Greg. What are you doing?"

"Getting this geometry assignment done. Didn't I hear you tell Dad you actually like this stuff?"

"Always liked math." Lance leaned against the far wall. "Man, I wish I could be there tomorrow night." Lance dipped his head, clearly letting Greg know he was lamenting. "Big game."

"Don't worry. I'll take care of that business. You just make sure those Wildcats want to give you a scholarship. Besides," Greg's cheeks started to redden, "it's great having a tight-end who can actually get open this year."

Both chuckled.

"My heart'll be with you. Read your keys and keep that tight-end busy." Lance ruffled the top of Greg's head before slowly turning towards the door.

"Hey, Lance," Greg called.

"What?"

"Gonna' beat'em. You'll get to come to the game next Friday."

Lance threw back his head and laughed. "What is it with you quarterbacks? I hope you're right. See you in the morning, little brother."

Lance lay on his back and gazed up at the dark ceiling. Moonlight filtered delicately through the tan shutters covering his bedroom window. The house was wrapped in a blanket of silence except for an occasional cough and wind sporadically pushing against a windowpane. Although he felt content, sleep was not an option. His attention was first drawn to the elegance of Rupp arena then to Lisa, remembering their walk hand-in-hand down Massachusetts Street. He visualized her face, her cute nose. He recalled the smell of her hair as he pulled her close before saying good-bye. Images worked their magic. Sleep became an option and then Lance accepted.

Chapter 26

The oldest son thought he might be the first one up, but found he was second. Helen was already in the kitchen and had made a pot of coffee.

"Good mornin', Lance. This breakfast won't be as good as Nana's last Friday, but I'll try." She seemed determined.

"You don't have to fix a big breakfast. We'll all be fine. They might even feed me over in Lexington."

"Pancakes are easy and the sausage links are almost brown. If you can reach the syrup, I think we'll be in business," she said, setting out the butter.

"Let me see. Aunt Jemima is right here on the pantry shelf. My job's done." He placed the container on the table. "Need me to do anything else?"

"Why don't you check on Bubba? See if he needs anything."

As Lance swung the door open, he could tell it was going to be another gorgeous day in eastern Kentucky. The sun was trying to peek over the surrounding hills. Greg's oak tree, a few of its golden leaves scattered below, was once again hosting sparrows. The back porch swing hung silently from its chain links, the white planks moist with morning dew. A soft breeze brushed Lance's face as he watched Bubba run up onto the porch wagging his tail. His mouth was open and his dark tongue drooped down. Helen had let him go for a run before all the neighbors got up. "Come on. Let's get you some water. If Mom looks the other way, I'll get you a piece of that sausage."

Bubba licked his lips, as if to say, "You the man, Lance. You the man."

Lance stepped back inside, Bubba following right behind.

"Will you set the orange juice out?" Helen asked. "I'll be right back. Got to make sure everyone's getting up. It's a big day. I don't want anyone to start off late."

Bubba looked up at Lance. Big black eyes conveyed the same thing Lance was thinking. *Big mistake. Big mistake. You don't leave two hungry varmints like us alone with the sausage. Someone might just as well leave Butch Cassidy and Sundance alone in a bank.*

"Let's see. One for you and one for me," Lance informed his partner in crime.

Bubba's eyes expressed the need for more and Lance was not willing to stop with one little link himself. The two finished their second take when Helen returned.

"Everything OK?" she asked.

Lance quickly swallowed the sausage so he could answer, "Sure, Mom. Gonna go get dressed."

Lance rushed out, avoiding his arrest and leaving Bubba to face the consequences. Helen could see a little of her breakfast meat was missing. Looking down at her sweetheart, she saw the contented look on Bubba's face.

"You and Lance were up to no good while I was gone, weren't you?"

If Bubba could speak, he still wouldn't have squealed on his partner. He rubbed his head against Helen's long terrycloth bathrobe. Helen placed her hand on the bridge of his dark nose and patted him softly.

"That's why I always cook more than what's needed. You're family. Still plenty to go around."

The five Stolers sat happily around the table teeming with honey glazed, brown sugar sausage, freshly brewed French Vanilla coffee, orange juice, and golden pancakes. Morning sunbeams sneaked through the kitchen window. Helen's family was going to scatter for the weekend, but for the next few minutes she had them all together.

"You packed?" Milt asked of Lance. Everyone knew this was not his last question.

"Yes sir. Third time. Getting this traveling business down to perfection."

"Greg, Cherie, you notice anything about the Camaro?" Milt fired his second question.

Cherie asked, "What do you mean, Dad?"

"It's in one piece. One of you tell your brother to make sure he brings it back from Lexington the same way. Your mom will need it to go to work next week."

"I hear you, Dad. I'll be careful," Lance promised.

"Good. That's what I wanted to hear." Milt turned to Greg. "You sleep all right last night? How's the arm?" Milt served himself another pancake. "Goin' to wear it out tonight?"

"Feels good, Dad," Greg answered. "Hope the weather's OK."

"Radio says it's supposed to be sixty degrees and clear today," Cherie informed the family. "Perfect weather for a football game."

"I thought I broke that thing," Milt said playfully. "You're not listening to the stuff Lance and Greg listen to are you?"

"Milt!" Helen verbally slapped her husband upside the head.

"High of sixty?" Milt turned to Cherie. "That means it'll be cool at kick-off tonight."

"Yep, said sixty will be the high. Dad, you'd like my radio station. They play a little bit of everything. I even heard the Beach Boys on there once or twice."

"Now, that's music." Milt's family loved his smile.

"Lance, the keys are on the counter." Helen said. "Greg, you and your sister are going to have to watch after your Nana again. All right?"

"She seemed to enjoy herself last weekend," Greg said. "One thing I'll do, though." He looked straight at his dad, "Take the phone off the hook! Don't want any calls that cause me to have to rake leaves again."

"It's a shame you feel that way. You're one of the best rakers in Floyd County. If there were a trophy for raking, I'm sure it would sit on our mantel as we speak." Milt spoke with a straight face, eating the last bite of his pancakes. "It looks like the few lying around can wait till next week. You'll have your brother and sister to help you then."

"There is plenty of stuff in the freezer and refrigerator," Helen said to Cherie. "Dad got more milk and pop last night. So none of you will starve."

"Not with Nana around." Cherie served herself another pancake.

"You two saw a good game last week." Greg still wanted to talk football. "How will the Mississippi State game shape up?"

Milt was not bashful about throwing in his ideas. "Kentucky will destroy them."

"It's not a basketball game," Lance watched his dad gesture as if saying, "Oh yeah, that's right."

Milt shot back with a lighter remark. "We all know the big game this weekend is right here in Connsburg. Greg Stoler leads the Green Bears to the playoffs."

"Don't put pressure on your son like that," Helen demanded. She put her arms around Greg, kissing his cheek before clearing his plate. It was time to go.

"It's OK, Mom. I'm excited about the challenge." Greg's face brightened. "Besides if things go south on us, I can start playing that sissy sport with my brother."

The whole family shared laughter as they finished the last bites of their breakfast.

Milt was the first to leave. He took a sip of his coffee, pushed back from the table, said goodbye to his three children, then gave Helen a kiss on her forehead.

"I'll be home about four so we can finish packing and get ready for Greg's game."

Greg was next. He pushed back just like his Dad, and looked at his brother. "Say 'Hi' to Rupp Arena for me. Let that big beauty know the Stoler boys will be back next March."

"Got you covered," Lance said. "Pound that Belfry team tonight. I want to see you play next week."

Chapter 27

Lance's last duty in Connsburg before he shoved off for Lexington was to give the Stoler girls a ride to their schools, a task he was delighted to perform.

"Mom, I'm going to put my suitcase in the trunk. I'll be ready whenever you and Cherie say its time."

"Are you sure you have everything you need?" Helen asked for the umpteenth time.

"I'm all set," he assured her.

Lance cheerfully gave Bubba a pat, hopped up to his room, closed his closet door, and studied the room's orderliness. Grabbing the edge of his bedspread, he squared it off neatly. He wasn't quite sure why he did that, but sensed it would make his mom happy if his room looked a little tidier. Suitcase packed, the blue sweater ceremoniously placed on top, he headed for the driveway.

The Camaro was a fine looking machine. Milt and Helen had owned a used Camaro back in the early seventies. This one was probably purchased to help them remember a time in their youth. Lance loved it. It was Kentucky blue with a T-top roof and had a soft interior that always smelled brand new. When Lance sat in the bucket seats, it gave him the same thrill a new NASCAR driver might feel when starting his first race.

Milt loved driving to school in the spring with the top open, windows down, and the remains of his hair blowing in the wind. Citizens of Connsburg walking on the sidewalks could hear two speakers blasting and Milt singing backup for Brooks and Dunn, Rock *My World, Little Country Girl*. On one occasion, Coach Hunter pulled up beside him at a red light, noticed the fifty-year-old teenager, and told him he'd better take that thing home before he got into trouble.

Lance opened the trunk and threw in his suitcase. The trunk was much smaller than the one in Nana's Buick. *Not much room*. He returned to the house, saw his passengers were ready, and they all headed back to the car.

A twist of Lance's right wrist, and the blue machine purred. The radio blasted an Alan Jackson song. Lance turned down the volume, but didn't change stations. He liked several of Jackson's songs. This one was heaven sent: *When Daddy Let Me Drive*.

As they pulled up in front of Helen's elementary school, Lance remembered it wasn't too long ago when he was a student there. The playground, covered with children, hadn't changed since he had first played on it in kindergarten. Two sets of monkey bars, two sets of swings, and four basketball hoops. He had played there during recess, after school, and on weekends when he and several of his buddies could escape from chores at home for some good old hoops fun. Terry had broken his arm there, Bruce bloodied his nose, and Lance had routinely scuffed both knees and elbows on its hard, unforgiving surface.

The baskets were exceptional. Lance smiled. At least he and his friends thought they were pretty exceptional. White backboards were painted every summer so the orange rims stood out, making easy targets. Metal nets made a harsher sound than the one standing guard above the Stoler driveway. Nonetheless, their clinking sound rewarded many young hoopsters throughout the years. Lance was one of them.

He pulled the Camaro next to the curb and turned to his mom. He was about to get out when Helen spoke.

"Stay there. I'll see you tomorrow. Cherie, see you tonight, Honey." Helen leaned over and placed a kiss on his cheek. "Have a good time, now. And be careful."

"I will. Love you, Mom." Lance looked as happy as Helen had ever seen him. She rested her eyes on him for several seconds before answering.

"I love you, too, Son."

Helen slid out of the car. Lance watched her move away. His mom's perfectly trimmed blonde hair attractively sparkled in the morning sun, as her petite body walked with the light tread of a Cherokee scout. She blew her two children a kiss, and entered the school.

"Let's take the sun panels out," Cherie pleaded.

"Your school's only right down the road."

"I know, but look at that sun. It's going to be a fabulous day."

Lance was about to put the car into drive. *Why not?*

"Ok, let's do it."

Cherie unfastened the one on her side and Lance got his. "Put them in the back seat," Lance ordered. "There isn't enough room in the trunk."

They jumped back into their seats and stared up at the cloudless blue sky. Cherie switched the radio channel to her favorite station and they were soon cruising down the road. The drive lasted but a few minutes, but it was pure bliss for Cherie. Lance pulled up next to the curb at her school and shifted into park.

"You should drop me off at school like this every day."

"Would, if Mom would give me the car." Lance traded smiles with his little sister.

Cherie leaned over and gave her brother a hug. "Enjoy the ride to Lexington. See you Sunday."

"You bet. Have a great weekend, Kid!"

Cherie opened her door and stepped on the sidewalk just as Bobby Lee Johnson appeared out of nowhere. Bobby had told more than one friend that he was working on being the next Lance Stoler of Connsburg basketball. Cherie had a crush on him.

Windows down and the roof wide open, it was easy for Lance to hear the conversation.

"Hi, Cherie. Nice car." Bobby started walking by her side towards the school. "Was that Lance dropping you off?"

Lance watched the two stroll for a little before he shifted into drive. He suspected young Bobby was feeling pretty good being the escort of Miss Cherie Stoler.

The Camaro buzzed through town and headed west. He made no attempt to change radio stations; Cherie's choice was just fine. Near-perfect traveling conditions made it easy for his thoughts to ramble. *Lisa's probably still sleeping. She'll go to class then probably do something with Marla.*

"It sure would be nice if she lost that phony ID. That thing is an accident waiting to happen," Lance said to the open air. "Maybe she'll stay in her room and study all weekend." *Are you stupid, or what?*

She has the right to do what ever she wants. Come on, we only had one weekend. *But what a weekend.*

He nudged his thoughts towards something he knew a lot more about: catching Greg's passes. *Won't be catching one of those spirals tonight.* He made the choice to not play football his senior year. He made the choice to visit in the fall, sign early. Not interfering with the football team or the basketball team's chance to repeat as state champs was a big factor. *Had to. I mean, I had to.*

He started to second guess himself. His imagination wasn't interested in stopping him. It was happy to be an enabler. The windshield became a TV screen. He could see himself running a fifteen yard square in, as he turned, the tight spiral from his brother settled in his hands and Akers High had another first down. The windshield video rolled on. The ball was on Belfry's twenty-yard line. The Green Bears needed a touchdown. Greg first checked the wide receiver on a post route. He was covered. His second read saw the tight end dragging across the middle. Touchdown Akers!

"Oh, I wish I could have my cake and eat it too," the driver mumbled selfishly to himself.

The air was getting cool. He pulled over at a filling station and put the T-top back to its original form. Stepping inside, he purchased a bottle of orange juice, some Fig Newtons and then returned to the Camaro, ready for the rest of his trip.

His focus switched to the Wildcats. The head coach, Lamar Jones, was a classy guy. So were the assistant coaches. He was especially partial to Coach Dave Hudson. He had met Dave during a summer basketball camp. Hudson had worked with him on his form. That instruction led to his personal record best consecutive free throws made.

Kentucky's tradition in basketball could stand toe- to-toe with any in the nation. The Wildcats had been to countless NCAA tournaments. They had taken on all challengers and walked away with several national champion-ships. The coaches throughout their history were an elite class. From Rupp to Jones there had been no letdown. When an opponent showed up on Kentucky's court, they'd better be bringing their "A" game.

He exited the Parkway and followed Route 60 straight into Lexington. This path would lead him right smack dab into the bastion of that tradition -- Rupp Arena. His hotel, the Hyatt, sat next door. It was still early so he had plenty of time to get checked in and relax for a few minutes. Coach Hudson wasn't picking him up until 11:30.

The Camaro approached the parking lot across the street from the hotel. Lance pulled into a spot, locked his mom's car, and headed to the lobby rolling his suitcase after him. *Where is Michael Lee when you need him?* Lance smiled as he thought back to his Kansas visit.

The lobby was decorated with a variety of elegant pictures, pottery filled with vibrant flowers, and furniture begging travelers to take the load off of their feet. He speculated this grand facility had served some mighty interest-ing guests. *Ashley Judd, for sure. She loves Wildcat basketball.*

Ashley was known to attend games regularly. She would sit with the students and "get it on" for the Wildcats. Lance humored himself. Maybe he would get the opportunity to let the actress cheer on his hoops act.

Room 503 was pleasant. He opened the draperies and surveyed Lexington. Recollections crowded his mind. Milt and Helen had brought the family to this city many times, often to athletic events. UK basketball tickets were hard to get, but others were not. They attended several football, a few women's basketball, and a half dozen baseball games.

The best visit was last spring, during the greatest show in hoops: the Kentucky Sweet Sixteen. Sixteen teams start playing on Wednesday and finish on Saturday. A team that wins on Saturday morning earns the privilege of playing Saturday night for the title. Win, and the state championship trophy is carried home.

Lance prized reading and re-reading the tournament program. The list of former players who participated was loaded with superstars, such as Cliff Hagen, Wes Unseld, Butch Beard, Allan Houston, and Jack Givens. *Next year*, he got goose bumps, *his name would appear.*

Last March, Connsburg temporarily relocated to Rupp Arena. The championship game against Lexington Catholic was a keeper. Chet Johnson was spectacular --twenty-five points and fifteen rebounds. Lance threw in twelve and had seven assists, five of which were perfection passes to Chet. Lance made one basket and went three for three from the free throw line in that last minute. It was a fantastic game. The Green Bears won by one. The nets were cut down and Connsburg had a team to remember for the ages.

He unzipped his suitcase and set the blue sweater out on the twin bed. Wrinkles were going to be kept to a minimum. Jumping on the other bed, he stretched his long legs full length, and grabbed the *Hyatt Magazine* on the nightstand.

The pages were stockpiled with ads about clothes, jewelry, and food. It had a map of the city that showed the location of Rupp Arena. He figured he was lying right where the two P's in "Rupp" appeared. It was not as detailed as Milt's *State Farm Atlas*, but it give him a good feel for where everything was, including the University. He had been on the campus many times, but today Coach Hudson was scheduled to give him his first personally guided tour. He was flipping through the final pages, admiring the top eating establishments when the phone rang. Lance sat up on the side of the bed. "Hello?"

"Hello, Son, you get in all right?"

"Sure, Dad. No problems."

"Well, I just wanted to make sure everything was OK. You know your mom, how she worries."

Lance knew he hadn't talked to his mom. They were both nailed down to schoolwork. "Let Mom know everything is all right." It made him feel good not to question Milt's excuse for calling. "And Dad, don't leave Connsburg without a win."

"We sure could use another tight end. If you start now, you could easily be back here for the kickoff."

"I wish. Don't I wish! Greg will take care of both of us."

"I have that feeling, too. Enjoy your visit. See you tomorrow morning. Love you, Son."

"I love you, Dad."

The phone was no more than placed back in the holder when it rang again.

"Hello?"

"Lance Stoler, how you doing? This is Coach Hudson. Welcome to Wildcat country."

"Morning, Coach. I'll be right down."

Lance found Coach Hudson standing right outside the elevator. "It's good to see you."

"How was your trip?" They shook hands. "I hope traffic wasn't bad."

Hudson had been with Coach Jones for nine years. They worked together at South Carolina before Jones was hired as the head coach. He was a tall, slender man with dark penetrating eyes, capable of encouraging a player to dig deeper and work harder with one blazing glance. His compassionate demeanor, positive attitude, and Southern charm were always on display.

"Beautiful. Mom let me drive her Camero."

"Your mom and dad are still coming tomorrow, right?"

"Wouldn't miss it. They both earned graduate degrees here. My brother, Greg, has a huge football game tonight."

"Sorry you won't get to see him play."

"Me, too. They'll win, though." Lance tried to sound confident. "I'll get to see him play next Friday."

"Well that makes me feel fine, real fine," Coach Hudson gave him one of his blazing glances. "If you're at his game that means you won't be visiting another school."

"No, Sir. This is my last visit."

"I say we get something to eat, meet with Coach, and then I'll give you a little tour of the campus. We're scheduled to be in Coach Jones' office at two. Coach really wanted to be here, but he's the guest speaker at a basketball luncheon and he couldn't say no.

"No problem," Lance said. "Wildcats should be really good again this year, huh, Coach?"

"We look good on paper. Four starters back." Hudson seemed pleased he asked and more pleased to answer. "Lance, did you know that in the last eight years, only two teams have won their regular season title or conference tournament title every year?"

"Kentucky has got to be one." Lance smiled confidently at Hudson, but couldn't guess the other team.

"Valparaiso."

"They have a great coach." Lance was enthused with that information. "Met him at a camp last summer."

They jumped into Hudson's car and after a short drive, Dave steered into a small parking lot. Lance glanced up at a blue and white sign that read "The Bluegrass Bar and Grill".

The hostess greeted them warmly. "Hi, Coach. Same table?"

"Sure, if it's available."

"Right this way." The hostess gave Hudson a practiced smile. Her smile improved as she surveyed Lance. Remembering her role, she led them to a table. "Hope you and your guest enjoy your lunch."

Hudson nodded a reply. The hostess set two menus on the table as they sat down. A waitress passed, carrying a tray filled with another customer's lunch. Everything looked delicious. They ordered, and then enjoyed a hearty conversation containing a dab of humor, sports, and business. All in all, it was a wonderful meal following a perfect morning.

The head basketball secretary, Mrs. Teena Shepard, was waiting for them. Mrs. Shepard was the Dayle Jarrett of Kentucky basketball. On the ride over, Hudson enlightened Lance as to her importance within the program. She had been an employee of the Wildcats for twenty-two years. She knew more about Kentucky basketball than any of the young puppies now coaching and was quick to remind the staff of that fact. She had many favorite players, but she was most partial to those boys who called the state of Kentucky home.

"The lady loves shooters, those who could drain it over anyone," Coach Hudson gave the impression he did, too. "She's been known to say, 'Dan Issel, Kevin Grevey, or Kyle Macy -- who would be stupid enough to play them in a game of pig?'" Hudson also explained that Teena recognized how important recruiting was to the success of any basketball program. Especially her Wildcats.

"She's going to make darn sure Kentucky looks good. That woman knows as much or more about you recruits as we do. For Pete's sakes, she types up the background information on each of you. Commits it to memory, by God." Hudson scratched the side of his face. "If some young man -- of course not you, Lance -- decides to go to another school, it wouldn't be because Teena didn't do her best to persuade him differently."

Teena greeted him as if he were already wearing the Blue. "Hello, Lance. We've been expecting you."

Her dark brown hair was cut in a pixie. Compassionate blue eyes were hidden behind thick glasses, and perfectly manicured nails sat in readiness at her computer like a fine piano player, undoubtedly resting from the last performance. *Could she be the one who typed the recruiting letters I received? How many letters had she printed then mailed to some young man dreaming he might one day become a Wildcat?* Lance still had his first letter. Postman West delivered it. At that time, he had no clue hundreds of basketball players were receiving the same letter. It would always be special to him. Coach Jones warned that the Wildcat staff would be watching him. And they did.

"Just fine, Ma'am." Lance greeted Teena with a great deal of anticipation.

"This is the lady I was talking about. If there is a better college basketball secretary in the nation, I dare you to show me. And good looking, too." Coach Hudson's Southern charm was hitting on all cylinders.

"Stop, David, you're making me blush." Teena stood up from her computer, not blushing at all. She was completely in charge of her world.

"Lance, how are your mom and dad? We like to keep up on our alumni. I bet your mom's still having every first grade parent wishing their kid was in her class."

"Doing fine. They'll be over tomorrow."

"Staying for your brother's football game?" Teena winked.

"Coach, she's good." Lance turned towards Hudson then back to Teena. "What position does he play?"

"Come on. That's a lay-up. Greg's a quarterback and if he had you-know-who as a tight end this year, well, they might beat Belfry." Teena smiled boldly.

That was it. Lance became just another of the hundreds of young men who found it easy to admire Ms. Teena and her delightful personality. The secretary stepped into the head coach's office and announced the arrival of the recruit from Connsburg.

"Lance Stoler. Welcome." A cheerful Coach Jones stuck out his big bronze hand and shook with the firmness of a seasoned farmer getting off his tractor.

As he walked into the office, the first thing that caught Lance's eye was the National Championship trophy, won in Jones' first year. Its place of honor was on a cherry hardwood stand to the left of a matching executive desk. An overstuffed couch upholstered in plush blue-and-white fabric was offset to the right.

Jones gave Lance a minute to absorb the Wildcat heritage staring back at him from every wall before asking, "How's my buddy, Coach Hunter doing? You guys are coming back over here next March, I presume?"

"Coach is doing great, Sir." Lance answered the second question with pride. "Sure would be nice to repeat."

Jones left no doubt as to whom he worked for. He was wearing a white shirt embroidered with Kentucky Wildcats on the chest, tan dockers, and Nike shoes that looked like they had just been taken from a box.

Did Nana dress this guy today, or what?

Coaching Kentucky basketball obviously generated unwanted side effects. Since Lance's first meeting with Jones at a Wildcat's basketball camp several years ago, his black hair was now streaked with gray, his cheeks sagged, and wrinkles had become more plentiful. Nonetheless, Lamar Jones stood out among men. His tall stature and imposing posture was worthy of any military general.

"If your team can repeat, it says a lot about Coach Hunter. And might I add, a lot about your leadership."

"Thank you, sir; I think the credit has to go to Coach Hunter. He really makes a difference."

"I like your modesty, Son."

Lance was flattered once more, but still didn't forget what his dad always preached. "Sales pitches." He meant no disrespect, but just like in Kansas, the prospects were all complimented. "Any other recruits in this weekend?"

"Two, and I'm sure you know one of them."

"Who's that?"

"Matt Hassel." Coach watched for the expression on Lance's face.

"This will be an interesting weekend." Lance tried to keep a blank face.

"You'd already told us you wanted to come this weekend. Matt's also visiting Arizona. His grandparents moved out there a few years back, this happened to be the best time for him to visit us, too."

Last March, it was Matt's followers who were certain the state championship would remain in Lexington until Akers High contested that conviction in the finals. Matt was the star player for Lexington Catholic. Like Lance, he was tall and had a hankering for crew cuts. There wasn't a soul within a hundred miles who didn't know Matt could shoot the rock and that he was a superb defender. Lance could well testify to that. In the championship game, he held Lance to twelve points while adding twenty to his own team's total. But what crippled his team was their star's fifth foul. With just five seconds remaining, Lance posted Matt up on the left low block. Recognizing the advantage, Bruce hit him with a pass. Lance spun to the right, cocked, and released a fade away jumper from twelve feet. The Rupp Arena crowd heard the noise Lance had come to cherish --swoosh. Then another -- the ref's whistle.

Black shoes, black pants, and a striped shirt galloped towards the scorers' table. Screaming fans heard, "Foul on number 24."

The ref's arm slashed down, causing another roar from the Connsburg faithful. The basket was good and Lance would step to the line for a bonus.

Matt lumbered towards his bench, his head down in disbelief. Lance walked over and grabbed his hand.

"You're one heck of a ballplayer," Lance caught himself saying.

Matt's eyes flashed misery. He managed to whisper, "Thanks."

Primed by persistent practice and hands blessed by Hoover, Lance stepped to the free throw line, received the ball, dribbled two times, then drained the bonus. Akers won by one.

"I'm sure Matt and I will enjoy meeting on a weekend we aren't expected to guard each other. I guess that can wait till March." He grinned. "We'd both relish having another battle in Rupp, I'm sure."

"I wouldn't mind seeing you two guarding a few of those boys from Tennessee or Florida. Sending them packing with their tails between their legs."

"That'd be nice."

Lance knew both he and Matt's coming to Kentucky offered problems. One would have to become a point guard or learn to like getting splinters. Sitting during a game was not one of Lance's ideas of a good time. Still, he had judged Matt to be a quality person. The idea of playing next to him was agreeable, if Fate willed it.

Teena stuck her head in the doorway and alerted Coach Jones that Hudson was back and ready to give Lance a cruise around campus.

"Sounds good." Jones stood up. "I'll see you at practice. Let Coach know if there is anything special you want to see."

"You bet." Lance's gesture made sure Coach and Ms. Teena knew how thankful he was for their time.

The sunny afternoon polished the Lexington campus, giving it a unique dignity all its own. Well-tended brick buildings, robust trees, and pleasant courtyards made the tour quite charming. Students were walking to and from classes. Some were sitting on benches, immersed in their textbooks. One was throwing a Frisbee. His dog caught it with ease. Another stood by his bike, one leg on the ground, the other resting on the pedal; he spoke with an elderly man, possibly a professor. In Lance's mind, the grounds were what a college campus was all about. He could sense the strong call of becoming a college student, not just a basketball player who went to school.

He would love walking up steps, then through halls to classrooms where he would learn more English, more math, more history, more "stuff". He did not know for sure what the "stuff" would be, but he wanted to learn more "stuff".

I'd get one of the seats up front in each classroom. Helen had taught him well. Her words echoed clearly. "Sit up front. You can improve your grades and show the teacher you're interested." She would giggle knowingly. "Or at least make them think you are."

The tour completed, they headed downtown to Rupp Arena. The team was on the floor surrounding the interlocked UK logo. Lance watched as the strength coach took the team through stretching exercises. Jones was leaning on the front edge of the scorers' table talking with two young men. Lance immediately recognized one. He had not seen the other before.

Approaching the table. Lance gained eye contact. He suddenly bent his knees and spread out his arms. "I can't help it. On this floor, when I see the pride of Lexington Catholic, I'm trained to assume the position."

The group laughed. Matt Hassel threw out his right hand and caught Lance's by the palm. Their thumbs intertwined.

"It's nice to see you when I don't have to worry about you lighting me up." Matt's voice was confident.

"After practice, maybe you two guys want to try a little one-on-one?" Coach Hudson jested.

"We'd better save it for next March. There is no way Matt will get five fouls again." A sincere compliment to the Lexington Catholic star.

Matt nodded appreciation.

"Lance, meet Eric Donaldson. He's from Cincinnati Princeton. People up in his area think he might be able to play this game in college," said Coach Jones.

Eric was a physical replica of Melvin Howard and looked like he could go one-on-one with Melvin on a moment's notice. Lance fervently hoped he would not have to counsel Eric through any situations like Melvin had last weekend.

Jones shared that Eric was a premier big man who could run the floor, which was perfect for Kentucky's up-and-down-the-court style of play. At Princeton, he was all-state last year, averaging twenty-one points a game and twelve boards. "And he loves to pick for you little guys." Jones winked at Matt and Lance, then he suggested the three spectators move to first-row seats. There they watched with amazement the crisp and marvelously organized practice. No time was wasted. Each player seemed to be receiving superb instruction. As the team began a three man weave drill, Eric broke the silence.

"So you guys have bumped heads?"

The two Kentucky boys glanced at each other. It was easier for Lance to answer. He remembered the pain on Matt's face after his fifth foul sent him off the floor.

"We sure did. On this very floor," Lance said. "Matt played one heck of a game."

Lance noticed a slight glimpse of thankfulness soften Matt's steel expression. Through his short testimonial, he tried to make Eric recognize that Matt was the star of the game.

"So who won?" Eric asked.

"Matt's team ran out of time and we snuck by them. But next March, the clock will be reset." Matt returned Lance's gaze. The steel expression was completely gone.

They returned their attention to the action on the floor. Lance loved watching his home state team. He had watched the Wildcats so much that it was not hard for him to evaluate how good the team might be. They would be awesome this season. But it wouldn't hurt to get a second opinion.

"What do you guys think? Pretty good, huh?"

Matt was first to reply. "No doubt. Look how quick those guards are."

"Why doesn't it surprise me?" Eric complained good-naturedly. "You *would* watch the guards first. Did you notice they have three pretty exceptionally big men? And two of them are seniors. That's good for me."

"They can make it to the Final Four?" Lance thoroughly believed his statement. Grandad Hoover never asked if the Wildcats would be good. He stated it with complete conviction.

Matt answered without hesitating. "Absolutely."

But what about him? Where would he fit in? Lance fell into an old habit of self doubt. He started asking himself questions. *Can I play here? Can I start here? Are Eric and Matt asking themselves the same questions?* Lance understood this wasn't little league basketball where everyone got to play so many minutes no matter how good they were. Players came and players competed. Kentucky started a senior and sophomore at the guard spots. A junior was the backup. *I could earn a spot here and possibly start after a few years . . . What am I thinking?* Self doubts always made him angry. *I'd start next year!*

Practice finished. A few players stayed to shoot some extra shots as Coach Jones addressed his recruits. "Well, Gentlemen, that was a Kentucky practice. We work hard, know what we're practicing, and get out. On time."

Matt fired right back, "You look mighty good, Coach."

"We have to be. Here, it's a big game no matter who we play. What coach wouldn't love to put a victory over the Wildcats on his resume?" He folded his hands together. "We have to improve. And we will."

Chapter 28

It was only 5:50 when Lance returned to his room. Having plenty of time, he jumped onto the bed, closed his eyes, and willed himself to see Greg warming up at the football stadium. It was agonizing.

"Dang, my little brother is going to war and here I am sprawled out on this bed."

His mind skipped out of Kentucky and floated to Kansas. Lisa's bright smile and peachy soft skin hung on the front of his brain like an alluring World War II pinup. He didn't want to rush this recruiting trip, but he could hardly wait to call her on Sunday.

Suddenly aware of the time, he hopped off the bed, stripped, and stepped into the shower. Ten minutes later, wearing Dockers, a white shirt, and the favorite blue sweater, he was walking across the lobby. Matt was already there.

The lobby had a bar and lounge nestled under a huge atrium ceiling where a few Wildcats congregated, no doubt, after watching Kentucky pound a visiting opponent. Matt sat in an overstuffed plaid chair in the reception area opposite the bar. Gazing at a large wood-burning fireplace, he seemed to be mesmerized by the crackling hickory logs. The flames blazed their radiance on a bronze statue of three thoroughbred race horses, the pride of this part of the state. Chattering guests busily milled about the lobby. Lance approached the fire and broke Matt's solitude. "How did you beat me here?"

"Lexington Catholic boys are fast. I thought you knew."

"I do know. I do know." Lance smiled agreement. "So, you're taking a look at Arizona, I hear?"

"Yeah, kinda. My grandparents live in Scottsdale and Coach Olson is really nice." Matt sounded almost apologetic. "I'm like you. A Kentucky boy. But my grandad begged me to visit."

Lance wished Hoover were alive to beg him to visit any school. His heart spoke instead. *Young Man. You're at that school -- UK.*

"It will be nice for you to see your grandad."

Eric joined them just as Coach Hudson walked through the lobby doors. The group packed into a waiting van and were soon parked in front of Malone's Restaurant, the finest steakhouse in Lexington.

Coach Jones, his wife, and three Wildcats who would act as hosts were waiting for them in a private dining room. Yvonne Jones was enchanting. The First Lady of Kentucky Basketball wore a blue dress with a white scarf wrapped proudly around her dainty neck. Kentucky colors. The three hosts were Mike Kelley, a back-up shooting guard, Dave Phillips, the starting strong forward who was good for at least ten points in any game, and Aaron Miller, the starting point guard, a Wildcat co-captain who also ranked third in the nation in assists last year.

Jones asked Lance to sit next to Mrs. Jones and told Aaron to pick any spot he wanted, as long as it was next to Lance, then made similar suggestions to the other recruits and hosts. Lance stared around the room, content to be in such good company.

Once again, his imagination drew his thoughts away. At this table were the makings of not a high school, but an NCAA championship team. With only six players, no one could get into foul trouble. Eric and Dave Philips could handle the high and low post while Aaron and Matt could start at the guard spots. Lance would be invited by the coaches to play small forward. Not a problem. They would operate as a three-guard offense. The six of them would be the college version of the well-oiled machine Norman Dale coached in *Hoosiers*.

Mrs. Jones would sit in the stands, hair perfectly groomed and smiling pleasantly for the cameras when the team was doing well. When things were not going well, which would be rare, she would still smile, allowing no one to know the pain she was absorbing in an effort to help protect her beloved husband. Lance examined the talent around the table one last time. *Yep. This group would beat Connecticut, maybe even Duke for the championship.*

"Lance, we'll all say a little prayer for your brother," Yvonne Jones' angelic voice delayed the imagined team's run at a championship. "I know it would have been exciting for you to be there tonight."

Her words demonstrated that she cared about more than just Lance's basketball talent.

"Thanks, Mrs. Jones. They kick off pretty soon."

The dinner went deliciously well. Waitresses brought sizzling porterhouse steaks and jumbo twice-baked potatoes. Dialogue centered on UK and Kentucky High School basketball. Everyone was involved, even Big Eric. His hometown, Cincinnati, wasn't in Kentucky, but might just as well be. Its airport was.

Coach outlined the game plan for Saturday after dessert was served, and then closed the meal by charging the hosts to take good care of their recruits. The dinner party pushed away from the table, said their good-byes, and headed to the exit. Lance watched eager heads turn as he and his "National Championship team" exited the restaurant.

Aaron immediately took charge. "Mike, let's all go over to the Moonlight. See what's going on."

"You guys interested?" Mike expected approval. "You'll like the Moonlight."

"Dave, what do you think?" Lance quipped. "You're the bodyguard in this group,"

Dave gave Lance a playful push on the shoulder. "A few coeds have been known to show up at the Moonlight. And, yes, I'll make sure you guys stay out of trouble."

When they arrived, the line into the Moonlight was about twenty deep and growing. The group waited their turn.

"It would be nice to go up to the bouncer and ask him to let us take cuts, but we don't want any privileges that could cause an 'extra benefits' problem with the NCAA," said Aaron. Evidently, Jones and Hudson coached their players on proper behavior off the court as well as on.

Once inside, they found an upscale establishment that specialized in dancing and more than a little matchmaking. The place was stuffed with people trying to do both. Matt looked around and gave his immediate approval.

"I like this place. Look at all the babes." He stressed his last three words.

They all moved to a side table. Dave didn't wait to take anyone's order. He ordered Cokes.

"Any problems?" Dave asked with such force in his voice that no one questioned his choice. "Remember, I'm the bodyguard of this excursion."

Lance was delighted. It was like Kansas. He didn't have to deal with taunting questions demanding why he wouldn't have a beer or something stronger.

A tall, curvaceous blonde walked towards their table. She stopped with a model's pose directly in front of Lance. "Hello, again. Two times in one day."

The room was not well lit. Lance realized she was the hostess from the restaurant where he had had lunch with Coach Hudson. The blonde had changed from her hostess outfit. She wore a tight black skirt that was barely there at all. Her ponytail was taken down, freeing a long, thick mane curling softly on her shoulders.

"Nice to see you again." Lance said, trying desperately to overcome a sudden squeak in his voice. "These are some of my friends." He introduced everyone.

"Nice to meet you all." She smiled coyly. "And this is Mary and Darlene," she identified two friends who joined her.

The boys took immediate pleasure assessing the new arrivals. Mary was a short, well-proportioned redhead, while Darlene, with black shiny hair that hung immaculately straight, could easily pass herself off as a California starlet.

Dave stood up, apologizing for his friends. "Excuse these guys. They're working on manners. Would you ladies like a seat?"

The three women looked at each other in silent communication. The redhead shrugged, "Why not?"

More chairs were hastily gathered around the table. The blonde slowly squeezed between Matt and Lance. She took a sip of bourbon and soda. "You introduced everyone else, but we didn't get your name."

"Lance, Lance Stoler." He managed not to squeak his answer.

"And we didn't get your name," Matt quickly inquired.

"Shelby, Shelby White." She kept her attention on Lance. "So, Lance, do you live in Lexington or are you visiting?"

Shelby looked measurably better than she had at lunch. Her voice was quite charming with its slow Southern drawl. He thought about Lisa. His brain was trying to do damage control. He wanted to enjoy the evening. Not have any problems. However, having someone like Shelby sitting next to him was a problem. He felt clumsy.

"Just visiting, like Matt and Eric. We're recruits."

Mike excused himself to get another round of Cokes, and Eric followed, offering to help carry glasses back. Aaron and Dave escorted Shelby's friends to the dance floor. Matt, Lance and Shelby were now alone at the table.

"What kind of recruits?" Shelby asked.

"Basketball."

"My gosh, you two are Kentucky basketball recruits? You must be pretty good." Shelby's words were entirely aimed at Lance.

"Matt is." Lance tried to escape her scrutiny. "He's the star of the Lexington Catholic team. Those other guys play for Kentucky. Well, the big guy doesn't. Eric is a recruit from Cincinnati." He wondered why his words stumbled out of his mouth like from a scared kid.

Shelby laughed. "I must be honest. Those two giants gave you away. The girls and I figured you all must be players. Coach Hudson is always bringing recruits into the restaurant. I remembered you from this afternoon, Lance."

"I guess we're hard to hide." Matt's eyes kept busy.

"Matt's the best player in the state. He can play college ball wherever he wants." Lance knew he was flunking his efforts to direct the spotlight on Matt.

Shelby purred. "How about you?"

"I'm fair. I try to do my best."

Matt broke out in a hearty laugh, seeming to delight in watching Lance squirm.

"Honey, don't let him fool you. That boy is the best three-point shooter in the state."

Lance smiled, appreciative of Matt's compliment. It at least made Shelby look Matt's way.

"Why, lucky me. I'm sitting between two future basketball stars."

Matt started talking more. Lance tried to say as little as possible. He wouldn't have wanted Lisa to see him now. Would he understand if he saw Lisa out with Marla, surrounded by dogs in heat? The dancers returned to the table. A couple of minutes later Eric and Mike returned with Cokes and a bowl of nuts for the table.

Lance noticed everyone becoming more relaxed and enjoying themselves. Mike asked the redhead to dance and Dave gleefully strolled off with Darlene. Shelby remained with Aaron, Eric, Matt, and Lance.

"Do boys from your town dance?" Shelby asked Lance.

"Back where I come from, we've been known to dance a few jigs, but Matt is the best dancer in his high school. Why don't you give him a whirl?" Lance suggested. If Matt would just look directly into Lance's eyes, he would see they were begging. *Come on, you got to take Shelby out for a spin.*

Shelby showed an instant of disappointment in her face, but just as fast regained composure. She took Matt's hand.

"Let's do it." Matt smiled like he won the lottery.

When the couple left the table, Aaron looked at Lance in disbelief.

"Are you crazy, Man? That hot babe wanted to dance with you."

"I'm not brain dead. I know. But I have someone special and I don't want to mess it up." Lance's firmness made him feel proud of himself.

"I can dig it. I wish that I had someone special. Haven't found her yet," Aaron lamented. "Hey, look at what just walked in. Maybe she could be real special to me."

Lance and Eric turned their heads and caught sight of another beautiful Kentucky woman strutting long legs towards the bar.

"Yep, she's your kind of woman," Eric declared, licking his lips.

Before the rest of the group returned to the table, Lance leaned over and asked Aaron if he could give him a ride back to the Hyatt.

"You sure you want to leave?" Aaron pleaded. "The night is still young."

"We have a lot to do tomorrow. Don't want to mess anything up."

Aaron flashed a sneer at Lance. "I got ya. You don't want to mess up anything with the coaches and you don't want to mess up anything with a certain special little lady."

The three couples returned from the dance floor and started to sit down when Aaron stood up. "I'll be right back. Goin' to give Lance a lift back to the Hyatt."

"Where you going? It's early." Mike asked.

Matt stared at Lance in disbelief. "You can't go. We got plenty of time."

"I know. It's just that I need to go. Got to check on my family."

"Oh, yeah, right," Matt said. "Hey, Man, I forgot about your brother. Hope he won." Shelby put her arm around Matt as if it might make Lance jealous. Two weeks ago, maybe. But not tonight.

"Thanks, Matt." Lance gave a quick nod to everyone at the table. "See you guys in the morning."

On the ride back Aaron resorted to snooping. "Tell me about this special girl. You must have known her a long time to let Matt have his shot at Shelby."

"Actually, I've only known her for a few weeks. Met her in Kansas. Haven't seen her since."

"You've got to be kiddin' me." Aaron cursed, swerving the car slightly. "You met her on your recruiting trip?"

"Yeah. Never met her before." Lance wasn't offended. He understood what often happened on visits. "She was with a friend of mine. We had a great time together."

"How do you know she's special? Especially if you just met and you don't really know her."

"She's special, all right. I think about her all the time. She's perfect. She's warm, cute, and has a precious smile."

He was silent for a moment. *What am I doing? I don't even know Aaron and I'm spilling my guts out to him. These are things I wouldn't even tell Mom or Dad.*

"Is she a student?" Aaron asked.

"Yeah, she's a freshman at Kansas."

"Does Coach Jones know you got a girlfriend back in Kansas?"

"Until now, no one knew. I guess not even me."

Aaron pulled up to the entrance of the Hyatt. "Good luck, Man. I bet she is special. See you in the morning."

Lance waved as the car pulled away from the Hyatt.

The first thing Lance did after unlocking the hotel door was to pick up the phone and dial home.

"Stolers."

"Cherie. How's my counselor? Is it OK to talk to Greg or --"

"It's more than OK!" She almost screamed. "You missed another great one."

"Well, put him on."

"What's happening, My Man?" Greg sounded like a general who had just turned the tide of a war.

"Don't play with me! What happened?" Lance begged. "What was the score?"

"Let's just say that little brother made sure you get to watch at least one more game this year." Could a voice hold more pride?

"Congratulations, Greg! What was the score?"

"Akers 21, Belfry 14."

"How did they get fourteen points?" Lance asked.

"Easy." Greg reported like he was doing a sports radio update. "They got them all in the first half. We were down 14 to 7 at the start of the fourth quarter."

"You've got to be kidding me. How'd you guys do it?"

"You know that bootleg pass Ohio State used last week to beat Iowa? Bruce caught one just like it to get us to 14."

"Super! How'd we get the last touchdown?"

"It was a beauty. Remember the play I described to you on Monday?"

"That one?"

"Brett Bloom was in at halfback. I pitched him the ball and he took off to the right. He acts like it's a reverse. Boom! He stops and looks to the left. There I am, all alone with the twenty-yard line. I catch it on the fifteen and dance into the end zone. And did I mention there was only six seconds left on the clock?"

"Sweet. I mean sweeeeet!" Lance shouted. "I'm so happy for you and the team. Great job. I can't wait to be there next Friday for the playoffs! When will we know who we'll be playing?"

"Coach says we should know by Sunday."

"Is Dad still up?"

"Lance! You know better than that. He's grabbing the phone right now."

"You're missing some good pizza here, son." Milt's voice was glowing as it always was when his children made him proud.

"You can have my share, Dad. It was a good one, huh?"

"What a comeback. Your brother actually has some hands. I heard him tell you he caught it on the fifteen. He bobbled it on the fifteen and finally caressed it on the twelve. He said there were six seconds on the clock when he scored. Well, there were two minutes left when he was bobbling it. You do the math. How fast was he going?"

Lance could hear loving laughter from the family room and wished he could be part of it. But he couldn't. That's life. Part of growing up. It felt awfully good to talk with his family. He never wanted to forget -- it's the simple things in life that make a difference.

"Here's your mom. You better say 'hi'."

"Everything OK, Sweetheart?" she asked.

"Sure, Mom. It was a nice evening. The coaches are great."

"Did they feed you anything?"

"No different than the other trips, Mom. A bunch of cornbread."

"Stop it." She giggled. "You would have been so proud of your brother. It was quite a comeback. I'm a happy girl tonight."

"I'm happy too, Mom. Happy for the whole family." There was a sudden catch in his voice. He took a deep breath.

Helen must have noticed. Her voice softened. "Dad and I will see you first thing in the morning. Who do we watch tomorrow?"

"UK plays Mississippi State."

"I swear I thought you were making basketball trips, but we keep watching football games." Helen was trying to sound lighthearted.

"All part of the process, Mom. All part of the process. See you all in the morning. Love you."

"I love you, Son." He knew she meant it with all her heart. "Good night."

Chapter 29

Lance was up early, headed to Rupp Arena. He wanted to breathe in her charm all by himself prior to attending the 8:30 brunch. Before stepping through the hotel doors, he heard a scratchy voice call, "Good morning, Lance."

He turned and saw Shelby walking towards him, black skirt in need of an iron and hair falling in tangles.

Lanced managed a surprised "Good morning".

"I work the early shift today," she muttered.

Lance wanted to ask, *Who did you stay with last night?* "That's nice. How late did you guys stay out?"

"We got back here about one."

Who is we? No, I can't ask that. "Whoa, you didn't get much sleep."

"We sure didn't." Shelby perked up with a suggestive voice.

Was she still trying to make him jealous? He wanted to know who "we" was. *Quit jacking around. Just ask.* "So, you and Matt had a good time?"

"Matt?" Her eyes opened wider as she laughed. "After Aaron came back from dropping you off, we danced. Several times." She said it gradually, as if she wanted Lance to visualize their dance. "He offered to spring for a room here. So we did. Aaron doesn't have to play a game tonight does he?" She straightened her sweater. "He might be a little worn out."

Lance now knew who "we" was. No more questions were asked. She needed to get to work and he needed to see Rupp.

"I've got to go. Nice seeing you again." Lance walked out of the Hyatt and did not look back.

Lance had three points of pleasure this morning. One, Greg's team won last night. Two, after encountering Shelby, he was doubly thankful for Lisa. And three, the cleaning people were in Rupp. The arena was open. He reverently walked inside, hoping not to be thrown out. He scampered down a few rows and sat down. This was the home of Kentucky basketball. The polished hardwood floor collared with blue trim seemed to be begging for someone to come on down and start shootin'. The only thing preventing Lance from doing so was the lack of a ball.

He sat alone in silence and admired her beauty. Even the Coke and Dodge advertisement signs looked good to him. Rupp was home to three National Championship teams. He surveyed all 23,000 seats. Sitting in what was probably one of the big donor's seats, he stared way up at the top of the arena. A few of Lance's friends made some noise up there last March. This place tugged at him like a mother to its cub. *What do I do? Is this where I belong?*

Should he leave the nest? Was going west and being with Lisa the right choice? Ohio State flat out said they needed Lance. Coach Meadors was exceptional. Was going north the answer?

A janitor moved on to the court and soon started to mop under the far basket. He looked up at Lance a couple of times, but went on with his work. Lance checked his watch and realized he had been sitting there for almost an hour. He thanked the cleaning people for letting him sit for a while, then retreated up through the blue exit doors. He looked past the escalators at the shops on the lower level, swung the side doors open, and walked back into the hotel lobby.

To his surprise, he found the Akers High School principal and his wife sitting on a wooden bench enjoying the warmth of a morning fire.

"Good mornin'."

"Well, he's still here. We rang your room and there was no answer. We figured you were in the shower." Milt pulled his son into a hug.

Lance gave his mom a kiss on the cheek. "I was sitting over there in Rupp. Forgot the time."

"I hope you know a good son will bring his momma back over here to Rupp next spring. With a team," Milt was in a good mood.

"Now there's a happy family." All turned to see Coach Hudson stepping through the revolving doors. "Akers had a good game last night. Heard about it on the radio as I drove over."

"Hi, Coach. I was getting ready to ask my dad for the play by play."

"I bet he remembers every play," Hudson said. "It's good to see you again, Milt. I'm surprised Lance can still move this morning with the size of that steak he had at Malone's last night."

"Those steaks were awesome, Dad."

"Come on. I'll show you the way to the brunch." Southern manners showing, Dave offered a hand as Helen rose from the bench.

Saturday morning Lance and his parents listened to professors, staff, and a team physician. All were entertaining. Each voiced the beauty of being a member of the University of Kentucky basketball program. They toured the athletic facilities including locker rooms, players' lounge, training room, and weight room. The Wildcats took a back seat to no one with their first-rate facilities. Lance could tell that his mom and dad more than ever loved hearing people brag about "their" university.

There were two major differences from his other trip -- the football game and the degree of Saturday night suspense. The game was a battle, but not of the same caliber as in Columbus, or the lopsidedness of the one in Lawrence. Kentucky won the game by scoring two touchdowns in the third quarter. Neither team scored in the fourth. The game ended Kentucky-24, Mississippi State-14.

Saturday night, there was little to worry about. His relationship with Lisa was not put in jeopardy and Lance didn't have to bail out any friends. After a delightful dinner hosted at the home of Mr. and Mrs. Jones, the recruits went to a party at Mike Kelley's apartment. Other than a little loud music, all was safe at UK.

Around 10:30, Lance asked Aaron for a ride back to the Hyatt, hoping he might see his mom and dad before they tucked in.

"Sure Man, no problem," Aaron responded. "Anyone else need a ride?" There were no takers.

Throughout the day neither he nor Aaron had mentioned Shelby. The trip back to the hotel would not take long, so Lance started some gentle jabs as soon as Aaron put the car into drive.

"So how'd you sleep last night?" He glanced at Aaron with disguised eyes.

"Fine." He slowly returned Lance's glance and saw his passenger now grinning broadly. "What? You know? Come on, you know, don't you?"

"Know what?" Lance was doing a poor job of masquerading.

"Hey Stoler, don't be conning me. You know, don't you?"

"Let's just say I got up early this morning to have a look at the arena and to my surprise, Shelby was walking out of the hotel."

"What did she tell you?" Aaron asked. "She tell you everything?"

"She did. Including the X-rated stuff."

"Come on, man. You acted like you wanted nothing to do with her. For some reason, she was hot for you. But might I add it didn't last long after my charm meter started clicking in."

"No problem." Lance said, then spoke with more seriousness. "I explained my situation to you last night."

Aaron turned onto High Street and pulled into the Hyatt entrance. "Stoler, you're something." The car came to a stop.

Lance started to open his door. "Thanks. You've been an excellent host."

"I like you, Stoler." Aaron stared at him. "We could use you. Hey, good luck this season. Win it all again."

"You, too."

Aaron headed back towards Mike Kelley's. Lance dashed through the revolving doors. He found his parents sitting at a lounge table having an after dinner drink with a few new friends. The place was packed with Wildcats. His dad had no problem finding people with whom to celebrate a couple of victories. "Isn't this early for you?" Milt asked as Lance pulled up a chair.

"I was at a party. At a player's apartment. But I knew if I wanted to catch you two before bed, I'd better get back."

"That was sweet of you." Helen squeezed her son's hand. "Everyone in here knows Akers is in the playoffs. Guess who told them?" Helen's face glowed. "And, oh yeah, they all know the quarterback's name, too."

"Did this person mention his other son was on a recruiting trip?" Lance launched a friendly stare at his dad.

Helen leaned back in her chair. "Only about a dozen times."

"So what's up?" Milt loved the attention. "This is a great place, isn't it?"

"Sure is. The visit has been really good. I meet the coaches in the morning and then I'm finished."

"Time's getting short. Week from Wednesday, you got to get off the fence." Milt challenged.

"Let him enjoy the weekend," Helen said.

Lance was thankful for the protection and happy to be with his parents. Tonight he didn't want to struggle over what he should or should not do. The three sat in the lounge talking about Greg's game, relishing a Kentucky football victory, and chatting about different parts of the beautiful campus.

Milt and Helen loved being in Commonwealth Stadium and once again paying homage to Memorial Coliseum. Milt treasured re-reading the plaque in front of the old basketball arena that gave a brief history of Adolph Rupp. He made a special note to anyone listening that Kansas had delivered Rupp to Kentucky.

Helen praised the UK Art Museum. "It's a shining star for the campus. Cherie would really love spending some long afternoons there."

Lance mainly listened, enjoying the blatant love his parents were expressing for their school. Milt reminisced through a few more stories, then spearheaded a reluctant closing of a fine day in Lexington.

"What time do you meet the coaches?"

"Nine. In their offices."

"We don't have to check out till noon. I need to leave early so I can go over to the high school to tackle a few things. You want to wait and ride back with Lance?" Milt looked at Helen for approval.

"That'd be great, Mom." Lance interjected before an answer could be offered.

"Are you sure?" Helen asked.

"I'd love to drive back with you. The three key words are: I drive back."

"You can drive." She playfully skimmed the hairs on the back of his head. "I'll shove your dad out early and then sleep in until you get back. Nana and the rest of the family are in great shape back home. Let's do it." Contented, they retired to their rooms.

Chapter 30

At sunrise, without much fanfare Milt was headed for Connsburg. Helen snuggled under the covers, enjoying a few precious extra hours of rest. Lance was preparing to drive over to the coach's office for his nine o'clock appointment when the phone rang.

"Hello?"

"Stoler? This is Thomas Hillcrest."

Lance was shocked. "Sir, how'd you get this number?"

"That's not important. Making sure everything turns out right for your grandmother is what's important."

"Grandmother?" Lance was suddenly chilled. "You mean my Nana?"

Hillcrest told Lance what no member of his family knew. Hoover's medical bills had stockpiled when the insurance companies refused to pay. They argued he had exhausted all benefits. Nana had obtained a lawyer to fight the insurance company, but to no avail. She was about to lose the farm and every penny of her savings. Through nearly half a century of carpentry work, Hoover had used his hands to earn those savings, buy their house, and maintain the treasured farm. His life's work, lovingly willed to Nana, was in jeopardy of being snatched away.

"It's been too long," Hillcrest stated flatly. "Those bills have to be paid."

Lance weakly sat down on the bed. Vivid memories of the last time he was alone with his grandad flooded his mind. Hoover lay in a Hospice bed with oxygen tubes supporting his lungs in their fight for air. Lance entered the bedroom and pulled a chair close to the bed.

"Hey, Grandad." He tried to sound happy. "What are you doin', trying to sleep on my visitin' day?"

"It's all your Nana's fault," Whispered Hoover, trying to sit up. "She puts me to bed when I've been a little stinker."

"Now, I don't believe a word of that. Here, let me help with those pillows."

He helped Hoover lean forward, fluffed the pillows, stacked them firmly, and watched him slowly lean back, pretending to be comfortable. Lance focused on the soft whir of the oxygen machine and mechanical ticking of the clock which almost blocked out the sound of a sudden gasp for breath.

Lance shared stories of what had been happening since last week's visit. His middle school was planning a dance. The kids were teasing him because Wanda Akers said she was going to find out if he could really slow dance. Basketball practice was going great. Greg would visit tomorrow and Cherie on Saturday. Mom still wouldn't let all three visit at one time. She argued they were too much for Grandad at one time, because sometimes they were too much for her. Boxes still needed unpacking since they moved into the new house, but Dad kept his promise and already had one sweet basketball hoop installed at the edge of the driveway. Lance went on and on, until he noticed Hoover's eyes were shut. He opened them, little by little, with tears forming.

"Oh, my dear boy. How I'll miss your stories."

Lance was scared. Trying to act jolly, he went on, "I got a tractor load of stories, Grandad. Take years for me to tell 'em all."

"Come closer, Son." Hoover breathed deep. He told a story about a boy who always was getting into trouble from the day he was born. He made his momma so mad the little thing would jump up and down in exasperation. The boy promised her that one of these days, when he felt the Lord a callin', he'd come forward in the church so he could be baptized. Have his sins swept away in the river.

Hoover worked hard for a breath. "Was me," he whispered. "Stand over by that door."

"Sure, Grandad." Lance walked over to the door, "What do you want me to do?"

"Come forward."

He walked over to the bed and took his Grandad's outstretched hand.

"Are you at peace?" Hoover asked.

"Well, yeah, Grandad." That seemed a strange question.

"Do it again." He tried to gesture, but the free arm fell limply to his side.

"Walk to the door and back?" Lance asked, totally stumped.

Hoover nodded.

Lance walked back to the door, turned around and returned to the bed.

"Are you at peace?" His question was more earnest this time.

"Yes, Grandad." If this was a game, Lance would blindly play along.

"Do it again." Hoover whispered.

His mind racing, Lance walked slowly to the door then back to the bed.

His mind unexpectedly solved the puzzle. Quietly, heart crying, he moved to the bed. "Grandad, am I comin' forward for you?"

Hoover didn't speak. Tears trickled down each cheek.

Lance took hold of the sturdy hand. "Are you at peace, Grandad?"

Lance felt the grip tighten. "Yes."

Nana entered the room with medication, unaware of what had just occurred. "Grandad needs to rest now, Sweetheart."

She spoke something else, but Lance didn't hear. He blindly moved towards the door, but stopped to grab the ball from its worn box in the closet. He stepped off the front porch into a gentle rain. Holding the ball closely, he stood silently in mud. The basket stared down, its rusty rim held firm. Lance desperately tried reaching back in his mind to another time, when love was gathered all around him, and every shot hadn't followed this steady rhythm: *swish, swish, swish.*

"Lance Stoler. You still there?" demanded Hillcrest.

Lance was startled by his voice. "Sorry."

"Look Son, this doesn't have to be a problem for you or your family." Hillcrest's voice was cold.

"How could that be? You just told me Nana doesn't have the money to pay all those medical bills. It would kill her to lose that farm."

Hillcrest snarled his words. "That's where you can make a difference."

"Mr. Hillcrest, I still don't understand. What do you have to do with all this? How do you know all this about my family?"

"Let's make this simple. When I hear you've signed your letter of intent with Kansas, those bills will be history."

"How?"

"Kid, you don't ask questions. And, by God, you don't say anything to anyone. You say one thing to that high school coach or to your family, you might just as well kiss the farm good-bye." Hillcrest was shouting now. "Time's up, Son. Your grandmother, you say you call her Nana? Well, Nana can't fight those insurance companies any longer. She's got to pay her bills. Now do you understand?"

Lance didn't know what to say, what to think. He felt as if he had taken a powerful blow to the stomach. "I think so," he mumbled.

"See how easy it is? You finally get to do something good. You sign with Kansas and your family gets rid of a lot of pain. And the best part is, no one else needs to know."

"But --" Lance wasn't allowed to finish his sentence.

"No buts. You sign and life is good. End of story. It's been nice talking to you, Son. I will expect good news on signing day."

Lance heard the phone click. He held it tightly to his ear, willing the conversation to have never occurred. It started to beep. Apprehensively, he set the phone down.

Completely alone in the sterile room, he recognized there was no one he could confide in, no one who could make him understand why this was happening. He looked at the clock. *I'm late.* After a few powerfully deep breaths, he gathered himself and numbly headed to the car.

Chapter 31

Coach Jones had an assortment of fruit, breakfast sandwiches, and rolls waiting on a small table set for two.

"Sorry, Coach. Had a phone call just as I was leaving the hotel."

"Everything OK?"

"Sure, Coach." Lance hoped his face didn't expose the turmoil racing through his body.

"Hope you had a good time last night."

"Sure did. Aaron was an especially fun guy to be around."

"That's good. Aaron is a fun guy to be around in Rupp arena, unless you're competing against the Wildcats. Then he can make life difficult."

They each filled a plate. Lance could barely look at the food.

"Straight out, Lance: we want you to wear Kentucky Blue. You're exactly what we look for in a player."

Jones' words were wonderful. This was the day his family had hoped for, dreamed for. But that phone call. One phone call sucked away all the joy, all the pleasure; faster than a viper striking its innocent prey. "I'm extremely flattered, Sir."

"When will you make your decision?" Coach wasn't pressuring.

Lance responded as he had to Coaches Booth and Meadors. "This won't be an easy one, Sir. I told everyone I would wait until after all my visits."

"Then it's for sure you're not going to visit anyone else?"

"No one else, Sir. It's hard enough as it is. I don't need any more complications." Lance tried to suppress his stomach's effort to make him run out of the room. "Coach, I have grown up knowing Kentucky is super. Your staff is great. It's just that the other schools are special, too. I'm humbled to have such wonderful offers.

Coach Jones answered honestly, displaying class. "I know, Lance. I know."

There was no way Jones could have known what turmoil Lance was dealing with inside. He had to think that Lance's only problem was picking a great school. He sought one last chance to convince Lance to join the Blue and White.

"We recruit only the best, Lance, because we are the best of the best. I'm not bragging. That was true before they hired me and it will be true when I retire and the next coach takes over the reins. We want you to be part of our future. I wish you Godspeed in your decision."

They continued a cordial conversation, finished their breakfast, and said amiable good-byes. At 10:15 Lance was again in front of the Hyatt. As he had on Friday morning, he pulled into the parking lot, ran across High street, and sprinted up to his room. He sat on the bed, dazed, contemplating what to do. Why hadn't Nana told the family she needed help? He couldn't let her lose all she and Grandad had worked for. Already packed, knowing nothing could be done right now, he took another deep breath and called room 420.

"Hello?" Helen sounded so happy. What would happen if she knew about Hillcrest?

"Good morning, Mom. I'm back. Are you ready?" he asked, begging his voice to act normal.

"Sure, Honey. I figured you'd be back by ten or a little after. I'm ready for a great drive home."

Mother and son pulled their black suitcases through the Hyatt doors. They crossed the road and hiked up several steps to the parking lot. The sun peeked through a few cotton ball clouds and beamed warmly on Lance's crew cut as he placed his suitcase into the trunk, his Mom's in the back seat. The fresh, crisp air gave him a moment's relief as he opened the passenger door.

"It's nice to be around a gentleman," Helen thanked him.

Lance forced a smile. He snuck one last peek at Rupp Arena and tried to gain his composure. The joyful possibility of having his Green Bears return to Rupp next March for the Sweet 16 Championship was buried under a heap of anxiety.

Within minutes they were on route 60, and then to the mountain parkway for their return trip. Helen watched the driver staring at the road in front of them. She knew her son would have a tormenting week ahead making his decision. She just did not know how tormenting. Unaware of the phone call, her heart was rooting for him to become a Wildcat, but that same heart told her it was Lance's life, not hers.

Mother's intuition caused her to probe. "Honey, have you met anyone on your visits you especially liked?"

"You mean like players? Guys that I would like to play beside?" Lance was hoping his mother would say yes.

"Yes." It was not the yes he had hoped for. Helen's voice let him know she hadn't meant players. "Or anyone else you thought was nice or interesting?"

Silence stood between them. It seemed like hours, but had only been a few minutes.

Helen was puzzled at his reluctance to talk. She tried to help.

"You still like J.C., right?"

"You bet, Mom. He showed a lot of character giving back that car. I still hope he doesn't have any trouble with the NCAA." This was good. He could talk about J.C., or other people he met, just not Lisa, and he could silently continue to gather his thoughts about Hillcrest. "Jay at Ohio State is a keeper. Didn't you like Jay and his girlfriend, Sherry?"

"They are a sweet couple." Helen didn't take the perplexed look off her face.

"Aaron was an interesting guy, here at Kentucky. I think he's a great player. I know the coaches like him."

"Anyone else?" Helen politely urged. She hadn't forgotten all the phone calls her son had made to Lawrence.

The rolling hills outside of Lexington were no competition for the mountains surrounding Connsburg. The Camaro crossed the Red River several times. They passed horse farms, herds of cattle, miles of fences, hay barns, big houses, small houses, trailers, fallen rock zones, and countless churches with white steeples piercing the blue sky. Lance was blind to the countryside. All he could think about was how he would explain Lisa to his mother. How could he tell her the trouble Nana was in? Hillcrest. How to explain him? Hillcrest had made it perfectly clear that his lips better be sealed about their conversation. Reluctantly, he chose to address Lisa. His voice cracked, but his words still came out sincerely.

"I did meet a real nice girl."

"A real nice girl?" Helen's eyes sparkled.

"Yeah, J.C.'s friend. The one I mentioned. Cherie gave me a hard time about her last week. The one I called."

"What's her name again?"

"Lisa. Lisa Gosline."

"She's from Kansas. Isn't she?"

"Yes. Well, not actually. She's from Missouri. Lisa lives in Kansas City. Did you know that Kansas City is in Missouri? She's a freshman at KU."

"An older woman? A-ha!"

Lance welcomed his mom's smile. It lifted his spirits.

"Just a year older."

"What do you like about her? Did you spend much time with her?"

Lance thought, *She's beautiful, she's real smart. I loved it when I held her.*

He said, "She played high school basketball," evading the second part of his mother's question.

"Tell me all about her. What does she look like? Was she a good player? Does she play for Kansas?" Helen's questions kept coming.

"Oh, no, she played ball in high school, but wasn't good enough to play at Kansas. She's a really good student... and she's beautiful. I mean really beautiful." He was surprised that those words came so easily, but was still too nervous to look at anything other than the road straight ahead.

"Wouldn't you know it?" Helen's head tilted back in the seat. "My boy goes all the way to Kansas to find him someone he cares about," Her lips turned upward. She looked content.

"Is it OK with you, Mom? You know, that I like her?"

"Lance, you don't have to ask me to like someone. You've never asked my permission before and I know you've had lots of girlfriends. Whether she's the right or wrong person, it's up to you. The Lord doesn't even tell you when someone is the right person. He lets you figure it out for yourself." Helen released a quick chuckle. "Sort of a hunting for Waldo thing. He's kind enough to give you a few signs along the way if you watch for them." She touched the side of her face, but the smile would not go away. "Left me a few breadcrumbs that led me to the guy you call Dad. Fortunately, his crumbs were pretty big too." Helen looked over at her son and strengthened her voice in an effort to boast. "You are aware that your father followed me to Eastern Kentucky. We got married, and I've never regretted it one day since."

Lance smiled. He remembered the way his dad told his version of the Eastern Kentucky story. Milt had looked around mischievously making sure no one could hear him tell it his way. *Mom's story was probably more accurate.*

"We were a little further along than you are right now. I mentioned marriage only because that is what we ended up doing." She looked at him seriously, as if to ask, "Is this the one -- the one you will eventually marry?"

"I know, Mom." Lance tried to show control and wanted to convey he knew what she meant. "Lisa and I have only known each other for two weeks." His heart missed a beat, declaring it was in control and demanded he confess. "But I think about her all the time."

"If she's as beautiful and as smart as you say, then she's worth thinking about."

"Thanks. I knew you'd understand." Lance was relieved. But relief was short lived. *Would she understand Hillcrest? Did she know about Nana and was not saying anything?* Setting one elbow on the armrest, he asked, "Is Nana all right?"

"That's the second time in two weeks you've asked about her. What's wrong? Nana's fine. Son, do you know something you're not telling me?"

"Have you noticed that her car needs to be tuned up?" Lance exploded. "And Nana ran out of chicken a few months back when Greg and I were having supper with her. When doesn't Nana cook enough for an army? She ran out of Pepsi! You know she never does that."

"Mom would tell me if something was wrong," Helen answered weakly. "Those aren't big things, Lance. Besides, maybe Nana's finally cutting back." He could tell by her expression he had scared her.

Lance's hands were tied. Hillcrest's voice kept ringing in his ears, "You don't say anything . . . You can kiss the farm good-bye . . . You sign and life is good."

Lance stopped his inquiry. Things seemed hopeless. Maybe predetermined. For the rest of the ride, he numbed his mind with talk about Greg's big game next Friday while Helen talked about who would probably come down for Thanksgiving. Nothing else was mentioned about Lisa, Nana, or Lance's decision.

Chapter 32

Before Helen or Lance could get out of the Camaro, Cherie ran out the back door ready to greet them. Bubba was also part of the welcoming party.

Lance gave Cherie a hug. "It's good to see my favorite sister."

"I'm your only sister, Boy," Cherie said as she gave Lance a mock blow to his right side.

Helen rubbed Bubba's head then hugged Cherie. "You and Greg been good for Nana?"

"Absolutely. Just ask her."

"I'll get the suitcases, Mom." Lance leaned down to pet Bubba who finally came to him after Helen was out of view.

Nana was busily preparing lunch for the family. After an embrace, Helen asked how she could help.

"Nothing, Honey, the roast is close to being done and the potatoes will take just a little bit longer. Cherie helped me make a salad and Greg coaxed me into baking some oatmeal raisin cookies." She wiped her chin. "Don't have too many left -- he ate half the dough."

Greg got up from the game on TV when he heard voices. He walked into the kitchen laughing. "Now Nana, you ate about as much of the dough as I did." His brother hadn't been one of the voices he heard. "Where's Lance? He need any help?"

"You're too late." Lance said as he entered from the back door. "The bellman already has the luggage."

"Give me Mom's before you mess up her clothes."

"Are you sure a playoff quarterback should be carrying this much weight?" Lance sat the suitcases down, joyfully giving his brother a high five. "Thanks for saving me, Man. I really wanted to see you guys play again."

"Me too," Nana said before she was enveloped by her oldest grandson.

Lance cherished the frail body enclosed in his arms. He didn't want to let her go. Without words, he wanted to find some way to let her know that everything would be fine. He would take care of her problems.

"What are we having?" Lance choked, coughed to cover it. "Sure smells good in here."

"Just a nice rump roast, green beans, and mashed potatoes. Your dad called and said he would be home in about an hour. We'll eat then."

Helen and Lance unpacked. When Milt arrived, the Stoler family sat down to enjoy the special company of each other. Greg's performance in last Friday night's game was completely evaluated again and Lance gave his review of everything that happened in Lexington, excluding the phone call and a girl named Shelby.

Everyone started to clear the table. "You guys go in and see who's winning," urged Helen. "I'll finish up in here." Nana declined the offer. She did not expect an argument and got none. Her daughter knew better.

Milt and the boys didn't hesitate. They headed to the family room. Cherie followed. She wasn't that much interested in the football game, but seemed eager to hear more about the trip to Lexington and whether Lance had made up his mind yet.

Hillcrest's phone call was banging around inside his head. Watching the game and talking about his visit offered a convenient mask for his pain.

"You know all three schools have made it to the Final Four and won national championships." The family room experts heard Lance's controlled voice.

"Any idea who won the most championships?" Milt asked.

"Even I know that answer," Cherie called out as if it were a game.

How about the most football championships?" Greg joined the game spirit.

"Kansas will win their first one when you show up," Lance said. "Dad, you know he could play quarterback there tomorrow."

Milt brushed away Lance's effort to score one for Kansas. "In my mind, your brother could play quarterback at any of your three schools!"

Lance had no way of knowing exactly what his sister was thinking, but a devious smile appeared when they made eye contact. She seemed to be asking, "Why don't you just come out and tell them about Lisa?"

His firm stare transmitted, *The word secret mean anything to you?*

While the analysts continued their debate in the family room, the two women finished their work, grabbed sweaters, then retired to the back porch.

They rested peacefully. The swing moved gently as the afternoon sun comfortably warmed them. Helen was gathering her thoughts. She had some questions to ask. Nana spoke first. "Well, Honey. Where do you think he'll go?"

"It's hard to say." Her voice clearly indicated she did not know. "He loves Kentucky."

"But." It was a forceful but. Nana always wanted to get to the heart of the matter. Fast.

"Ohio State is special to him. He feels the coaches there want him, but more importantly, I think he has confidence he can make a difference there." Helen looked right at her mom. "You know the Wildcats could sign an All-American from somewhere else in a second if he chooses another school."

"What about those Jayhawks?" Nana seemed to notice Helen was skirting them. "My gosh, Helen, it's way out there next to Nebraska."

"I know, Mom. He was moved by the people of Kansas. I haven't heard him say anything glowing about their coach, but for some reason he has looked past the coach. He loves the tradition at Kansas."

"What else? You're not telling me something."

Helen took a deep breath, and prepared an honest answer. "Two things, Mom."

"Well, tell me."

"Lance seems worried about you." Helen peered into Nana's eyes.

"Well, Lord, Honey, I'm the least important factor in his decision."

"No. I mean he thinks something's wrong."

"Now, Helen, I'm fine. You know kids. Always worryin' about their grandparents." Nana's face turned pale. "Tell me the second thing."

"He's developed a friendship with a star player from Kansas City. And . . ."

"And what?"

"And... he might have fallen in love for the first time."

"Who?" Helen could tell that her mom had not expected love to be part of the equation.

"A girl he met on that visit. His friend introduced them."

"What's she like?" Nana was full of questions now. "Do you know anything about her? What's her family like?"

"Well you know Lance. He won't say much. What he did say was that she's beautiful." Helen looked out at her garden. "I suspect she's gorgeous."

Both women knew Lance inside and out. "Then she's gorgeous." Nana stated flatly.

"So, I don't have a clue as to what he'll do." Helen sighed. "Brace yourself. Love...sure is powerful."

"Don't I know it! When Hoover gave Milt a hard time, I remember how you acted." Nana freed a tender grin. "You'd have followed Milt anywhere."

The women kept the swing moving but no words were spoken for several minutes. Each gazed out into the yard and clear sky. A band of cardinals chirped majestically, as if harmonizing a new song just for the two of them.

Nana finally broke the silence. "Who'd have thought it?" She huffed. "You can kiss Kentucky and Ohio State goodbye."

Helen didn't say a word. She welcomed her mother's arm gently slipping around her shoulders.

In the family room the TV had just been turned off. The Miami Dolphins had no problem beating the New York Jets. Greg and Lance decide to go for a run. Lance said he needed to run off Nana's cooking, but he wanted it more for the therapy than a workout. Milt's exercise was to simply change positions in his favorite chair, but he did offer to hold down the fort. "You guys have a good time. I'll turn the TV on in a little bit, just to make sure the Forty-Niners get off to an early lead on the Cowboys.

Greg was sitting on the back porch when Lance came through the back door. The women had departed the friendly confines of the swing and were investigating the garden. Lance shouted out, "Hey, Mom, Greg and I are going for a run. We'll be back in a minute."

"OK." Helen made a slight wave. "Be careful."

The boys prepared to take off when Bubba came racing up to them. Tired of gardening talk and sensing where the boys were headed, he joined the journey.

Stride for stride, the boys ran down the concrete path with Bubba happily galloping behind. After a mile, the runners headed down the only street that ever had much traffic on Sunday afternoons. Lance noticed a coal truck coming up behind them. They were running into the oncoming traffic lane, but he still encouraged Greg to move over a bit more.

Lance turned to check whether Bubba was safely off the street. The powerful truck moved closer, noticeably not following the speed limit. The engine roared louder and louder as it approached.

Greg had moved ahead of Lance about ten paces and was unable to hear Bubba barking at the approaching red beast. The barking had no impact so Bubba squared up to the truck as it passed him, surely an attempt to protect his boys. He moved a few feet onto the road, continuing to bark at the beast.

A green Dodge driven by an elderly woman suddenly came around the corner, passed Greg and Lance and was headed straight for Bubba, who was still barking at the red monster that had just passed by. She slammed on the brakes, and skidded.

Greg, far enough ahead, did not realize what was happening. Sadly, Lance witnessed the whole thing. Horrified, he watched as the Dodge hit the magnificent Lab from behind. Bubba spun clockwise and rolled over several times before his poor body came to a halt on the road's apron.

"Bubba!"

Greg heard Lance's scream. He turned back immediately. "No! Not Bubba!"

Both boys sprinted to their beloved pet. Blood dripped from Bubba's mouth. Unable to move, his dark eyes were clouded in pain. The lady in the Dodge pulled over and got out of her car.

"I'm so sorry." Sorrow was evident on her frail face. "I didn't mean to hit him. He jumped out right in front of me as I came around the corner after that truck."

"I know, Ma'am. I saw it. It wasn't your fault," Lance was crying as he sat on the ground stroking the lab's side. "Greg, go get Dad. I'll stay with Bubba."

Before Lance could finish his words, Greg was gone. The Lord had blessed him with speed -- it was now used to full capacity. Within minutes he was back at the house, screaming for his dad to come fast.

"Bubba's hurt!" Greg shouted, trying to catch his breath.

"Get in the Tahoe!" Milt burst from his chair. "Show me where he is."

The whole family heard Greg's screams. They all ran to the front yard as the Tahoe peeled down the driveway, around the curve by the Big Sandy River, and out of sight.

Milt saw Lance leaning over Bubba as he turned the corner. He slammed on the Tahoe's breaks and jumped out.

"We've got to get him to the vet." They gently lifted Bubba into the back of the Tahoe. He let out two feeble howls of pain, then seemed to be unconscious, yet still breathing. Lance and Greg jumped in beside their friend.

Dr. Sherwin's home was less than two miles and his office was right next door. Milt veered the Tahoe into the Sherwin driveway, honked the horn, then flew out of the truck. His determined knock on the door quickly summoned Mrs. Sherwin.

"May I help you?" she asked with a friendly smile.

"Yes, I'm Milt Stoler. It's an emergency. Is Doc Sherwin in?"

Dr. Sherwin, a small man with dark curly hair and a freckled complexion, had treated Bubba since he was a puppy. Most of the time it was for routine shots, never anything serious. He got up from the Forty-Niners - Cowboys game and came to the door.

"Milt, what are you doing here? What's wrong?"

"It's Bubba," Milt said with a shaky voice. "He's been hit."

"Where is he?"

Lance and Greg had the back door of the Tahoe opened.

"Let me see him." Dr. Sherwin moved quickly to the car.

Lance and Greg jumped out and stood quietly by their dad. After carefully placing his hands about Bubba, Dr. Sherwin said, "I have a stretcher in my office. Let's get it. He needs to go inside so I can get a better look."

His expression did not bode well for the condition of their precious pet. Carefully they moved Bubba and Dr. Sherwin started his procedures. The mourning Stolers accepted seats in the waiting room.

The walls, covered with beautiful black and white framed photos of Jenny Wiley State Park, would normally draw raves from the good Doctor's customers, but on this Sabbath day, they had no impact. A glance at the photos, a peek out the window, a stare at the magazine stand, a trip to the water cooler, could not stop the anxiety. The slightest sound, the ticking of the clock, a deep breath, a sniffle, a crossing of the legs became magnified, causing even more apprehension.

Milt rubbed both hands along the side of his head. "I'd better call." Milt pulled out his cell phone. "They'll be worried sick."

"Hello?" Helen answered rapidly.

"It's me. Bubba's been hit. We brought him over to Dr. Sherwin's."

"How is he? Please tell me my sweetheart will be alright!" She pleaded.

"He's in with Doc." Milt looked at his sons. "The boys are taking it pretty hard. Lance saw the whole thing happen."

"Oh no!" Helen sighed.

"Let's pray for the best."

"I'll tell Cherie and Mom." Helen rallied all of her power to control her grief. She gathered herself. "Milt, I love you."

"Me, too, Honey. Me, too."

Dr. Sherwin stayed in his office with Bubba for a long time. The men patiently waited, hoping Dr. Sherwin would perform a miracle. The door cracked open.

"Milt, can I see you?"

Not a word was said. Milt got up, walked in, and the doctor closed the door. Ten minutes later, Milt opened the door. He could not conceal the tears streaming down his face. The boys had rarely seen their Rock cry. Milt sat next to his sons and offered an explanation.

"Things aren't good. Bubba has shattered his shoulders, broken both front legs, and has a terminal concussion. He's still breathing, but in great pain. Doc recommends he be put to sleep."

This tragedy was taking their friend from them -- forever. Tears were impossible to hold back. Devastated for the second time in one day, Lance wiped his forearm across his eyes. "What do we tell Mom and Cherie?"

Sunday night was a rough time for the family, especially Helen. Bubba had been her soul mate in her garden, on walks down by the river, and on the back porch. The whole family was familiar with the frequent picture of Helen in the swing, Bubba resting quietly by her feet. Efforts to hide her pain were unsuccessful. Unlike her son and mother, Helen had no mask.

The day of painful loss came to a close with hugs that lasted a little longer and seemed to have a little more meaning. By ten, most of the family was tucked away, trying to rest for the next day. Lance was not. He desperately searched for the safety of sleep, but the events of the day haunted him. Bubba's passing, Hillcrest's proposal, and his impending decision raged like a storm inside his head. Abruptly, there was a bolt in his thoughts. *I told Lisa that I would call.* He flew out of his bed, slid down the hallway, and into the kitchen.

"Hello?" A sleepy voice answered.

"It's Lance."

"I've been worried sick." Lance heard concern in her voice. "You said you'd call when you got back from your trip," She scolded.

"Lisa." He tried to stay composed. "It's terrible."

"What is it?"

"The trip went fine, but when I got back, Greg and I went for a run and well . . . Bubba, our dog, got hit."

"Is he OK?" Lisa gasped.

"No, he was hurt real bad." Lance explained. She listened silently to every word. His voice was raw with emotion. He shared memories about how adorable Bubba was as a puppy. How he would scare away salesmen, work in the garden with his mom, run with him and Greg. It felt comforting to talk about it. "When I came home, he was always there to greet me, Lisa. Always. Now he's gone."

Lisa finally spoke, calmly, "Lance, the Lord is faithful. He'll strengthen you. I just know He will."

Lance wanted to share more. *Can I say something about Hillcrest?* As much as he wanted to, he knew better, he knew the consequences. He wished they could be sitting on the back porch swing, holding hands and dreaming of their future. His troubles would be gone and life would be easy again. He looked at the stove clock. It was late.

"I better go, Lisa. Thanks for talking to me."

"Try to get some sleep, Lance."

Her voice was reassuring. He willed it to echo through his mind till sleep finally came.

Chapter 33

Monday morning saw the family trying to manage the first day without their friend. There were no arguments, no problems waiting for the bathroom, and no complications with breakfast. They all gathered together around the table eating their cereal. Conversation was limited.

Milt was first to speak. "Your mom and I feel it would be best if we pick up Bubba's body from Dr. Sherwin, have a service in the garden tonight, and bury him there.

"Thanks, Dad," Lance knew Bubba would have wanted to come home.

"I would love that." Cherie had tried sleeping with cool cloths on her eyes—but they were still red.

"Is that what you want? You'll want him forever in a corner of your garden?" Greg asked his mom.

"Yes, Son."

"We'll do it right after dinner," said Milt. He pushed silently away from the table.

On the schools steps, Lance shared Sunday's tragedy with his friends. Bruce, Terry, and Dale were no strangers to the big black lab's loving personality. They were heartbroken.

Little was mentioned about his Kentucky visit. Everyone assumed his reluctance to talk was generated by Bubba's death.

During third period, Coach Hunter predictably pulled Lance out of study hall. Nothing was mentioned about Bubba nor Hillcrest. Lance swallowed hard and tried to give his coach the best answers he could. Lance could tell

Hunter figured his peculiar behavior was nervousness about his impending decision.

The school was aglow with excitement about the football playoffs. Surrounded by such festivity, Lance hid easily. He simply wanted to finish school, have practice, and get home.

Nana arrived before six o'clock. The family sat down and Milt said grace. The meal was over in less than fifteen minutes. Little was eaten from anyone's plate.

Milt and Lance headed outside. A grave had already been prepared and a big rock for a headstone rested by the mound of dirt.

"I came home this morning and got things ready," Milt informed his oldest. "Last night, your mom showed me where she wanted Bubba." He set his shovel down. "After school, she went down to the creek and found this rock for his headstone."

"That'll be perfect," Lance said, weakly.

Next to the site was a rolled canvas that enclosed Bubba's body.

"If you'll help me, let's set him down and cover him up. Your mom and I agreed it would be best if just the two of us saw this part."

"I'm glad Greg and Cherie don't have to watch." Lance helped his father do what was necessary.

They smoothed out the site and slowly rolled the stone to the head of the grave. When Greg brought out the three women, they saw a smooth patch of dark, Kentucky dirt and a sturdy headstone. The rock was strong, solid, splendid -- just as Bubba had been.

The family gathered around the site. Milt urged Helen to say a few words first. The sky was dark. Stars were everywhere. Wind blew gently through the hills. The howling of neighborhood dogs could be heard in the distance. They seemed to know that one of their friends was no longer with them.

"Dear Lord, please bless all of us as we remember our precious friend with the love you taught us for all creatures. Let us all be strong and cherish his memory. In your honor, Amen." She placed fresh cut flowers from the garden on the grave.

Cherie was crying. "I love you, Bubba."

Greg held her up with his strong arm. "Me, too." He couldn't say more.

Lance spoke with the same tight jaw Milt had been displaying for the last twenty-four-plus hours. "You were a dear friend. Sleep tight, Boy." He felt empty.

"God speed, Bubba. This family will miss you. Amen." Milt ended their service.

Arms around each other, the six mourners walked back to the house, with Lance silently praying for strength to move on.

The rest of the week moved rapidly. Lance continued to grieve for Bubba and plow the fields of decision. He talked to his friends, he talked to his high school coaches, and he considered everything each of the college coaches said as they called the house for their NCAA permitted phone calls. On Tuesday, J.C. called to work his friend over about coming to Kansas and he found out about Bubba. He reacted like Lance's other friends; he compassionately left him alone with his thoughts.

J.C. was not told about Hillcrest; however, not telling his friend caused him to burn even more. He was reaching the boiling point. Something needed to be done.

He approached the laundry room. Helen was finishing a last load of clothes. "Mom, would you do me a favor?"

"Sure, Honey. What do you need?"

"Would you just go check on Nana?" Frustration caused the words to explode from his lips.

"You really are bothered, aren't you? You're making me a little scared."

"Mom, please just go check." His voice was begging. "It won't take long."

Helen left the clothes and drove out to the farm. As she pulled up, she saw the old basketball hoop, the tattered grey barn, and was surprised that only one light was on. She stepped onto the front porch, knocked at the door, and walked in calling, "Hello! It's Helen."

She found her mother sitting in the brown recliner Hoover had always considered his private chair. Helen saw right away she had been crying.

"What's wrong?" She sat down right beside her.

"Oh, Helen, it's nothing."

"Mom, this isn't like you."

"I didn't want to be a burden to you, to Milt, to the kids." She sounded so tired.

"You're no burden, Mother. What is it?"

Nana pulled out a white handkerchief and wiped her face.

"It's the farm. The insurance people say they won't pay for the last year of Hoover's bills and I've got to sell it to make everything whole." She was sobbing. "Honey, I've tried. Those times I said I was in church or at Aunt Normie's, I wasn't. For the past two months, I've been driving to Lexington every Thursday to meet with attorneys. I've got to pay them, too." Now she was choking with sobs.

"So that's why you didn't stay with us the night before Lance went to Ohio State." Several unanswered questions were suddenly resolved. "What did the attorneys say?"

"They thought that they could do something at first, but now they say it's hopeless. The insurance companies won't pay."

Helen was furious. "No, Mom. You are not losing this farm."

"There is nothing you can do. The attorneys have done all they can." She got out her handkerchief again.

"Daddy didn't save and work all his life to have something like this happen. He paid his insurance bills every month." Helen put her arm around her mother. "I won't stop until this is handled right. I don't care if I have to call every politician in this state. I'll call the governor if I have to."

The women sat in silence and held each other.

"We won't say anything to the family. This is a rough week because of Bubba, Greg has his game, and Lance . . . Mom, don't ask me how he knew, but Lance is the one who told me to come see you tonight."

"He did?" She wiped her nose. "I didn't want to interfere with his decision. I didn't want any of you to know. I didn't want to mess up your family's special time."

"You're not, Mom. For right now, not even Milt will know. Let me go to work on this."

They hugged each other, said a prayer. Helen headed back home.

Milt was the first one to greet her. "How's Mom doing?"

"She's all right. Still feeling bad about Bubba."

Lance had been listening for the car to pull in and was only seconds behind his dad.

"She's all right?" Lance was shocked.

"I sat with her for about an hour. Wants Greg to throw a couple of touchdown passes on Friday. And she's not wondering like you are where you should go to college. She'd have you signing with Kentucky before daylight." Helen set her keys down on the counter and headed towards her bedroom. "It's been a long day."

Lance knew his Nana. She wouldn't budge. It didn't matter what his mom said. Nobody would find out until it was too late. Lance knew what he had to do. Nana will not lose the farm.

Wednesday, everyone prepared to be on their way, except Helen. She told Milt she was not feeling well and was going to stay home. It was unusual, but no one, not even Milt, questioned her. They all felt she deserved a day off. Only she knew her real motive.

Lance e-mailed Lisa every day. Each day she responded. She hoped she would be one of the first to be privileged to know his decision. Wednesday came and went, though, and she still heard no resolution. She would have to wait.

Thursday night brought a taste of normalcy for the family. The family walked to Billy Ray's Restaurant, home of the original "Poolroom Hamburger." The double burger with bacon and cheese was a handful for anyone, including all three Stoler men. Helen particularly liked Thursday's menu because the special was pan-fried country chicken, pinto beans, and macaroni and cheese. Comfort food.

The restaurant was located just three blocks away, right down Front Street with the Big Sandy River flowing behind. The Stolers arrived in good spirits. Recovery from Sunday's darkness was still a work in progress, but the excitement about Greg's game had caused a welcome diversion.

The Stolers were regulars at this establishment, and received plenty of greetings as the five strolled back to their favorite table. Sheila waited on them. She had graduated from Akers High only three years earlier. She loved waiting on the Stolers, not only because Milt was generous with his tips, but she also took pleasure in waiting on his good-looking sons.

Billy Ray's did nothing to damage their reputation. Once again, they served the best dinner in town. The Stolers finished, said goodbyes on the way out, and started an unhurried walk back home. Milt and Helen strolled a few steps ahead, followed by Greg and Cherie while Lance brought up the rear. Helen kept looking up at the sky, naming stars she saw. She seemed to be in much better spirits today.

Cherie dropped back and walked with Lance. "You calling Lisa tonight?" She whispered.

"Maybe."

"No maybes. You're calling her." Cherie said a little louder.

"Now what are you all talking about back there?" Helen asked.

"Oh, nothing. Lance was explaining to me how beautiful the stars are."

"Lance talking about the stars?" asked Milt. "Yeah, right. You two must be up to something."

"He's probably telling Little Sis where he's going." Greg's voice was a mixture of humor and a tad bit of envy.

"Nope, I'm just enjoying the evening. Not bad company tonight."

They turned up their driveway and everyone scattered. Lance had a half hour of homework, which he easily handled. Restless to make a few phone calls, he headed down the hallway and into the kitchen. It was empty. He cracked open the back door slightly. Helen and Milt were quietly swinging. "Could I make a couple of phone calls?"

"Who you wanting to call now?" Milt asked.

"Honey, you can make some calls," Helen interrupted. "Milt, I need your help on something," Helen said as an excuse. "Come on. Let's go inside."

Milt seemed puzzled, but he understood his wife quite well. He followed her commands. They went through the kitchen and headed back to their bedroom where he could help Helen with her "something." Passing Lance, Milt gave him a squeeze on the shoulder and his mom gave him an understanding smile.

In the master bedroom, Milt asked, "What the heck was that all about?"

"Lance met a girl in Kansas and I think he feels something special for her."

"No way, not one in Kansas. What's wrong with a girl from Kentucky?"

"Everyone can't be as lucky as you, Milt."

Lance's first call was to J.C. He wanted to talk to him about the Jayhawks, but more importantly he wanted to get some more feedback on Lisa.

"Burbridges."

"Is this Mrs. Burbridge?" Lance recognized her voice.

"Yes it is."

"This is Lance."

"Well, hello. My boy sure wants to talk to you. He is wondering every day when you are going to come and be his teammate."

"He'd be a great teammate, Ma'am."

"Here he is, Honey."

"It's about time you called," J.C. proclaimed. "You still sitting on top of that fence?"

"Yeah. I'm trying to get off. No later than next Wednesday."

"Coaches here are relentless. They're still worried you might stay home and be a Wildcat."

Lance wanted to spend only a little time on basketball. "Thanks for the surveillance. Have you seen Lisa lately?"

"You've got that one covered. She asks me all the time. Are you coming? Are you coming? She really likes you. What do you want me to tell her? I'll see her this weekend."

"Tell her you think that I really like her," Lance answered.

"Whoa, so things are heating up. I'll tell her. That only helps Kansas."

Comfortable about his feedback on Lisa, Lance aimed to fortify his most inner thoughts, to make sure his camouflage was working.

"So you think that Kansas is still my best option?" Lance asked. He had come to grips with Hillcrest's offer. Knew his responsibility. Nana would have no more worries. No one would know, family or friends. It was over. As far as they were concerned, he would still be seeking advice and making his decision next Wednesday.

"You know that's what I want. I see only Kansas." Lance heard a change in J.C.'s voice. He sounded more sincere, more reverent, and full of wisdom. "You should do what's in your heart."

There was silence. Lance could not believe what he just heard. His friend really did care.

"Listen to me." As if recovering from a turnover, J.C. relinquished his softness and toughened up. "I'm becoming some big-time advisor."

"No. I think you're becoming a friend. A great friend."

"I better get going. Keep me posted," J.C. insisted. "Have a great weekend."

"You too," Lance said as he hung up the phone.

The next number was easy to dial.

"Hello?

What a beautiful voice.

"Hi, Lisa, this is Lance."

"How are you?"

"Fine." His voice feigned enthusiasm. He was determined to not reveal what was ripping him apart. "We had dinner at one of our favorite restaurants. Got my homework done, so I thought I'd call."

"That's nice. Who ate with you?"

"The whole family. We tried to get Greg ready for his playoff game tomorrow night." His voice could win an Academy Award.

"You mentioned that in your e-mail. Is he ready?"

"Greg's ready. The entire town would love it if we could win."

"Tell him I'll be rooting for him."

The girl in Lawrence and the boy in Connsburg rambled on; their words traveling back and forth over miles of countryside.

"Have you decided, yet?"

"Not yet, Lisa." Lance noticed the concern in her voice. His determination would not let him share. He had to stay on task. No one could know. Again he heard Hillcrest's voice, "And, by God, you don't say anything to anyone."

"Well, maybe it is best you have the weekend to keep gauging what you should do."

"I think you're right," Lance sighed. "What a mess, huh?"

"No. This is the biggest decision you have had to make and you want to get it right. Those are three good schools you are considering. You have to do what is right for you and your family."

Her words hit like thunder on his heart. *Nana is my family.* He forced himself to concentrate.

"Thanks for describing it that way. You know," he stopped, bravely gathering words. "You know I really like talking to you."

"Me too, Lance. Me too."

"Hey, I better go. You're probably studying for a test or something."

"No, I'm fine. I've been studying all night. I stayed in. It's Thursday night. I hoped you would call."

Lance was happy she didn't have to hang up. He listened to her talk about Marla, her classes, and her family. She mixed in a little humor. "Dad would be happy if you didn't go to Kansas. The Missouri Tigers like it any time the Jayhawks don't get what they wanted." Lance could sense she was smiling. "They didn't get me, though."

They both realized that the time had come to end their conversation. "Good-night, Lisa."

"Good-night Lance. Good luck tomorrow night."

Lance quietly placed the phone into its cradle.

Chapter 34

Friday night was cold, but the fear of rain had subsided. The stadium was filled to capacity. This was not the infamous Massilion-Canton McKinley football game in Ohio or one of those big high school contests in Texas. But to all the fans of Akers High School, it didn't matter. Their team was in the playoffs and they had a good shot at winning.

Every available parking place had been captured and the brisk air had brought out heavy jackets, caps, gloves, steaming coffee, and plenty of hot chocolate. The team was ready, the band was ready, the cheerleaders were ready, and for sure all the fans wearing Green were ready.

The Cawood team, cheerleaders, and fans were also ready. It was just bad timing on their part that they ran into a good team with a tremendously focused quarterback. By halftime, number 11 for the Green Bears had thrown two touchdown passes and had run for another one. The score was 28 to 7. The people from Connsburg were delighted to stretch awhile and buy something to warm themselves up.

The third and fourth quarters were stalemated with Akers scoring in the third and giving up a touchdown in the fourth. The players cleared the field. Lance would get to watch at least one more playoff battle.

Greg jogged towards his family. He hugged his mom, Nana, and then his sister. Milt and Lance proudly marched him to the locker room.

"You did good, Son, you did real good," Milt was elated.

Lance grabbed his brother by the shoulder pads and drew him close. "I'm proud to be your brother. Thanks for getting me another game to watch, Mr. Quarterback."

Greg pointed his finger to the sky. "That one's for Bubba," he said.

Saturday was a better day. Lance was beginning to accept his fate. He understood life's decisions are often made *for* you, not *by* you. Practice was early, so he was out the door by 8:30. The quarterback was not far behind. Greg needed the comforts of the high school's whirlpool. His therapy was over before the end of basketball practice, so the little brother peeked into the gym. Bruce, who had also been soaking a few deserving muscles, was with him. Being in the playoffs was fantastic, but they were eager to join Lance and the rest of the team for hoops season. They sprawled out on the bleachers and watched. With each dribble or shot Lance was like an artist trying to get a painting just right. Someone else might use a brush and slap paint on a canvas, but the great ones make paint come alive. So it was with Lance. He was fine art in motion.

Before Greg could say anything, Bruce declared, "He's good. Isn't he? Look at that form."

"He's fun to watch." Greg answered. "Where's he going to school, Bruce?"

"You're his brother. You mean you don't know?"

"In this one, being a relative is no advantage. I don't think he even knows yet. What happened to Bubba last Sunday has really affected him."

"What do you mean?" Bruce asked.

"I'm not sure. He's just been quieter around the house. And then there's that girl he met in Kansas."

"What girl?" Bruce was surprised. "He's been holding out on me."

"Her name is Lisa. He's been calling and e-mailing her. It all happened in the last two weeks."

"A girl. Dang! He's going to Kansas? There goes my football scholarship to Kentucky or Ohio State. Lance would have told those coaches that they should take me. Kansas couldn't care less about a tight end from a small Kentucky high school," Bruce whined. "They go get those studs from Texas."

"You're going to play in college," Greg reassured his tight end. "And that doesn't mean he's going to Kansas. He just seems to be acting a little different. But let's be honest. Lisa isn't hurting the Jayhawks' chances."

Greg waited to walk home with Lance after practice. They were almost out the door when Bruce ran up behind them.

"So Lance, how's the decision coming? You've told the Ohio State people that you and I are a package deal, right?"

"Bruce, you know the only reason they had me visit was because they figured that was the only way they could get you," Lance joked with his friend.

They cut across the football field and headed towards the Big Sandy. It was a warm Indian summer day. The three seemed to silently agree in unison to take the long way home. They stopped next to the riverbank. Bruce picked up a small rock and skipped it across the water's surface. They moved over to some logs in the spot where they used to catch crawdads when they were little. They sat in silence, enjoying the river's rhythm. Finally, Bruce broke the stillness.

"Hey, Big Guy, what's this I hear about a Jayhawk woman?" he asked, as if setting a trap.

"That's classified. Who said something to you?" Lance's eyes took his brother into custody.

"Hey, I got my sources."

"Greg, what have you been telling him?"

Throwing up his hands the younger brother called out, "I know nothing."

"Look, she's someone I met on my visit."

"Is she good-looking?" Bruce asked.

"I can answer that one," Greg replied for his brother. "She's lights out."

Lance burst out laughing.

"Greg, look at him." Bruce chuckled. "That boy's in love."

The three got up and strolled along the river. Lance forced a new subject. "Who's on this afternoon?" He threw another rock across the water. "I hope there's a good game."

"I think it's the Georgia-Florida game." Bruce said. "It should be pretty good. I'd like to be there in person. They say it's the biggest tailgate party anywhere."

"Sounds good to me," Lance said, slapping Bruce on the back. "Let's go watch some football." They picked up their pace and jogged home.

Lance welcomed the diversion of watching football. It didn't cure his problem, but temporarily soothed his inner turmoil. Georgia lost to Florida, Ohio State won, Kansas and Kentucky had another bad day. That evening the boys went over to Bruce's for a party to celebrate Friday's victory. Cherie had a slumber party with some of her classmates, and Milt took Helen to a movie.

Two days in a row, it appeared to be a happy time for the Stolers. All problems were well disguised.

Chapter 35

Sunday morning, the Tahoe pulled into the First Baptist Church. Lance had missed the last three Sundays and was glad to return. Winter coats were on display everywhere because the temperature had dropped to 30 degrees during the night. The service started at eleven. As usual, Milt had his family in their pew by 10:50.

This church was a secure haven for Lance. The white walls and plain wood trim always comforted him. The stained glass windows glistened, ushering in additional light and warmth. Lance gazed up at the magnificent cross hanging behind the pulpit. It encouraged him. To the congregation, he appeared to be silently waiting for the service to begin. They little knew he was vigorously praying for his family, for J.C., and for Lisa. Then he concentrated all meditation on Nana and the farm.

He surveyed the church. The pews were full of family and friends he had known most his life. People who had cheered for him at little league games, football games, and who made the trip to Lexington last spring for the state championship. *What would they all say on Wednesday? It didn't matter! Nana would be fine. Everybody would...* The minister walked in. Lance grabbed a hymnal. The choir began the first verse of *Onward, Christian Soldiers* and the service began.

The ride home was quick. The family returned to a kitchen filled with sweet smells of a honey baked ham. The only thing missing was being able to share the bone with their beautiful black lab. To no one's surprise after the fine meal the boys slipped into the family room. A few NFL games were available. The Bengals played in the first game and the Browns were scheduled to be broadcast in the second against the Oakland Raiders.

Between games, Milt asked Lance if he wanted to shoot some free throws. The sun was breaking through the cloud cover and the temperature had risen to 51 degrees. Perfect weather for any real basketball player.

"I'd love to, Dad."

Milt darted to the bedroom, slid on the tattered Wildcats sweatshirt he always wore on the driveway, then met Lance at the backdoor. Milt picked up Lance's favorite ball out of the basket, "Here, you shoot. I'll rebound."

Lance took a couple of dribbles then nailed three in a row.

"I'm glad all that traveling has not affected your shooting." Milt released a bounce towards Lance.

"I love that sound." Lance started to shoot again, then stopped. "Dad, where do you want me to go?" He rolled the ball in his hands, silently hoping his Dad had not eliminated Kansas. "Have you and Mom talked about it?"

"Your mom and I think and talk about it all the time. It's not easy letting your first son go, you know." He pondered. "Where do we want you to go?" Milt stood with hands on his hips. "That's easy. We love Kentucky. We love our home." He pulled the ball away from Lance's hands while gazing deeply into his eyes. "Son, it's your life. What if Columbus had never sailed? What if Abe Lincoln hadn't gone to Illinois? What if Adolph Rupp had stayed in Kansas?" Milt quickly dribbled the ball one time. "What will make you happy? What will cause you to feel good about yourself? Where will you make a difference?" He dribbled the ball harder and faster. "Make a difference, Lance." Milt cuddled the ball. "I hope I have made a difference at Akers High School."

"You have."

"Well, some school is waiting for you to make a difference." Milt handed back the ball. "Today in church, while we were waiting for the service to begin, I was praying... giving thanks for your brother not getting hurt on Friday. Praying for our family to give Bubba up to the Lord and cherish his memory." Milt wiped the bottom of his nose across his sleeve. "I prayed for Nana's health, and Son, I prayed that some of the sunlight shining through those windows would be the Lord lighting a candle for you. He is with you, Lance, and in a couple of days He will have helped you choose a path." Milt's eyes were suddenly red. His voice deepened as he slapped the ball. "Can you hit ten in a row?"

The net swooshed nine out of ten times. Milt tucked the ball under his arm. "The Browns are on and the sun is running out of gas. Let's go inside." Milt put his other arm around a cherished son.

Walking up the porch steps, Lance ached. It was hard not to share his problem. But once again, he accepted the burden of responsibility. Besides, the decision was made. *No sense bringing another problem to Dad's plate.*

The rest of the day was peaceful. Lance even slept well. His dad's comforting words had created a calm oasis, however brief.

Chapter 36

On Monday, all were out the door as usual. But school was anything but usual. Akers was in high spirits with the challenge of another playoff game and everyone knew, in two days, it would be the first fall signing day for college basketball. The day Lance would step into his future and choose the new course for the rest of his life.

He walked up the steps with Greg and met the gang. They wanted answers and they wanted them now. The only problem was Lance was resolved to wait until the last possible moment. Was there a miracle out there?

Terry spoke up first. "What'll it be, Stoler? Kentucky Blue, Kansas Blue, or Buckeye Red?"

"It's scarlet," Bruce corrected Terry. "Not red."

"Big deal." Terry pushed his head back and joined all the other stares waiting for a response.

"Still too close to call, Terry. But I'm working on it."

"He's not going anywhere. He's staying in Kentucky," Dale calculated.

"What do *you* know? He's headed to Columbus," Bruce predicted.

"Bell's going to ring, we'd better get going." Lance left his friends standing on the steps.

Coach Hunter darted into third period study hall, no doubt wanting to make sure the Lexington coaches had nothing to worry about. He wasted little time getting Lance down the hall and into his office.

Lance examined the room with a new sense of awareness. The desk was old, hardwood maple. Coffee stains decorated its surface. Papers were shuffled in several directions. A whistle lay silently by the phone. The office didn't have the expensive trimmings of the three college coaches he visited, but it had character. It was the sight of hours of labor, plenty of player meetings, and had produced more than its fair share of winning seasons. A bounty of great photos hung silently on the walls. The prize location went to last year's championship team. It was displayed right above Hunter's head. Visitors could not enter without noticing its magnificence.

Coach had been as polite as possible for as long as possible. "Now Lance, you're getting short on time." His tone left no question he was about to fight for Kentucky. "Kansas is good, and Ohio State is real good, but they're not the Wildcats." His lips started to form an apology. "Don't get me wrong. Homer Meadors is a fine man." Apology over, Hunter attacked again. "But we need you at Kentucky. That's the place for you. I know it's your decision, but I thought you ought to know straight up how I feel."

"Thanks, Coach, but which school needs me most?" Lance was steadfast in his resolve to save Nana; he just caught himself asking an honest question. It intrigued him what his coach might say

"Are you kidding? They all need you."

"At which one will I make a difference?"

Hunter leaned back in his chair and looked out his window. He cursed softly to himself.

"Look, the way I see it, Homer Meadors can't win the Big Ten unless he gets someone like you. He's figured it out. Ain't just basketball. Things you do on and off the court, well, they're tied together. Helps a team." Hunter tightened his jaw. "Heck, what am I saying? We need you in Lexington. It'll be great bringing fans over to watch you. It'll be fun watching my point guard on TV." Hunter came close to begging. "You know what I mean, don't you?"

"Sure, Coach." Lance knew he couldn't say any more. "I'd better get going."

That night, Lance approached his dad. "Ok, if I make a phone call?"

This was one of those times the less said, the better. "Sure, son. Make sure you hang it up when you're through." Milt was making a living working with teenagers, helping them with their problems; his smile conveyed he was good at it.

Lance dialed. To his dismay, he heard an answering machine. It's only nine o'clock in Lawrence. Where's Lisa? *Yeah, right. As if she's supposed to sit in her apartment waiting for my calls.*

Lance waited for another ten minutes then placed another call.

"Hello?"

Lance was relieved. "Hi."

"Did you try to call earlier? I went outside for a second and I heard the phone ring. By the time I got back there was no answer."

"Yes, sorry, I hung up." Lance apologized. "I reckoned you were probably out."

"No. I've been waiting. Hoping you'd call."

They talked about small stuff at first, trying to avoid the real issue. Lance explained his conversation with Coach Hunter and that he would be deciding soon. He wanted so much to let her know about Hillcrest. To confess what was going to happen. Determination and focus formed his next words. "Only got a couple of days."

It was easy for her to pick up weariness in his voice. "Don't worry, Lance." She seemed to be trying hard to help him. "I have only known you for a few weeks, but I feel like I've known you all my life. You'll use the direction that God has provided you. I have no doubt." Lisa paused for only a second. "Will you call me tomorrow night?"

"I sure will."

Chapter 37

On Tuesday, excitement was building. The school was buzzing about the game on Friday and predictions about where Lance Stoler was going to play. Basketball practice wasn't until six o'clock, so Lance sprinted home right after his last class. He headed for the back porch. The afternoon air was cool, but his body temperature was spiraling. The heat generated by his thoughts was more than enough to keep him warm.

"I'm home!" Hearing that voice was not a surprise.

"I'm out back."

Helen did not take off her coat. She wrapped it snugly around her as she stepped onto the porch. "Can I sit down with you?" Helen asked. "Don't you need a sweater or something?"

"I'm fine, Mom. Just thinking."

"I have some great news."

Lance was surprised. "What about?"

"You were right about your Nana." Helen gave him one of those looks that always made him feel like he was pretty smart after all. "She's been worried sick about Grandad's hospital bills. Turns out those jerks, I'm sorry, I shouldn't talk that way, the insurance company wasn't going to pay the medical bills. Nana tried." Helen continued to tell Lance what he already knew. "Every Thursday she was driving to Lexington to talk to attorneys. The attorneys finally gave up and said she had no choice but to pay. That's where she had been the night before she drove you to the airport."

"You're kidding." It was easy for him to act amazed.

"Last week when I stayed home, I called every politician I could find a number for. Well, this morning, I got a phone call at school. It was Senator Pletz's office."

"What did they say?"

"They said, "Mrs. Stoler, Senator Pletz was upset when he heard about your situation. They said they didn't think it was fair; Hoover had paid into the carpenter's insurance for over fifty years. When he needed their coverage, they wanted to weasel out. They promised he would have the insurance company call me.""

"When will they call?" Lance asked eagerly.

"They already did. About 2:30 this afternoon they called me at school. They apologized for not handling it properly. They'll cover all of Dad's bills, and they asked me to get Senator Pletz off their backs." Helen glowed like a prizefighter who had just thrown a knockout punch.

Lance could not hold back. He grabbed his mom, and hugged her tighter than he ever remembered.

"The Lord sure does work in mysterious ways!" He shouted with pure joy.

"We couldn't say anything. I didn't want this to impact Greg or you. Not this week. And you know your dad." Her voice was trembling. "I'm thankful you said something. The car, the food, not taking Cherie shopping. Mom was running out of money. She was going to sell the farm to pay for everything. But, now it's over."

"Yes, Mom, you're absolutely right. It is over." Lance sighed happily.

Helen read nothing into Lance's sigh. What she didn't know was she had solved two problems.

Having revealed her secret, she studied her son. "Nana's fine. And Honey, you're fine." She assumed Lance was on the swing contemplating, worrying about his decision. Helen grabbed her son's hand. "Stop worrying about what other people want, what will make them happy. You go make a difference. You go be happy. Wherever that takes you, Dad and I won't be far behind.

Lance threw his arms around his mom once more. "I love you, Mom."

Proudly wearing his varsity jacket, Lance walked home from practice. The cool November air invigorated his mind. His mom had unknowingly put him back on track. Hillcrest's demands were beaten. He thought about his re-cruiting calls, visits from coaches, suggestions from friends, advice from fans, and information gathered on visits. It was as if he had a headset on and was listening to a CD. He heard Coach Hunter's voice, his Nana's, his brother's, his sister's, J.C.'s, the sweet sounds of his Mom and Dad, and finally, the far-off delicate voice of Lisa.

The ones he loved all agreed it was his decision. They made it clear they would be behind him no matter what he decided. He was pulled to stay home, to please everyone in his school and family. But his mom and dad both said for him to be happy, to make a difference. He wanted to make a difference. It was no secret Kentucky could win the SEC and National Championship with or without him.

He was also pulled to stay home because of his roots. But Milt had helped him see that many a man had to step outside the known to become what destiny had planned for them. Was he any different?

What about Kansas? Kansas could be an excellent choice. Hillcrest didn't represent the beautiful people of that state. Booth? He couldn't will himself to admire that coach. But not going to Kansas meant he couldn't be J.C.'s teammate. Only a week ago, his friend demonstrated great courage as a person, not just as a basketball player.

He stopped right in his tracks with his next thought. *Lisa. No Kansas means no Lisa.* What would happen to the fire that had started burning inside of him if he didn't go to Lawrence?

He snapped the top button on his coat and forced himself to concentrate. *I must go where my heart leads me.* *Make a difference.* A place where he could grow and pursue the purpose for which he was created, not just play basketball.

Walking up his driveway, he passed the hoop and moved back to Bubba's grave. He couldn't find peace. He ended up by the back porch swing. He sat down and grabbed the ball from the basket. Once again, the feel of worn leather against his palms soothed his thoughts. He stared at it as though it were a crystal ball that could mysteriously answer his questions. He peered through the kitchen window and saw all was as amiable as ever.

It took only two dribbles of the basketball. *I need to make a difference. I want to make a difference.*

Confidently, Lance pushed off the swing, tucked the ball under his right arm, and entered the back door. Cherie was watching a rerun of *Seinfeld* with Helen. Lance stepped into the family room.

"Where's Dad?"

"Back on the computer." Helen looked up only briefly. "How was practice?"

"Good," Lance said, his voice self-assured. "I need to tell everyone something."

"Oh, boy." Cherie gasped. The force of his voice and his posture got their attention. "I'll get Dad and Greg." The two women knew it was delivery time.

"I'm happy for you son. I'm glad you're ready to share with us." Helen grabbed the remote control and turned off the television.

"What's up?" Milt asked as he followed Greg into the family room.

"Your son has something he wants to share." Helen motioned them to sit down.

Lance looked at each of his precious family members. He clutched the ball in front of him.

"Tomorrow, I'm going to let Coach Meadors know I'm coming to Ohio State."

"Congratulations, Son. We're proud of you." Milt wrapped his arms around Lance in celebration.

"A Buckeye . . . All right!!" Greg high-fived his brother and pulled him into a hug.

Cherie was showing her braces again. "When will the Ohio State soccer coach call me?"

"No later than tomorrow night." Lance good-naturedly predicted.

Helen got up off the sofa. She embraced Lance. "You'll make a difference there. I knew deep down inside that you would." Helen wiped her eyes.

"You need to call Nana," Milt urged, still smiling like he had just sunk a thirty foot putt.

"Absolutely. And I need to call a couple of other people. Then that's it." Lance was relieved the decision had been made.

"I'll get Nana on the phone," said Helen. She dialed her mother's number and talked for just a few seconds. "Here's Lance; he wanted to tell you something pretty special."

Lance remembered Hillcrest's ugly words, "And the best is, no one else needs to know." Neither Nana nor anyone else would ever know about Hillcrest's phone call. Helen handed him the receiver. "I've got some news, Nana."

"Well let's hear it," Nana demanded lovingly.

Lance braced for a second. He knew full well his Nana's love for the Wildcats. "Nana, I'm going to Ohio State."

As Lance would grow older, he would learn more about how powerful unconditional love is. Nana was about to demonstrate.

"Honey, that is great. You're going to dazzle those Buckeyes." She sprinkled love all over his news like it was sugar on a Christmas cookie. "Your mom told me on Saturday that the team in Columbus might really need you and you would make a huge difference with them. I'm happy for you, Lance."

"And I'm so happy for you Nana. You've got to be relieved, too."

"That's nothing, Honey. Tonight's your night." He could hear her giggle. "I'm going to go buy myself something red. Whoops! I mean scarlet!"

Lance was struggling with his emotions. His gut felt tight. He was not sure he could make the next call. He hesitated, sat down by the phone, looked out the kitchen window, took a deep breath, and dialed.

There was no answering machine. A soft voice quickly answered, "Hello?"

"Hi Lisa, it's Lance again."

"Hey, I know who it is. I'm getting to know that voice real well." She was cheerful. "Have you decided?"

"Yes."

"Well, tell me."

"Lisa you know meeting you was one of the best things that has ever happened to me. And I really like the people at Kansas."

Before Lance could continue, Lisa jumped in, "I know that, I know that, but where are we going?"

Lance heard eagerness in her voice. *Why did she say, 'we'?* He paused.

"I decided on Ohio State."

"I'm so happy for you. Ohio State is a great choice."

Lance was confused. Did he underestimate how Lisa felt about him? She really did seem happy.

"I thought maybe you might be unhappy I didn't choose Kansas."

"I'll miss Kansas."

"What do you mean you'll miss Kansas?" Lance asked.

"I have a dad who hates paying out-of-state fees to Kansas. He's a Missouri grad, remember? Also, you have a great sister."

"Sister? How'd Cherie get involved in this?"

"Last Tuesday, I got an e-mail I thought was from you, but it was from Cherie. She wanted to let me know she couldn't figure out where you were going, but she knew if you didn't come to Kansas, you'd be sad. It would cheer you up if you knew I might transfer. So she sent me the e-mail address of the admissions office at Ohio State. She actually covered both bases. She sent me Kentucky's, too. What a sister, huh?"

"Cherie did all that?" Lance was amazed.

"She sure did." Lisa didn't stop. "I e-mailed them both explaining my intention to enroll. Both informed me that because I was a merit scholar in high school, it would be no problem. So, Ohio State is going to get two new students next fall."

"Unbelievable! Lisa, I'm so happy."

"Me, too, Lance."

"I need to call J.C. Do you think he'll understand?"

"He's a friend. Being a teammate is secondary to him. Call him."

"I will."

"Call me tomorrow. I can't wait to tell my dad. He'll be happy he won't have to watch you play for the Jayhawks." Her pause was too short for Lance to respond. "Get ready for him to tease you about what a worthless nut a Buckeye is!" She was still laughing as she hung up the phone.

Lance sat and smiled. *Unbelievable.*

He dialed again. No way would his friend read about it in the papers or find out from one of the Kansas coaches. He had to hear it from the source.

"Hello, Burbridges."

"Hello, J.C."

"Hey, what's going on, Man?"

"I've decided."

"Cut it to me straight."

"It's got to be Ohio State."

He responded like Lisa said he would.

"That's for the best. I'm happy for you, Man. Sad for me, but happy for you."

"It pulls at my heart to know I won't be your teammate." Lance's voice was genuine. "I wanted that very much."

"I know." J.C.'s voice was also genuine.

Lance tried to explain. "In Columbus, I think I can make a difference."

"You will....Hey, who said we can't be teammates? Let's give it five years. I'll meet you in L.A. The Lakers will want both of us."

The ballplayers talked and laughed for another couple of minutes and then closed their conversation. J.C. hung up in Kansas City, and Lance in Connsburg. Each knew roots of a lifelong friendship were thick already.

Sleep was not a problem for Lance. The people he loved most had rallied behind him and were supporting his decision. Tomorrow would take care of itself.

There were no changes in the demands for the shower on Wednesday morning at the Stoler house and the race was on to make certain at least a few Wheaties were still available. Helen's smile was lovely. Her child was going to fly away. But not today.

Cherie was bubbling. She loved it when Lance came by her room last night to talk about a certain phantom e-mail.

Milt was always proud of his children, but this morning, he was filled with pride, ready to burst. Most might say his red tie was a dead giveaway.

Greg enjoyed walking to school with his brother on any day, but especially on this November morning. The few autumn leaves still clinging to their branches gleamed in the morning sunlight. The two talked nothing but football in anticipation of Greg's next game. As usual, the gray sidewalk led the boys right by the Hallmark lady's house. As fate would have it, she was walking out to get the paper.

Both Stolers called out to her. She waved at both. "Good morning, Greg. Good morning, Lance."

About the Author

Allen Bohl's extensive career in athletic administration began at The Ohio State University, then continued at the University of Toledo, Fresno State, and the University of Kansas. For nearly 25 years, Bohl provided impressive leadership for athletic programs across the nation. Throughout his career, he worked diligently to enhance academics, compliance, and fiscal affairs, as well as improving each university's fundraising, marketing, and equity efforts.

Dr.Bohl has always been an educator, a role he continues to this day. From 1971 to 1974, he was an instructor of electronics at Keesler Air Force Base in Biloxi, Mississippi. After finishing his military career, he became a math teacher and coach in New Carlisle, Ohio. During his years in athletic administration, he regularly integrated teaching into his active schedule. His college courses focused on helping students improve management skills and their leadership abilities. Presently, he serves as an adjunct professor in the Sports Management Program at Flagler College in Florida.

A native of Vermilion, Ohio, Bohl earned a bachelor's degree from Bowling Green (1970), a master's of education from Southern Mississippi (1973), and a Ph.D. from Ohio State (1978).

Bohl and his wife, Sherry, live in St. Augustine, Florida where he is working on his second novel. They have two sons, Brett Allen and Nathan Gregory, and one daughter, Heidi Cherié Sherwin.

For more information on Allen Bohl or to order additional copies of this book please visit www.AllenBohl.com.